QUEEN OF

Allen Raine (Anne Adaliza Puddicombe)
1836–1908

QUEEN
OF THE RUSHES

A Tale of the Welsh Revival

by
ALLEN RAINE

with an introduction
by
KATIE GRAMICH

HONNO CLASSICS

Published by Honno
'Alisa Craig', Heol y Cawl, Dinas Powys
South Glamorgan, Wales, CF6 4AH

First Impression 1906
This edition © Honno Ltd 1998

Introduction © Katie Gramich 1998

Illustrations reproduced by permission of the
National Library of Wales, Aberystwyth

British Library Cataloguing in Publication Data

A catalogue record for this book is available from the British Library

ISBN 1 870206 29 0

Published with the financial support of the Arts Council of Wales

*Cover photograph from the film **A Welsh Singer**,*
based on another novel by Allen Raine

Cover design by Chris Lee

Typeset and printed in Wales by
Gwasg Dinefwr, Llandybïe

Contents

Preface

This is the first of a new series of Honno Classics. Honno, as the Welsh Women's Press, has up to now concentrated on publishing works by contemporary women authors, though it has also brought to the light of day the auto-biographical writings of Welsh women, putting on record their experiences of life earlier in this century. This important process of rediscovering and chronicling hitherto hidden women's history will be complemented by the new Honno Classics series, which will bring back into print neglected and virtually forgotten literary texts by Welsh women from the past. Side by side with the English-language Honno Classics will be a sister series entitled Clasuron Honno, which will rediscover and re-present Welsh-language texts from the past. Texts in both series will include introductions setting them in their historical context and suggesting ways of approaching and understanding these works from the viewpoint of women's experience today. It is also intended to give a flavour of some of the generic diversity of the literary material available, ranging from novels and short stories to poetry, plays, and non-mainstream genres, such as letters and diaries.

There is a huge range of material to choose from and our aim, as editors, is to select and bring back into print works which are not only of literary merit but which remain readable and appealing to a contemporary reader-ship. An additional aim for the series is to provide texts for students of Welsh writing in English, who have until now remained largely ignorant of the contribution of women writers to the Welsh literary tradition simply because their works have been unavailable. As the texts in the series appear, therefore, it is hoped that a new, more complete picture of the Welsh literary canon will emerge.

The spirit in which these books are brought back into the public domain is one of excitement and celebration. We, as editors, have been surprised by the wealth of literature lying there in the research libraries, waiting to be re-discovered. We hope to bring some of our enthusiasm for these works to a new readership. Nevertheless, we hope that our enthusiasm does not lead us into uncritical praise; we feel that it would be unrealistic, for example, to expect all Welsh women writers in the past to display sound feminist principles in their work! Therefore, we intend firmly to reject the temptations of 'presentism', namely the judging of the past by the criteria of the present. Indeed, the conflicting portrayals of Welsh female identity found in these works bears witness to the complex processes that have gone into shaping us, Welsh women of today. Being able to read, examine and ponder on these portrayals will surely help us to understand our own situations better.

Series co-editors:
Jane Aaron and Katie Gramich

Introduction

SANDCASTLE EMPIRE

Allen Raine is one of those sterling performers in a side-tent of the circus of the literary tradition: the amazing disappearing woman. How many have disappeared over the centuries? The disappearance of Raine and other phenomenally successful female authors of the past can be justified by an academic and literary establishment concerned to uphold high aesthetic standards. The argument is that they deserve to be forgotten because their work has no literary merit. However, it is curious to note that more self-consciously highbrow, serious writers like Dorothy Edwards and Margiad Evans, who were highly regarded by the male literary gurus of their day, also fail to be incorporated into the established canon. It is difficult to avoid the conclusion that female writers' exclusion is a direct result of a patriarchal bias against the supposedly inferior literary productions of women.

Aesthetic value judgements are the albatrosses hanging from our necks. Allen Raine is a thoroughly bad writer, the argument goes: why should we bother to re-read her work, to re-assess her achievement, when the perusal of a few pages is enough to confirm our worst fears? But, as Terry Eagleton points out, "Literary theorists, critics and teachers . . . are not so much purveyors of a doctrine as custodians of a discourse . . . Certain pieces of writing are selected as being more amenable to this discourse than others, and these are what is known as literature or the 'literary canon' . . . [but] since literary critical discourse has no definite

1

signified it can, if it wants to, turn its attention to more or less any kind of writing . . . Literary criticism cannot justify its self-limiting to certain works by an appeal to the 'value' [since] . . . criticism is part of a literary institution which constitutes these works as valuable in the first place . . . there is no such thing as literature which is 'really' great, or 'really' anything, independently of the ways in which that writing is treated within specific forms of social and institutional life."[1] Most feminist critics have been weaned on the received values of the academic establishment, too. We know that W. H. Auden is a 'good' poet, Idris Davies a 'bad' one; Aldous Huxley a 'good' novelist, Richard Llewellyn a 'bad' one; Galsworthy a 'good' dramatist, J. O. Francis a 'bad' one. But I have chosen these examples of male writers in order to demonstrate that absolute value judgements are not always particularly useful. Idris Davies may be a 'bad' poet, according to the common aesthetic criteria which we have all internalised but it is of course more than obvious that Idris Davies is much more important, pressing, urgent, relevant to a Welsh reader than any of his more polished English contemporaries. Indeed, as both Tony Conran and Dafydd Johnston have shown in editing his work, it is precisely those places of tension, of gaucheness, of outright embarrassing 'badness' in his poetry which are the sites of the most fascinating revelations – about language, about culture, about what it is to *be* Welsh in the way that Idris Davies was, painfully, Welsh. My argument is a simple one: that the value of literature is not simply accountable in aesthetic terms. And that it is not only defensible but essential that we, as Welsh readers, as women readers, as novel readers, re-publish and re-read the work of Allen Raine.

BIOGRAPHY

Anne Adaliza Evans, known as Ada to her family, but better known elsewhere by her androgynous pseudonym, Allen Raine, was born in Newcastle Emlyn on October 6th, 1836. Her dates, 1836-1908, correspond fairly closely to the reign of Queen Victoria and this is no doubt apt for she strikes one as a typically Victorian writer, despite the fact that she did not publish her first novel until almost the turn of the century. As a woman in her sixties trying to cope with a mentally ill husband, a retired banker, Allen Raine certainly did not strike either her readers or her acquaintances as a New Woman of the period. If we are to believe Virginia Woolf when she asserts "On or about December 1910 human nature changed"[2] it was fitting that Allen Raine did not live to see this new, Modernist age, for she belonged firmly to the high Victorian ethos of her youth.

Although she chooses rural settings for her novels, her own upbringing was as the daughter of a solicitor in a small market town. She thus belonged to a very small middle class and her education reflected the aspirations of that class, for she was sent to school at Carmarthen and later bundled off to be 'finished' at Cheltenham and London. She was thus separated from her family and from her Welsh roots for a key period during her youth. She returned to Newcastle Emlyn for some years before her marriage to a London banker, Beynon Puddicombe, in 1872. The childless couple lived on the outskirts of London for most of their married life until, during the late 1890s, Beynon Puddicombe began to show symptoms of a severe mental illness which forced him to take early retirement. The Puddicombes then moved to a house which they had built in Tresaith, on the Cardiganshire coast, a village which Allen Raine was very familiar with, since she had spent summer holidays there with her family ever since her childhood. Tresaith and the surrounding countryside is recognisably the setting for many of her novels.

For some ten years after her marriage, Allen Raine manifested symptoms of what one might recognise as a typical Victorian lady's illness: fatigue and prostration which confined her to her couch. Florence Nightingale, Amy Dillwyn and countless other middle-class women of the period seemed to go through these prolonged bouts of semi-invalidity which it is tempting to interpret as signs of frustration with the lack of opportunities afforded to women in their situation. This is not to say that the illness was feigned; such feelings may well have resulted in severe depression, which was not properly diagnosed or treated. The women I have mentioned were roused from this state when they found something they could commit themselves to; in Allen Raine's case, this seems to have been writing novels with a patriotic purpose.

Although Raine had written in a sporadic and unfocused way during her youth, she did not begin writing in earnest until she was in her sixties and she was prompted to do so then by that most Welsh of promptings: an Eisteddfod competition. She shared a prize in the 1894 National Eisteddfod for "the best serial story . . . characteristic of Welsh life." The text, entitled *Ynysoer,* was serialised in both English and Welsh in newspapers but was not published as a single volume (under the title *Under Billows Roll*) until after her death. Her first best-seller was her second novel, originally entitled *Mifanwy* (sic) but retitled by her publishers as *A Welsh Singer*, which appeared in 1897.

Once Allen Raine had made this successful start, she became a prolific writer, publishing eight novels over the next ten years. Sally Jones, in the only substantial critical work available on the author,[3] argues convincingly that it is unlikely that Raine was forced to try to make money from her novels in order to pay for the expensive treatment and care which her sick husband required, for the Puddicombes were fairly well off in any case. However, her husband's illness and his periodic stays in a North Wales asylum is no doubt of significance for Raine had, in effect, a room of her own (overlooking the beach in Tresaith) and an income to go with it. She certainly made money from her writing: the sales figures show that she was an enormously successful novelist during the brief period of her publishing career. One index of her popularity is the fact that a number of her novels, including *A Welsh Singer* and *Torn Sails* (1898), were made into silent films during the first decades of the new century.

By Berwyn Banks (1899), revolving around a 'mixed marriage' between Anglican and Methodist, exhibits Raine's characteristic religious tolerance. Her own religious background, being a mixture of Unitarianism and Anglicanism, may have contributed to her apparent impatience with sectarianism. *Garthowen* (1900) could have been a watershed in Raine's career as a writer, for it is an ambitious novel which eschews many of the more clichéd elements of the romance plot in favour of a more serious exploration of social themes. It is certainly a novel which deserves to be republished and re-evaluated by a new generation of readers. Unfortunately, however, sales of *Garthowen* were considerably fewer than those of the previous novels; it seems likely that Raine was urged by her publishers to return to the trusty romance formula in subsequent novels. *A Welsh Witch* (1902), as the title suggests, does contain more fantastic and romantic elements than *Garthowen* but it also ventures further afield in terms of setting, for it features not only scenes in a Glamorganshire coalmine but a mine disaster. This might seem to be stereotypical Anglo-Welsh material but it is as well to remember that the material was innovative in 1902. Indeed, the subject matter of the typical Anglo-Welsh industrial novel of the 1930s is already here in embryonic form; given that the 1930s novel is so male-dominated, it is a useful corrective to note that it was a female novelist who might be said to have initiated this tradition.

On Wings of the Wind (1903) concerns a family feud, while *Hearts of Wales* (1905) is an historical novel set at the time of Glyndŵr's rebellion. *Queen of the Rushes* (1906) was the last novel Raine completed before her death and arises directly from the author's observation of the events of the 1904-5 Revival. Her interest in the Revival is evident from a letter which she sent to the *Western Mail* in December 1904; in it she expresses her reservations about the "scenes of frenzied excitement" which accompanied the Revival meetings but finally expresses her hope that the Revival (or, as she prefers to have it, the *Diwygiad*, for the Welsh word "implies reform as well as repentance") will lead to "a real reformation in our national character."[4] Beynon Puddicombe died in 1906 and Allen Raine did not survive him for long, dying of breast cancer in June, 1908. There were several posthumous publications, including a collection of short stories, entitled *All in a Month* (1908).

Interestingly, when the furore over *My People* began in 1915, Allen Raine's name was repeatedly invoked as an example of a good, wholesome Anglo-Welsh writer, whom Caradoc Evans *should* have emulated. In a sense, the Caradoc Evans controversy created not just notoriety for Evans but also a false impression of Allen Raine, a false impression which has unfortunately persisted to the present day.

ALLEN RAINE AND THE ANGLO-WELSH

That Caradoc Evans is the founding father of Anglo-Welsh
literature, razing the "sandcastle empire"[5] of Allen Raine
and her like with the stamping boot of *My People* in 1915 is
a statement which remains generally accepted, despite
having been challenged from several quarters. Raymond
Garlick and Roland Mathias have demonstrated that English
writing by Welsh authors may be traced back at least to the
fifteenth century.[6] Moreover, feminist critics have begun to
rebel against the tacit acceptance that female authors do
not count as founding mothers of any kind of literary
tradition. Sally Jones made the plea for a reassessment of
Raine in 1979 but, hitherto, few have heeded her call.[7] As
Jones points out, Raine was instrumental in "popularising
Wales as an acceptable subject for novelists"[8] at a time
when Wales in the London literary establishment was not
simply deeply unfashionable (as it still seems to be today)
but virtually did not exist on any literary map which they
were able to read.

It is, I think, important to differentiate between Allen Raine
and the majority of the female novelists both before and
after her lifetime who have used Wales as a kind of theatrical
backdrop to their work. In the Romantic period Wales did
temporarily begin to come into being as a literary landscape
for the English-speaking world; it was regarded as an area
of titillatingly horrid scenery where Gothic characters and
situations would feel suitably at home.[9] My argument is
that Allen Raine's novels are different in kind from these
often amusing and entertaining Cymric romps. Raine is an
Anglo-Welsh novelist in the modern sense in that she does
balance on that bridging hyphen between a Welsh Wales
which she knew at first hand and an Anglicised or English
reading public. She is not simply using rural Cardiganshire

as a convenient backdrop or as a means to sell her books; she is evidently committed to this place, feels that she is part of it, to such a degree that she transforms it and recreates it in her work. She stated as much herself: "This has been the great desire of my life: to shew the poetry and interest of Welsh life to the nation with which we are linked."[10] One indication of Raine's desire to give an authentic account of rural South-West Wales is her insistence on using many untranslated Welsh words in her texts. She does provide a brief glossary in some editions of her novels but by no means all of the Welsh words are translated. The words are, moreover, dialectal and are – unlike many of Caradoc Evans's inventions – accurate renderings of Cardiganshire speech. A very brief glance through *Queen of the Rushes*, for instance, turns up words such as the following, *bwcci, whintell, clôs, cryman, anwl, merch-i, ach-y-fi, bwthin, crydd, ladiwen, howyr bach, lodes, caton pawb, hysbys, b't shwr, tân, can diolch, Dakee*. Given this very overt display of Welshness, it is odd that a critic such as Ernest Rhys should have claimed that there is nothing distinctively Welsh about Allen Raine's novels.[11] On the other hand, she was the recipient of fan mail from no less a figure than O. M. Edwards. It seems to me that her patriotic credentials are impeccable, though she is certainly capable of criticising aspects of Welsh society, as *Queen of the Rushes* shows.

Recently Alun Richards has written that two of the first questions one should ask of a writer are "Has he or she got a voice of his or her own?" and "Has he or she created a world?"[12] I think one can answer "Yes" to both questions in the case of Allen Raine. She has suffered from disparagement of having reputedly created unreal, idyllic pictures of life in rural Cardiganshire, pictures which were replaced by the supposedly more harshly realistic ones of Caradoc Evans's *My People*. Such a judgement is untenable when one actually reads the authors' works. Caradoc Evans's world is no more realistic than Allen Raine's is idyllic. Although she tends to polarise her main characters, creating impossibly virtuous heroines and thoroughly reprehensible villains, the other *dramatis personae* of her works are by no means idealised. Village life as it is depicted in *Queen of the Rushes* is not all bucolic harmony: the vividly individualised minor characters like Het, Ben Stable, Hezek, Jerri, N'wncwl Sam, Betsy Jones and Nelli Amos are, variously, prone to gossip, bad temper, vindictiveness, envy, vanity, and more gossip. As Sally Jones observes in her discussion of Raine's 1898 novel, *Torn Sails*, the character Gwen "suffocating her dying baby with roast mouse . . . is a sister to Nanny in *Be This Her Memorial*."[13] Raine's novels are not as 'nice' as the critics seem to think.

Having laboured the point above that we do not have to confine our literary interests to canonical texts, it must be acknowledged that Allen Raine's work is not bereft of those qualities which we traditionally associate with 'good' literature. Her characterisation is vivid and authentic, her use of setting is skilful and often poetic, her grasp of the social ties and conflicts in the community she depicts is secure. Above all, she creates a 'world'; she has a 'voice'. The formulaic aspects of the romance genre she adopted in virtually all of her published works can be irritating, certainly, but perhaps no more so than the quirks of more illustrious writers – the sentimentality of Dickens or the schoolma'mish touches of Charlotte Brontë.

THE REVIVAL

The fact that *Queen of the Rushes* is set at the time of the 1904-5 Revival, precisely when Raine was writing the novel, indicates that she was not a novelist who necessarily wanted to escape into the never-never land of romance but rather wanted to comment directly on contemporary events. Allen Raine was not wasting her time building sandcastles on the beach at Tresaith; she was interested in the much more substantial Empire of Nonconformity and the very solid edifice of the Chapel. Raine is not hostile towards the Chapel but she is, like her mouthpiece in the novel, Gildas Rees, extremely suspicious of the Revival. She suspects that the extreme manifestations of conversion in the Revival meetings are not indications of true faith. Like Gildas, and her heroine Gwenifer for that matter, she believes in reason and restraint.

In a sense, Allen Raine's suspicions about the Revival and her fear that the extreme manifestations of religious fervour would not result in a long-lasting conversion were borne out by events. As R. Tudur Jones puts it: "Yr oedd y llwydrew wedi cyrraedd cyn i dân y Diwygiad lwyr ddiffodd."[14] [The frost had fallen almost before the fire of the Revival had been quenched.] Raine depicts the rapid extinguishing of the 'flames' in the closing chapters of her novel; it is seen as a return to normality, though for certain individuals, the conversion has been quite genuine.

One actual historical figure appears in the novel, namely the Revivalist preacher, Evan Roberts, a twenty-six year old ex-miner from Loughor, "of whom the much abused word 'charismatic' can be used with absolute correctness."[15] Roberts was often accompanied on his missions by young women converts, who also preached and helped spread the word. In the adulatory account of his work by a fellow Revivalist, the Reverend D. M. Phillips (Tylorstown), it emerges that Roberts was also something of a poet. Extracts from his own work can perhaps best convey the intensity of the message he was taking to the people of Wales:

> *Cymru! Cymru! annwyl Gymru,*
> *Cefaist dân o'r nef;*
> *Ar dy liniau, dan y fflamau,*
> *Codaist allor gref . . .*
> *Mil o ddysgawdwyr,*
> *A'r wlad ar dân;*
> *A phawb yn awdur*
> *Emyn a chân;*
> *Iesu yn marchog,*
> *A'r gelyn yn brudd,*
> *A thyrfa ardderchog*
> *Yn rhydd! yn rhydd!* [16]

> [Wales! Wales! dear Wales,
> You received fire from heaven,
> On your knees, under the flames,
> You raised a strong altar . . .
> A thousand teachers,
> And the country on fire;
> And everyone the author
> Of hymn and song;
> Jesus riding triumphant
> And the enemy laid low
> and a great congregation
> Set free! set free!]

The important role of women in the Diwygiad is indicated by the list of people Evan Roberts drew up to go with him on his first missionary journey: eight of the ten names are those of young women, such as Florrie Evans and Maud Davies. A vivid first-hand account of a Revival meeting

featuring Evan Roberts and one of his 'helpers', Annie
Davies, is found in Gwenallt's autobiographical novel,
Ffwrneisiau.[17] The prominent role played by Nance in the
depiction of the Diwygiad found in Raine's novel is therefore
faithful to the 'facts' found in the accounts of historians and
eye-witnesses.

Philip Jenkins argues that the Chapels' hierarchical
structure which "exclu[ded] from power and spiritual
status . . . younger men and all women . . . was a muted or
potential source of grievance. [This] is suggested by the
explosions that occurred during revivals that offered a
democratic access to grace, a chance that was seized above
all by women and the young. The appeal of revivalism to
women . . . was remarked on by observers of all revivals."[18]

One might argue that this outbreak of female self-assertion
was a Welsh substitute for suffragism. The first organization
for women's suffrage was not established in Wales until
1907, and the suffrage campaign tended to be waged by
English, middle-class visitors to Wales, and to take root in
Welsh soil only in the major urban centres and in the narrow
coastal strips of the extreme North and South. It can never
be said to have been strong in rural Cardiganshire.
Nevertheless, in such a setting, challenging the chapel
hierarchy could be seen as analogous to challenging the
Government itself. The behaviour of the suffrage campaigners was certainly described by contemporary critics in
terms similar to those used of the Revivalists; Virginia
Woolf quotes from the memoirs of Sir Almeric Fitzroy,
decrying the 'suffragettes' after they had kicked a male
politician's shins and squashed his hat: "an attack of this
character upon a defenceless old man by an organized
band of 'janissaries' will, it is hoped, convince many people
of *the insane and anarchical spirit actuating the movement*."[19]
(my italics)

Certainly, Allen Raine has nothing ostensible to say about female suffrage or education in this novel. Implicitly, perhaps, she is critical, if we are to interpret the actions of the women associated with the Revival in the novel as indicative of the 'excesses' of women suffrage campaigners. As Ceridwen Lloyd-Morgan has shown[20], in Wales there was something of an overlap between the two apparently dissimilar movements in that both took an interest in temperance. Many of the leaders of the temperance movement in Wales, such as Cranogwen and Ceridwen Peris, were also active in the suffrage campaign. The saving of men from the 'demon drink' is one of the effects of the Revival mentioned several times in the novel in very positive terms. John Davies remarks that the 1904-5 Revival *did* give a significant boost to the Temperance movement, as is evidenced by the campaign during 1908 to close three-quarters of the public houses in Wales.[21]

In her silence about female suffrage and education, Raine provides a striking contrast to another Cardiganshire woman novelist, 'Moelona.' Moelona began publishing her work in Welsh just a few years after the death of Allen Raine and certainly the example of the latter must have been an inspiration and encouragement to an aspiring author from the same area. Moelona's commitment to the feminist cause is evident from the outset, though, and is expressed perhaps most clearly in the semi-biographical novel *Ffynnonloyw* (1939), whose protagonist, Nan, a teacher, becomes a suffrage campaigner. It is remarkable to note how refined and wise the heroine of *Queen of the Rushes*, Gwenifer, is without the benefit of any education; contrast this with Moelona's heroines, who are formidably educated, and who use their education to further their political and personal aims. Gwenifer is an isolated romance heroine, a heroine who is a Rousseauesque child of nature, with apparently no need for schooling. Moreover, when she begins to speak, she does so with no trace of the 'rough accent' characteristic of all her peers and this without benefit of a single elocution lesson!

Allen Raine's work testifies to the fact that women's writing is not necessarily oppositional. The ideology implied in Raine's novels is a conservative one, which is not overtly critical of patriarchal society. Nevertheless, as Roland Barthes has shown, even the most conservative of writers may unconsciously reveal some of the contradictions or deficiencies of a system which they wholeheartedly support. The key is in the *reading* of the text; in offering this feminist reading of *Queen of the Rushes*, I am certainly not suggesting that Allen Raine consciously concealed a feminist message in her work. No text is fixed with a monolithic meaning; this novel 'means' very different things to a reader of 1906 and a reader of 1996. One can go further to suggest that the novel means something slightly different to every single individual and to the same individual at different times in her life or in different frames of mind. Sally Jones describes Allen Raine's texts as being "of a dual nature. On the one hand there is the sober, precise, even witty depiction of the rural society of which she was herself a part, and on the other hand there are passages of what can only be described as romantic gush."[22] While I see exactly what Sally Jones is suggesting, I think that some aspects of the "romantic gush" are not without their interest to a feminist reader.

VOICE

The speaking voice is the central metaphor of the novel. For more than half the text, the heroine is dumb. During this time, the anti-heroine, Nance, who is inconveniently married to Gildas, the man whom Gwenifer loves, is distinguished by her volubility. By the end of the novel, however, the roles are almost entirely reversed, in that Nance, deranged by the effects of the Diwygiad, is reduced to virtual silence, broken only by some incoherent babble, while Gwenifer's speech is fully restored and she "revel[s] in her new-found power." As Betsy Jones observes, "Time for her to be looking out for a husband, for she's got a tongue now, to give him a trimming sometimes."

One of the male villagers rather callously remarks in the opening chapter, referring to Gwenifer's sudden affliction: "perhaps 'Twill be a good thing to have one woman amongst us who won't clabber and jabber." Evidently the common male in this society regards the female as particularly prone to "jabbering." One of the other foils to Gwenifer in the novel, her co-worker Het, is another example of female garrulousness who tends to scorn "milady's" aloofness. Gwenifer is thus marked out as different, not as other women, and her otherness is confirmed by her own solitary habits, which earn her the half-derisive nickname of "Queen of the Rushes."

The issue of speech becomes central in the Revival. The climax of the revival meeting is the individual's public confession of sin and her or his personal commitment to Christ. It is this communal voicing of the most intimate feelings that fills Gildas with dread and suspicion. When he hears the voice of Ben Stable articulating his confession, it is significant that Gildas scarcely recognises Ben's voice. It is as if someone else is speaking through him and because

Gildas is sceptical of the possibility that this might be the Holy Spirit, his impression is one of falseness, of inauthenticity. The climax of the alienation between Gildas and Nance is the Revival meeting where Nance raises her voice in public prayer and confession when, according to Gildas, she ought to be at home preparing his supper. Gildas is astonished and repelled by the extent of her rebellion: "how dared she thus defy his wishes!" She even takes the name of her Lord, Gildas, in vain, praying for his salvation and encouraging the whole congregation to join in the prayer to "bring [Gildas] to his knees!" Gildas is mortified and ashamed, preserving his independence, refusing to be coerced into joining this communal fervour.

Gwenifer is immune to the Diwygiad by virtue of her dumbness: she is prevented from entering into the public voicing of religious enthusiasm. For a novelist, it would no doubt be tempting to restore the heroine's speech at the critical point in a Diwygiad meeting: such a miracle would surely be proof of the presence of the Holy Spirit. Significantly, Raine rejects this possibility and restores Gwenifer's speech in a melodramatic episode when she is seen to be undertaking an act of selfless Christian duty *outside* the confines of the Chapel.

In a community such as this, where everyone gossips, the voice itself becomes suspect. What people say – for example, that Gildas has murdered his wife – is often false, while those who remain silent – Gwenifer, perforce, and Gildas, by choice – are perceived as maintaining truth and integrity. Captain Jack's affectation of a rough, country accent to conceal his status as a gentleman is an index of the potential duplicity of his character.

The motif of female dumbness is common in literature from the earliest times. The Greek legend of Philomel/Procne/Tereus is archetypal. The female victim is mutilated by the male rapist in order to prevent her from announcing his guilt. The loss of the female voice is an emblem of injustice, of the female as passive victim of a brutal, rampaging male sexuality. She is Eliot's "infinitely gentle, infinitely suffering thing."[23] Shakespeare's *Titus Andronicus* resorts to the same motif, but it is one which is obviously appealing to female authors, too, as the recent film *The Piano* shows. It lends itself to use as an indication of a common female voicelessness in an oppressive, patriarchal society. The motif also owes something to the common stereotype of the female as excessively loquacious. This 'folk' tradition is alluded to in *Queen of the Rushes*, where Gwenifer's misfortune is viewed, jocularly, as a blessing by some of the older male villagers. The 'silent woman' is a kind of oxymoron, a singular figure who might become an object of the fatigued, nagged male's desire. But she is also beyond the pale, as Gwenifer's isolation shows, such an oddity that she is outside 'normal' human society, with its gender polarisations and battles. The silent female is an observer of the scene, rather than a participant.

Hélène Cixous in her influential text, *La Jeune Née*, extols the mother as the fount of the voice to be heard in all female texts. Woman's voice for Cixous is the voice of the Mother: "The Voice, a song before the Law, before the breath was split by the symbolic, reappropriated into language under the authority that separates."[24] Though one might feel some scepticism at the excessively Romantic tone of Cixous's paean, not to mention the hovering at the edge of some essentialist definition of the Eternal Mother, yet Cixous's ideas are peculiarly apposite when one applies them to a reading of *Queen of the Rushes*. In the first chapter Gwenifer loses her mother and immediately, as a direct result, loses her voice. Attempts are made to coax her into entering the symbolic order by unsympathetic male voices, but Gwenifer refuses to enter this order, remaining true to her mother, though the latter's voice is forever silenced. The mother drowns in the sea, which for Cixous, as for many other writers, of course, is the feminine element. Gwenifer, as she matures, becomes increasingly identified with the solid ground of the moor, and with the solid common sense, the dependability and unshakeability of Gildas. She is gradually drawn from the sea, her mother, to take her place in the prosaic reality of Gildas's land.

In the novel a female body emerges from the womb of the sea, while that element is associated with the more unstable characters, such as Captain Jack and Nance. Captain Jack's character is fluid, unfixed – indeed one might argue that there is a homosexual element in his make-up. He is strongly tempted by the Diwygiad and especially by the charismatic gaze of Evan Roberts: the moment when their eyes meet across the crowned chapel is a quasi-romantic one. Where Jack's character is unfixed, Nance's is increasingly unhinged. Gildas is often described in phallic terms as upright, unbending and rigid. Interestingly, however, the portrayal of Gwenifer echoes this, for she is like a rush – upright, like Gildas, but more pliant and vulnerable.

Though Gwenifer and Nance obviously function as heroine and anti-heroine in the novel, there are some interesting similarities in their backgrounds. Both are orphans, their lost mothers being substituted by father figures: Hezek in the case of Nance, Gildas in that of Gwenifer. The latter continues to cherish her mother's memory and to identify herself with her, as the lost voice indicates, while Nance is totally cut off from any maternal influence, thus becoming totally brainwashed by the patriarchal symbolic order which she enters wholeheartedly. Nance is one of those anti-heroines who remain child-like and irresponsible, despite the buxom nubility of their bodies

– she is therefore an embodiment of the patriarchal view of women as not entirely adult, fickle, superficial, vain and garrulous. It is an indictment of Gildas's masculine prejudices that he chooses such a woman rather than the woman who is his intellectual and moral equal, namely Gwenifer.

Male genealogy is important in the society depicted in the novel; the male protagonists's status as "mishteer" of the village is underlined by the fact that the village actually bears his name: Tregildas. However, this patriarchal inheritance is not idealised, for we learn that the father, Jonathan, was by no means an ideal master nor an efficient farmer, for Gildas inherits "unkempt" lands. Gwenifer, meanwhile, is emphatically a member of the peasantry, for her mother labours all day in the fields. Both Gildas himself and the villagers perceive the orphaned Gwenifer as his property: "tis to you she belongs". Gwenifer accepts her status as chattel while Gildas accepts his new responsibilities. The novel opens, then, with a catastrophe which binds the hero and heroine together indissolubly: each loses a parent and is suddenly transformed by that loss.

In contrast to Gwenifer and Gildas, whose status in their own society is clear and unambiguous, both Captain Jack and Nance are what Sally Jones calls "mongrels", namely, products of a union between a gentleman and a peasant woman. Hezek is ruined by his marriage to "a beautiful but uneducated peasant girl." Nance has experienced no check, no restraint in her upbringing by her indulgent grandfather, whereas it is implied that Gwenifer has already learned a strong sense of duty and propriety from her mother. At the opening of the novel, the ten-year-old Gwenifer has performed all the domestic chores at home while her mother is out labouring. Arguably, Raine may be seen to suggest that the mother's influence, the mother's education of her

daughter, is indispensable. For Gwenifer, like her friend
Nance, receives an education by Nature, but is not rendered
wild and unstable by it.

Although both Gildas and Captain Jack have received an
education, it is interesting that Gildas neither regards himself
nor is regarded by the villagers as a "gentleman". The
household at Scethryg, which we observe fairly intimately,
is one where master and servant sit down at the same table.
This is made clear when Gildas and Captain Jack confront
each other and Gildas identifies Captain Jack as "other", a
gentleman (though he tries to conceal this by speaking with
a different accent) and therefore "not one of us".

On the surface, it would seem that Nance is the character
whom we would today identify as a feminist heroine, in
her self-assertion, her refusal to be bound by her husband's
wishes, her passion, her unabashed sexuality, her desire to
escape from the galling confines of domesticity. But Allen
Raine makes it very difficult for the reader to recuperate
Nance as a feminist heroine, for she is vain, childish,
emotionally incontinent and self-centred. Once she has
been labelled "buxom" and "pouting", we know that she is
heading for perdition! Moreover, she is not really a feminist
rebel for, when she attempts to escape with Captain Jack,
she abnegates herself before him in the acceptable feminine
fashion. There is no doubt that the sobriety, self-sacrifice
and obedience of Gwenifer is being held up as an example
to female readers of the novel; the fact that the rebel,
Nance, is punished so cruelly for her misdemeanours acts
as a warning to any potential dissident amongst us. The
overall message of the novel seems to be in favour of the
status quo: collaboration with the social system is more
likely to result in personal happiness than overt rebellion
against it. Moreover, Raine is capable of modulating her
own voice as narrator of the novel in order to command

our assent to the projected ideology: the pronoun "we" is used at strategic points in the narrative in order to draw us in to the novelistic world and to confirm its values. At other times Raine manages a dramatic switch to the present tense, a hackneyed technique to create an effect of immediacy perhaps, but still used very effectively by this supposedly unskilled writer of romance, for instance in the melodramatic confrontation on Maldraeth beach in Chapter 13 or the atmospheric scene in the kitchen of Scethryg at the opening of Chapter 18.

In her account of Allen Raine's early life, Sally Jones talks of the novelist's mother, Letitia Grace, as "a shadowy figure."[25] As we all know, that phrase recurs in so many accounts of artists' mothers and grandmothers. The perpetual shadow in which they seemed to exist may be construed by a feminist reader as that cast by the Father, blocking out the mother's outline, erasing her, drowning her voice. Feminist theorists such as Hélène Cixous and Luce Irigaray are urging us to disinter the mother, to find that lost or silenced voice. It is all the more interesting to me to find the haunting figure of the lost mother and her drowned voice in the ostensibly reactionary pages of Allen Raine's *Queen of the Rushes*.

NOTES

1. Terry Eagleton, *Literary Theory: An Introduction,* (Oxford: Blackwell, 1983), pp. 201-2.
2. Virginia Woolf, "Mr. Bennett and Mrs. Brown" (1924), in *Collected Essays*, vol. I (London: Hogarth, 1966), p. 321.
3. Sally Jones, *Allen Raine (Writers of Wales),* (Cardiff: University of Wales Press, 1979). I am much indebted to Sally Jones for the biographical material included in this introduction.
4. ibid. p. 55.
5. Gwyn Jones, "The First Forty Years: Some Notes on Anglo-Welsh Literature," in Sam Adams and G. R. Hughes (eds.), *Triskel One*, (Llandybie: Christopher Davies, 1971), pp. 75-95.
6. Raymond Garlick and Roland Mathias (eds.), *Anglo-Welsh Poetry 1480-1990,* (Bridgend: Seren, 1992).
7. John Harris is one of the few. In his article "Queen of the Rushes", (*Planet* 97, Feb/Mar, 1993, pp. 64-72), he asseverates "Anglo-Welsh literature began in 1897 with the publication of *A Welsh Singer*", p. 64. However, he does blot his copybook rather with his patronising closing remarks: "Is the silence now perpetual? One has to imagine so, while admitting that a publishing house like Virago has raised a few unlikely candidates from the dead."
8. Sally Jones, op. cit., p. 74.
9. See Jane Aaron, "A National Seduction: Wales in Nineteenth-Century Women's Writing," *The New Welsh Review* (No. 27, Winter 1994-5), pp. 31-38.
10. John Harris, op. cit., p. 64.
11. Sally Jones, op. cit., p. 75.
12. Alun Richards, "The Art of Narrative," *The New Welsh Review* (No. 33, Summer, 1996), p. 31.
13. Sally Jones, op. cit., p. 86
14. R. Tudur Jones, *Hanes Annibynwyr Cymru,* (Abertawe: Undeb Annibynwyr Cymru, 1966), p. 236.
15. Philip Jenkins, *A History of Modern Wales,* (London: Longman, 1992), p. 208.
16. Y Parch. D. M. Phillips, Tylorstown, *Evan Roberts a'i Waith,* (Dolgellau: Y Goleuad, 1912), p. 400.

17. D. Gwenallt Jones, *Ffwrneisiau*, (Llandysul: Gomer, 1982), p. 79ff.

18. Philip Jenkins, op. cit., p. 208.

19. Virginia Woolf, *Three Guineas*, (Harmondsworth: Penguin, 1997), p. 168.

20. Ceridwen Lloyd-Morgan, "From Temperance to Suffrage?" in Angela V. John (ed.) *Our Mothers' Land: Chapters in Welsh Women's History 1830-1939*, (Cardiff: University of Wales Press, 1991), pp. 135-158.

21. John Davies, *Hanes Cymru*, (Harmondsworth: Penguin, 1990), p. 487.

22. Sally Jones, op. cit., p. 31.

23. T. S. Eliot, "Preludes" (1915), *Collected Poems*, (London: Faber, 1975), p. 25.

24. Quoted in Toril Moi, *Sexual/Textual Politics*, (London: Routledge, 1988), p. 114.

25. Sally Jones, op. cit., p. 4.

CHAPTER I

The Boy-Master

It has always been a matter of great annoyance to Jonathan
Rees of Scethryg that the sea made a deep curve into the
middle of his farmlands, forming a miniature bay which
divided his two best fields from the rest of his property, thus
obliging him and his labourers to make a circuit of the little
creek whenever work had to be done in the further fields.
Rather than make this addition to the day's labour they
would often cross the intruding tide in old Jerri Jenkins's
boat; and this Jonathan had done on the morning of the
day on which our story opens, accompanied by his band of
reapers, grumbling as usual at the inconvenience of the
crossing.

They had worked all day in the sunshine, where the yellow
wheat was taking a rich red tinge and the oats were
beginning to shed their grain, and in the chat and jollity of
the harvest field he had forgotten his ill-humour. At sunset
he was returning with his labourers towards the boat which
was waiting for them.

On the other side of the cove a child stood looking at them
with a happy smile on her lips and in her brown eyes, for
the boat which she was watching with such interest held all
that was dear to her upon earth – the mother for whom she
had waited all day and for whom she had laid the tea-things
before she had left the house; the kettle was even now
singing its song of welcome on the cosy hearth.

She heard the laughter and jokes of the reapers as they stepped into the boat, hustling each other with good-humoured roughness, their sickles gleaming in the sunset light.

It was a small boat for so large a party, and she noticed that it was rather heavily laden, for little Gwenifer Owen was thoughtful beyond her years, and of a rather anxious, nervous temperament. However, she forgot her fears in listening to the merry talk and laughter which drew rapidly nearer, when suddenly the boat listed heavily, there was a rush to the other side, a lurch, a plunge, and, while the child looked on, it capsized, and a moment afterwards all its occupants were struggling in the water; and in that calm sunset hour the tragic event occurred that stirred the whole countryside to sympathy and compassion, for out of the eight reapers who entered the boat four only reached the shore in safety.

Few of the peasantry even on the sea-coast can swim, and for those who could not, on this occasion there was small chance of life, for the little bay ran deep between its craggy shores. For a time they tried to keep afloat by clinging to the upturned boat, but one by one they had loosened their grasp and sunk into the tide, while the frantic villagers ran hither and thither, unable to do more than weep and wring their hands; for Jerri's was the only boat their tiny strand possessed, and that was lying keel upwards right in the golden pathway made by the setting sun.

Two of the younger villagers swam out and helped to rescue four of the boatload, and succeeded in righting the boat; but four had already sunk, amongst them little Gwenifer's mother. Two were strangers who had asked and obtained a day's work and wage in the harvest field, while the fourth was no other than Jonathan Rees himself, the owner of the most unkempt farm in the parish. The few thatched cottages which stood perched each on its own hillock above the shore also belonged to him, their occupiers looking up to him as their 'mishteer' as well as their friendly neighbour.

He had been a good landlord on the whole, seldom refusing their labour on the farm in lieu of any deficit in their small rents of thirty shillings or two pounds a year.

Standing on the rocks alone, watching the approach of the crazy boat, the child Gwenifer had been an eyewitness of the tragedy, and it was some time before the villagers found her lying unconscious on the ground.

She remained in this state for many hours, awaking at last only to the delirium of fever; and the sorrowful sympathy of the villagers reached its climax when it was discovered that not only the cheerful buxom mother lost her life in those shining waters, but that the sight of the disaster had deprived her child of the power of speech.

Long little Gwenifer hung between life and death, nursed by a neighbour who, having no household ties of her own, consented to take up her abode in poor Jinni's cottage until the child should recover or die; and Gwenifer lived, grew well and strong again, but her power of speech did not return. She was not alone in her bereavement, for at Scethryg the sudden death of the head of the family had plunged his home into confusion as well as sorrow. Being a widower, there was no one left to take on the management of the farm except his only son, Gildas, a boy of sixteen, who had hitherto, under the somewhat grudging and strict surveillance of his father, shown but little aptitude for farming. The sudden and tragic manner of his father's death seemed to overwhelm the lad with sorrow, and he called to mind his past misdoings with a poignancy of regret that magnified his small delinquencies into serious faults, and he awoke from the stupor of a first grief with a strong determination to do better, and to master the adverse fate which seemed to his youthful imagination to have cruelly deprived him of help and counsel just when he was most in need of them. His father's irritating and niggardly ways were all forgotten, and only his acts of kindness and his seasons of tenderness were remembered.

With all his carelessness and his headstrong ways, Gildas had fine traits in his character, and the sad occurrence which had deprived him of a parent seemed in the mysterious dispensation of Providence to be the very thing calculated to call out these good traits. His dark eyes lost a little of their sparkle perhaps, and his lips took a firmer curve as he turned to the duties of his farm life. His first important step was to take his father's half-brother to live with him as steward and manager; and although there had been much shaking of heads and forebodings of evil in the village, when the boy first declared his intention of keeping on the upland farm in his own hands, the news of this first step met with general approval, and old Jerri the boatman was heard to declare that 'perhaps the lad would *behave*, if he can only keep that hot, proud spirit of his in order!'

'Proud spirit!' said Ebben the carpenter. 'I'd like to see the man or the spirit that Gildas couldn't master.'

Jerri deliberately cut a fresh quid for his cheek before he answered: 'I'm not denying that the boy is strong, but he may manage the devil himself and yet not be able to master his own spirit; that's what I'm saying, man!' and with a shove of his oar he thrust his boat from land.

The few thatched cottages that bordered the creek were known by the high-sounding name of Tregildas – Gildas town or home. Who this Gildas had been nobody knew with any certainty, but tradition averred he was an ancestor of the Scethryg family – a man of proud overbearing spirit, who kept not only his own dependents under his despotic sway, but carried his raids and cruelties into the surrounding districts, until his name became a terror to the neighbourhood. Jonathan Rees treated this tradition with a show of incredulity; but when his son was born he had christened him Gildas, and as the boy grew up he bid fair to emulate his fierce ancestor in the boldness and determination of his character, though those traits were counterbalanced by a warmth of heart that was probably wanting in the first of the name. His father was often heard to declare, 'There's a fool I was to call him Gildas; as sure as I'm alive, I believe the name puts things into his head and makes him penstif.' However that might be, it was evident that after his father's death the lad seemed to have taken upon himself not only the management of his own headstrong self, but of all those who came in contact with him. Up early and late, he and n'wncwl Sam tilled and hoed and planted, and compelled the hitherto bare and badly farmed fields to yield their full meed of produce, until at last his neighbours said: 'There's a good farmer is Gildas Rees! Dei anwl! Old Jonathan would stare to see the farm so tidy; but fair play to him, he gave the boy good schooling.'

'Yes indeed!' said another, 'but 'tisn't that, I am thinking; because there's our Ben has had the same schooling, but Gildas knows how to put his schooling into the farm, seems to me.'

'That's it, that's it. Got a good heart too, the bachgen! See how he was feeling for the los'ach Gwenifer, and wouldn't let her be sent to the workhouse.'

'No, but in my deed I'm thinking we'll repent that. What will we do with a girl that can't speak a word? She'll be no use for dairy or field!'

'Well, I dono,' said the first speaker, laughing, 'perhaps 'twill be a good thing to have one woman amongst us who won't clabber and jabber. Poor thing! when she's well she

can come to us to mind the geese and turkeys for a bit.'
And so Gwenifer's fate was settled for her, and when at last
she was considered well enough to leave the cottage where
she had spent her happy childhood, the bits of furniture were
sold and old Jerri Jenkins, taking the child by the hand,
said, 'Don't she cry, 'merch-i! She shall come and mend the
nets, and row the boat across for me sometimes.'

He had meant it kindly, but the girl had dragged her
hand away with a scream and run into the empty cottage,
where all that remained of the 'bits o' duds' that had made
the place habitable was the framework of an old bedstead,
which, being built on one side into the mud wall, was not
removable. Upon its bare boards Gwenifer had sprung and
crouched on the furthest corner, her little brown fingers
clasped round her knees, her eyes glistening with the tears
which she restrained with difficulty. One by one the villagers
who had gathered to the sale had tried to entice her from
the corner, but blandishments, entreaties, and even threats
were all in vain. Not even the storm of wind that rose at
sunset had the effect of moving her from the corner of the
bed, where she had often slept, her head upon the bosom
which those shining yellow waters had hidden from her for
ever.

At last, as the storm increased in fury, the villagers
wearying of their importunities began to look at each other
in puzzled annoyance.

'I was told you we should have trouble with her,' said
one. 'My advice is, lock the door and let us go home. No
harm can come to her, and perhaps in the morning she'll
have come to her senses.'

'Listen to me,' said Jerri, who was always considered to
be a man of strong sense (especially by himself), and with a
turn of his quid and a shrewd wink, he continued: 'Who
brought this bother upon us? Wasn't it Gildas himself,

refusing to let her be sent to the workhouse? Well, then, let him manage the girl. We'll lock the door and go straight up to Scethryg and tell him about her, and let him settle the matter. After all, 'tis no business of ours, eh?' and thinking that Jerri had solved the difficulty discreetly, two or three of them accompanied him up to the farm, locking the door on the wilful child, who sat on the bare bedstead with the look of a frightened animal which seeks in the faces of those around it for some explanation of its trouble.

At Scethryg the fury of the storm was more felt than in the hut, which was somewhat sheltered by a rising of the moor.

In the cosy kitchen, lighted up by the blaze of the logs which n'wncwl Sam had just brought in, Gildas sat with a knitted brow jotting down his 'counts' in a leather-bound volume, in which his father and grandfather had recorded their losses and gains, together with the births, deaths, and marriages, and other events of importance in the family. He had just written 'Oction at poor Jinni Owen's to-day. 'Moelen' had a fine red bull calf,' when the thumb latch was raised to admit Jerri and his followers.

'Jari! here's a sudden storm! Look here, mishteer, what are we to do? 'Tis Gwenifer Owen won't move from her mother's bed, not for kind words, nor threats, nor sweets, nor nothing. What will we do?'

The lad looked up from his writing, with a flush of annoyance. 'How do I know?' was his first hasty answer.

'Well, we've done our best with her, whatever,' said Jerri, 'but we didn't like to carry her out by force without asking you, 'machgen-i, because, of course, you see 'tis to you she belongs.'

'Oh, I see,' said Gildas, with a sudden intuition, 'you are throwing her upon me because I wouldn't let her go to the workhouse,' and he laughed with a little flash of sarcasm.

'All right! go home all of you to your beds, and leave the key here; I'll see to the child.'

The men were profuse in their denials of his suggestion.

'No indeed, mishteer! nothing could be further from my thoughts,' said Jerri. 'I'll go at once and carry her up here, with your leave, kick and scream she ever so much.'

'No, no, go you home,' said Gildas; 'I'll manage her.'

'*I'll manage her!*' scoffed one of the men, as they fought their way home through the wind; 'that boy thinks he can manage the world!'

'Well, indeed! he is doing very well with his world,' said Jerri, but the wind carried his voice away.

In the farm kitchen the lad continued to bend over his diary; n'wncwl Sam rearranging the logs on the hearth, till the old room glowed with their blazing light, and every pot and pan shone out, and every quaint brown stool threw its shadow on the floor. Het clumped in and out in her wooden shoes, and Ben Stable came in from the yard carrying his lantern, which blinked and sparkled through its numerous eyes.

'Don't put it out,' said the boy-master, seeing that Ben had inflated his cheeks in readiness for the puff: 'I'm going out.'

No one was surprised, as it was his nightly custom to inspect the animals in their sheds before drawing the clumsy wooden bolt for the night; but n'wncwl Sam called out as he struggled with the wind at the door, 'I'd see to the horses first if I was you. Leave the 'croten' in the dark a bit, and she'll be ready enough to come.'

Without answering, Gildas closed the door and turned to the yard, carefully inspecting the sheds, and, last of all, looking into the barn, to be sure that the beggar who he had permitted to sleep there was not smoking, and so endangering the safety of the place.

All was safe and in order, and, drawing the string latch behind him, he turned towards the moorland side of the hill, where Jinni's cottage stood. The wind had risen to a gale, rushing up against him from the sea, and lifting the clumps of heather and furze in his path as if it would tear them from their roots. The cows, who loved the short herbage on the moor, were lying here and there under the shelter of the blackthorn bushes; they raised their heads a moment in wonder as the lantern flashed by them, and a forlorn sheep who had lost her lamb woke up, and, reminded of her loss, bleated out her sorrow to the stormy night. Gildas pressed on with that curious look of set purpose in his face that hid so completely from others the feelings that prompted his actions. It must be confessed that there was much annoyance mixed with the generous pity that incited him to brave the elements on such a night. 'Bother the chit!' he muttered as his lantern swung round, and his cap flew skywards behind him; for in spite of the pity he had felt for little Gwenifer Owen, when his own heart was softened by the same loss that had brought such disaster to her, and though he had firmly opposed the idea of sending her to the workhouse, his kindness had gone no farther, and he had almost forgotten her existence while she had been laid up fighting so hard a fight with fever and death.

During that time he had found himself and his own tangled affairs a hard enough problem to grapple with; but the sale at Jinni's cottage had recalled the tragedy to his mind, and he had determined as he hoed the turnips that day to inquire for the child and do something to help her if possible, for he had rather an exalted idea of his responsibility as a landlord.

Perhaps this accounted for his apparent willingness to take upon him the burden which he saw the villagers were thrusting upon him. At all events, here he is at the door of the hut, which under the driving clouds, and beaten by the storm wind, looks desolate in the extreme.

He knocked at the door, then at the tiny window, but no sign of life appeared in the cottage.

'Hai! Gwenifer!' he called at last. 'Gwenifer Owen, dost hear, then?' But no sound reached his ears except the roaring of the wind as it rushed up from the north, and bent the scrub and heather on its way.

'I am going to unlock the door and bring a light in, child, so don't thee be frightened'; and in another moment the perforated lantern shed its dancing patterns upon the bare whitewashed walls and earthen floor of the cottage – upon the figure of a child also, who sat crouched up in an empty bed, her hands clasped round her drawn-up knees, her dark hair hanging dishevelled and tumbled over her shoulders, her lustrous brown eyes looking at the newcomer with the terror and helplessness of a hunted animal. Gildas had felt nothing but annoyance and impatience as he had fought his way over the moor; for girls and children were but insignificant objects in his prospect of the world, and Gwenifer was just the age that made her less than nothing to the boy full of new-born plans and projects. Nevertheless, the sight of that forlorn creature, looking at him with fear and distrust, touched something deep down in his heart, and some manly feeling of protection rose in his nature.

'Come, child,' he said. 'Thee must not stay longer here in the dark. 'Tis autumn, and the nights are cold. Thou seest the furniture is all gone, and it is not fit for thee to sleep here alone. Come, get thee down.'

But the child only shook her head slowly.

'Wilt not come with me, and sleep with Het in the loft at Scethryg to-night?'

Another shake of her head was her only answer, and in vain did Gildas coax, command, and even threaten; the child grew firmer, and continued to shake her head. Her obstinacy, however, only moved the lad's own unyielding temper, and laying hold of her hand he endeavoured to draw her towards him; but she screamed and struggled so much that he desisted suddenly, and said in an altered tone of voice:

'Gwenifer, listen! Thou art ten years of age, and I have heard thou hast sense beyond thy years. Knowest thou that I am thy mishteer? Knowest that I came down through the storm because I was sorry for thee, and could not sleep in my bed, knowing that thou wert here in the dark and lightning? Yes, it *does* lighten! Dost remember that I, too, am an orphan since that red sunset? Art not sorry for me too?'

Now he had touched the chords of tender memories and love, and the brown fingers were unclasped from the knees. Slipping on to the ground, she drew nearer to Gildas, and, leaning her cheek on his rough coat, sobbed heavily, the tears dropping slowly down her cheeks.

'That's a brave maid!' said Gildas encouragingly. 'Why, thee and I ought to be good friends if any one ought. Come, trust to me!' and opening the door, they were met by a furious gust of wind which blew over the lantern and left them in the dark. Locking the door, he took her by the hand once more, and, she, yielding to his guidance with no further demur, they turned towards the open moor, where the blast blew up behind them, hurrying Gildas's pace into a run, and almost tearing the girl from his grasp. 'Seems to me I had better carry thee,' he said, stooping and gathering the little thin form into his arms.

Scarcely feeling her weight and helped on by the gale, he made good progress, and Gwenifer sobbed with her cheek on his breast. Gradually her tears ceased, and she lay still, and more content than she had been since her mother's death.

Reaching a gap in the hedge, Gildas rested a moment, leaning on the bank to recover his breath, and looking down at his light burden saw that she had fallen asleep, her long, dark eyelashes resting on her pale cheek, on which the tears glistened. 'Here,' he cried, entering the farmhouse door, where n'wncwl Sam was waiting for his supper – 'here, Het, here's a new shepherdess come to Scethryg!' And he dumped his burden on to the floor with the awkward unintentional roughness of a boy.

Het drew near, looking rather scared as the rudely awakened brown eyes looked round the comfortable kitchen.

'Diwedd anwl! What am I to do with her?' she asked, not in the most gracious of tones; and instantly detecting the reluctance in her manner, the sensitive child turned again to Gildas, who, rather tired of the whole affair, was already sitting down to the table.

'Why, a basin of bread and milk and a good warm by the fire, and then off to bed with thee,' he said, ''tis full time'; and Het knew by the tone of command that further demur would be useless, so she thrust the round-backed oak stool towards the hearth, and gently pushed Gwenifer into it.

Before many minutes the girl was hungrily supping her bowl of barley-bread and milk, for she had scarcely tasted food that day, the sale having occupied everyone's attention too much to allow them to think of the silent child, who had crouched behind the garden hedge, her heart bursting with feelings that she was unable to express. No wonder that the large tears rolled down her cheeks, as she hid there in the shadow – no wonder that a little wail broke from her dumb lips, as one by one the few rough articles of furniture were brought out and sold. It has been a bitter experience, one to be ever remembered, and the long day endurance had only been lightened by Gildas's kind though firm tones; but when the lad's strong arms had enfolded her and borne her safely through the wind and storm, the sorely tried child had sunk into trustful slumber, and from that moment he had taken his place as her master and her owner.

Unconscious of this, the matter-of-fact Gildas, as soon as

he had ordered her in Het's safe keeping to bed, dismissed the subject from his mind, and was soon arranging with n'wncwl Sam for the threshing next day.

'And what'st going to do with that dumb girl?' said the latter, when the subject of the threshing had been settled. 'Mark my words! she'll be a burden upon thee for ever!' For although Gildas often sought and followed his advice in matters of farming experience, yet he felt that he was generally controlled and dominated by his wilful nephew, and he consoled himself for this by systematically objecting to everything that the younger man proposed.

'Didn't you say Twm had grown careless, and had given notice three times this month?'

'Pouf! I don't take no notice of him, not I!'

'But I do,' said Gildas. 'Let him go. This child will be well soon; she can take his place. Let's to bed.'

N'wncwl Sam put his pipe away, and followed Gildas up the crooked stairs, still grumbling to himself – 'Mark my word, thou'lt see then! As true as there's rain after wind, thou'lt repent!'

They had reached the turning in the stairs when both stopped and looked at each other, for above the roaring of the storm they heard a timid but distinct knocking at the door.

'Who can it be this time o' night?' said Gildas.

'Be bound 'tis some tramp; let him be!' answered n'wncwl Sam, but without replying, his nephew went down and unbarred the door.

CHAPTER II

The Old Storehouse

When he opened the outer door, Gildas's first encounter was with the stormy wind, which blew out his candle before he had more than a moment's glance at the visitor who knocked at his door so late.

That glance, however, was sufficient to reveal the figure of Hezekiah Morgan, an old man who for two years had been permitted to occupy a loft over the storehouse, paying a small rent for this poor refuge from the storms of life. He had once filled a responsible position as master of 'Bryn Austin', one of the best schools in South Wales; but now, broken in health and spirits, he was thankful to find a shelter in the old loft, which had before his advent been used as a receptacle for old boards, broken harness, rusty tools, and many other unconsidered trifles connected with farm life.

'Hezek!' exclaimed Gildas in surprise. 'Come in, man, while I light my candle and hunt for your key. In the dear's name! where have you come from in such a storm, and so early in the year? Is Nance with you?'

'Yes,' said the old man in a gentle voice, which trembled a little from the stress of the wind with which he had battled. 'Yes, here she is'; and he drew aside the folds of his shabby brown cloak, disclosing the figure of a child, who clung to him closely and looked out from her hiding-place with laughing blue eyes and a dimpled roguish face.

'*She* has only played hide-and-seek with the wind under

39

my old cloak. It has buffeted me sorely, but everything is fun to Nance.

'We were on the Wildrom Mountains when we heard of the calamity which has befallen thee and deprived me of a good friend. Gildas, my heart aches for thee, lad; and so I returned, thinking perhaps I might be of some service to thee. The herb o' gold has not ripened yet, and the moon-wort was only beginning to seed; but I could stay no longer after I had heard of thy sore loss. One of the servants at the farm where we lodged brought a newspaper home from the fair and lent it to me, and in that I read of the accident.'

'Here is the key,' said Gildas, finding it between the plates on the dresser, where he had been fumbling, partly to hide his awkwardness, for a lad of sixteen shrinks from speaking of his sorrow.

'Will I put the 'cawl' on again?' he asked. 'A bowl of it would warm you before you go.'

'No, no,' said the old man. 'I have all we want in my wallet, and little Nance will soon kindle a fire and put things straight. Good-night, my lad; I see thine eyes are heavy with sleep.'

'Good-night,' said Gildas, unbarring the door again; and as the old man went out, a bright round face peeped smilingly from under his cloak. The wind caught them at the doorway, and a peal of merry laughter from the child reached the lad's ear with the swirling blast. However, neither laughter nor wind prevented his falling into a heavy dreamless sleep as soon as he had thrown himself upon his bed, while out in the 'old storws,' as it was generally called, the old man and his grandchild spread their simple supper in the light of the fire of wood which they had soon kindled. In its warmth and brightness, Hezek – or, to give him his proper name, Hezekiah Morgan – lost the tremble in his voice somewhat and regained his usual placid demeanour.

His had been a life of strenuous efforts, ending in the failure and disappointment that generally attend the man who allows himself to be led captive by a headstrong passion. As a schoolmaster he had been very popular, so much so that to have been a pupil of Hezekiah Morgan was considered the best stepping-stone to success in life; but in a weak moment he had given way to a foolish fancy, and had married a beautiful but uneducated peasant girl.

This was the commencement of his reverses; for, finding, to his disappointment, that he could not raise her to his standard of grace and refinement, he became dissatisfied and depressed, and turned for solace more and more to his own desultory and curious studies, interesting himself much in astrology as well as astronomy, and, most of all, devoting himself to his favourite study of botany; for in the herbs of the field he believed was to be found a cure for every ailment to which humanity is liable.

Gradually he lost interest in his school, the numbers of his pupils dwindled away, and his wife, keenly alive to her own shortcomings, sank into ill-health and died at the birth of her first child, leaving her eccentric husband and his helpless offspring to face the journey of life without her. This child – a girl – had grown up somehow, and married early a well-to-do farmer, who had willingly taken her old father also to live with him, as out of his former earnings he still possessed sufficient to pay his son-in-law for his board and lodging. But misfortune had not done with Hezekiah Morgan; for his daughter, inheriting her mother's malady, died soon after the birth of her first child.

For the next six years the old man lived on at the farm, feeling himself, as his small savings diminished more and more, an unwelcome encumbrance.

He was devotedly attached to his little granddaughter, and upon him fell the chief care of the child, her rough father taking no interest in her, although she was an attractive little creature, full of sportive and enticing ways. It was convenient to feel, when the harvest, the sowing, the corn-grinding called all hands to work, that the child needed no care or nursing while 'Dacu,' or in English pronunciation, 'Dakee,' was ready to watch over her and guard her from every danger. And so it came to pass that every day, and in every season of the year, the old man and the child might be seen roaming about the farm lands, sunning themselves on the gold-starred hedges, or sheltering behind the hay-stacks; anywhere away from the house where they were both made to feel that they were only in the way.

At last there came a day when the hard-fisted and hard-hearted farmer announced his intention of bringing home a new mistress to the farm, and Hezekiah, who was now generally known as 'old Hezek, the herbalist,' had said, 'Then perhaps you will not want to keep me here any longer?'

His voice trembled, and his hands closed and opened nervously, for he felt that banishment from the child would mean death to him.

The farmer had seen his anxiety and at once taken advantage of it.

'Well,' he said, 'most like, look you, a second wife won't care to see the first wife's father here. 'Twill be enough for her to have another woman's child to 'tend.'

'No doubt, no doubt,' said the old man, his tongue cleaving to his parched mouth. 'You wouldn't let the little one come with me, would you?' To him the favour seemed too great to expect. 'You know,' he continued eagerly, 'I have still enough to keep me in food and lodging. You have the capital, and for Nance's sake you would send me the interest regularly. I would go back to Tregildas to end my days in my own neighbourhood, I think.'

'Ten shillings a week,' said the farmer grudgingly. 'Tan-i-marw! 'tis a fine thing to have money and nothing to do! But, look here. If you make your will to her, and sign it before you go, you may take the child. 'Twill be a great bother, but I'll send the interest regular. You'll take care of Nance?'

'Yes, yes!' said Hezek, 'and whoever wants, she shall not.'

'Very good,' said the farmer. 'This day week I'll be bringing my wife home.'

Before the day was over he had written out the simple document, and the old man had signed it with trembling fingers, trembling not in sorrow at having to leave the house where he had had little love or tenderness shown him, but in fear lest his son-in-law might change his mind, and refuse to let him take the child away with him.

'When can I go?' he asked, standing with his old battered hat in his hand.

'That is as you will,' answered the farmer. 'There is no hurry for a day or two.'

'Well, 'tis a fine day,' said the old man, 'I had better start at once; you will want to see little Nance sometimes, so we will come here on our rounds, perhaps, eh?'

'Very good,' said the farmer, reaching down his bill-hook, and turning towards the door as if tired of the conversation.

'Good-bye, then,' the old man called after him, for he had already reached the gate of the close.

'Oh, fforwel!' said the farmer, stopping; 'I didn't think you were going so soon. And here,' he continued, returning slowly with his hand in his pocket, 'give her this – this shilling,' he said, with a burst of generosity. ''Tis better for me not to see her. Perhaps she'll cry, and not be willing to go. And mind you, I wouldn't be willing to let her go, only I know you'll treat her well, and if I kept her here she'd worry our lives out fretting after you.'

'Yes, yes! b't shwr,' said Hezek, 'and I thank you for your kind consideration. Good-bye!'

One more 'fforwel' from the farmer, and he was gone to 'trash' his hedgerows and give a general tidy up, in preparation for the new wife who was to arrive so soon.

Hezek had never felt much affection for his son-in-law, nevertheless he felt sad and sorrowful as he tied up his few belongings in his knapsack, for, alas! his heart was warm and tender, and therefore open to many a wound that one more callous would have escaped. 'Come, dear heart!' he said, affecting a jocose and lively mood which he was far from feeling, 'come, tie up thy bundle. We are going to run away together to-day, thou and I, as we have often planned. Come! and we will travel over the blue hills to where the sea is tossing and frothing; I will show thee the white-winged ships that sail over it to far-off lands, and the sea-pinks growing on the rocks, and the white sea-gulls that float through the air. I will show thee the house where I was born, and we will find a lodging somewhere near, and live there.'

'Yes, for ever and ever, Dakee,' said the child, executing a whirling dance around him, and flipping her tiny pink fingers. 'Oh! there's happy we'll be! and father and the new mistress won't ever find us.'

'No, no, 'merch-i.' And with his first week's allowance in his pocket, the old man set forth with a flow of hope in his heart which had long been a stranger to it, Nance tripping beside him, her little blue bundle hung over shoulder, and her shilling tied up in the corner of her pocket-handkerchief.

Leisa, the servant, had filled a capacious wallet with sufficient food for two or three days. 'Well, in my deed,' she said, 'I don't know what will we do without you, when we are sick.'

'Thou art never sick, Leisa, so thou wilt not miss me,' answered Hezek, with a gentle smile, and he bade the girl 'good-bye' with real regret in his simple old heart. 'But surely,' he thought as he trudged along behind Nance, who fluttered like a butterfly from side to side of the mountain road, 'surely there are kind hearts in the world somewhere still, and where if not in my old neighbourhood?' His step became lighter and his voice more firm, as visions of his old home rose before him and old memories awoke within him.

'I'll go straight to Scethryg,' he thought. 'Jonathan and I were good friends long ago, perhaps he'll find us lodging,' and with this vague prospect reviving his spirits, he journeyed on over moor and fell, ever like the wounded deer, drawing nearer and nearer to his old home.

'Tell me about the sea,' Nance would say, when tired of her fluttering, she would return to the old man's side, and, nestling her hand into his, would walk soberly for a few minutes.

'The sea! Oh, it is broad and shining, stretching as far as we can see. The sea-pinks grow on the cliffs above it, and shells, pink, white, brown, and yellow, crowd in the chinks of the rocks around its edge.'

'Shells and sea-pinks? Oh, Dakee!' and Nance would look up at him with wondering blue eyes, and again ejaculate, 'Oh, Dakee!' And so they wandered on together side by side, often hand in hand, the child oblivious to all but the present happiness, the old man rejoicing in the feeling that at last his darling was all his own.

It was late on the second day when they reached Tregildas, Hezek weary and footsore, but Nance still brimming over with vivacity and excitement, for here in very truth was the broad blue sea that she had dreamt of; here were the cliffs, the white-sailed ships, and here the sea-pinks growing on the bare grey rocks. Here, too, were the ruined lime-kilns which Hezek had told her of, at the curve of the inlet, which in his youth had glowed like two fiery eyes looking out to sea, and when, on the strand, she picked up shells, real shells! her delight was unbounded, and she shed some petulant

tears and pouted her red lower lip when the old man turned
from the shore toward the higher lands of Scethryg.

'Don't cry, dear heart,' he said. 'But a little way further
and we'll be at the end of our journey.'

'But I don't want to go further,' said the wilful child. 'Go
you, and leave me to pick up shells.'

'To-morrow, my little one; to-morrow thou shalt play all
day on the shore.' But Nance still sulked and lagged behind,
until suddenly out of the gloaming a dark-faced boy caught
them up dangling a bundle of fish. In a moment Nance was
eagerly interested, and while Hezek inquired the way she
danced round the silver mackerel and clapped her hands
with pleasure.

'Did they come from the sea, too?' she asked. 'Oh, there's
pretty things are in it. Will I carry them for you, boy?'

'No,' said the boy rather curtly, 'but if you are going to
Scethryg I daresay you will have them for supper: that is
where I live.'

'And that is where I want to go,' said Hezek. 'Jonathan
Rees no doubt is your father, 'machgen-i; have you ever
heard him speak of Hezekiah Morgan?'

'Yes, I think,' answered the boy, slackening his pace a little.
'There is Scethryg,' he said, pointing to an old farmhouse of
grey stone.

'Yes, yes, I know it well, my boy; I asked the way because
that new bit of road puzzled me; now we're on the moor I
know every step of it – och-i, och-i!'

Jonathan Rees, waiting in the farmyard for the return of
his son, was not in the best humour for granting favours
when Hezek, preceded by Gildas, arrived.

'So thee'st seen fit to come home at last, idle-pack!' were
his first words of greeting, words which his son took no
notice of as he passed into the kitchen and delivered his
fish to be cooked for supper.

'You don't know me, Jonathan Rees?' said Hezek, with outstretched hand.

'No, I don't,' said the farmer, 'but coming so late, you must be wanting a lodging, and there are two tramps in the barn already – so . . .'

'No, no, I am no tramp; but indeed I thought perhaps you would give us a lodging – just for to-night, at any rate. Don't you remember Hezekiah Morgan?'

'Caton pawb! Where did you come from this time of night? Of course I remember you now'; and he took the proffered hand, but with no warmth of greeting. 'Come in,' he added grudgingly, preceding his visitor into the comfortable farm-house kitchen, where Hezek proceeded to explain the reason of his advent and to make his request known. 'I had a longing, you see, to end my days in my old neighbourhood,' he said, when, after many hums and haws, Jonathan seemed inclined to make room for him.

'Couldn't he have the old storehouse?' said the brown-skinned boy, who was watching Het frying the fish.

'Of course I will pay whatever you like to charge me, in reason,' said Hezek.

'And if Dakee hasn't enough, I have a shilling,' said Nance, who thought it was time to suggest something definite for the warm glow of the fire was pleasant and the smell of the frying fish appetising.

Jonathan Rees took no notice of the child's remark, but, seeing a chance of turning the old storehouse to some account, agreed to his son's proposal; and finding that the old man made no demur to his rather exorbitant charge, added in an effusive manner, 'Well, look you! You're an old friend, so I'll throw in the vegetables for your cawl into the bargain; and I daresay you and your grandchild will weed the garden in return.'

'That we will, indeed,' said Hezek; and so it was settled.

And feeling that he had made a good bargain, Jonathan waxed more amiable, and over their supper the two men vied with each other in recalling old memories, though the farmer was ten years younger than his guest, until at last Nance fell asleep, and was carried by Het up to the only spare bed the house possessed. Here Hezek, following soon, sank upon his pillow with a heart full of gratitude; for although he had not been received with the warmth and friendliness which he had associated with a return to his old neighbourhood, he was used to coldness and rebuffs, and was thankful that Jonathan Rees had agreed to his request, though grudgingly.

And so he and Nance settled down to the rude but safe shelter of the 'old storws,' where Hezek was to end his days and the child to grow up to womanhood.

'Maldraeth! Maldraeth! When will we go to Maldraeth?' she cried impatiently next morning, when the old man, assisted by Gildas, was endeavouring to bring some order into the confusion that reigned in the loft.

'By-and-by, by-and-by,' said Hezek, trying to pacify the wilful girl, who stamped her little foot and grumbled while the others worked.

'By-and-by!' said the lad irritably, for children, especially girls, were to him simply impedimenta to be ignored and avoided as much as possible. 'By-and-by, if I was your grandfather, I'd give you a whipping!'

Nance stood still a moment to stare at him in astonishment before she answered, her eyes flashing, her cheeks burning. '*You* my grandfather!' and pointing her finger at him she continued disdainfully, 'You, indeed! There's a fine grandfather *you'd* make! Not if you put on Dakee's spectacles, and carried his wallet of herbs, you wouldn't look wise! Tush! I don't care that for you! Grandfather, indeed!' and she snapped her fingers derisively; but Gildas was too busily occupied to notice the little irate fairy. He was entering into the business of domiciling the newcomers with real zest, and his father, who presently came to see how the work was progressing, said, with a little sarcasm in his voice, 'Oh, yes! Come to Gildas for anything but the farm work!' and he turned away before the boy, colouring hotly, had time to defend himself.

At last everything was arranged to his satisfaction, 'And I'll come to-morrow to board off the end for the two little bedrooms for you,' he said, preparing to leave the scene of his operations for a time, when he was surprised to hear a sob from Nance, who was standing with her pinafore to her eyes.

'What is it then, dear heart?' said the old man, with tender pity.

'I want to make friends with him,' answered the child, looking at the brown-faced boy.

'Oh yes, you must forgive her,' said the old man.

'Alreit, alreit!' he said, turning towards to the door; but Nance, with her face to the wall, wept aloud.

'Give me a kiss, then,' she cried, for that was the only form of reconciliation she knew of.

'Ach! no,' said the boy, 'I can't bear kissing.' Then, seeing another wail was imminent, he hastily dived his hand into his pocket and extracted a screwed paper of sweets.

'Here!' he said, thrusting them into the child's hand.

Nance smiled and accepted the peace-offering. 'You *shall* be my grandfather, if you like,' she said, sucking her sweets; but Gildas showed scarcely as much gratitude as she expected, for he was off at once and running down the ruinous flight of stone steps that connected the loft with the farmyard.

In the afternoon, however, he returned, full of interest and energy, having collected from all sorts of odd nooks and corners, and eked out by a small outlay in the village shop, a sufficient assortment of articles for the primitive ménage. A few cups, plates, and bowls ranged on a shelf which he had himself fixed on the wall, a crock for the cawl, a kettle, and a tea-pot, and behold Hezek and Nance settled into their new abode and quite content with its arrangement!

Once more, as the sun was setting, the child began to reiterate her cry for Maldraeth, a lonely cove under the cliffs; and he set out not unwillingly to gratify her desire, for it has been a favourite resort of his boyhood and often in his mind of late.

He had laid the scene of most of his legends and 'stories' on Maldraeth, stories that had beguiled many an hour when he and Nance had roamed about the fields of Penwern together, and for this reason she was now impatient to see it for herself. So over the moor and down the rugged path they made their way, even the excitable child consenting to 'hold tight on Dakee's hand' as she looked over the dizzy height to the shore below. And when at last they reached the pebbly strand her voluble tongue was silent, and her little hand clung to his in a solemn awe as she saw the tall crags towering over the lonely beach, which even at noontide looked dark and forbidding.

'See here!' said Hezek, pointing to the bank of seaweed, driftwood, and starfish left by the tide on the sand. ''Twas here most likely that Gwrgan found the chain of gold with which he bought his freedom long ago, as I told thee. And then in that cave, perhaps, the white lady lived, who came out every night when the moon was shining, and sang so sadly and so sweetly that the shepherds on the hills would weep when they heard her. Dost remember? I have found wonderful things on this shore myself, for here comes everything in from the sea; the tide sweeps in here and leaves its treasures, because the rocks close almost round it.'

Nance, however, refused to stoop over the garlanded shore, turning even from the shells that lay scattered under her feet; and when at last the sun went down like a fiery red ball behind the grey sea, she began to whimper, 'Come home, Dakee! Ach! I am not liking Maldraeth,' and the old man was never afterwards troubled by the petulant cry of 'Maldraeth, Maldraeth; I want to go to Maldraeth!'

Day in, day out, they roamed the fields, the moor, and Tregildas sands together – Hezek with bent shoulders and peering eyes, ever seeking for herbs and flowers, the child tripping about and making little excursions on her own account whenever a brighter flower or butterfly attracted her attention; and his expostulating cry of 'Come back, dear heart!' made no more impression upon her than did the sea-wind whistling over the moor, until, tired out, she returned of her own free will, and nestling her hand into his, looked up into his face with such bewitching contrition that she seldom heard the word of reproof which she knew she deserved. The other village children seemed but little attracted by Nance's volatile ways, and left her rather severely alone, while she seemed inclined to shrink disdainfully from their stolid manners. Little Gwenifer Owen alone seemed to take to the stranger, who was of the same age as herself. They soon became much attached to each other, and Gwenifer was almost as close an attendant upon old Hezek the herbalist as his own grandchild, taking far more interest in his collection of herbs than did Nance, who was much too busy with her own affairs to waste her time upon 'old plants that smell nasty, and haven't got flowers on them.'

To Hezek the peace and safety of the old loft was as a haven of refuge from the storms of life which had buffeted him so sorely, and he thankfully settled down to his uneventful life. In autumn he made excursions inland, to some locality where the plants he required bloomed more freely than in the keen sea-air, and it was during one of these pilgrimages that he had learnt from the shepherd of a mountain farm the history of the disaster which had befallen his old friend Jonathan Rees. As we have seen, he hurried back to Scethryg, and, after a journey of many days, reached there on the stormy night when Gildas and n'wncwl Sam had been suddenly disturbed on their way to bed.

How they rejoiced in the shelter of the old loft when Nance had kindled the fire! How Hezek had basked in its light! How Nance laughed at the spluttering and crackling of the wood! And when they spread on the board the simple fare which they had had the precaution to bring with them, what simple happiness was theirs! What sweet content!

CHAPTER III

'Gwenifer'

Eight years have passed away when we next see the little village of Tregildas – years that have made but little difference to its outward appearance, and none to its craggy heights. A few roofs of slate, straight and bare and ugly, replaced the soft brown thatch of former years; but the gates that had been out of repair when Hezek Morgan first took possession of the old storehouse still hung loose upon their hinges, or upon one hinge, as the case might be. Jerri's crazy boat still crossed the tide occasionally, and the accident which had invested him and his boat with a tragic interest had been almost forgotten.

Above the village the grey walls of Scethryg still stood in apparent confusion, though, approached more closely, it was evident that not one ivy-covered gable, not one flight of stone steps, not one door, but had a good reason for being there. Use or comfort only had been considered, as a shed had been added here or a dairy there, and the result was a dwelling-house both beautiful and comfortable. The lichen stains on the roof were a little yellower perhaps, the ferns round the horse-pond a little thicker and greener than when we saw them last. Certainly the fields and hedges showed more signs of care and cultivation, for the master of Scethryg was energetic and thrifty, and had the reputation of being the best farmer on the coast.

On the human beings whose acquaintance we have

made in these pages the years have left their impress. The aged stooped more as they crossed the fields to plough or harvest; there were a few more wrinkles round the eyes, a little less vigour in the step. With the young time had been busy too, imperceptibly but surely leading the youth into full manhood, the girl into womanhood, so that when we next meet Nance Ellis it is difficult to recognise in the buxom young woman, the little elf-like child who had trotted by the old man's side all the way from an inland county to the sea-girt cliffs of Tregildas. There was still the same sparkle of fun and mischief in the blue eyes, the same crown of golden hair; and Nance was called a 'purty girl,' in spite of her irregular features and a suspicion of coarseness in the square build and bright complexion. The nose was too short, the mouth rather too wide; but why seek out the flaws in Nance's face? for it was never the same for an hour together, and if her pretty, pouting ways did not please her swains today, depend upon it to-morrow her smiles and jokes would lead them captive.

The day had been dark and lowering, brooding clouds hanging over the sea with the persistent gloom of a November day; but suddenly, towards evening, the weather seemed to remember it was March, and began to storm and bluster. Over the leaden sea came fitful gusts that curled the tips of the waves into little white streaks, scarcely distinguishable from the seagulls that were settling down on the surface in expectation of what the north wind might bring them.

Around Scethryg it swirled and eddied, blowing the straw about in the farmyard and making the old thorn-hedge round the horse-pond sway and creak. Gildas Rees, grown tall and broad and manly, taking advantage of a momentary lull, went round his barns and outhouses to see that no doors or gates were swinging open.

At the further corner of the yard he reached the flight of stone steps leading up to the storehouse, and, looking through the gathering twilight at the closed door at the top, stood a moment as if debating within himself whether he should mount the steps or not.

It was unusual for him to hesitate long, and it was not many seconds before he had run up the rude approach and knocked at the red-painted door.

Having knocked, he did not wait for an answer, but raised the thumb latch, and entered in a swirl of wind, turning to close the door at once.

'Only to see how you are here,' he said. 'I have been to Caermadoc to-day, and just come home. Are you frightened of the storm?'

'Frightened? No, not a bit,' answered Nance, coming forward with a smile. 'If it was not getting dark I would go out and play with it. See! Dakee is asleep through it all!'

At that moment the wind seemed to wake from its momentary calm, and hurl itself against the door with a roar and a rattle that awoke the old man and set Nance laughing defiantly. She shook her fist at the door, and, with a gesture that had clung to her from childhood, ended up with a snap of her fingers.

'I don't care that for his blustering!' she said, as another furious gust clamoured for admittance.

'Dear anwl! 'tis strong up here,' said Gildas, looking with an amused smile at the girl who pitted herself so recklessly against the powers of Nature without.

'We are going to have tea, Dakee and I,' she said. 'Let *him* whistle out there, and stop you with us, mishteer, and have a cup of tea. Be bound Het is not ready for you.'

'Yes, indeed she is whatever,' said Gildas. 'Tea is ready and n'wncwl Sam waiting, so I must not stop; only I thought perhaps the wind would be frightening you up here with these shaky doors and windows.'

'Oh, twt! A fig for the storm!' said the girl, helping him to close the door; and Gildas went across the stubble, his head bent against the blast, and bearing in his mind a distinct picture of the scene he had just left: the quaint old raftered room, its whitewashed walls all aglow in the firelight, the simple cooking utensils hanging each on its nail round the hearth, the rude oak furniture, Nance's rounded figure moving up and down amongst them, and the old man dozing by the cheerful blaze.

Hezek, awaking, looked round at the cosy brightness with a glow of content, and turned to the rough table which Nance carried up to the hearth, pursing up her full red lips and mocking the whistle of the wind.

'Thou art a brave little lass,' said the old man, who never seemed to realise that his pet was no longer a child; 'but thou art forgetting, 'merch-i, that the storm-wind is sure to bring trouble, if not sorrow, to somebody. What about the poor sailors out at sea to-night?'

'Well, of course I would be sorry for them if I could *see* them,' said Nance, as she cut the bread-and-butter; 'but look now, Dakee: it can't bring *us* any trouble whatever. We have no one belonging to us at sea. Let the old wind roar and howl its best – it can't come in here. So there's your nice hot tea, and there's your herring frizzled up as you like it'; and Nance made it a cosy merry meal, in spite of the noise and bluster of the storm.

'Gildas might have stopped to tea with us,' she said, with the little pout on her lips that was so pretty and provoking. 'One thing I know, he'll be older when I ask him next; that he will!'

She had scarcely spoken when a loud knocking startled them both, the knocking being followed by a rough shaking of the door. Recalling her vaunted bravery, she rose, calling out, 'Who is there?'

At that moment there came a slight lull in the storm, and a voice answered, 'Nance Ellis! Open the door for the dear's sake! Here's a man has been hurt, and wants to see Hezek.'

Before he had ended his request, the door was opened and two men entered, almost hurled in by the wind. One of these Nance recognised as John Davies, the mate of the *Liliwen.* The door closed, and for a few moments there was a comparative calm, during which the visitor began to account for his sudden arrival. 'Hezek, man! 'Tis to you we are coming for help; this is Cap'n Jack – you've often heard me talking 'bout him. Well, he has had an accident to his hand, and I told him, if any one would cure him, 'twould be Hezek Morgan.'

Captain Jack had sunk on the chair which Nance brought him, his face white and drawn, while her grandfather, gently unwrapping the outheld hand, examined its injuries.

'Ts, ts!' ejaculated Nance as she caught sight of the crushed fingers. 'How did it happen?'

'Oh! 'twas this deuce of a wind,' said the mate, 'coming on so sudden; loosened something in the hold, and the cap'n and me, we was trying to right it, when down came Joshua Jones' wife's tombstone, slap on his hand. Bringing it home for him from Liverpool we were, and, Dei anwl! I thought the cap'n was gone, so white he was till I moved the weight off him; then he soon came round; and now, you see what you can do for him. Well, Nance lass!' he added, suddenly turning to her, and gripping her hand, 'how art thou? In my deed I'll soon be failing to know thee, growing prettier and prettier and taller and taller every time I come home.'

Nance blushed and laughed a little, as much as she dared while her grandfather was probing and examining the injured hand.

'You have broken your fingers, lad,' said the old man, 'besides a nasty wrench of the wrist. There's a good doctor at Caermadoc; what d'ye think? Will you rather trust to me or get Gildas to drive you there in the car?'

'Oh, go on,' said the captain, speaking for the first time. 'All the way to Caermadoc and this infernal pain to bear all the time? Not I!'

Nance, at a sign from her grandfather, had already mixed a glass of hot brandy and water, and now held it towards the stranger, who raising his eyes to hers stared for a moment at her piquante face.

'Well,' he said, 'your permission, doctor? Well, then, here's to a continuance of our acquaintance and a little Dutch courage to me. Now, heave ahead,' he added when he had gulped down the steaming potion.

'Come you then, mate, and hold his hand,' said Hezek, who was already in his element sorting out his herbs and bottles. 'Nance, go you out of sight a bit, 'merch-i,' and the girl, who had paled a little, turned away and shut herself into her tiny bedroom, laying her head on the bed and drawing the quilt over her ears.

She need not have done so, however, for the stranger, though shrinking at the prospect of pain, was brave enough under its actual endurance to bear it with stoical firmness.

At last a long-drawn 'There!' from Hezek, followed by an 'Ah!' of satisfaction from the patient, proclaimed the dressing over, and Nance was called upon for a sling, as well as for its proper adjustment, during which operation the captain was sufficiently recovered to make very good use of his eyes; eyes of the lightest shade of blue, which looked out from a face of sunburnt brown with a very striking effect of contrast. They were eyes that could dance and sparkle with fun and mischief, or flash with dare-devil recklessness, but they were also capable, in their owner's infrequent moments of seriousness, of expressing a strangely wistful sadness. Nance did not seem to dislike their appearance, for she smiled and blushed under their gaze, as she helped her grandfather to put away his herbs, his oils, and his pipkins, very well satisfied with the result of his dressing of the injured hand.

'There, my lad,' he said, 'a good job, and well done, though I say it myself. 'Twill heal for certain, though not at once, mind you. You must let me see it every day at first.'

'Of course,' answered Captain Jack, 'the two John Davieses will be here again to-morrow right enough,' and answering Hezek's look of inquiry, he added, laughing, 'We are both John Davies, d'you see – I and the mate, and that's why they call me Captain Jack.'

'Oh, that's it. Well, well!' said Hezek. 'Lemme see. Aren't you a son of Davies Rhiwgollen?'

'To be sure. His only son. He's dead these two years.'

'So indeed! an old pupil of mine he was long ago, in Bryn Austin School.' And Hezek sighed as he recalled his past importance.

'Well indeed!' exclaimed the patient, evidently not unwilling to prolong the interview, but he was interrupted by his mate.

'Excuse me, cap'n,' he said, pointing towards the window which rattled in its frame, while outside the wind roared and blustered with increased violence, 'there's the little *Liliwen* waiting for us, and I think we're going to have a rough night, so the sooner we're aboard the better.'

'What do I owe you, doctor?' said the captain, diving into his pocket with his left hand, 'for I must go, I suppose, since the mate calls the captain to order.'

'Nothing, nothing, till your hand is well,' said Hezek. 'You can pay me a trifle then if you like.'

Nance wished them a smiling good-night, which the captain evidently appreciated, for when they reached the stubble yard he shouted to his mate, 'You never told me old

Hezek had a pretty daughter, man!' but John Davies's answer was carried away by the wind.

'He speaks like a gentleman, Dakee,' said Nance, returning to the interrupted meal. 'Ach y fi! this tea is quite cold; wait till I make some fresh.' When the brown teapot had been refilled and they had sat down again, she returned to the same subject, her grandfather looking thoughtfully into the fire.

'Dakee! Cap'n Jack speaks like a gentleman, doesn't he? Is he a gentleman?'

'No, 'merch-i,' answered Hezek, with more decision than usual. 'His *father* was a gentleman, an old pupil of mine, Nance, and the best fellow in the whole school; so straightforward he was, so merry, and with it all so warm-hearted. 'Twas a pity he had a son like him who had just been here; he spent his money, and he broke his heart. I remembered the whole story as soon as he said his father was dead. He tried everything to bring this lad to his senses, but nothing would sober him. A drinking, idle rascal, until at last he ran away from his uncle's office (a lawyer he was in Merthyr) and left his debts for his father to pay. So there's your gentleman!'

'Ts, ts,' said Nance, turning her cup round, and looking at the tea-leaves at the bottom. 'Well, he seemed all right tonight whatever. Perhaps he has turned over a new leaf.'

'Perhaps indeed, 'merch-i. I have heard that since he went to sea he is not so wild. The ship is his own, you see; only his uncle and the mate have a few ounces in her; so that will make him look to his ways better, perhaps.'

'Pwr fellow!' said Nance.

'Yes, yes, we must be kind to him, for his father's sake. His hand will get well before long, and then we won't see any more of him. I wouldn't like him to be coming here often, mind you, and Gildas wouldn't, I'm sure. He knows about him no doubt.'

'Gildas!' said Nance, with a little wilful set of the lips, 'what has he to do with it, I would like to know?' and – yes, undoubtedly, though unconsciously, she snapped her fingers in the folds of her blue gown.

'Well, he is our 'mishteer' whatever, and so kind he is, we wouldn't like to offend him, 'merch-i.''

'No,' said the girl laughing. 'Oh! anwl, how he would knit those black eyebrows, and how his eyes would flash! *I* know him!'

'He is never cross to thee, Nance?'

'Cross to me? No, indeed. What for? He'd better not, too!'

The old man muttered something about a woman's tongue, while Nance hummed about her work. At last she lighted a candle, and Hezek, putting on his spectacles, began to sort the herbs he had gathered in the morning, tying them up in separate bunches, which he hung on the rafters to dry; and without, while they chatted and worked in the warm lighted storehouse, the storm wind still roared, and the *Liliwen*, riding at anchor in the bay, bowed her tall mast and creaked and strained under the blast.

At the other end of the irregular block of walls and gables called Scethryg stood the farm kitchen, more sheltered from the wind than the old storehouse, and, like that, aglow with light and warmth. N'wncwl Sam and the master of the house were sitting at their evening meal under the wide chimney. Gildas seemed to have returned from Caermadoc in a thoughtful mood; he stirred the glowing logs aimlessly; at last, opening the door and looking into the darkness, he asked, 'Is Gwenifer here?'

'No,' said Het, who was always touchy on that point. 'She's in her old hut, I suppose. In my deed I don't know what draws her to it so much.'

''Tis very natural,' said Gildas; ''twas her home once, and home is very . . .'

'That's what I say,' interrupted n'wncwl Sam, who ever since he had been saved by his nephew from the penury of his home, was always hankering after it, or persuading himself that such were his sentiments. 'Nothing will make up for the loss of home'.

Gildas's black brows contracted as he turned to the discontented old man. 'Why talk nonsense about it, though?' he asked. 'You know very well you would not like to go back to yours.'

'No, no, caton pawb, no! I wasn't thinking of such a thing, but thinking of Gwenifer I was, out there on the hillside in such a wind as this.'

'Oh, I see,' said Gildas with an incredulous smile, 'but I daresay she has a good fire, and the little bwthin is fast bolted and barred. Gwenifer knows how to make a bright hearth, and to turn the blackest weather into light.'

'Dear anwl!' said Het. 'Couldn't be a brighter fire than you have here to-night, and I'm sure no one could set on the table a better meal than you have had! The fish you brought home fried as brown as dried bracken, and bread that I baked to-day! But some people are never satisfied, and you may . . .'

'Hsht! enough, woman!' said Gildas, 'or out I go. The storm wind is better than a woman's tongue!'

Thus it will be seen that while without the north wind raved, within the house, too, there were elements of discord; and perhaps it was due to this that Gildas went out in such inclement weather, turning his face toward the black moor and crossing it with difficulty, so strong was the wind. Across its broad expanse he saw in a momentary gleam of moonlight the little brown hut which Gwenifer Owen still called home although her daily work took her often away from its rude shelter. She spent most of her time at Scethryg, and her life was a busy one, and full of interest in spite of the spell of silence which held her in its thrall; for Gwenifer had never recovered the power of speech, and the girl was still as silent as the sphinx. Like the sphinx, too, her dark eyes seemed to hold within their depths the memory of thoughts and feelings born of her long silence alone on the hills and moors.

Frosts had whitened, harvests had ripened, the years had come and gone, but Gwenifer was still condemned to silence, and seemed to stand alone, looking calmly on at the follies and unrest of the world; and it was to this solitary and thoughtful creature that Gildas Rees, with his practical rustic outlook, expressed in the bright black eye, the firm tread, the rather loud voice, and the powerful limbs, was making his way through the wind and storm.

'She's not blown away whatever,' he thought when he caught sight of a glimmer from her two-paned window; and while he fights his way across the moor, we will leave him and relate how Gwenifer came to be still living in the hut in which she was born. Ever since that stormy night, eight years ago, when Gildas had carried her home in his arms, she had quietly succumbed to his strong will, and taken her place in the household with complete self-surrender, and with a feeling that in his strength and his imperious ways lay the safest shelter for her imperfect life. The child could not have given expression to this feeling even had her lips been unsealed, neither had it ever dawned upon the boy-master that she had so completely transferred to him the loyal fidelity which she had once given her mother only. Absorbed in the work of his farm, he was much too busy to notice the little silent waif who went in and out amongst them, attracting as little attention as possible, effacing herself entirely and seeking only to serve the master who had conquered her warm impulsive heart.

Jinni's old cottage far up the mountainside had fallen much into decay, and Gildas, generally more neat and thrifty than his neighbours, surprised them all by leaving it unrepaired.

'Pull it down, master,' said Ebben the carpenter, 'and build a nice stone house with a slate roof and two chimneys, and a square wall round the front. That's how they do now.'

'Let be, let be,' said Gildas. ''Tis not wanted up here so high. Nobody but Gwenifer would live in it'; and the girl, who listened anxiously, heard the words with relief, for the old cottage was dear to her, and she spent every hour that she could spare within its walls, decorating the empty shelves with shells and broken crockery, where once her mother's much-prized jugs and plates stood in bright array. Or sometimes, sitting in the open doorway, she gazed over the broad shimmering sea that stretched beyond the moor, often until the sun had set and the stars came out and crowded the dark blue vault above her. No wonder that as she grew older her dark eyes seemed to see more than was visible to those around her, for to her many a sight and sound unseen by the denizens of the busy world were familiar as the broad noontide. The falling stars that shot at midnight across the zenith, the pallid stars that sometimes span the sky of night, the quivering rosy light that spreads from out the deep mysterious north, the lambent flicker on the rippling tide – Gwenifer knew them all. She had spread upon the old oak frame a bed of sweet dried heather; and it had become an understood thing that after supper she should steal silently away, and be no more seen until the sunrise called her once more to her duties.

'Let her be,' Gildas would say when Het or n'wncwl Sam complained; 'the child has sorrow enough! And do thou, Het, take her a blanket and quilts from the Cist'.

'And can't milady sleep with me, then?' Het would answer, 'when I have widened my bed for her, and given her a box to keep her clothes in?'

'Let her be!' was Gildas's reply; and she was left in undisturbed possession of the hut, whose thatched eaves came down low over door and windows. Here she would often play at housekeeping, alone and silent, but with a face full of smiling interest.

Once when a shadow passed the window and a firm step crossed the threshold, she stood expectant, shy, and frightened; for it was Gildas who stood before her, his young face set in the unnatural seriousness that had fallen upon him since he had become Master of Scethryg. He was still young enough to remember his own boyish games, but for a girl's foolish fancies he had nothing but contempt. He took in the scene at a glance: the bits of broken crockery, the bread and cheese – her daily provision for her mountain lunch – that little tin jug of whey, all spread as if for a feast, while in the tiny grate flamed and crackled a branch of dried furze. 'Silly child,' he said, with a frown which he thought due to his position as the mishteer, 'art pretending to have company?' And Gwenifer, who stood convicted, could only say, 'Yes; are you angry?' and Gildas had no difficulty in understanding her, for though deprived of the power of speech, she was still able to communicate her thoughts with ease to those around her, most of whom had become as familiar with her signs and gestures as she was herself. For every person in her small circle of acquaintance she had an unmistakably descriptive sign; and though it would be wearisome here to detail her *répertoire* of signs and motions, yet they were to her, and to those accustomed to them, as real and intelligible a medium of communication as a written or oral language is to others.

'Angry?' said Gildas, who after all was but a boy, in spite of his masterful ways, 'not I, b't shwr! What do I care where thou eatest thy food?' and sitting down on the edge of the old oak bedstead, he drew from his pocket the hunch of barley-bread and cheese which he was carrying with him for his own lunch.

Delighted and happy, Gwenifer began to drink her whey and attack her bread and cheese as the frown relaxed on the mishteer's face.

'Thou art an odd girl,' he said, looking round at the bare walls and the heather-spread bedstead. 'What wilt thou do when I pull down this hut and build it up afresh?'

In a moment Gwenifer's face altered – a shadow fell upon it like the shadow of a cloud upon a sunny landscape. Her eyes filled with tears, but rising from her mimic table she stood before the autocrat with her hands crossed on her breast, endeavouring with a little wintry smile to adapt herself to her master's wishes, unconsciously taking upon her the look of a martyr. It was self-effacement beyond the lad's comprehension, but it stirred within him the nobler feelings which lay at the foundation of his dogged resolution to fill worthily the place of master.

'Twt, twt! lass,' he said, 'I was but joking; thee can'st have the old hut if thee likest, I will not take it from thee. I have told Het to bring thee a quilt and blankets. Go fetch the brown mare from the long meadow for me; I am going to Treberwyn.' And off ran Gwenifer, content and happy.

After this Gildas would often turn in to the cottage to eat his frugal fare, and as they both grew older he would sit beside the girl on the heather, watching with her the white-winged ships that crossed the bay, they knew not whence nor whither – often, too, consulting her in her difficulties, always sure of a sympathetic listener and a wise counsellor, but noticing little how the childish ways were laid aside as the years went on, nor how in their fleeting course they had changed the thin and rather plain child into a maiden of rare beauty.

Let it not be thought that during this digression Gildas

had been kept waiting at the cottage door; on the contrary, it had been opened to him at once, for scarcely ever did a *stranger* cross the moor. Sometimes Hezek, his shoulders bent and his eyes peering on the ground, would pass that way, and sometimes Nance would run across between the heather mounds; but in the storm and wind Gwenifer had recognised the mishteer's step at once.

'Didn't I say,' he said as he came in and helped her to close the door – 'didn't I say to n'wncwl Sam, 'Gwenifer knows how to make a bright hearth, and how to turn the darkest night to light and cheer'! Well! who would think,' he added, looking round the tiny hut, its whitewashed walls all aglow in the firelight, and recognising the air of peace and comfort reigning over everything, 'who would think this was the hut they wanted me to pull down? I came to see if thou wast blown over the rhos, lass.'

The girl, smiling, shook her head and placed a chair for him, drawing from the corner a rush stool for herself, though all in perfect silence.

CHAPTER IV

Hezek's Patient

There were two faces that Gwenifer Owen read like an open book – the face of Nature and that of the man who had just entered at her cottage door, and was now sitting opposite her in the firelight. It required not a word to tell her that behind those dark eyes some new and powerful feeling was kindling, but she asked no questions with the quick and expressive gestures which sometimes made her face and figure alive with interest, but waited patiently until her visitor should choose to enlighten her.

What was it that moved the mishteer so? What brought that light into his eyes and that curve of content upon his lips? It was surely no disquieting thought, so she tried to ignore it and to turn the conversation to the ordinary channels of sea-coast events.

Holding her apron up by one corner, she made her companion (well accustomed to her signs) at once aware that she meant, 'There is a ship.' As quick as thought, certainly quicker than she could have expressed the thought in writing, she drew an imaginary wavy line horizontally before her eyes, and thus said 'The bay.'

'A ship, is there?' answered Gildas. 'What is she?'

Again Gwenifer held on her apron, this time making the two corners stand up like two sails side by side, then turning to the windowsill she drew from a little box of treasures a scrap of red ribbon and fluttered it in the air.

'A schooner?' said Gildas, 'with a red pennon? And not known to Gwenifer. Must be a stranger, lass. Well, she is having a rough welcome to the bay; but she'll outride this if she is a sound craft; I think we've reached the worst of the storm; 'twill go down before morning.' A nod from Gwenifer dismissed the subject, and Gildas, gazing into the fire, seemed to have returned to his first subject of contemplation, from which raising his eyes to the girl's form, a sudden appreciation of her beauty startled him. The firelight threw its glamour over a face and figure that required no enhancement of their charms, for in the long silent years Nature seemed to have been lavish in her gifts of outward beauty to the human being whom Fate had smitten so sorely. When Gildas, looking at her so suddenly, saw the slender shape, the pure oval of her face, the look of almost angelic patience that sat upon her brow and lips, he was filled with a warm glow of admiration, and with rustic simplicity of manner exclaimed, 'Dear anwl, Gwenifer! thou hast grown into a beautiful creature while we have been busy sowing and reaping and fishing.'

A flash of pleasure swept over her face and she smiled even while she shook her head. 'No?' said Gildas. 'I say 'Yes', then. Come sit thee down, Gwenifer, I have something to tell thee; something that I thought perhaps thou would'st have seen for thyself, though in my deed I have done my best to hide it; but thine eyes, or something within thee, seem to see further than most people. Well,' – and the strong man seemed strangely moved. 'Hark to the storm,' he interpolated. 'Well, Gwenifer, there's not much comfort on the hearth at Scethryg. N'wncwl Sam and Het are both as prickly as hedgehogs sometimes; and I – well, I am hard and obstinate, I daresay,' and he paused a moment as if recalling some subject of dispute. 'But, lass! I am never hard and cross to thee, am I now? Come! thee'lt say that for me?'

Gwenifer shook her head emphatically, and her deep brown eyes seemed to grow humid with the warmth of her denial.

'No indeed! how could I when we've been together so much, and thou hast listened to all my grumbles without losing patience with me? In my deed I don't know what would the world be like without thee.

'And now,' he continued, 'thou'lt wonder perhaps that I am not satisfied with such close friendship as thine and mine. I think I ought to be too; but I'm not. I want a *wife* to share my home with me, to brighten the hearth, to make it cosy as thou hast made this, Gwenifer. Tell me, lass! dost understand me and see the reason in it?'

She bowed her head, and all the feelings which through the long silent years had been suppressed and stifled sprang into life that could never be extinguished.

'Yes? I knew thou woulds't. 'Tis a pleasure to talk to a sensible woman. Now I expect Het and n'wncwl Sam will be dead against it,' and he laughed as if he rather liked the prospect of their opposition.

Gwenifer's hands lay clasped on her lap, her eyes fixed upon them, the long dark lashes outlined on her cheek, while her bosom rose and fell with every fluttering breath.

The fire in the grate leaped up and died down again, but Gildas remained silent for some time. At last he roused himself, and, as if dallying with a pleasant thought, smiled, as he asked, 'Can'st not guess, Gwenifer? Well, indeed, I have been clever to hide it even from thee, lass.'

A blinding flash of lightning startled them both. It was followed by a loud peal of thunder, which seemed to burst over their heads and roll away over the moor. The wind dropped for a moment, and in the silence all nature seemed to be waiting for the next crash.

'Come,' said Gildas, suddenly awaking to the necessity

for hurrying home; 'come lass, be quick; put out the fire; we will run after the next flash'; but Gwenifer shrank a little, and trembled strangely.

'Come,' he said in an authoritative voice, ''tis not a fit night for thee to be here alone,' and obediently she reached her cloak and drawing the hood over her head was ready to accompany him over the moor. It came again, the scathing flash, and as its reverberating peal rolled away in the distance they went out into the darkness and ran before the wind.

To steady her footsteps, Gildas laid hold of her arm and was surprised to find how it trembled.

'Don't be frightened, 'merch-i,' he said. 'We'll be in Scethryg before the next flash.'

'Merch-i! It was spoken kindly, almost tenderly, and at any other time would have called the responsive colour to the girl's cheeks and a smile to her lips; but the spirit of the storm seemed to have suddenly cast its shadow over her: the roar of the blast, the rolling thunder, the rolling sound of the breakers on Maldraeth – all seemed to hold the very atmosphere under a spell.

When they entered at the farmhouse door, she approached the hearth, where the fire had burnt down to a few dying embers; raking them together, and adding a fresh log, she soon brought warmth and light into the darkened kitchen, while Gildas barred the door and lighted the lamp.

It was really only nine o'clock, but they kept early hours at Scethryg and she was not surprised to find that n'wncwl Sam and Het had gone to bed.

'Come, lass, sit down,' said Gildas, lighting his pipe, and appearing to prepare for a long talk. The logs spluttered, the clock ticked, and Gwenifer sat silently looking into the fire.

'Here's peace and quietness at last! – inside the house at least,' he added as another flash lighted up every corner of the room.

'Tan-i-marw! seems to me there's something in the weather against me speaking tonight,' and he laughed with that sparkle in his eyes that made the charm of his rugged face. 'Well! I was going to tell thee, Gwenifer, what I have been trying to hide for so long, and I don't know why would I hide it, only that I suppose I was not sure whether Nance would have me; and I am not sure now, for the matter of that, for I know I am not good enough for her, and I come to thee, as I always do when I'm in a puzzle. Dost think I dare ask Nance Ellis to have me?'

While he spoke the timid hopes, the happy thoughts, that had for a moment blinded Gwenifer to the truth, took wing, and left her filled with a heavy sense of loneliness. Never before had she been glad that she was dumb, now she was thankful that only a bend of the head was required of her. Gildas, in his new-found enthusiasm, took all the rest for granted, and launched into the usual panegyrics of a lover, his companion listening with what patience she could.

'Hezek sits late over his herbal,' he said, when, having recounted all his reasons for choosing Nance, he rose from the hearth, and with many directions to Gwenifer to get warm and dry, moved towards the door. 'I will go to the storws for an hour or two,' he said, 'but, say once that thou art approving! for, on my word! if thou art not, 'twill spoil everything; eh, Gwenifer? dost think I am wise?'

Disturbed by so direct an appeal, she rose, and following him a few steps, laid her hands on his arm and looked searchingly into his face.

'What art asking me? Am I sure what I want? Yes, indeed, I want Nance'; and his face lighted up with that rare smile which so completely altered its expression.

For answer, Gwenifer only waved her hand towards the door with a placid smile of consent, as though she said, 'Go, Gildas, and God bless thee.' That was the meaning he put into her action, and he went out with a pleased look and a firm step.

When he was gone, she returned to the hearth, and stood for some time looking into the fire, which had burnt up brightly, and was bringing into relief all the old familiar furniture – the stools, the brass pans, the benches. She looked round at them all, and wondered why everything looked so different.

Outside, the lightning still flashed occasionally and the thunder rolled over the moor, but Gwenifer, standing there and gazing into the fire, scarcely heard them, so absorbed was she in her own thoughts.

At last she went slowly up the stairs and sought her place beside Het, who grumbled a little at being disturbed, but soon slept again.

Not so Gwenifer, who, lying awake, listened to the storm, and thought the next hours were the longest she had ever passed. She seemed to see the warmth and glow of the old storehouse, Hezek bending over his herbs, Nance, fresh and buxom, moving about in the light and shadow. There is a knock at the door, a finger on the latch, a dark-faced man enters, and she buries her face in her pillow and tries to shut out the picture that follows. She hears the distant thunder of the breakers on Maldraeth, she pictures vividly the foam that flies in lumps against the cliffs, she hears the creaking of the thorn-hedge by the horse-pond, but nothing effaces the vision of a well-known face changed and softened by a new and overmastering emotion.

At length she hears the opening and closing of the outer door, a footstep mounts the stairs, stops outside her door, and Gildas speaks in a low voice. 'Gwenifer, lass, I thought thou woulds't like to know 'tis *alright*.'

An acknowledging tap on the wall from Gwenifer, and the happy lover passes on to his loft in the further gable.

Het tosses in her sleep, and Gwenifer – lies still and waits for the dawn.

It comes at last, with a blush of rose in the east and a sense of life astir everywhere. The clouds break up, the wind sinks down, the waves dance joyfully on the bay, and the daffodils on the garden hedge nod approvingly, as Gwenifer, rising before the other members of the household, takes her way to the hillside with her milking-pail. Afterwards, instead of returning as usual to breakfast at the farm, she turned towards the dewy moor and the little brown cottage, where she would be free to think, to wonder, to weep perhaps. She dreaded to hear a happy call at the window, to see the door open to admit Nance, blooming and fresh; to be called upon to listen again to the story of Gildas's love, to rejoice with her friend over the bright prospects opening out before her as mistress of Scethryg. Her fears on this score, however, were needless, for Nance seemed in no wise anxious to share her news with anyone. In the old storehouse she moved about her work in a strangely absorbed and silent mood, tossing the logs on the fire, pushing the clumsy furniture roughly into their places, clattering the cups and saucers so noisily that Hezek looked up and grumbled a little. 'Such a noise, Nance! Thee'lt break the things, I'm afraid.'

'Well,' said the girl crossly, 'it wouldn't matter much if I broke the whole cracked lot of them.'

'Ah, well!' said the old man, 'they've served us very well. Thou'lt have better things in Scethryg. I'm afraid thou'lt be too proud to peep into the old storws then!'

'Oh, Scethryg! Nonsense,' said Nance, tossing her head, 'that's a long time to come yet; perhaps never!'

'Oh yes, 'twill come,' said Hezek encouragingly, and in his voice there was a tone of the pride which he deprecated in his granddaughter. 'I hope those lads won't be late to-night,' he added. 'I must see that hand before I go to the prayer meeting. Art coming, 'merch-i, or art going to wait at home for Gildas?'

'I'm not going to wait for him or any man,' said Nance. 'Besides, he never comes in till late.'

They were interrupted by the arrival of the two men whom they had expected, Captain Jack assuring them that his hand was getting on 'first rate,' and that Hezek was a 'slap-up doctor and no mistake.' He spoke with a broad, rough accent of the sailoring folk around him, for Captain Jack found no difficulty in adapting himself to the manners and language of the company in which he happened to find himself, but, on the contrary, rather enjoyed doing so, and was often heard to boast that it would be hard to find any class of men with whom he had not been at home at some time of his adventurous life, although he was as yet barely thirty years of age. His rough manners were, however, only a cloak put on at the promptings of an innate refinement of feeling, which forbade his appearing in any way superior to those amongst whom his lot was cast. At a moment's notice he could drop that cloak, and in better company could at once take his place as a man of gentlemanly behaviour and educated speech and manners.

Perhaps it was this underlying refinement that, with all his rough ways, lent a charm to his personality – a charm that was felt by everyone who was acquainted with him, more especially by every woman, though she herself might be rough and ignorant.

Nance was sympathetic as Hezek examined the crushed fingers, and Captain Jack, though making little of his injury, was not ill pleased with the interest it created in her.

'Oh, don't you look at it,' he said, as he saw both Nance and the mate were peeping over the old man's shoulder. 'The mate and me, we're used to rough sights, but I wouldn't like you to remember me with a shudder. That's a good ointment of yours, whatever, doctor,' he continued, 'wonderful soft and healing.'

'Yes,' answered Hezek, ''tis made from the flowers of the marigold. Ah, 'tis a rare herb for healing. Gildas lets me grow a bed of it in the garden. You tell him what good it has done you; for he doesn't believe much in my herbs and flowers. Well, well, there's never anything the matter with him, so he has no need of any 'weeds,' as he calls them.'

'I'll tell him, you bet,' said the captain, as Hezek finished the dressing and Nance refitted the sling. 'I don't know him. As far as I can remember I've never had a word with him yet, but he looks a *man*, whatever they say.'

'I never heard say anything bad about him,' said the mate, 'except that he's proud and hard, and cold as a stone.'

'That's plenty bad enough,' laughed Nance. 'He's very kind to us, whatever.'

'Well, of course, what else could he be to you?' said the captain, smiling, and raising those wonderful eyes of his to her blushing face.

'He's all that a man ought to be,' said Hezek, a little irritably. He was annoyed and disturbed at the condition of secrecy upon which alone Nance had given her consent to be married – a stipulation which Gildas had only been too glad to agree to, for he carried his reserve and pride to a morbid extent in his dislike of being talked about. To be the subject of gossip would have been an ordeal which he would have shrunk from, as he said, 'like fire on my skin'; so Nance carried her point, and Hezek was obliged to keep the news of which he was so proud to himself.

'Well,' he said, when he had put away his pots and bottles, 'we are going to the meeting in Brynzion to-night. Will you come with us?'

'Yes, will I indeed,' said the mate. 'I hear there's a grand Revival about here now. Come on, cap'n; be bound there'll be good singing.'

'Oh, diwss anwl!' said the captain. 'Not I. I haven't been to a prayer meeting these years. Go you and sing 'Hallelujah'; I'll wait for you outside. Are you going?' he asked, turning to Nance.

'Yes, I suppose,' she answered. 'They are all going to the prayer meetings here lately, though indeed I don't see any difference in them from the old meetings, except that they are longer.'

'I've heard my father tell about the last Revival,' said Captain Jack. 'He was a boy then, and he went to chapel, like all the rest, to see what was going on; and a woman sitting near him, getting warmed up, took off her hat and threw it up, shouting 'Bendigedig!' and all the others shouted too. Then she began to look for her hat, crying and singing at the same time, and whispering like, between the shouting, *'Oh, dear anwl! where's my hat?* – Bendigedig!' 'Hallelujah! – *What was it like?'* whispered another woman. *'Black with red lining.* – Praise the Lord!' And somebody pushed it into her hands.'

Nance and the mate laughed, but Hezek looked grave.

'Well, look you, my boys,' he said, as he turned the key in his old cupboard door, 'I don't hold myself to be a good man – no, indeed – but if you knew my inner self, the spirit inside this body, you would see that it has never been the same since that old Revival. Before that I lived with my eyes closed as it were; since then I have always been wide awake to see what was right, though I have not always followed it, d'you see? So I can't join in your laugh, my boys, though I could tell you a good many funny stories about those times too. Come, Nance, put thy hat on, 'merch-i.'

When they reached the village they found the long windows at Brynzion ablaze with light, and the congregation beginning to assemble. Nance and Captain Jack had loitered a little, so Hezek and the mate waited for them, the latter looking somewhat disturbed as they emerged from the darkness into the light that streamed through the doorway. He was divided between his desire to attend the meeting and hear the singing and his habit of keeping watch over his friend. 'You won't come in then, cap'n?' he asked in an undertone.

'No,' said the other, 'I'll go and have a smoke on the kiln.'

Packed in the narrow seat in a corner of the chapel, John Davies's thoughts often went out to his friend. At all events Nance was safe beside him in the chapel, and this was satisfactory. The strong friendship existing between these two men was a psychological puzzle, for it would have been scarcely possible to find two more opposite natures: the one careful and wary, the other headstrong and rash; the one incapable as he would have been unwilling to diverge from the narrow groove in which his ancestors had walked before him, the other ready to welcome any breeze of amusement or romance that would fill his sails and waft him pleasantly over the sea of life. In spite of this, from their earliest boyhood John Davies had constituted himself Jack Davies's guardian, and seemed to hold himself responsible for all that young man's follies and eccentricities. Over and over again had Jack as a boy been punished for companying with the blacksmith's son, a common street boy! and one, too, who had the reputation of being self-willed and bold, as his father had been before him; but, in defiance of all restrictions, the two boys were often together, shooting, fishing, hunting. Few pleasures were perfect to Jack unless John Davies were somewhere near to watch his exploits, to help him out of his scrapes, to carry his gun, to hold his horse; in fact, the humblest office was gladly accepted by John Davies if it only brought him into touch with Mr. Jack. Later on, when Jack was sent to school and afterwards to college, there to run a reckless course of dissipation and folly, John Davies went to sea, and thus lost sight of his friend for several years; until at last Jack, fallen from his high estate, lighted upon John Davies once more, and, following his advice, embarked on a seafaring life. Here, finding himself in the position for which he had always had a hankering, he tried to patch up his broken fortunes by plodding steadily at work, soon proving himself to be well fitted for his duties; and, as we have seen, he was now captain of the *Liliwen*, with John Davies for mate.

As he turned from the door of the chapel, having seen his mate elbowing his way through the fast-gathering crowd, he laughed and shrugged his shoulders. 'On my word,' he said, 'not even for the sake of sitting by Nance would I go into that stifling place,' and he turned towards the old disused limekiln which stood but a short distance from the chapel, its crumbling wall making a convenient seat for the village gossips, and thus giving a sociable appearance to the little mound on which it was built. It was the general rendezvous of the village, where the latest bit of news was retailed and the affairs of the world (the Tregildas world) were discussed. Here the men loved to smoke their last pipe when plough, or boat, or tools were done with for the day. Here, on the moss-covered wall, a few men were sitting in conclave as Captain Jack turned from the chapel door. They were the flotsam and jetsam of the coast who had not yet been drawn within the influence of the revival, but liked to sit near and pass remarks upon those who attended the meetings. One woman sat there a little apart, in a crouching position, her two elbows on her knees, her lined and rugged face lit up by the red glow of the setting sun at which she was staring.

'Na, na,' she muttered to herself. 'The wind does not blow through the closed door, the tide can't flow in where the rocks stand high against it, and the Spirit won't flow into Brynzion while the hard 'black rock' prevents it.' But nobody listened to her; they were too interested in the subject of their conversation, their figures outlined against the crimson sky.

'Tell you I saw him myself,' said one. 'Cap'n Jack, of the *Liliwen*, and John Davies; and the cap'n's hand was in a sling. Going down to Maldraeth they were, and across to the ship. They say he won't be able to use his hand for a month, though Hezek dressed it beautiful.'

'A good thing too,' answered another. 'Keep him out of mischief, perhaps. A regular scamp he was, and owing a lot of money, they say, till his father paid his debts.' But there was a sudden silence, as out of the twilight came the figure of Captain Jack himself. There was a general shifting of seats to make room for him on the low wall, and many of the men touched their hats respectfully.

Captain Jack accepted the proffered seat, looking round at the company with a genial 'Nos da chi'.

'Going to the meeting, sir?' said one of the men.

'No, no,' answered the newcomer. 'It's not much in my line. I haven't been to one for years, and I might do something out of the way, d'you see; might stand up when I ought to sit down, or something,' and he laughed as he struck a light for his pipe.

'You might do worse,' said Jerri the boatman. 'There's powerful prayers in there, I can tell you.'

'Go in, man,' said the old woman, 'the Spirit might come to you.'

'And why don't you go in?' asked Captain Jack.

The sun was gone down, and in the dim light she looked a strange, weird figure. 'Ah, well, you see,' she answered, 'I am waiting to see will it be any use to go.'

At that moment a man, who was evidently taking a short cut across the green, approached the kiln and walked rapidly on towards the chapel door, which his figure darkened for a moment as he entered. The woman, watching him, rose from her seat and with a curious motion of her hands, half comical, half despairing, turned away.

'Not I,' she called back as she went. 'The Spirit won't come to Brynzion while the 'black rock' stands against it.'

'What does she mean?' asked Captain Jack, as his eyes followed the figure passing in through the lighted doorway. 'Who was that? Wasn't it Gildas Rees?'

'Yes, 'twas mishteer,' said Jerri. 'He might have given us a 'Nos da' in passing.'

'He was in a hurry,' said another. 'Late for chapel, you see.'

'He's a grand man, whatever,' said the captain. 'Make a fine soldier.'

'Oh yes, that he would,' said Jerri, 'and it's my belief he'd walk straight into the middle of the bullets and never bend his head. But, mind you, bullets are all very well; but when it comes to opposing the Spirit,' – and he shook his head gravely.

'The Spirit! Diwss anwl! what are you all talking about?' said the captain, looking round the company. 'You're rather creepy, with your Spirit; what d'you mean by it?'

'Well,' said Jerri, 'there's *something* comes to the meetings for certain. Not here yet; but at Moriah, at Beulah, and at Graig they've all felt it. Here we're as dry as the sand yet, but if prayers will bring it 'twill visit us soon. I wouldn't be outside here to-night if it wasn't for Joseph the shop's cartload of goods expected, and I've promised to help him with the horse.'

Here a full tide of harmony swept out through the open chapel door, filling the night air with the rise and fall of its music. Again and again the refrain was repeated before the second verse was begun: the old well-known tune that had soothed the cradle of their ancestors and accompanied them to their graves! the words that their mothers had often sung them to sleep with!

Who could refuse to join in those swelling tones?

Not Captain Jack, certainly; for with all his wild and head-long ways, the memories entwined round his boyhood's home, and the love of his mother, had always the power to reach his heart; and as the refrain began again he hummed the tune in a musical voice, Jerri joined with his quavering bass, and the other four men came in in correct harmony, until the night air was full of music. Many times the hymn was sung in the chapel, and answered by the voices on the kiln.

It was a strange and new experience to Captain Jack, and he enjoyed it all: the swinging rhythm of the chorus, the soft night sky, where one bright star hung over them like a lamp.

At last the singing ceased, and was followed by the sound of a voice, that rose sometimes into a paean of rapture, sometimes fell into the depths of sorrow.

'How much longer will they go on?' said Captain Jack, beginning to grow weary. 'I think I'll go down to the Ship Inn for a glass. Come on, all of you, and I'll treat you to a 'blue', to wash the salt out of your throats.'

Jerri drew his hand over his lips. It was a tempting offer, and one that two months earlier he would have readily accepted; but to-night he shook his head. 'No, thank you, sir,' he said, 'we're most of us totlers about here.'

'No? Well, tan-i-marw,' said Captain Jack. 'You're a strange lot about here, with your spirits, and your prayers, and your . . . ' He paused as another figure appeared in sight. A girl this time – slender, silent, beautiful. She approached, and Captain Jack stood transfixed with admiration.

What was Nance's buxom beauty? what was any woman he had ever seen compared with this simple, graceful child of the hills, as she stood a moment before turning to the chapel door?

'Thou'rt very late, 'merch-i,' said Jerri. 'First prayer and first hymn is over; perhaps thee can slip in unnoticed though.' But she was gone and already entering the chapel.

'Didn't I say you were a strange lot here?' said Captain Jack, starting from a dream. 'Who's that? Is she the Spirit you've been expecting? In my deed, I don't think there's any woman living so . . . so . . .'

'So silent,' said one of the men. 'No, you're right there, cap'n – 'twould be a good thing if they were. That's Gwenifer.'

'Gwenifer?'

'Yes, Gwenifer Owen, the dumb girl. Her mother was drowned before her eyes, when she was a child, and she fell down like one dead, and she's dumb ever since.'

'Well, well!' said Captain Jack, sitting down again as if the better to grasp the idea. 'Dumb! What a cruel fate!' he said to himself, unconsciously dropping the broad Welsh accent which he generally affected. 'Poor thing! poor thing! And such a beautiful creature too.'

'Beautiful creature? Well indeed! She's only Gwenifer; nobody's taking much account of her about here. She's quite used to her silence by now, and I don't think it's troubling her at all; she's speaking as well with her hands and eyes as most people do with their tongues.'

'Dear, dear!' was all Captain Jack's answer, and he fell into a brown study in which he heard as if in a dream that bursts of harmony which came occasionally through the chapel door. The men puffed at their pipes, the waves broke on the shore with their recurring rush, and Captain Jack watched the lighted doorway closely for another glance at Gwenifer; but when at last the black mass of people emerged into the night air, he only saw for a moment the slim figure of a girl who passed quickly through the crowd and took her way alone towards the hillside above the village.

CHAPTER V

The 'Liliwen'

In the bright afternoon sunlight the sea, smooth and green, rose and fell gently round the side of the *Liliwen* as she rode at anchor in the bay; the tide flowed slowly by, carrying on its surface little beady wreaths of bubbles; overhead the sky was blue and cloudless, in the rigging a soft west wind was singing, the cabin boy sat humming at the prow, his keen eye marking every movement on the shore. He saw the fishermen who slouched into the Ship Inn, the cows that grazed on the uplands, and Gildas Rees who worked steadily at his plough in the field across the cove. John Davies down in the stuffy cabin was stooping over a letter, through which he toiled with apparently less ease than did Gildas at his furrows. He was writing to the 'owners' of the *Liliwen*, explaining the cause of her detention in the bay; the 'owners' in reality consisting only of Captain Jack, his uncle, and the mate himself, who owned a humble 'ounce' in her, just enough to make him scan her graceful proportions with pleasure, just enough to make him love the tinkling of her anchor chain, the swelling of her sails. 'There!' he said at last, with a stretch of satisfaction, 'there! 'tis finished, thanks be,' and he read it over to himself, afterwards carrying it with him up the narrow cabin steps to the deck, where he found the captain leaning over the rail and smoking.

'Done?' he asked, taking the letter from the mate's hands and conning it over rapidly. 'First rate, couldn't have done

it better myself; we'll post it to-night on our way to see
Hezek,' and slipping his hand out of its sling, he examined
it as though he could see the injury through the wrappings.
"Tis pretty painful to-day, I don't know the reason why,' he
said; but as the sight of the white bandage did not enlighten
him much he slipped it back into its sling again, and both
men leaning over the rails continued to smoke in silence,
gazing over the undulating green waters towards the land,
where every path and hedge and furrow showed distinctly
in the clear spring sunlight.

At last the mate, knocking the ashes out of his pipe, said,
'Diwss anwl! we'll turn into jelly-fish if we stop here until
your hand is well.'

'Well, old Hezek says it must be dressed once a day for a
fortnight or three weeks if it's to heal, and I don't want to
lose my right hand.'

'No, no; there's nothing for it but patience, I suppose. The
owners know the reason, and the cargo won't spoil with
keeping. Do'no what Joshua Jones will say, though.'

'A tombstone won't spoil, man,' said the captain.

'No, but he's in a hurry,' answered the mate. 'I've always
noticed when a man's in a hurry to put a tombstone on his
wife's grave, he's going to be married again. That's human
nature, d'you see,' he added, 'it's kind of honourable to pay
her the last compliment before he begins again! You bet,
you'll hear he's going to be married soon.'

'Well, if he's in a hurry,' said the captain, 'he's better send
a cart for it; 'tis only twenty miles as the crow flies, and we
might land it here.'

Again silence, broken only by the creaking of the mast
and the liplapping of the sea against the side of the ship.

'Going to have a spell of fine weather, I think,' said the
mate at last.

'Good thing for me, being crippled like this,' answered
the captain.

'Oh, as for that, if rough weather came, I'd take your place, and get Jim Craddock to take mine.'

'If it wasn't for this confounded hand wanting dressing every day we could do that now,' said the captain, 'and set Joshua Jones at ease to marry again if he likes. Ach-y-fi! there's something mean in that marrying again, to my mind. Whatever my faults are, I'd be faithful to the memory of my love.'

For answer the mate broke into a loud peal of laughter, his tarry hands holding his sides, his broad shoulders shaking with merriment. 'Oh, good lor!' he said at last, 'where's Jinny Pritchard in Bristol, and Ellen the Mill at Trebowen? and Miss Jones the Post Office at Cardiff? and the little widow that made your new shirts? and Jane Lewis? and . . .'

'Oh, taw! hold thy tongue,' said the captain. 'They're where we left them, I suppose. I didn't care a cockleshell for one of them.'

'No, no. Like Joshua Jones is going to do, you put a tombstone on every one as soon as you saw the other.'

The captain was silent, gazing across the land at Gildas Rees still ploughing, and the cows still grazing in the sunshine.

'What's that?' he asked suddenly, pointing up the hillside; 'I thought it was a rock, but I see now it is a hut.'

"Tis Gwenifer's cottage,' said the mate.

'Gwenifer! the dumb girl?'

'Yes. Lives there alone.'

'Alone! that young creature, and silent always! Dear anwl! the girl who lives alone up there must have a – a . . .'

'A what?' said the mate.

'Well, she must be different to thee and me.'

'Mh! She's used to it, d'ye see.'

The captain was not sure what he was going to say when

he was interrupted – a clear conscience, a clean heart, a good record, perhaps.

Anyway, he kept it to himself, for what had he to do with any of these? Instead, he asked, 'Are Nance and she friends?'

'Oh, first-class,' said the mate.

'Perhaps we'll see her in the storws some night. I think there's something moving behind those broom bushes. Dash it! I can't hold the spy-glass steady with my left hand.'

'What do you want to see?' asked the mate, turning to look at him. 'What's the great concern you take in Gwenifer? Look you, cap'n,' he said, with an altered look, 'she's not like other girls, and 'twould be a blackguard shame to try any of your enticing ways upon her.'

'Hisht, man,' said the captain, turning upon him suddenly. 'Confound thee! Keep thy coarse tongue quiet, and let me go my own way.'

'Oh, heave away, then,' said the mate. 'But look here, cap'n, steer clear of Gwenifer Owen.'

The subject of their conversation was at that moment sitting on the grassy bank that encircled her little garden, her eyes fixed on the fluttering pennon of the *Liliwen* as she rocked on the gently flowing tide. Her hands had fallen listlessly on her coarse blue skirt, her whole attitude was one of deep abstraction. What was she thinking of as she sat there in the afternoon sunlight, the Scethryg flocks spread over the plain before her? Was she counting up her small wages to see whether she could afford to buy a ribbon for her bare neck? Or did her thoughts travel back to the sun that had set so long ago upon her happy childhood? Or did she count the seagulls that floated on the sea? We cannot tell, for Gwenifer's thoughts, whatever they were, were hers alone.

Suddenly through a gap in the bank a sturdy figure entered, Gildas fresh from the plough, his strong hands stained with the brown upland earth, his neck bared to the sea breeze. Gwenifer turned towards him with a smile of greeting, and climbing up the rough bank he sat down beside her, between the broom bushes.

'I saw thee from the field, lass, and came up as usual to tell thee what is in my mind,' he said with a laugh, in which lurked no discontent, no doubts, no worry – but only the fulness of happy life that seems by right to belong to the tiller of the ground.

'Hast seen Nance yet?' he asked. 'I mean, has she told thee our plans?'

Gwenifer shook her head.

'Well, indeed; she's careful as I am to keep the villagers from talking. That suits me well, for all my life I have hated to have my name on every old woman's tongue. Dear anwl! I think I could bear to be *murdered* if I could keep it all to myself, or to be *married*,' he added, with another laugh; 'but to be talked about, ach-y-fi! 'twould be like fire on my skin.'

Gwenifer laughed too, and pointing to her lips, with a shake of her head seemed to say, '*I* won't talk about thee.'

'No, no, but listen then; 'tis this I want to ask thee,' and he plucked at the grasses, biting off the ends, as he continued, '''Tis this way now. Nance is slow to make up her mind, and there again she pleases me; a forward girl I can't bear; I like them modest and . . . and . . . like thee, Gwenifer. But when a man has made up his mind to be married, he likes to make haste about it, eh, lass?'

Gwenifer nodded.

'Well, I want thee to help Nance to make up hers. I'll give her leave to tell thee; no doubt she has waited for that, poor little thing; and thee'll advise her, Gwenifer, to do as I wish?'

The girl bowed her head.

'Yes; everything's ready, thee see'st; and there's no reason to wait. N'wncwl Sam is going to live in the storws with Hezek. Nance will be able to tend them both there, and the

two old men will be company for each other. There's Flower
and Rattler getting restless, I must go back to my ploughing;
and now, lass, I'll leave it to thee. Persuade Nance to be
married next month, wilt, Gwenifer?'

Again Gwenifer bowed her head, and Gildas slipped
down the bank on to the moor, adding as he turned away,
'There's the *Liliwen*, idling her time, like me. A bad job the
captain hurting his hand like that; but in my deed, I think
Hezek's herbs will cure him. I believe in them, mind thee,
though I do plague him a bit about his weeds.'

He took two or three steps towards the cliff, but turning
back said, 'Oh, Gwenifer; thee wast at the meeting last night.
Well, did'st ever see such a thing? Old Marged Jones crying
and moaning! and Jossi Penlan sobbing and praying in
another corner! In my deed, if a man had got to make a fool
of himself like that before he is forgiven, then Gildas Rees,
Scethryg can never be saved.'

As he walked away over the moor, Gwenifer looked after
him thoughtfully, and sighed as she returned to her weeding;
the west wind blowing in from the sea echoed her sigh, and
fluttered the *Liliwen*'s red pennon.

It was not till the next afternoon that she got a chance of
advising Nance, whom she had of late seen less of than
usual, for the latter's time had been taken up, not only by
Gildas's frequent calls, but also by her grandfather's patient
and his mate.

They were frequent visitors to the old storehouse, more
especially the captain, who generally arrived about teatime,
and stayed till the clock in the corner struck seven, when
he was careful, as he said, 'to clear out and make room for
his betters.' Seeing that Gildas's visits were pretty regular
and punctual, he had guessed the state of affairs, and one
evening had laughingly questioned Nance on the subject.

'Come, lass,' he had said, for he had grown very familiar

with the girl, 'you might tell a poor man how the land lies, for fear he may be shipwrecked before he knows it. Gildas is courting thee, 'tis plain to see; come now, how soon is the wedding?'

Nance's colour came and went, and a little hardness came into her voice.

'Well, indeed, perhaps he is courting me; but when the wedding is to be is another thing; he wants it to be soon.'

'Of course he does, and small blame to him. I can understand that, lass; I'd want it to be soon myself!' and his light blue eyes sought hers, which drooped before them. 'But there!' he added, 'that is life: some men get nothing but fair weather, full sails, and gentle breezes, while others toss about amid the rocks, and have to sail alone over stormy seas.'

Nance made no answer, but continued to pleat up the hem of her apron.

'Well,' said the captain, changing his tone and manner, 'I must 'wish you joy'; and I tell you, Nance, I think Gildas is a lucky man. Come, he wouldn't grudge you walking with me to the gate, that is only friendly.'

This conversation had all been carried on in an undertone, while Hezek at the farther end of the long room was stooping over his books.

Nance only too readily yielded to the suggestion, and with a nod of acquiescence slipped out of the door, and ran down the steps to the yard; Captain Jack following caught her up by the horse-pond, and side by side they walked not only as far as the gate, but down the lane and over the fields.

To Captain Jack the little episode of a flirtation with Nance meant no more than had a score of other such experiences; why, she was all but a married woman, and therefore safe to joke and flirt with!

But Nance's erratic, wilful heart had been given all took readily to the handsome sailor; and as she flew back over the moor to meet her affianced husband, she felt the first pangs of the guilt and barbed unrest which was never to die out, for she still meant to keep her hold upon Gildas Rees, and be mistress of Scethryg, although had Captain Jack asked her to marry him, she would have thrown Gildas's love to the winds.

He was already waiting for her when she reached the storws, Hezek seizing the opportunity for dilating upon the virtues of his herbs.

'There's that lad's hand,' he said, ''twas as bad a crush as you ever saw, but 'tis getting well rapidly, and he'll be able to sail when he likes, I think.'

But Gildas scarcely heard, he was looking round the room expectantly. 'Where's Nance?' he asked.

'Well, gone to look for Gwenifer, seems to me,' said the old man. 'She went out when I was dressing Cap'n Jack's hand, I suppose. Girls can't bear that sort of thing you see. She'll be back soon, depend on't,' and while he was speaking the latch was raised and Nance entered, heated with running, flustered, and, if the truth must be told, a little cross.

'Here she is!' exclaimed Gildas. 'In my deed, lass, the old storws looked empty without thee. Where hast been? with Gwenifer?'

'No,' said Nance. 'I have been as far as Pensarn looking for Jinni the sewing girl.'

'Ha!' said Gildas, well pleased. 'To make thy wedding dress, I hope; for I tell thee, Nance, I am going to have it settled to-night. Come, put on thy shawl, and let us walk down Maldraeth; the moonlight is bright as day, and no one will disturb us there.'

'Ach, no,' said Nance, 'not to Maldraeth; I hate the dark old shore.'

'Dark?' laughed Gildas. 'No place would look dark to me if thou wert there, lass; but where thou pleasest,' and he turned towards the thorn-hedged lane, where but half an hour earlier Nance had listened to Captain Jack's merry talk and banter. There had been no love in it, of this her womanly instinct assured her; and if she married Gildas Rees, Captain Jack would flirt as merrily with the next woman he met. And here beside her was one who loved her with all his honest heart; why, why, could she not love him in return? And Nance's false and fickle heart was torn with restless longings. But through it all she adhered to her determination to be mistress of Scethryg, and hold her head high above the village girls.

When on reaching the edge of the cliff they looked down over its dizzy height to the shore below, Gildas pointed to the sands lying smooth and white in the moonlight. 'See,' he said, 'where is the darkness there? 'Tis light as day; we can see the blue of the sea; and there's white the waves break on the shore.'

But Nance shivered a little as she looked over the edge.

'Art cold, 'merch-i? We must go in then,' and he drew her red shawl a little closer round her shoulders.

'No,' she answered, 'I am not cold, but, ach-y-fi I am not liking Maldraeth; ever since I was a little girl I am afraid of it.'

Gildas laughed loud and heartily, for to him no corner in the realm of nature held anything to dread or shrink from, and as for the deep mysterious fears that haunt the minds of the learned and the doubting, why, he had never heard of them, never dreamt of their existence; and so he laughed, the healthy, whole-hearted laugh of a strong man to whom there was a God in heaven, who having created man was not above taking an interest in him and his concerns. He was not a religious man perhaps, except in as far as every honest, truthful man to whom duty is a law is religious. Indeed of late, since the strange wave of fresh spiritual life had begun to flow over the land, Gildas had been called irreligious. 'Ach-y-fi,' said one, 'what wonder Brynzion is passed over, with mishteer sitting there so hard and stiff, and never an Amen nor a prayer from him!'

'Don't I tell you,' said Nelli Amos, the old woman who had crouched on the kiln when Gildas had entered the chapel, 'don't I tell you the Spirit won't come where the 'black rock' stands up against it.'

'We can't turn him out, whatever,' said Jerri, 'because he's our mishteer you see. I don't lay the blame on him altogether, mind you; not altogether, because Evan Roberts has never been here; if he would come just once, to open the door like, and bring the Spirit down, perhaps we could keep him here, in spite of mishteer.'

'One thing I advise you,' said Nelli Amos, 'get rid of the 'black rock'.'

She was not a tenant of Gildas Rees's, but lived in a hut which her grandfather had built and thatched, so she was not afraid to speak her mind, and often to give herself the airs of a landed proprietor.

Meanwhile Gildas and Nance had roamed back to the thorn-bordered lane, and he was well pleased, for he had extracted from her a promise that as soon as the banns were 'out' she would marry him. In the shadow of the thorn bushes they had parted, and she had returned to the old storehouse looking strangely pensive and sad. 'As well then as ever! and what do I care?' she exclaimed, as she took off her red shawl and flung it on the bed.

Next day, in the Scethryg fields, she sought out Gwenifer, calling over the moor and startling the birds from their nests in the stunted thorn bushes, until at last Gwenifer came through a gap in the hedge, clasping to her bosom, throbbing with pity, a wounded rock pigeon which she had rescued from the hawk. With little cooing sounds of tenderness she smoothed the ruffled plumage and soothed the terrified creature, more frightened than seriously hurt.

'What is it?' said Nance, drawing near. 'Oh, an old rock pigeon! Let him go, lass; n'wncwl Sam would wring its neck pretty soon. Let him fly, and come thou and hear my news.' And side by side the two girls sat upon the heather, the broad bay stretched before them, the sea-crows calling overhead, the Scethryg herds browsing audibly around them.

The pigeon, getting over its fright, fluttered its wings, and Gwenifer, raising her two hands above her head, gave it a helping toss, and straight as an arrow away it flew to its nest on the side of the rugged cliffs; and the girl turned to her companion with that smile upon her lips which spoke so much of chastened and patient endurance – a smile that Nance did not return, as she sat there, silent awhile and almost sullen, her eyed fixed on the sea, where the *Liliwen* rested like a bird on the waters.

'Thee can smile at such trifles!' she said at last.

'Yes,' nodded Gwenifer. 'Why this sadness?' she added, raising her eyebrows inquiringly, and putting on the mournful expression which she observed on Nance's face.

For answer Nance only pointed to the graceful schooner that seemed as immovable as a painted ship before them.

'The *Liliwen*?' queried Gwenifer in astonishment; and it was Nance's turn to nod this time without having recourse to words. She followed up her nod by a silence, in which her full lips fell into the little pout which had been so fascinating in her childhood. Suddenly she drew herself up, and, as if forcing her thoughts into another groove, said, 'Listen then, lass; what dost think? I am going to be married. Yes indeed then,' she added, with a natural pride, her face brightening a little as she thought how much not only Gwenifer, but every girl in Tregildas, would envy her. 'Yes indeed, and who to, dost think?'

Again Gwenifer's inquiring eyebrows.

'Why, to Gildas, the mishteer himself, and I will be mistress of Scethryg – there's for thee; and thy mistress too. Ah, well, I won't be hard on thee, Gwenifer, because we're friends these many years now. What will Leisa Owen say? and Jane Bryncelyn? I would have told thee sooner, but thou know'st how Gildas can't bear to be talked about, and 'twas only last night he gave me leave to tell everybody, for our banns will be out on Sunday.'

She had been too absorbed in the news she had to impart to notice that her companion had paled a little, and that her fingers had nervously plucked quite a little heap of heath blossoms.

At last she took Nance's hand in her own and pressed it warmly, with a look which required no word to wing its message of love.

'Yes, I knew thee'd be glad,' continued Nance, 'but, Gwenifer, lass;' and she pointed to the *Liliwen*, on whose deck they could see the captain leaning over the rail and looking straight towards the Scethryg fields. Again Nance pointed towards him, and, turning her finger to her own heart, she pressed her hand upon her bosom, using Gwenifer's own sign of appreciation or love.

Into the latter's face the blood rose slowly, as she questioned within herself what this might mean. But of this her companion did not leave her long in doubt, for none were afraid to tell Gwenifer their secrets. 'Yes indeed,' she said, 'he is handsome and pleasant as no words can tell, and I love him, Gwenifer; yes *indeed* then, and if he only called to me I would go to him as his dog runs to him when he whistles.'

Gwenifer started to her feet, flinging from her Nance's hand, which had rested on her lap; the blood rushed through her veins, and, unable to repress her burning feelings, she wrung her hands as she tried to control her indignation.

'What's the matter, lass?' said Nance, laughing. 'Well, in my deed, 'tis no wonder the boys in the village call thee 'Queen of the Rushes'. Sit down again, and fear nothing, for I tell thee, lass, *he doesn't care a cockleshell for me*, so it'll be all right when I am married to Gildas; and perhaps Captain Jack will be sorry then. Yes, yes, I'll be a stupid old married woman very soon, going to chapel every Sunday with my hymn-book and my pocket-handkerchief in my hand. Fear nothing, Gwenifer; it's all right.'

CHAPTER VI

Brynzion

Gildas Rees of Scethryg was not the man to let the grass grow under his feet when he had once made up his mind to a course of action.

Thus, his marriage with Nance was a thing of the past when we next see him at work on his farm.

The hay harvest of another year was ripening fast. In the brilliant sunshine of a May day he had hoed his roots and sown his corn, with the happy satisfaction of a man who knows he is working for his own home.

A year had passed since he and Nance had settled down as man and wife in the old farm where he and his ancestors had lived and died before him, and Hezek Morgan's sorrow at the loss of his little lass had been considerably lessened by the knowledge that she was not far removed from him, and moreover was 'Mestress of Scethryg'.

In the course of the day she paid frequent visits to the old storehouse, where n'wncwl Sam had also settled down more contentedly than he ever had in the farmhouse itself. He took much interest in Hezek's collection of medicinal plants, and would often accompany him on his rambles in search of some rare herb. In the evening, when the door stood open to admit the sea breeze and the sunset light, the two old men busied themselves with the many small jobs that form part of the routine of farm life. They wove the round potato baskets, or fashioned the long wooden spikes for haystack or thatch, so that their time was fully occupied, though none of their work was compulsory. Generally, after sunset, they found their way into the house, and smoked the last hour away with Gildas, under the chimney, while Nance moved about at her work in the background. She had developed into a famous housekeeper, and had taken up her duties as mistress with a zest and interest which had, in a great measure, banished the discontent she had felt upon her first betrothal to Gildas. Forever on the alert, she dusted, and swept, and cleaned, until not a speck or a spot was there, on shelf or table.

She routed out the corners which had harboured many a cobweb before her advent, and Het, who was at first inclined to rebel, had been obliged to adapt herself to the ways of her energetic mistress; for Nance was resolute and sharp of tongue, and ruled her household with a rod of iron.

Even Gildas had perforce to submit to her rule, and when called to order, would laughingly return to the door to shake off the lumps of brown earth which clung to his shoes. Sometimes he would pull his forelock with mock humility, and ask, 'Please, mestress, may I take a few breaths of air to keep me alive?' and they would laugh together, Nance blushing a little at her husband's implied rebuke.

That is not to say that her little wilful ways did not sometimes disturb the even tenor of their domestic lives; for as the months went by and she seemed every day to grow more shrewd, more sharp, and overbearing, and to rule her household more vigorously, Gildas began to look grave sometimes, his dark eyebrows lowering, and his lips falling into that firm set which, had Nance been wise, would have warned her from trying him further, but that just what Nance was not.

Returning from his work on the hedge-bank one day, he entered the farm kitchen with a light step and a cheerful

countenance, which broadened into a smile as he saw Nance
sitting on the hearth holding up for inspection a new hat
which she had trimmed for herself.

'Ho! Well done,' he exclaimed, 'a sign thou art coming with
me to the fair to-morrow, I hope?'

'The fair? Not I,' said Nance, 'There's a meeting at
Brynzion at seven to-night, and to-morrow at Graig; seems
to me thou'st a good memory for everything but thy
meetings, Gildas.'

'Well, there's so many here lately, 'merch-i, 'tis hard to
remember them all. Come now! I'll go to Brynzion with
thee to-night, and thou wilt come with me to the fair to-
morrow! Remember 'tis our wedding day, and I met Jones
Bryndu to-day, and he asked would we go in and have tea
with his mestress on our way home if we went to the fair?'

'Well, I don't see why we should neglect our meetings
because we were married this time last year,' said Nance as
she laid away the hat and sat down to the tea-tray.

'Oh! is the hat for the meeting, then?' said Gildas with a
look of amused annoyance.

'Well yes, it is, then,' said Nance, with a wilful set of the
mouth, and an extra sparkle in her eye. 'I've been to plenty
of meetings in the same old hat; 'tis full time for me to have
a new one. There's Mary Thomas has had two new hats
lately, and I going on and on with the same.'

'Indeed thou art very careful, 'merch-i,' said Gildas, 'and
'twould please me well to see thee in a new hat. But surely
thou can'st spare one evening from these prayer meetings
to go with thy husband to see a friend.'

'And to a fair,' said Nance.

'Well yes; to the fair too – why not? Seems to me all these
meetings are making thee too anxious and careful, 'merch-i.
Put all thy cares aside for one day, and come with me for a
little jaunt.'

'Oh, I daresay I am all wrong,' said Nance, with a pout on her lips and a frown on her brow, 'and I daresay I am a very poor wife for thee, and perhaps . . .'

'Stop, stop, Nance!' said Gildas, 'thee'rt a very good wife; I haven't a word to say against thee, except perhaps thou'rt a little too much given up to these prayer meetings.'

'Oh, say what thou please'st about me,' said Nance, 'only I won't hear a word against the prayer meetings. There's a Master who has more right to our service than even a husband.'

There was a little break in her voice as though the tears were not far off.

'Stop, Nance!' said Gildas again. 'Are we going to have our first quarrel about such a trifle . . .?' He was going to say 'as a hat,' but Nance had taken the bit between her teeth, and rushed headlong on her way.

'Trifle indeed! Trifle, are you calling a prayer meeting? I'm not calling it so whatever; and let me tell thee, Gildas, 'tis paining me to hear how the people are blaming thee. 'Never,' they say, '*never* will the Spirit visit Brynzion while Gildas Rees is there.' And in my deed 'tis no wonder they are thinking so, because thou hast turned so cold and hard against religion I am quite ashamed of thee.'

While Nance had poured forth her harangue, Gildas had sat looking across the tea-table through the open doorway to the moor, which stretched away beyond the farm lands till its hazy outline merged into the blue of the sea, while the foreground was gay with bushes of gorse and broom; but the sunny landscape on which he gazed did not lift the shadow that had fallen over his face. He was silent for some moments, looking fixedly at the scene. At last rising, he said, 'Well 'tisn't often I have been to chapel lately, b't shwr, and 'tis only for company to thee that I go at all; for I tell thee, Nance, I don't like these wild ways they have got into lately. My mother was a good woman, but I never heard her crying aloud about her sins; but there, I'll say no more, thou shalt do as thou please'st – thou art mistress here. Only one thing, 'merch-i (but I know I need not tell thee that) – thou'lt never make me ashamed of myself and thee as Owen Davies must have been last week when Laissabeth made such a fool of herself. Tan-i-marw! I could never bear that,' and passing over to the fire he lighted his pipe and puffed away in silence, while Nance with a good deal of clattering washed up the tea-things and gave her orders to Het.

At last Gildas, knocking the ashes out of his pipe, said, 'Come, 'merch-i! put on thy pretty new hat, and we will go to chapel together.'

Nance tossed her head a little angrily while she dressed, but Gildas, taking no further notice of her petulance, endeavoured as they crossed the moor to smooth over the little disagreement by chatting on the everyday occurrences of the neighbourhood. When they entered the chapel it was already packed almost to suffocation, the heat but little tempered by the fresh sea breeze that blew in at the wide-open doors.

One of the occupants of the sêt fawr with energetic gestures invited Gildas to join the deacons seated there; but ignoring the invitation, he followed his wife to the Scethryg pew, where they found themselves just in time for the opening hymn, which a white-haired labourer gave out, and began to sing, the whole congregation joining in.

The mellow tones of the middle-aged, the fresh young voices of the lads and lasses, and the clear ringing strains of the children filled the chapel with a volume of harmony. Over and over again the hymn was repeated, with ever-increasing warmth, until at last the old man raised his hand, and the singing was discontinued. One after another, old men and young, old women and young, followed each other in earnest prayers, alternating with the fervid hymns which had come down to them form their forefathers, and which seemed to express their own feelings as no spoken language could have done.

In full rich harmony they sang, swaying with the rhythm, and visibly affected by their long tension of expectancy, for Brynzion had been for a whole year alternately buoyed up with hope and sunk in despair by the absence of the religious fervour which in other places had attended the revival services. True, Ebben Lloyd the carpenter had 'taken the pledge' and kept to it, thus changing the miseries of a drunkard's home into an earthly Paradise. True also, Jerri the boatman had become a sober man and a shining light in the congregation. The Sunday school was well attended by pupils whose ages ranged from eighty downwards. The quarrels and bickerings of the little village had disappeared – in fact, Tregildas had become a pattern village in its great desire for the coming of the Holy Spirit; but all this did not satisfy Brynzion, for there had been none of the excitement and uplifting that had marked the meetings at the other chapels in the neighbourhood.

'There must be something wrong,' said Jerri; ''tis we are in fault, not the Spirit,' and old Nelli Amos had not hesitated to lay the blame on Gildas Rees – 'the black rock' as she continued to call him; so that when they saw Gildas, instead of taking his place amongst the deacons, follow his wife into the Scethryg pew, there had been a flutter of mixed feelings in the hearts of the elders of the congregation, while Nelli Amos was distinctly elated and put an extra ring in her voice as she led the refrain of the hymn. Towards the close of the service, a stranger entered, and quietly placed a paper in the hand of the preacher, who had taken but a very modest part in the proceedings of the evening. When he rose from his seat and spread the missive on the open

Bible before him, there was a dead silence in the chapel; one might have heard a pin drop, and the crackling of the paper seemed full of import. Gravely and slowly, and with a tremble of eagerness in his voice, he read aloud the short message.

'Evan Roberts will visit Brynzion one day in the present month. What day, the Spirit has not yet revealed to him.
(*Signed*) ROBERT OWENS, *Deacon, Tregarreg.*'

There was a moment's silence, ending in an outburst of song, which seemed the only fitting expression for the tide of jubilant gratification that swept over the congregation like a strong south wind. From every corner of the chapel came ejaculations of praise and prayer.

In the pew in the corner Nance had risen to her feet, her excitable nature moved to its very depths by the strong emotion of the moment. She clasped her hands and joined in the exultant refrain; and when the first verse was ended it was her voice that led on the second without a break, Gildas sitting beside her calmly observant of all that passed; and naturally reserved and sensitive, fearing lest she might lose control over her feelings, he laid his hand quietly on her arm, but with an impatient jerk she flung it from her and continued to sing in a kind of ecstasy. Hymn after hymn was sung, prayer after prayer was outpoured, until the clock on the front of the gallery pointed to half-past nine; and the meeting was brought to a close at last in a scene of enthusiastic congratulations. Evan Roberts was coming! and doubtless with him would visit them the Spirit for which they had so long prayed.

Gildas looked at his watch impatiently, and whispered, 'Time to go home, 'merch-i, follow me close,' and, though a little reluctantly, Nance took his advice, and followed close behind her stalwart husband, as the quickest means of reaching the doorway.

After a few breaths of the pure fresh air, she said in great excitement, 'There's a grand meeting it was, Gildas! Wasn't it wonderful to hear little Jane the Mill praying like that? In my deed, I felt something rising up in my heart, that I could almost fall down and pray myself.'

'Caton pawb, Nance!' said Gildas, 'Never, I hope, before strangers like this. Thou'st got to keep a strong guard on that heart of thine, 'merch-i; 'tis warm and true I know, but 'tis too ready to blaze up like the dried furze on the mountain; 'tis the slow-burning peat lasts longest, and warms the hearth and cheers our hearts; this blaze of prayer and noise will soon die away.'

'Die away?' said Nance. 'No indeed, I'm not believing thee, Gildas, and I can't think how thou could'st hold up so straight and stern, when the old hymns were filling the chapel! I was looking at thee, and thou wert as cold and hard as a stone, and old Dafi Lewis praying too!'

They were walking over the short grass of the moor. A light in the Scethryg kitchen gleamed through the soft gloom, the May night was heavy with the sweet perfume of the earth and the gorse, the landrail called from the lower hayfields. The stars were hidden by a mist that came up on the wind that bore with it also a distant threatening murmur.

Gildas was silent for a time, some strange weight oppressed him. The mysterious upheaval in the spiritual life of those around him disturbed him; it seemed to hold for him a foreboding of evil, against which his own spirit rebelled. Not from any antagonism to real religion, but because his blunt and honest nature, and his instinctive reticence, made him shrink from the publicity given at the revival meetings to the most secret feelings of the heart. As usual when he was deeply moved he answered in a calm voice.

'I am not saying, Nance, that that old tune did not touch me; 'twas because of that I looked so straight and hard perhaps. 'Twas a hymn my mother used to sing when I was a boy, and, Nance, I am not the hard man thou seem'st to think me; but to wail and cry, to shout Hallelujah, and to tell all the people that I am a sinner – ach-y-fi! 'tis not the way I think of religion. Wasn't it the Lord Jesus who said, 'Enter into thy chamber, and when thou hast shut to thy door, pray to thy Father which is in secret'? No, Nance, I would rather die than show my heart to strangers. Come, 'merch-i, we won't speak any more about it, for 'tis plain to me that on this matter thou and I will not agree.'

'We must disagree then, I suppose,' said Nance, with a toss of her head, which in the darkness Gildas felt rather than saw, 'for I will never desert the prayer meetings. I will ask them to pray for thee, Gildas, that the spirit may come and soften thy heart.'

'Pray for me? in public!' said Gildas, recoiling in horror. 'Nance, lass, thou *would'st* not do a thing that would anger me so much.' He paused with his fingers on the door latch and stood in a listening attitude, while on the still night air came the sound of a booming threatening thud which seemed to reverberate in the ground under their feet.

'What is that?' asked Nance, listening also.

''Tis the sea breaking on Maldraeth,' said Gildas, 'and 'tis a sign we are going to have a storm. The wind changed when we were in Brynzion. I thought indeed the air was heavy,' and he drew a long breath as if oppressed by something.

'On Maldraeth!' said Nance, with a little shiver, ''tis gloomy always there, but 'tis worse with that thundering noise. There it is again! Ach-y-fi! I never heard it before.'

'No,' said Gildas, entering the house before her, 'most like not; 'tis very seldom the wind blows straight from that point, but when it does the sea feels it down there I can tell

thee. Come in, 'merch-i, let us blaze the fire and shut the door
on the storm and darkness – it need not come near thee and
me;' and he tried to close the door, but stopped as he felt a
slight resistance. 'Gwenifer!' he exclaimed, as a slender
girlish figure entered. 'What! hast been to the meeting and
we never saw thee there? Come in, lass, and have supper
with us.'

Nance, too, was pressing in her invitation; and gathered
round the homely table, they chatted as easily and as unem-
barrassed as though Gwenifer were able to express herself
in the same manner as themselves.

'A storm coming?' said Gildas in answer to a sign from
her, which they had no difficulty in understanding. 'Yes,
and a bad one. Hast heard the thundering on Maldraeth?'

The girl nodded, and in her own picturesque way said,
'Far out in the bay there is a ship tossing badly.'

'A ship? A schooner?' asked Gildas.

'No.'

'A smack?'

'Yes, far out; 'tis very rough.'

'Yes,' said Gildas, 'and we have only the swell of it yet,
before midnight 'twill reach us. Thou must go before it
comes, Gwenifer.'

Nance was rather silent; and as she ate her supper, the
pout on her lips was very pronounced.

Gwenifer, sensitive and tender, noticed it as once, as well
as the little shadow of vexation on Gildas's face.

'What did'st think of the meeting?' the latter asked. 'Dost
like all that fever and confusion? Mestress and me, we are
not quite agreeing about it. Dost like it, Gwenifer? Is that
religion? Out there alone, so many years in the silence, thou
must know if anyone does. Come, tell me, lass, is this
pleasing to the Almighty and to thee?'

It was some little time before Gwenifer answered; she

seemed troubled at the difficulty of explaining herself, as she rarely was. At last, with a smile, she pointed upwards and bowed her head, then wringing her hands with an expression of misery on her face, she shook her head.

'What dost mean, lass? That part of it that comes from above pleaseth thee, and the noise and the excitement thou dost not like. Is that it?'

'Yes,' nodded the girl.

'I knew that would be thy thought. Well, Nance shall have her way, and go to as many meetings as she likes; she goes with it heart and soul, but for me, I am not liking it.'

Gwenifer glanced swiftly from one to the other; and by some mysterious instinct which had grown upon her in her years of silent seclusion, she felt the mutterings of a storm which was gathering round Gildas's head. And as she ran over the moor through the fitful moonlight she heard again the booming thunder of the waves on Maldraeth, and in some unaccountable manner seemed to connect the threatening sounds with the shadow on Gildas's face; and she trembled as she heard the recurring boom which spoke of resistless power, more forcibly than the foam and roar of the breakers would have done, and of the heavy impact of waters which the south wind was driving against the cliffs of Maldraeth.

CHAPTER VII

A Fairing

All night the storm continued to rage, and to Gwenifer, lying awake in her lonely cottage, the sound of the night wind rushing by, the roar of the breakers, seemed like a threatening of trouble to Gildas. Why to Gildas she could not tell, and the early hours of dawn found her still awake and disturbed in spirit. The sun rose bright and clear, and in his slanting rays the sea turned to gold and the moor became resplendent with the purple and yellow of heather and furze.

On the bay, no ship with snowy sail or flaunting pennon could be seen, only the great wild waste of water stretching to the horizon.

Gwenifer's thoughts flew to the tiny bark which she had seen the night before tossing dangerously amongst the breakers. What had become of her? she wondered. Had she reached some port of safety? Had she folded her sails and dropped her anchor in some sheltered haven? or had that wild storm wreaked its fury upon her, and compassed her destruction?

She knew from experience it would be useless to try to sleep, so she dressed herself and prepared her simple breakfast, and while she did so her thoughts returned persistently to that frail craft which she had seen but for a moment through the twilight haze. What had happened to her, and what was she? Not the *Liliwen*, she knew; smaller, and with but one mast, her sails unfurled, the seas breaking over her

– her chance of safety was small indeed. But as the sun rose
higher and higher, brightening the moor and gilding the
sea, the depression and the gloom fled from her heart.

'Perhaps the little ship was safe in port!' and as she raised
the latch, and saw the Scethryg cows lying safe in the shelter
of the furze bushes, she was lightened of her burden; and
although she did not sing aloud, in her heart rose a paean
of youth and life and health.

What a foolish girl she had been! was her thought as she
ran over the moor, every cow rising as she passed and
clumsily following to the milking-yard. What had the
booming thunder on Maldraeth threatened after all? Nothing
worse than this boisterous storm, which could not reach the
cosy hearth in the old farm kitchen, or the loft where Gildas
lay sleeping; what mattered anything else? 'No, too ready is
my heart to fear,' she thought, 'the storm will pass, the world
is beautiful, and the cows are coming home to be milked.'

Yes, Gwenifer, the world is beautiful, the cows will be
milked, and in due time the storm will die away; but far out
upon that stormy sea are floating a few spars and broken
boards, all that remain of the ship that had so persistently
haunted Gwenifer's thoughts. Many fathoms deep under
those foaming billows the captain, the mate, and alas! the
young wife who had accompanied her husband are lying;
no trace of these remains to tell the tale of their sad fate.

Surely Gwenifer's forebodings of trouble for Gildas were
groundless; at all events they seemed to have taken flight
for the time, as she carried her pail to meet the cows in the
farmyard.

A little later and the whole Scethryg household was astir,
for under Nance's energetic rule none were allowed to waste
the early morning hours in sleep; so that when Gwenifer
returned from the milking she found the plain and plentiful
breakfast already prepared: the brown teapot sitting close

on the embers, the flat loaf lying on the table, with the butter
as yellow as the cowslips that decked the Scethryg fields,
while over the fire Nance held the spluttering pan that was
filling the kitchen with its savoury odour. Gildas entering
upon this scene, required no pressing to draw his chair up
to the table at once, with a cheerful 'Well, I'm ready!' He
was not ill pleased that the strong wind shook the windows
in their frames, that Ben 'Stable' took out his red pocket-
handkerchief and tied his hat down over his ears, for it all
went to prove that Nance could not have gone to the fair,
although doubtless (as he wished to believe) she would have
accompanied him had it been a fine day.

'No indeed, this is not a day for new hats and ribbons,'
he said as he proceeded with his breakfast, 'but I must go,
and sell that horse. I will be home early and bring thee a
fairing.'

He shrank from saying anything about the meeting in the
evening, and Nance was apparently as anxious as he was
to avoid the subject.

'Good-bye, 'merch i!' he called out, as he mounted his
horse at the door, where Ben Stable joined him, riding the
horse that was to be sold.

Down in the village he passed Brynzion, which, in spite
of the wind, two or three people were busily engaged in
cleaning and adorning. A burly sea captain perched on a
ladder was cleaning the windows, Jerri the boatman polished
the brass thumb latch, while another stalwart sailor weeded
the path that surrounded the walls.

'Preparing we are you see, mishteer,' said Jerri, 'and tidy-
ing the place up a bit against Evan Roberts comes, because
no doubt there'll be some strangers coming too.'

'Like enough,' said Gildas, passing on without any further
remark. An unreasoning feeling of antagonism was growing
in his heart towards the chapel and everything connected

with it, for he attributed all Nance's altered ways to her devotion to it, and to its services; and as he rode into the town, his thoughts returned to his rugged old home with an aching dissatisfaction. He made a bad bargain over his horse, and returned home not in the most equable frame of mind; but still, his just and honest nature prevented him showing any signs of his discontent to Nance.

The storm still raged, the whole bay tossing as if in a ferment of boiling anger. The booming thunder on Maldraeth was no longer heard, for the air was full of the rattle and roar of the wind.

'I told thee 'twas not over,' said Gildas, entering the kitchen where Nance already seated at the tea-table awaited his coming, while in the background Gwenifer stood holding up a quilt of brilliant colouring, the work of her clever fingers. Her dark eyes, bent down on the quilt, were raised inquiringly to Gildas's face as he entered, and, as if in answer to her question, he said, 'I got on pretty well, though in my deed that road goes straight in the teeth of the wind to-day – 'twas hard sometimes to keep on the saddle.'

''Tis a beautiful patchwork, lass,' said Nance. 'Take it up to the coffer, and come thou down and have tea with us before thou goest.' But Gwenifer shook her head and showed she was going a-milking.

'Oh, I thought Het had milked,' said Nance, dismissing Gwenifer and the quilt from her mind.

'Come, Gildas,' she said in her managing brisk tones, 'come, sit thee down; 'tis getting late for tea.'

'Well,' said Gildas, doing as he was bid with an indulgent smile, 'I am ready for my tea, too, but thou dost not ask me who I saw in the fair to-day.'

'Who?' said Nance, with but little interest, for her mind was full of the prayer meeting.

'Well, first I met Jones Bryndu, and he asked would we

go and have tea with his mestress on Monday. Wilt come, 'merch-i? Jones and I we are old friends, and I like to please him.'

'Yes will I,' said Nance. 'On Monday there is no meeting.'

'Right. Well then, who should I meet but Cap'n Jack! and for a wonder without John Davies.'

'Cap'n Jack!' exclaimed Nance, with a strange flutter in her breast, a flutter of uneasiness as well as pleasure. To do her justice she was thoroughly in earnest in her devotion to what she considered the claims of religion, but this was a sudden strain upon her courage and steadfastness which she was unprepared for.

'Yes, Cap'n Jack,' continued Gildas, 'with his voice as pleasant and his eyes as wonderful as ever! I've been asking him is it true what they say, that he can see twice as much as other people?'

'What did he say then?' asked Nance, with curiosity.

'Oh, he laughed as usual, and says he, 'That depends upon what I am looking at.' The *Liliwen* has been badly damaged, a collision in the Channel, and she's in Cardiff undergoing repairs; and 'twill be a long undergoing, I am thinking, by what the captain tells me of her condition. He's coming to stop with John Davies's aunt in Tregildas, old Marged Jones.'

'Oh!' was all Nance could say.

'Yes, and I told him to come up to Scethryg as if he was at home, and we would be glad to see him, eh, Nance?'

'Yes, of course,' she said, and in silence went on with her tea, Gildas also doing full justice to the loaf of 'plank' bread, occasionally interrupting his meal with little items of news which he thought might interest her.

But she seemed strangely silent and preoccupied, and at last when tea was over rose rather hurriedly, calling to Gwenifer, who had returned from milking. 'Come, Gwenifer, and take my place with these tea-things, for 'tis late and I must go to the meeting.'

'Stop a minute, 'merch-i,' said Gildas, who had reserved what he thought would be his crowning bit of news till the last, 'I have brought a fairing for thee. What dost think it is?' and he rose to search in the pocket of his greatcoat for a little green box which he laid on the table, looking at Nance with a smile. ''Tis something I heard thee say thee would'st like to have,' he said, 'what is it then? Guess.'

'Oh, I can't wait,' said Nance impatiently, 'I must go and dress.'

'Well then, here it is,' he said, raising the lid and displaying a brooch, which at another time Nance would have received with delight.

'Oh, a brooch,' she said, 'well indeed, 'tis pretty, Gildas, and I did say I wanted one; but after all, I have the one thou gavest me before we were married, and what do I want with two? Put it there on the shelf, and when I come back I will look more at it. Thanks to thee, bachgen! Look at it, Gwenifer,' and she hurried up the bare stairs to the loft, where they could hear her moving briskly about on the uncarpeted boards.

The pleasure in Gildas's face died out, and an impenetrable look of hardness seemed to veil his eyes.

Gwenifer, alive to every change in his face, felt aggrieved at Nance's coldness, and longed to be able to soften its bitterness to Gildas.

'Nance likes it,' she signed, 'only . . .' and she waved her hand towards the door.

'Yes, yes,' said Gildas, 'she wants to go to the meeting. Indeed, lass, I am afraid I am not fit to be the husband of such a religious woman!'

To this Gwenifer made no answer, but looking down at the old oak table, drew imaginary figures on it with her forefinger. Her dark lashes lay upon the smooth ivory of her cheeks, the red lips had fallen into a curve of sadness.

'To tell thee the truth,' said Gildas, rising, 'I am getting to
hate these meetings; they are changing Nance entirely. Well,'
he added, 'I will go to the stable and see to the horses,' and
Gwenifer looked after him with a depth of pity in her eyes,
for she thought the revival had made no change in Nance,
but it was her real nature which her husband was now
discovering. For the first few months of their married life
Nance had succeeded in hiding from him the faults of temper
and character of which she was dimly conscious, and now,
under the influence of a new excitement, she was growing
more careless in her endeavours to conceal them. What could
Gwenifer do? Should she speak to Nance? To Gildas? Ah no!
too much she feared lest she might reveal the secret which
she had kept so safely hidden in her heart; and Gwenifer
did what Nance never did, she reasoned the matter out, and
came to the conclusion that the wisest course for her would
be not to interfere. She clasped her hands, as she had a habit
of doing when strong emotions surged up within her, and
called in vain for words. 'Oh, Gildas, Gildas!' was her
thought. 'Oh, would thou wert happy! then I would be
content.'

Half an hour later Nance was crossing the moor with her
grandfather.

'The storm is nearly spent, Dakee,' she said. 'There's odd
now! that Gildas would not come to the meeting. Ach-y-fi!
'Tis a shame to see how hard he is; they are all talking about
him in Brynzion.'

'Nance!' said the old man, 'wilt take my advice in this
matter? leave Gildas alone, 'merch-i. I have great faith in him.
He's all right, Nance. He does not talk about religion, but we
see the fruit of it, in my deed, so fret not about him, but let
him go his own way; 'tis very kind of him to let thee go thine.'

'Kind indeed!' said Nance, 'I don't see it then; 'twould be
more kind of him to come with his wife to the meeting.'

'Nay, Nance, thou wilt never alter Gildas Rees; he's as firm as the strong oak.'

'Yes,' said Nance, 'and as hard as the black rocks, as Nelli Amos says.'

'Come, Nance fach,' said the old man gently, 'the Diwygiad should teach thee to have kinder feelings towards thy husband.' But she walked on in silence, with the little pout on her lips which had been so charming in the child, but was not so becoming to the face of the woman.

Old Hezek too seemed lost in thought, till reaching the chapel door they were soon absorbed in the crowded congregation.

Thus Nance continued to attend her meetings, while Gildas gradually withdrew himself from them more and more. His lips took a hard firm set, the smile that used to lighten up his countenance so much, seldom visited it, and he grew more silent – 'as silent almost as Gwenifer,' Nance would say sometimes, at which remark he would rouse himself and join boisterously in the laugh or the joke, soon relapsing into silence, however.

His changed appearance began to be noticed by the villagers without securing their sympathy, but rather arousing their anger. 'Only a year,' they would say, 'since he married the purtiest girl round about here; and now see his serious face! and never coming to chapel! Pwr thing! ach-y-fi, 'tis a shame!'

Gwenifer saw it of course, and longed to chase away the gloom; but Nance, if she saw it, seemed indifferent, and continued to go her own way. Two or three times in the week the hearth at Scethryg was bare and empty in the evenings when Gildas, tired with his day's work, returned to it for cheer and rest; for Nance was at the prayer meetings, where nightly the spiritual influence which they awaited seemed increasingly felt, and she grew more and more wedded to the services of the chapel.

It was late one night in June when, returning from one of these services with her grandfather, she heard a voice that startled her, and in another moment a figure approached whom she recognised as Captain Jack.

With a little flutter of excitement and pleasure, she took his outstretched hand, with the usual Welsh greeting. 'Well indeed!' and she was thankful that the darkness hid the blush that rose to her face at his sudden appearance. Old Hezek was delighted to meet his former patient.

'Well, where did you come from so sudden?' said Nance as they turned towards the moor together.

'The *Liliwen* has got a crack in her side, and I have left her in Cardiff docks for repairs.'

'Oh yes! Gildas told me; and you are stopping in the village.'

''Tis an ill wind that blows no one any good,' said Hezek. ''Tis a good chance for us to see you again,' and he shook hands warmly with the captain.

'Yes, you can shake as hard as you like,' said the latter, laughing, 'you made a good job of my hand, doctor, 'tis stronger than ever now.'

'You'll come up to Scethryg, and have supper with us – eh, Nance?' said the old man.

'Yes, of course,' said Nance, seconding his invitation. 'Gildas will be glad to see you,' and they walked on through the gloaming. The air was laden with the scent of the hayfields, the sunset light still lingered in the sky, the bats flitted by them in the darkness, and Nance, poor Nance, walked on in a kind of dream.

When they reached Scethryg, it was with a strange nervousness that she ushered the guest into the old kitchen, where Gildas was sitting alone by the hearth.

He rose at once when he saw the newcomer, and welcomed him with true hospitality.

'Glad to see you, cap'n,' he said. 'I told mestress you would turn up some day.'

'Well, you see,' said the captain, 'I am stopping with Marged Jones, John Davies's aunt, and I will be glad to come up here sometimes to see you all.'

'As often as you can,' said Gildas. 'We are haymaking to-morrow; will you give us a hand?'

'Yes indeed,' said the captain, 'though 'tis long since I worked at the hay.'

'Come, sit you down,' said Gildas. 'We are going to have supper, aren't we, Nance?'

'Well yes, at once,' and she set the chairs to the table.

'Come, Het,' called Gildas, 'we'll try thy last brewing.'

'Het's brewings are always good,' said Captain Jack, setting the rush chair for Nance. 'There's glad I am to have a sight of you both, and of my old doctor here. Well, you've treated the mestress well, whatever; her roses are blooming as fresh as ever.'

'Oh yes,' said Nance, laughing, 'there's not much the matter with me, I think.'

'Is the singing as good as ever in Brynzion?' he asked, turning to Nance, and under his gaze her heart fluttered again. She remembered the walks in the moonlight, she remembered the kiss by the thorn bush, and wondered whether he had forgotten; but turning to her duties as hostess she answered as calmly as she could.

'Yes, better than ever; but come, here's the supper. 'Tis but plain, but I hope you won't mind that.'

'Dear anwl no,' said Captain Jack, 'I am so hungry I could eat a brick; and with a glass of this sparkling ale too, why, 'tis a first-class supper! And how's all in the village?' he continued as he drew his chair to the table. 'Dafi Pengaer as fond of a drop as ever?'

'No,' said Nance, 'never a drop does he touch, and Leisa,

poor thing, is having a happy life, what she never knew before. That's what the Diwygiad has done for her, whatever,' and she cast a swift glance at her husband, which the captain's keen instinct interpreted rightly into a rebuke of some sort.

'Well, well,' he said, 'if the Diwygiad has done that, 'tis wonderful indeed.'

'Yes,' said Gildas, 'that is the strange thing about it! I can see many good things it has done, and 'tis beyond me to understand; but I will not believe there is any good in crying, and moaning and shouting; d'ye call that religion, captain?'

'Perhaps,' said Captain Jack, ''tis the Spirit of God poured into earthen vessels.'

Nance looked up well pleased, Gildas somewhat in surprise, while Captain Jack himself seemed strangely disturbed. He had spoken on the impulse of the moment, and had unconsciously enunciated a great truth. Such a subject was not one upon which he was accustomed to bestow a thought, or to venture an opinion, so, a little confused, he tried to change the subject.

But Gildas added, 'The mestress and me don't agree about it you see; she is heart and soul for it, and I, well I am not against it, exactly, but I don't hold with their ways down there at Brynzion. She shall have her own way about it, and go to all the meetings if she likes, dear heart.'

'Well, I have never been to one yet,' said Captain Jack, ''tis time for me to begin, I think. 'Tis how you take it, I suppose, this Diwygiad,' he added carelessly, and the subject dropped.

'Come,' said Gildas at last, turning to the hearth where the logs were spluttering cheerfully, 'a smoke before you go, for I see you looking at your watch.'

'Well, one pipe before I start. 'Tis a good stretch to the village, and 'twas late to come up here; but I wanted to see you all, and to thank the doctor here for curing my hand so well.'

And under the wide open chimney they chatted on all the events that looked so big and important to the country eye, and seemed so small and insignificant to the outer world.

'Well, I will be here to the hay to-morrow,' said the sailor, at last rising to go. 'Nos da to you all. There's snug and cosy you look here! I'll be thinking about this bright hearth when I am trudging along; 'tis enough to make me long to be married myself!' and as they closed the door after his departure, they heard him humming cheerfully, as he began his way across the dark moor.

For two or three hundred yards he walked on almost unconsciously, so busy were his thoughts with the bright hearth he had just left: n'wncwl Sam sitting stolidly silent, old Hezek's bent shoulders and grey beard, Nance's trim figure moving about her household duties, the little imperious ways which seemed to have grown more pronounced, the shadow of care or vexation on Gildas's face – nothing was lost upon Captain Jack, he was alive to it all. Nance's dimpled charms, the embarrassment with which she had received him, the drooping eyelids, the changing colour – these too Captain Jack noted. Suddenly he was recalled to himself by finding he had reached the edge of the cliff.

'Jari!' he said, 'I've got wrong; lost my way somehow, and no compass to set me right. Where am I, I wonder? I thought I knew my way into the village,' and with a shrug and a laugh he turned round, but again took a wrong path. When he had followed it for a quarter of a mile or so, he came upon a tiny thatched cottage, through whose diminutive window gleamed a beacon light. No front garden or 'cwrt' separated it from the grassy moor, which reached right up to its whitewashed walls. Only a little bareness before the doorway showed it was ever trodden by human footsteps. Captain Jack approached noiselessly over the grass, and knocking at the low door, which stood open, called out, 'Hoi! is there anybody in who'll show me the way to Tregildas?'

In answer to his call a girl appeared, who seemed surprised but not startled at seeing a stranger. The light from the inner chamber, faint though it was, revealed her fully against the surrounding gloom – her gown of dark red frieze set close to her slender form, her dusky hair crowned her head with many coils, her bare neck and arms were smooth as satin, though tinged by sun and wind.

Captain Jack for a moment stood surprised at something unusual in the girl's appearance.

It was Gwenifer, who, having stayed late over her quilting at Scethryg, was now preparing her own supper of bread and milk. Here was a wonderful thing, a visitor in the midst of the moor – away from Tregildas, away from Scethryg! She was not at all frightened, no thought of danger entered her head; on the contrary, it was pleasure only that she would have wished to express. But the stranger, unacquainted with her signs and gestures, seemed at first puzzled by her silence; recalling, however, what he had heard, it flashed upon him that this was Gwenifer the silent girl, whom he had thought of so often since that night when she had appeared to him for a moment in the glow of the sunset. She smiled a pleasant greeting, raising her eyebrows inquiringly, and this at least Captain Jack understood.

'I am John Davies,' he said, 'captain of the *Liliwen*. About here they call me Captain Jack', and at once Gwenifer, remembering Nance's infatuation, could not help showing her change of feelings in her expressive face.

'Ah!' he said, 'you have heard no good of me. But you are Gwenifer, and I have heard nothing but good of you. Will you direct me to Tregildas?'

Instantly she was alive to his wishes, and anxious to help. Taking down a cloak which hung on the boarded wall, she flung it hastily over her, and, drawing the hood over her head, came out into the darkness.

'Oh, no, no,' said Captain Jack, 'you shall not come, 'tis late and the dew is heavy.' But she only waved a laughing rejection of his reasons, and continued to walk beside him over the moor.

Conversation was impossible, and the sailor could only follow his guide in silence. Once she turned to him as the moon peeped out from behind the clouds, and without the slightest embarrassment laid one hand on his arm, and with the other pointed to where the moonlight made a silver path across the sea.

'Yes,' said Captain Jack 'beautiful indeed,' and he looked, not on the path of silver, but on the girl's face which the moon shone full upon. She, however, seemed quite unconscious of his admiration, and arriving at a diverging pathway pointed to it and stopped.

'Yes, yes, I see,' said the captain. 'How stupid I was to lose my way! But in my deed I'm glad I did, because I have wanted to speak to you; and now we are friends, aren't we?'

She bowed her head, smiling in that proudly gracious manner which made the boys of the village call her 'Queen of the Rushes.' There was no excuse for lingering, so Captain Jack had perforce to follow the path which she pointed out.

'Good-bye,' he said, 'and thank you, and . . .' He was longing to tell her how sorry he was for her affliction, but suddenly stopped in confusion, feeling it would be an insult to do so; but Gwenifer had caught the meaning of his sudden hesitation and laid her finger on her lips.

'My silence, yes,' and again she bowed her head, and Captain Jack as he turned away took off his cap with an unfeigned and almost reverent admiration.

Gwenifer waved her hand, and was gone.

CHAPTER VIII

A Bowl of Buttermilk

The weeks slipped by, unmarked by any special events other than the gathering of the hay harvest, which was rich and plentiful.

Captain Jack had become a regular attendant at Brynzion, drawn there simply by a feeling of sociability and his love of music, for Brynzion was famed for its good singing even in that neighbourhood, where choirs and singing-classes were the mainstay of every congregation. He enjoyed the swinging rhythm of the old hymns, though with a little sense of awkwardness at finding himself inside a place of worship – an experience which he had eschewed for many years.

Nance saw him from her pew in the opposite corner and rejoiced. Why she so rejoiced it would be difficult to say. It does not do to look too closely into the motives and sentiments of the human heart. At all events, she thought her joy was over the saving of his soul.

Poor Nance! She was ill at ease, and had lost the buoyancy and spirit which had been her chief charm. Her face had lost some of its fresh colouring, too, and there were dark rings under her eyes; for though the mind may not be deep enough for harassing thoughts, the heart may still open to the ravages of stormy passions and insidious temptations.

To do her justice, it had not been without a struggle that she had allowed her infatuation for the roving sailor once more to enter her heart. Gildas she thought was hard, and callous to the religious wave that was bringing life into services that had grown somewhat time-worn and spiritless.

Here was a man who felt it all as she did, who attended every meeting, and who as regularly walked home with her and her grandfather, ever ready at stile or streamlet to help her over, with the little nameless attentions to which she was not much accustomed in her rough country life.

A perverse stubbornness seemed to be daily growing stronger within her against Gildas who was hard and proud she thought – not towards her, it was true, but towards the wave of the Spirit which to her and to her friends meant religion, and therefore it was right that she should show her disapproval, and that she should be more faithful than ever to Brynzion.

Gildas, meanwhile, showed no diminution of kindness and care towards her, though he had become more reserved and less cheerful than he used to be, letting her go her own way, and calmly taking his own to field and market; but towards Brynzion and the revival showing a cold and stolid front, taking no interest in the meetings, and receiving Nance and Hezek's glowing accounts of fresh conversions with indifference.

No suspicion of her feelings towards Captain Jack had ever entered his mind. As ready as ever to greet him with hospitable warmth, to drive him to market or fair, to smoke with him under the big chimney, he wondered why he so seldom appeared at Scethryg. 'What is the matter with him, Nance?' he asked one day, when the sailor had sat for an hour with Hezek in the old store-house, and had then returned to the village without entering the house. 'Has the revival altered him, too?' he wondered; but he kept his thoughts to himself, for he had got into the way of avoiding that subject as one on which it pained him to disagree with Nance.

'What is the matter with him? How do I know? Nothing, I should think,' she answered, turning to the dairy with the look of irritability which was settling down upon her face.

'Well indeed, perhaps I am fancying it. They're drawing the net to-night on Tregildas sands; there'll be plenty of fish – will I ask him to come and have supper with us? Wilt come down thyself to the shore, 'merch-i?'

There was an eager tremor in the man's voice, and a melting tenderness in his eyes, as he asked the question; but at Nance's reply every sign of eagerness was repressed, and the flash of light that had for a moment made him look like the Gildas of old died away.

'Caton pawb!' was her answer. 'How can I go down to the shore when it's churning-day and all!'

'Gwenifer is going to help thee, isn't she? and she is coming to see the nets drawn. There will be plenty of time when the churning is over.'

'Oh! let Gwenifer go then; I am too busy whatever.'

'So!' said Gildas, a flush of annoyance dyeing his face. For a few minutes he was silent, but rose at last and followed Nance into the dairy, where in the shaded light she was busy over her cream-pans. She looked very pretty and young with her tucked-up skirt and bare arms; a shaft of sunlight streaming in through the latticed window catching her yellow hair. Scarcely noticing Gildas, she continued to pour the golden cream into the churn, but when he closed the string-latched door behind him, and approached her more closely, she raised her eyes inquiringly, and it would have been no wonder if they had rested admiringly upon him; for as he stood there in his rough grey working coat, his blue shirt loosened at the collar, showing the manly brown throat, his red tie hanging loosely on his breast, his strong hand grasping the sickle which he was carrying to his work – he made a striking picture of rustic comeliness and strength.

Nance noticed nothing of this, or if she did she made no sign; but she saw the look of determination in his set lips and flashing eyes, and her own hot temper rose at once defiantly in opposition.

'Not so near the churn, Gildas,' she said, 'there are hay-seeds on thy coat.' He did not withdraw, however, but stood still a moment, looking at her hot with anger, but with a wistful seriousness which she had never seen in him before.

In that moment's gaze, while the thick cream flowed softly into the churn, he seemed to read her very soul; and, alas! Nance was beginning to harbour feelings that would not bear such close scrutiny.

'Dear anwl! What is it, then?' she asked at last, when her eyelids were beginning to droop a little under his steadfast look.

"Tis this then,' he said. 'Listen to me! Art coming with me to Jane and John's wedding to-morrow? Thou knowest I have promised for us both.'

'Jane and John's wedding! and me in the middle of clear-ing up the work after the haymaking! How can'st expect me, Gildas? No, indeed! I am not coming.'

There was another silence, during which the man's broad chest heaved a little, while, with folded arms, he stood looking out through the lattice bars, as though he took counsel from the shimmering sea that gleamed through the ivy leaves outside.

'Nance!' he said at last. 'Nance! Listen to me, 'merch-i, for I mean every word I say. Of late thou hast refused me every trifle I have asked of thee, though I have never refused thee anything. Once more, Nance, wilt come with me to the wedding? If not' – and he paused for a moment – 'if not, then *I will never ask thee anything more!*'

A peal of laughter was Nance's answer.

'Well indeed!' she said, when she had recovered her

breath. 'Well indeed! I thought something dreadful was coming. Is that all, then? Thou wilt never ask me anything more.' And she laughed again, with one hand to her side, while the other still held the dropping cream pot.

'Yes, that is all,' he said, and slowly turned away sickle in hand.

She expected a last reproach, but it did not come; on the contrary, Gildas seemed to have forgotten the matter as he passed out through the kitchen. He stopped at the doorway and called back in his usual manner, ''Tis a hot day; Dai and Ben will be glad to have their lunch: wilt remind Het of it Nance?'

'Yes, yes, I'll send it at ten as usual; 'tis only half-past nine yet.'

'Right,' said Gildas, and was gone.

In the lane that led to the fields two men were sauntering towards him, enjoying the cool shade of the overarching thorn hedges, and Gildas recognised Captain Jack and his mate, who had arrived the preceding day.

'Well, well! I was asking Nance this morning what had become of you, cap'n! and I am glad to see, mate, that you've not forgotten your way to Scethryg.'

'No, no, not likely! And how's the mestress?'

'Oh, quite well,' said Gildas. 'She's in the house. Go you in and sit a bit; 'tis as hot as noon already.'

''Tis that,' said Captain Jack, and his light blue eyes, whose long black lashes seemed to throw quite a shade over them, flickered and drooped under Gildas's straight, clear gaze; and the latter wondered what had disturbed the light-hearted sailor.

'Any hay to make?' asked the mate.

'No, 'tis all in, as the captain here can tell you.'

'We are bringing you news,' continued the mate. 'Evan Roberts is coming this week. He's to lodge with John Parry

and his wife, and there's to be a grand meeting at Brynzion
to prepare for him.'

'So indeed!' was all Gildas's answer, while Captain Jack
said nothing, but reached up to the pale June roses that
trailed over the hedgeside.

'Well, he has been long waited for,' said Gildas at last. 'The
mestress will be glad of the news. I must go to the fields, so
good-day to you both,' and he went on his way down the
shady lane.

'Dei anwl! There's a fool I was to say anything about it to
him,' said the mate. 'Did you hear how dry he answered? 'So
indeed,' says he, as if I had only told him the wind had
changed. Well, he was always as cold and hard as a stone. I
wonder how is poor little Nance getting on with him?'

'A grand man, I call him,' said Captain Jack. 'As straight
as a line and as honest as the day! If everybody was like
Gildas Rees there would be no need of any Diwygiad.'

'Oh yes, he is all that, no doubt,' assented the mate, and
in the silence that so often marks the companionship of old
and tried friends they passed up the lane to the farmyard,
where the sunshine was glistening on the straw, and in the
shade of the cow-sheds a few of the cows and horses stood
ruminating and lazily switching their tails at the flies.

Outside the farmhouse door the temperature was almost
tropical, and from this great heat the two men entered gladly
into the shady interior.

How refreshing the breeze blowing straight through the
house from front door to back! how suggestive of coolness,
too, was the swishing sound of the frothing cream in the
churn!

'Pouff!' exclaimed both the men as they entered, to find
Nance busily preparing the ten o'clock lunch, which Ben and
Dai were already waiting for under the shadow of the hedge
in the turnip-field.

She pulled down her sleeves and smoothed her ruffled hair with a shy embarrassment, and her face lighted up with the old sparkle and brightness, which had been absent too often of late.

With a great many 'dear anwls' and 'well indeeds' she greeted the newcomers warmly, fetched two horse-hair-covered chairs from the 'parlwr', and placed before them a brown jug filled with foaming new beer, pressing them to drink, 'for 'tis so warm to-day, and you must be thirsty.'

"'Tis warm, and no mistake,' said Captain Jack. 'We would not come up so early, only the mate here thought you would like to hear the news we're bringing you.'

'Yes,' chimed in the mate, 'we're bringing you good news, whatever! Evan Roberts is coming to Tregildas very soon.'

'Very soon?' exclaimed Nance. 'Oh, there's glad I am;' and all the interest and excitement that was wanting in Gildas's reception of the news was evident in her face and voice. Her colour came and went, there was a flutter in her breath and a restlessness in her movements which the mate had never noticed before.

'Now,' she said, 'I hope we will have the same grand things happening in Brynzion as they have had in Graig and other places. Well indeed, there's a good thing you are telling me.' Her hand trembled as she held the sparkling ale towards Captain Jack, who, however, declined it, saying laughingly, 'No, no, give it to the mate – he can never refuse a glass; but for me – a drink of buttermilk, if you please; I'm thirsting for it, with that swishing sound in my ears.'

'Oh, well, you can have plenty of that; 'tis Gwenifer churning in there; I will fetch you a jug of it.' But before she could prevent him he had started to his feet, and had pushed open the dairy door, where the sound of the swishing was growing less continuous, saying, 'No, no, I will fetch it myself.'

In the shaded light Gwenifer was standing peering into the churn, while Het stood expectant at the handle. 'Is it come?' she asked. Gwenifer smiled and nodded, and, raising her eyes, saw that Captain Jack had entered the dairy, and was looking at her with that strange gaze of wonderment and admiration combined which would have embarrassed most girls, but to her it seemed only the natural expression of those wonderful eyes . . . so light in colour, yet so deeply shaded.

Therefore there was nothing but pleased surprise in the look with which she greeted him as he drew nearer.

'I've come to beg a drink of buttermilk,' he said. 'If the taste of it is as good as the sound, this hot day, 'twill be better than all the cwrw in the world.'

Evidently this was the girl's own opinion, for she nodded emphatically as she turned to a high shelf that ran round the dairy walls. Reaching down a wooden bowl, she filled it from the churn and held it towards him, her slender, girlish figure showing its graceful lines against the whitewashed walls; and Captain Jack took the crude drinking-cup from her hands with a respectful, almost a deferential air, which Gwenifer seemed to accept quite naturally.

'Here's to our further acquaintance, then, Gwenifer,' he said, and, raising the bowl to his lips, he took a long and refreshing draught before he returned it to her with the same respectful manner.

Standing there in the green light that filtered in through the screen of ivy growing over the window, surrounded by the snowy milk-pans, and white-scoured dairy utensils, she seemed to him the embodiment of purity and innocence, and in her presence the reckless sailor felt a strange and wistful longing for – something – he knew not what, which she alone could give him.

Her neck was bared to the cool breeze, and her round

smooth arms rivalled the cream in their sun-kissed whiteness.

He lingered a moment, turning his cap in his hands as if with the intention of speaking; but Gwenifer interrupted him by laying her finger on her red lips, with the usual shake of her head, as though she said, 'I would remind you that I cannot answer what you have to say, 'and she turned to the churn where the butter was floating in yellow crumbs on the face of the frothing buttermilk.

'Yes,' he said, 'I know I ought to go, but I want to tell you first how much I wish those beautiful lips could speak.' As soon as he had spoken, he was filled with fear lest his words had offended her; a sense of refinement, which perhaps he owed to his early life and education, told him that it had been bad taste to allude to her affliction, and he left the dairy in an uneasy frame of mind, for this silent girl had some strange attraction for him, and as he entered the kitchen he seemed lost in thought, and left the dairy door ajar. As a consequence Gwenifer, looking after him, could see Nance who was sitting in her direct line of vision, and her brown eyes were arrested by something in that picture seen between the heavy black door and its clumsy frame. What was it that made her stand so still with that brimming platter of butter dropping its cream into the churn?

Nance was sitting in the full light of the window, her knitting fallen on her lap, John Davies slowly winding up the ball of worsted which had rolled on to the floor, when Captain Jack appeared, and over Nance's face came that change of expression which had arrested Gwenifer's attention.

The changing colour, the drooping eyes, the conscious smile of greeting, – where had these been when Gildas had entered – Gildas, who had chosen her to be his wife, to share his hearth with him, when she, Gwenifer, ofttimes

had closed the door upon them and taken her solitary way
over the moor? How often at such times had she envied
Nance as she looked back through the darkness and saw the
cheerful light in the Scethryg window! How her heart had
rebelled at the thought of Nance's happiness, and her own
silent loneliness! And now, what was the meaning of that
altered expression in Nance's face? of that beaming smile?
that blushing embarrassment? Och-i, och-i! she saw it all.
She called to mind the foolish infatuation that had prompted
the words – 'Gwenifer, I love him, lass, and if he called me I
would go to him as his dog runs to him,' and in one swift
flash of intuition she realised that Gildas was supplanted in
Nance's heart by this roving sailor. Gildas despised,
forgotten! To her it seemed terrible and almost impossible.
The very thought of it sent the blood surging through her
veins and dyed her cheeks with the hot blush of shame. She
could hear the merry talk in the kitchen, the captain's
bantering jokes and Nance's laughing repartees, and her
heart ached with an intolerable sense of wrong done to
Gildas. What could she do to help him? She, the silent one,
who could not even tell him how she pitied him. Pity him?
Pity Gildas, the strong, the firm man, who to her seemed the
embodiment of all that was brave and powerful!

She finished her work like one in a dream, her thoughts
as busy as her deft hands, as she cleared the dairy of every
sign of the churning, except that row of golden pats ranged
on the cool stone slab prepared for them. How white, how
pure, how sweet everything looked! Why was her heart so
full of dark misgivings? She must go, she must fly to the
lonely moor, where the west wind could whisper peace to
her, where the rushes would bow, and the wild flowers
would nod and tremble as if they understood the feeling
which she was unable to express.

It was noon before the two men rose to go. 'Are you sure

you won't stay and have your cawl with us?' asked Nance, as the captain stood hesitating a moment, cap in hand.

'Oh, diwedd anwl, no!' exclaimed both, 'not for the world; Peggi Jones would never forgive us, she thinks she makes the best cawl in Tregildas. One moment, mestress,' added the captain, and he entered the dairy where Gwenifer was putting the finishing touches to her work. 'Good-day,' he said, 'we are going now, and thank you again for the buttermilk.' She looked up surprised, not accustomed to such attention, and waved a deprecation of his thanks with the smile which was so ready to come to her lips, but with a cloud of sorrow in her eyes that the captain saw at once, and pondered over as he caught up his companion in the shady lane.

'What you been doing so long in the dairy, cap'n?' asked the mate as they walked on together, and there was a sly twinkle in his eye, though there was a note of more serious warning in his voice. 'No courting with Gwenifer allowed; 'tis hands off her, mind you.'

'Hush, fool,' said the captain, turning upon him for once with real anger. 'Would'st joke with an angel who came down to walk on earth for a time?'

'Well no, *I* wouldn't, b't shwr,' answered the mate, with the bantering twinkle still lurking in his eyes. But Captain Jack did not seem inclined to follow up the subject; on the contrary, an occasional remark on the heat was all that passed between them, until they reached the village and sat down to Peggi Jones's cawl.

When the shadows of evening fell over the sea, Tregildas made a sudden start into life and action. The lapping of the wavelets on the sands, the soft grey atmosphere, instead of soothing, aroused the inhabitants to a new sensation. There was something to do! Something to call them out from their cottages where the odour of the culm fires hung heavily.

They earned enough for their simple mode of life, and there-fore preferred to rust out rather than wear out. But when the net that had hung undisturbed for a month over the rafters in Jerri's cottage had been dragged from its place, by a sudden burst of energy that had seized two or three men simultaneously; when it had been carried out a few hundred yards from the shore; when a second boat had borne one end across the little bay, and the calling and the hurrying assured them that it was really about to be drawn in – then Mari and Sara and Marged and Ann began to bestir themselves, for there would be fish, b't shwr, without any exertion on their part, and if they were there in good time they would share in the haul.

So they reached down a special jug from the top shelf on the dresser – the very jug in which their mother or grand-mother had hoarded up her savings! – and picking out a few coppers, proceeded to the shore, where, in the fast falling darkness, they found a goodly company of friends and neighbours. They greeted each other with an unusual seriousness, if not solemnity; for were they not on the eve of an important event, which should bring salvation to their souls and glory to Brynzion?

At last the two boats neared the shore, drawing closer and closer together, and entrappping the silver mackerel that had shoaled in the bay all day.

Gildas was in one of the boats, his hands busy with the oars, while his heart was burning with a bitter sense of anger. When he arrived on the shore, he had been greeted respectfully by the assembled villagers with the usual 'Nos da chi, mishteer,' and he had not at first observed the coldness in their manner; but as they drew near the surf and launched their boats there fell upon Gildas a curious sense of isolation. There was no direct insult offered him – they dared not insult the man who owned their cottages –

but a sort of silent aloofness seemed to shut him out of the free comradeship which generally reigned on such occasions. He had been slow to recognise the fact, but at last it dawned clearly upon him that his attitude towards the revival meetings was embittering the feelings of his neighbours towards him, and his hot, proud spirit filled him with a defiant independence. What did it matter? He could live without their friendship; he could turn them out homeless on the bare shore to find new homes where best they could.

These were the thoughts that rose within him when for the first time in his life he felt himself avoided and insulted; but bending to his oar, with the peace of the sea around him, and only the sound of the oars in the rowlocks breaking the silence, he saw the dark blue sky of night above him where the stars were beginning to show through the haze, and in his heart a nobler spirit than that of revenge took the place of his first turbulent feelings of indignation. 'They know me better than to fear me, and so they venture far,' he thought, and with a scornful smile he helped in the work of drawing in the net. Again he found himself left alone on the rocks, while the rest of the company ran eagerly towards the spot where the silvery, flapping haul had been emptied on the beach.

'Jari! I must go, too, if I want any fish for supper,' he thought, and the smile of scorn changed to one of amusement as he followed more leisurely across the shore. A little heap of the best fish had been laid aside for him.

'Will I carry them up to Scethryg for you, mishteer?' said Jerri; but he declined in a voice that sounded perhaps a little colder and harder than usual.

Here a silent, slim figure with a creel on her shoulders appeared in the gloom, and, laying her hand on his arm, pointed to the fish and then to her creel.

'Gwenifer, lass, is it thou indeed? How dost find out

always when thou art wanted? Art sure the fish will not
wet thy neck?' But she showed him the seaweed laid thick
at the bottom of the basket, and slipping the creel over her
shoulder they turned to leave the shore.

'I'm glad, after all, that Nance did not come down,' said
Gildas. ''Tis rather chilly and damp to-night.' As he spoke
he stumbled over a woman, who crouched behind a rock
counting her fish.

'Nelli Amos!' he exclaimed, 'what in the name of the dear!
art doing here, with thy rheumatism so bad? Go home, out
of the damp.'

'What am I doing here? Well, I don't know; 'tis too damp
for me; but I'll tell you what I am *not* doing, Gildas Rees,'
she said, rising and straightening herself: 'I am not opposing
the Holy Spirit; I am not turning my back upon the chapel
where my parents worshipped before me; and I am not
leaving my young wife to come to chapel alone and to walk
home with a stranger.'

'Well done, Nelli; thy words flow like the mill-stream,'
laughed Gildas; but his laugh covered a flood of disturbing
thoughts, and a crowd of dark imaginings sprang into life
within him as he turned away and followed the path to the
moor.

'Only two fish she had in her basket, whatever, poor thing!
Thou canst slip two more on her table as we pass; she will
not know who did it,' he said.

'Yes,' nodded Gwenifer, and she made a little detour from
the path round Nelli's cottage.

They had reached the uneven ground that bordered the
moor; the stars crowded the sky above them, and Gildas
stood still awaiting Gwenifer's return.

Suddenly on the night breeze came a light laugh, then
voices, followed by the appearance of two figures who ran
down the hillside together; and Gildas recognised Nance

and Captain Jack as they emerged from the gloom. 'Nance,' he exclaimed, and for a moment she seemed embarrassed, but quickly regained her self-possession.

'Dear anwl! Gildas,' she answered. 'What! coming home? Are we too late, then? There's a pity.'

'Well, there,' said the captain, 'I was afraid 'twas rather late; but when I saw the boats going out, I thought 'twas a pretty sight, and a pity the mestress should not be there.'

'Yes, you are too late,' said Gildas. 'The fish has been divided, and the net is drawn up to the grass. I thought you were too busy to come, Nance,' he added. 'You have changed your mind.'

'Yes, I changed my mind,' said Nance, with a bold front. 'I suppose I have a right to do that if I like.'

'Was it a good haul?' asked Captain Jack.

'Yes, very. Gwenifer is carrying some up in her creel. Come you and the mate to supper with us.'

'The mestress has been asking me already,' said the captain. ''Tis kind of you both, but we have promised to go and have supper with Jones the preacher to-night.'

'Oh, well; some other night, then. Good-night now. My clothes are too wet to stand longer.' And he turned towards Scethryg; but Nance stood still.

'Go you home, Gildas,' she said, with an air of bravado. 'Gwenifer will give you your supper. I am going to see Nelli Amos.'

Without a word Gildas turned up the hillside, soon joined by Gwenifer, who had returned just in time to hear Nance's last words. She lingered a moment with her; but Nance had dismissed her impatiently, and Gwenifer, when she caught Gildas up in the lane, saw by his silent abstraction that he was troubled and ill at ease.

CHAPTER IX

The Revival Meetings

When Gildas reached Scethryg he found old Hezek seated alone on the settle, the little round table, on which stood a dip candle, drawn up at his elbow; by the dim light, he was poring over the weekly newspaper, which found its way to the farm with the groceries every Thursday evening.

Laying it down as Gildas entered, 'Dear, dear!' he said, ''tis wonderful what power that young man has over the hearts of the people! Evan Roberts, I mean; 'tis very plain God's blessing goes with him, eh, Gildas? What think you about it?'

Gildas drew his chair to the table rather wearily. 'I am tired,' he said, 'and hungry. Come, Gwenifer, lass, let's have some fish fried. Where is Het?'

'She's gone to the prayer meeting at John Parry's,' said Hezek, and while Gwenifer moved about the hearth the old man returned to the subject of the revival. 'Why are you against it, Gildas?'

'I am not against it; may be 'tis wanted; but I am against these wild ways – people showing their hearts to the world, and crying out that they are sinners! There's no need to shout that, 'tis plain enough when you come to deal with them; and d'ye think, Hezek, 'tis pleasing to God that a woman should leave her house empty, and her husband lonely, for any prayer meeting in the world? 'Tis a small job getting her husband's supper, I know; but if it's the job she ought to be doing, that is how she will be serving God best at that moment, and that's my opinion plain for you!'

'And you are about right, I dare say. Nance, where is she?' said Hezek.

'Down in the village,' said Gildas. 'There is something strange about her lately.'

'Dear anwl!' said the old man uneasily. 'I have seen no change in her myself, but she cannot be obstinate to you, Gildas, who are so kind to her,' and he rose to open the door and to peer out into the darkness.

'Where can she be,' he said returning.

'With Nelli Amos,' said Gildas. 'She *keeps* the chapel, so I daresay she is busy to-night; but what Nance wants there I cannot see.'

'But, 'machgen-i,' said the old man, 'can't you share in her feelings about it?'

'No, I cannot,' said Gildas and turned to the table, on which Gwenifer was laying the supper. When she had finished, she bade him good-night in her usual manner, by laying her fingers on his arm and nodding.

'Art going? Good-night, then, and, Gwenifer, I thank thee, lass.'

'Here she is!' exclaimed Hezek, as a light step was heard in the yard and Nance entered.

'Well indeed, I am hungry,' she said, sitting down. ''Tis helping Nelli Amos I have been to dust and clean the chapel.'

'And dost think, 'merch-i,' said Gildas, 'there was more call for thee to do that, than to come home with me?'

'Yes,' said Nance curtly. ''Tis working for the Lord!'

'That is not my opinion, then,' said Gildas, 'and I tell you, Nance, if you are going to follow the path on which you have started, you and I will drift far apart.'

'You and I!' She should have noticed the dropping of the familiar 'thee and thou', but, full of her new-found zeal, she heeded not the cloud that lowered over Gildas's face.

He finished his meal in silence, and at last rising, said, 'Well, good-night, I am rather cold after my wetting.'

When he had gone, Hezek turned to the hearth, and drawing Nance to a chair beside him, began to lay before her the danger of offending her husband. 'He's a stern man, Nance, though just and true; beware how thou dost anger him, dear heart.' But Nance listened impatiently, and the pout on her lips grew more pronounced.

'Dakee,' she said, 'I have felt the power of the Diwygiad, I have given myself to it, and if Gildas turns his back upon it I go not with him.' And when she rose to put out the lights, the old man felt, as he had often done in the days of her childhood, that his words had made no impression upon her, and he muttered something about a 'wilful woman' as she let him out before bolting the door.

Thus, in spite of her grandfather's warning, each day, as it drew to a close, found her rounding off her household duties with a view to being ready for the meetings at Brynzion. And Gildas, quietly accepting the inevitable, would take his sickle, his hoe, or his rake, and turn straight away from his meals to his work. But it was not without a pang that he noted the empty hearth and Nance's little rush chair vacant in the evenings.

In the first months of his married life, when the work of the day was over, he had been accustomed to turn to that hearth for cheer and companionship. Now, how changed was everything, he thought, and he looked rather wistfully round the comfortable old kitchen as he passed out to the farmyard, for it is a mistaken idea that the longing for the peaceful joys of homelife is reserved for women only to feel. On the threshold, however, the shadow that had fallen on his face lightened a little as he caught the sound of a woman's voice. Loud and clear it came on the evening air, and Gildas, listening, recognised the tune as an ancient Welsh drinking-song to which had been set the words of a modern hymn. It was Nance's voice, and as he listened the singer came out of the 'boidy,' carrying on her hip a pail of frothing milk. The sinking sun shone straight into her eyes, so that she saw not where her husband stood still to look at her. The tune was in a minor key, like much of the Welsh music, and she sang its mournful cadences with a strong realisation of the self-abasement which they expressed.

> Oh, wretched that I am,
>
> Adrift upon the sea!
>
> Oh, fill my sails with heavenly airs,
>
> And waft me home to Thee.

As she finished the verse she stopped, and leaning her pail on a low wall stood silently musing, her eyes fixed on the ground. Her full, round mouth had taken a curve of sadness, there were lines between her eyebrows which should have no place on the face of a young and happy wife.

With a deep sigh, she took up her pail again and passed on to the house, and Gildas, both pained and softened by the look of sorrow on the young face, turned aimlessly towards the moor.

There was no work to do there, and it was almost unconsciously that he turned his steps that way. But not for Gwenifer only did that great open tract of moorland bring a message of peace and solace; no one could tread its lonely paths or breathe its pure air without a feeling of the insignificance of things seen, and the overwhelming reality of the unseen.

Even sights and sounds that recalled to the senses the realm of nature around, seemed but to impress the mind more vividly with a sense of the immanence of a spiritual power behind and beyond it. To Gildas, as he walked further and further away from the house, and at last sat down where nothing was in sight save the moor below and the sky above, to him came those soft influences which we so sedulously banish by our devotion to the cares and pleasures of the world.

The lines smoothed out of his face, the shadow lifted from his brow, and a great wave of pity swept over him for the woman whose clear voice still rang in his ears. 'Oh, wretched that I am!' Poor little Nance! so young, so warm-hearted, so anxious to be good. Had he been selfish and cruel in opposing her devotion to the Diwygiad? From a furze-bush near him came a waft of sweet odour that seemed to say, 'Love her, Gildas, and forgive her.' From the sea came a western breeze that whispered, 'Thou art strong, oh, Gildas, and she is weak; forgive her and love her!' 'In my deed,' he exclaimed, as he rose hurriedly to his feet, 'I believe they are right, and I am a hard man. Poor little Nance!' And he wheeled round and strode back towards Scethryg, taking a short cut which he had avoided before, and which led him by Gwenifer's cottage.

'Hoi, Gwenifer, lass!' he called out as he caught sight of her in her garden. 'I haven't seen thee all day; where hast been?' He opened the little wattled gate and looked round. She was standing in the middle of her garden in the full glow of the sunset light; in her arms she held a large bundle of scarlet poppies which she had just weeded out; they trailed round her skirt, they clung to her shoulders, reflecting the crimson light like sparks of fire. Drawing nearer the gate, she looked over her bundle of brilliant colouring at Gildas, with the clear calm eyes that always reminded him of the brown pool in the little river that brawled down through the alders to Tregildas sands; pointing to her glowing bundle, she raised her eyes to his with so much meaning that he understood.

'Yes, beautiful,' he said, ''tis pity they are so troublesome.' As he spoke and looked at her – a recognition of her beauty swept over him, and with it a pang of regret. Regret of what he scarcely knew, and he had no time to consider, for he must return to Scethryg. He would show Nance that he at least was not changed; he would lighten her heart, and she should never more say, 'Oh, wretched that I am.'

'I am going to Brynzion,' he said to Gwenifer, 'so I mustn't stop; perhaps I have been hard to poor Nance. Good-bye, lass;' and he hurried on, bearing with him, however, an impression of a fair face that rose above a crowd of red flowers. Facing the east, he saw the moon rising clear and round over the landward hills, though at the right dark clouds were rising too. 'Dear anwl!' he said, as he hurried on, 'the moon reminds me of Gwenifer – so far above us, so silent, so fair, the storms of life touch her not.'

Drawing nearer home, he heard a loud boyish voice calling to him. Ben Stable, standing on the garden hedge, made a sign to his master to hurry, and long before Gildas reached him he had shouted his news. Rattler had hurt his foot – sprained it, Ben feared; and Gildas hastened to the stable to examine the injured limb and to apply the necessary remedies, so that his arrival at the farmhouse door was delayed a full half-hour.

He was not surprised, therefore, to find that Nance had already left the house. Well, he would follow; and hurrying through his change of clothes, he was soon tramping over the moor to the village. The sky had darkened with gathering clouds; like threatening hosts of gloom they spread from the south towards the rising moon, and the long line of golden haze in the west was all that remained of the sunny day that had passed away.

The air was heavy and murky as Gildas reached the village; no human being was in sight, no lounging smokers round the kilns.

'Thunder, most like,' he said to himself. 'Caton pawb!

Where are the people? All in the meeting, I suppose;' but, looking towards the chapel, he was surprised to see no light in the long windows. All was darkness, and no singing came surging out through the open doors. Entering a cottage, he found the only occupant, a crippled woman, sitting alone by the fire.

'Hello, Fani!' he said. 'What, all alone? Where's Deio and Maggi? What's become of all the people?'

'In chapel, of course,' answered Fani, and her pale face grew reproachful and indignant; 'where I would be myself if I could only crawl there.'

'But there is no meeting,' said Gildas, ignoring her angry looks, though he was quite aware of them, 'there's no light, no singing.'

'No,' she answered, swaying backwards and forwards, 'they are often praying in the darkness to save the lights, but they are all there; and go you, too, Gildas Rees – go you in and take your place by your wife's side, and if the Spirit does not move you to offer up a prayer, at least breathe an 'Amen' sometimes to warm the meeting. I am sitting here alone and watching, and I am seeing many things, mishteer; you at home instead of in chapel; mestress, pwr thing, going alone; and – come here, man, let me whisper to you. *Walk home with her yourself over the moor o' nights.*' She pressed her hand upon his arm, and then straightening herself, continued to look at him with meaning in her eyes, but Gildas turned abruptly away. 'I have no time for gossip to-night,' he said, and passed out through the doorway, a hot flush dyeing his face – a flush that faded and left his countenance set and hard as a white mask as he approached the chapel door.

Outside, the closing dusk and a rising wind that sighed through the thorn-bushed – inside, darkness, lighted only by the moon that shone full through the long windows, and only one voice that rose and fell in hushed accents of

prayer and penitence: old Bensha's, the shepherd on the next
farm to Scethryg, a man whose blameless life and gentle
disposition were proverbial. Gildas recognised it at once.
'Well indeed,' he thought, 'old Bensha's prayers come from
a good heart, whatever;' and he prepared to edge his way
through the packed congregation to the Scethryg pew, when
he was startled by a familiar voice that, breaking in upon
the old man's prayer, burst into a fervid petition for mercy.
It was Nance's voice! and Gildas, astonished and angry,
stood still to listen, scarcely believing his own ears. Nance
to raise her voice alone in an assembled multitude! Nance
to lay her feelings bare before this crowd! It was intolerable
to the proud man, whose idea of womankind had been
formed upon the retiring modesty of Gwenifer's character.
Such, too, he had thought, was Nance; but now her con-
fessions of sin, her fervid prayers for forgiveness, her rapt
uplifted countenance, all failed to awaken in his heart the
tender pity that had turned his footsteps so hurriedly from
the moor. The tenderness died away, and only strong disapproval remained. Already Fani's words were rankling and
kindling a fierce jealousy – of whom, of what, he scarcely
stopped to ask himself. The words, 'Oh, wretched that I
am!' returned to his mind again, but only to increase his
resentment of this publicity. Nance knew his feelings well;
how dared she thus defy his wishes! 'Ach-y-fi,' he muttered
to himself, 'I never dreamt that she would be raising her
voice before people like this.'

But Nance was quite oblivious to the crowd around her.
Alone in a whirlwind of stormy passions, she was pouring
out her soul in a fervid appeal for help. Oh for an anchor to
hold on to in the sea of unrest on which she was tossing! Oh
for a breath from Heaven to fill her sails, and waft her to rest
and peace! And as her voice rose in excited tones, a chorus of
'Amens' and 'Bendigedigs' arose from the assembled throng

around her, and Gildas grew hot and cold by turns with a shrinking sense of shame.

Again there was a chorus of 'Amens.' Nance's voice grew more impassioned, and what were these words that reached his ears from the darkness? Oh, God! he could not bear it. For Nance, carried away by the enthusiasm of the crowd, had embarked upon another wave of prayer: 'And yet another petition I make to Thee; hear me, O Lord. Dear friends, lend me the wings of your prayers to aid my own. My husband, Lord! he who is so near to me, so far estranged from Thee; save him, O Lord! Save him *now*; wherever he is, whether on the moor, or in the field, or in the house. Touch his heart *now*, and let him no longer oppose Thy Holy Spirit in this place. Bend his proud head, O Lord, and soften his hard heart.'

Here she had given voice to the general feeling; now at last she had expressed the thoughts that had permeated through the whole neighbourhood for weeks, and a hundred voices joined in her prayer: 'Save him *now*, O Lord. Touch his hard heart: humble it, break it, if need be, but bring him to his knees.' And a chorus of 'Save him, Lord! Save Gildas Rees!' burst from the whole congregation, while Nance sobbed and swayed in an ecstasy of fervour.

Just within the chapel door the subject of their prayers was standing straight and white, as if turned to stone. A few of those around him had, of course, recognised him at once on his entering the chapel, and, seeing his look of dumb misery, one man made room for him on the bench upon which he was sitting; but Gildas took no notice. He heard the ejaculations and pleadings that rose from every corner of the building, and, with a strange feeling of being overpowered by some mysterious influence that seemed to fill the darkness, Gildas, the practical and clear-headed, looked around him in bewildered astonishment. Was that old

Bensha the shepherd's face? Was this Nelli Amos who prayed so loudly beside him, 'Humble his proud heart'? and yet another voice rose above the sea of praise and prayer – a boy's voice clear and ringing, a voice as familiar to him almost as Nance's! But whence came this flow of eloquence – these fervid utterances, expressed in language that surely emanated from some other source than the heart and lips of an ignorant farm labourer? Could this be Ben Stable? And, as he listened, Gildas's own heart seemed to burn within him. His head throbbed, his pulses quickened, and for a moment he was in danger of losing his self-control; for what was this strange power that seemed to hold him in its grip, and to constrain him to cry aloud, 'God forgive me, for I am a sinner'?

But only for a moment was his firmness shaken. Every instinct of his strong and rugged nature rose up in arms against this feeling of coercion; and where a man of less strength of will would have succumbed, and added another to the number of 'conversions,' Gildas Rees refused to yield to the mysterious power that seemed to palpitate through the darkness around him.

'Yes,' he thought, 'I am a sinful man!' and never had he realised it more acutely than at the present moment. But was there not the wide moor, the fields, the barn in which he could pray aloud if he desired? Was not his own heart wide enough for repentance, for reformation, for bitter thoughts and wounded feelings? Yes, he felt the power of the Diwygiad; but he held firm to his convictions that the fervour and excitement around him were unnecessary adjuncts to the simple communion between a man and his God.

Gildas Rees had not thought much about these things. He had been too busy with his reaping, his sowing, and his mowing; but, while he had toiled in the pure, keen moorland air, they had unconsciously dawned upon him and had become ingrained into his nature.

Great beads of perspiration stood upon his forehead; he clenched his hands tightly as he stood there proud and defiant, while all around him surged the sound of sobs and prayers, 'Save Gildas, Gildas Rees! Save him *now*, O Lord!'

Slowly he turned towards the door, endeavouring to reach it through the throng who pressed around him; and shocked, almost awestruck, at the obduracy of the unrepentant sinner, they shrank back and made way for him to pass out into the darkness. Once in the open air, he seemed to regain at a bound his usual decision and firmness, and to shake off the strange sense of compulsion that had weighed upon him, and, reaching the kiln, he sat down on its low wall, feeling more exhausted than he had ever done before.

The dusky night was falling over moor and sea, the air was full of the soft splashing of the waves upon the shore, like the sound of a mother hushing her babe to sleep. Yes, here was peace and rest – the peace in which Gildas's honest nature had grown and thriven, and to which he returned with the natural satisfaction of a boy who throws off the restrictions of school for the freedom of home. Rising, he turned his back on the kilns, and made his way towards Scethryg, for he thirsted for the solitude and freedom of the moor.

He was filled with a bitter sense of indignation towards Nance; but the hotter the feelings that raged within him, the keener the dart that wounded him, the deeper did Gildas Rees bury them all under that mask of stony hardness that had fallen over his face.

When Nance returned from Brynzion that night, she expected an angry reception from her husband; for she had heard of his presence in the chapel, and knew that she had wounded his tenderest feelings and offended his proud, reserved nature irretrievably; so she came prepared with angry retorts and self-justifications, for the fervour of religious feelings that filled her within the chapel took wing when the meeting broke up, and the natural self asserted itself once more with more or less power. In some cases the warmth, the zeal, the awakened conscience remained to strengthen and mould the remainder of life; but not so with Nance. Her heart was aflame with a host of conflicting feelings: with fear of the material hell-fire which she had been brought up to believe in, with repentance, with longing for peace and purity, but, above all, with the guilty love which she had now ceased to make any efforts to banish from her heart. The thought of Gildas, whom until to-night she might have drawn to her with a smile or a caress, had become distasteful to her, and henceforth she thought, as she drew near the glimmering light in the farm kitchen window, she would be justified in hating him: for had he not turned his back upon the Holy Spirit, and disdainfully cast from him the prayers of the congregation?

She had walked home alone over the moor, for Hezek had often of late turned in to Fani's cottage to read to her or to refresh her with an account of the fervour of the meetings which she was unable to attend.

Where was Captain Jack? Nance wondered, and her lonely walk had not smoothed her ruffled feelings.

She was not prepared for the quiet scene that met her eyes as she entered the house, and the calmness and homely comfort only added fuel to the fire of unrest that was burning within her. She looked round and called loudly on Gwenifer.

The bread and cheese, the jug of buttermilk, were still on the table, though it was long past supper-time, and Gildas, sitting at the old bookcase-desk, was bending over his accounts. The face which he raised as Nance entered was that of a man ten years older than the Gildas who had hurried through the farmyard a few hours earlier, intent on winning back the love and confidence of his young wife.

Every vestige of colour had left his face as he looked up from his accounts; there were lines between the black eyebrows, and the bright flashing eyes looked dull and sunken.

There was no trace of anger in his voice, however, nor indeed of any feeling, as he answered: 'Gwenifer is gone home; it was getting late for her to cross the moor alone,' and turned again to his accounts.

'Cross the moor? Dear anwl! Nobody cares how often I cross it alone, seems to me,' said Nance, drawing her chair to the table. To this Gildas made no reply, but, closing his account book, rose and bolted the door before he turned to the stairs which opened into the kitchen.

Nance began her supper, a little subdued by her husband's unexpected calmness. Soon bringing her simple meal to an end, however, her mood seemed to change. She clattered the plates and dishes and swept up the stone floor with many thumps and thrusts against the clumsy furniture, which fortunately was strong and solid enough to bear its rough treatment without injury. As she worked she sang, and at last, flinging another log on the fire, sat down before the blaze; and opening her hymn-book of large Welsh print, with all the tunes in sol-fa notation, began the repertory of revival hymns which had become so popular in the neighbourhood that every ploughboy shouted them up and down the furrows, and every milkmaid sang them over her pail.

The clock had long struck eleven, and still the weird and mournful hymns continued, Nance turning leaf after leaf of her hymn-book in a kind of feverish excitement. Upstairs Het slept through everything, but Gildas sleepless and restless, heard it all, and longed for peace.

'Seems to me no one cares how often I cross the moor alone!' The words had recalled to his mind Fani's warning.

'Walk home with her yourself over the moor o' nights!'

What had she meant? Who had been Nance's companion in her frequent walks from the meetings? But he was not of a suspicious nature, and above all things hated village gossip; so, with a weary sigh, he turned his head on his pillow, and cast from him the thought as of no consequence.

Midnight! and the old clock seemed to throb with indignation at the unusual sound of singing at such an hour. As the ringing echo of its last stroke died away, Nance closed her hymn-book and began her way up the old crooked stairs.

CHAPTER X

'Rotten at the Core'

On the higher reaches of the moor, towards the uplands, where the peat was black and the cotton-grass trembled in the breeze, where the rushes stood in companies round the pools as if to guard their solitude, where the bog pimpernel grew in patches of delicate pink, and the blue-black whortle-berries spread their neglected dainties over rock and fell – there the little river Erva had cut for itself a deep furrow through the soft ground, and, having reached a pebbly bottom, babbled and laughed over the stones as if in perfect content. It must have carried with it from the upland plains, the seedlings which had taken root and flourished on its banks in clumps of alder and hazel; under their leafy branches it ran its course towards the sands of Tregildas, there to find the natural death of a streamlet by mingling with the blue waters of the bay.

Over the crest of the moor the solitary figure of a man suddenly appeared, looking in the distance no bigger than a fly, but stepping out so smartly that ere many minutes had elapsed he had approached near enough to be recognised as Captain Jack. Slung over his shoulder he carried a bundle which was evidently a heavy one, for he occasionally lowered it to the ground, taking off his cap and baring his heated forehead to the cool breeze.

At a curve of the mountain road he came upon the streamlet hurrying on its way through the bog. Loosening his bundle once more, he sat down, and, watching the brown waters as they curved and eddied by their banks, fell into a fit of musing, unconsciously plucking the luscious whortle-berries that grew in profusion within reach of his hand – a brown, shapely hand, which bore on the back the sailor's emblem, a tattooed anchor.

His light blue eyes roamed dreamily over the stream, the moor, the hazy distance, his look of abstraction showing how far his thoughts had wandered from the scene around him. The shadow of the low bush under which he lay had been gradually withdrawing its cool relief, until at last the hot sun shone full upon his face, and with a start Captain Jack awoke to the fact that it was nearly noontide, and rising to his feet he shouldered his bundle once more. At this point the stream grew narrower, the bushes meeting overhead, and he saw he must lose the company of his babbling friend, or follow it into its covert under the bushes.

He was wearing his sea-boots, and did not hesitate long, as he felt the scorching sun on his head, to slip into the stream and wade ankle deep along its course. There, under the overarching bows, the Erva seemed to talk to him; it whispered in the rushes, 'Come here, and listen to my secrets'; it laughed and sang over the shingle, 'Oh, foolish man, to let dare dwell within your heart!' What wonder that that fairy avenue cast its glamour over him, and filled him with dreams and fancies!

It glided softly under its canopy of green, saying as plainly as streamlet can say, 'Come, follow me; further, further, through the water-lilies, past the swaying ferns; come on and on and see what I have to show you.' And, smiling at his own childishness, he went; but the smile left a wistful seriousness, as such smiles often do. For thus had he waded as a boy in the little river that ran through his father's hayfields, John Davies splashing after him; the memory of the old days came strongly upon him as he crunched the brown shingle under his feet, and many a prank and boyish escapade returned to his mind. Yes, those were happy days; but the years that followed he would gladly have forgotten; and as usual when any unwelcome thought pressed in upon him with too great persistence, the careless sailor tried to whistle it away. Perhaps his merry notes disturbed some bird within the alders; there was a flutter, a rustle, and pushing his way through the bushes he came suddenly upon a fairy pool, where the streamlet widened under its screen of greenery, and where upon a miniature beach of golden gravel a girl was standing, her eyes fixed expectantly upon the rustling bushes.

'Gwenifer!' exclaimed Captain Jack, and his heart thumped under his Cardigan jacket. 'Well, in my deed, the stream was right. 'Come on,' it said; 'come on, follow me, and I will show you something beautiful.' 'Yes'll I', said I; and I waded down the stream, and here's what it had to show me. Gwenifer! there's glad I am,' and he slipped his bundle on to the grassy bank. 'Come, let us sit and rest,' he said, 'for I am tired, whatever.'

Gwenifer raised her eyebrows inquiringly as she sat down beside him.

'Where have I been? I am getting to understand you quite well, you see. Well, to Tregarreg. Marged Jones's sister in 'the Works' has sent her a present, and it has been three days at the station, so I offered to fetch it; but, in my deed, if I had known how heavy it was I would have hired a trap to bring it; must be a ham, I think; since a mile or two from the town, it has been getting heavier every minute.'

'Yes, I know,' signed Gwenifer, with two or three emphatic nods, and she drew out from the thicket behind them a bundle which she too had carried.

'You too? Well indeed! Why didn't you ask me to bring it

for you, Gwenifer? The heavier it was the better pleased I would be.'

But she shook her head, while she unfolded a square of gaudy calico, at last displaying a roll of brown and blue linsey.

'Oh! going to Jinni the seamstress?'

Gwenifer nodded, while she hung the material in folds over her arm, and held it up for the sailor's approval.

'For me,' she said, pointing to herself, and looking at him inquiringly. 'Do you like it?'

Evidently a new gown was a matter of importance to Gwenifer, and she looked well pleased when Captain Jack said, 'Oh, 'twill suit you first-class! Brown with a dash of blue in it, there's nice you will look! But, in my deed, lass, if your gown was of grey tatters you would look like a queen.'

'Queen of the Rushes!' laughed the girl, tearing a handful of her subjects from the river brink, and holding one in her hand like a sceptre.

Captain Jack had heard the term 'Queen of the Rushes' used by the villagers in derision of Gwenifer's proud manner, and his brown face flushed with annoyance at having suggested the thought in her mind.

'Well I don't know about the rushes,' he said, 'but queen over everything to my mind.'

He was longing to tell her of his love, but in her presence the rash headlong sailor was humble and diffident as a boy in his teens. His words seemed to have made no impression upon the girl, for she tied up her bundle again, with a look of abstraction that showed her thoughts were more concerned with her new gown than with anything Captain Jack had said. They had become very friendly and even familiar, for he had sought every opportunity of meeting her, and had haunted Scethryg with a persistence that was quite misunderstood by Nance, for it had never dawned on her that the lively sailor could be attracted to the silent Gwenifer.

The latter, meanwhile, had grown more at her ease in his company; she liked his merry sallies, and, moreover, had the comfortable assurance that while she could engross his attention she was keeping him safely away from Nance. That her companionship could have in it any danger to Captain Jack never entered her mind; she, the dumb, the silent one! Therefore there was absolutely no awkwardness or self-consciousness in her manner when she met him under the shade of the hazel and alders.

'Now stop you there,' he said, addressing his bundle and thrusting it under the ferns on the river bank. 'I will fetch you by-and-by. I am going to carry *your* bundle,' he added, and refusing to be denied he hoisted it on his shoulder, and, leaving the water-course, they walked together over the moor towards Jinni Seamstress's cottage.

As they neared the door he delivered up his 'pack,' saying, 'Now I will wait here till you come out.'

But she shook her head with decision, and pointing to the sun, drew her finger down to the west, where the sea was glistening like a sheet of silver.

'You mean you won't go home till sunset? Dear anwl! I didn't know it would be such a long job to fit a new gown. But, indeed, I have seen Jinni Seamstress fitting the mestress at Scethryg. 'A little bit by-here to take in,' and 'A little bit by-there to let out.' Oh, I know her.'

And laughing heartily at the sailor's imitation of the dress-maker's tugs and pinches, Gwenifer took her parcel, and disappeared into the passage which opened into Jinni's workroom, a black-raftered, yellow-washed room littered about with scraps and snippets of dress material.

'Well, I will come back and fetch you then?' Captain Jack called after her, ignoring the girl's vigorous signs of protest.

They had neither of them noticed that over the brown moor a man had been approaching as they walked and chatted together, for Captain Jack was becoming quite an adept in Gwenifer's mute language of signs.

Now he was startled to find that almost before he had got over her abrupt dismissal, Gildas Rees himself was coming up with him.

'Well, in my deed,' said the sailor, 'when you want to meet your friends, go over Scethryg moor. First Gwenifer, and now you!'

And looking at Gildas, he was surprised to see how pale and haggard he looked. He had not been at the meeting the night before, but Marged Jones had not failed to acquaint him with Nance's wifely concern for her husband's spiritual welfare, and with Gildas's shocking irreverence in leaving the chapel.

'''Tis enough to make his father turn in his coffin!' she said. 'He was deacon in Brynzion for thirty years, and a godly man! A good thing he died before his son brought shame on him. Ach-y-fi! how is he going to gather his harvest, I wonder? 'Tisn't many will be willing to work for him.'

'Well! 'tisn't much I know about such things,' said Captain Jack, 'but seems to *me* now, Gildas Rees is the best man in the whole of Tregildas.' But he said no more, for he saw by his landlady's lowering brows and her constrained manner, that he had roused the narrow bigotry of the ordinarily gentle woman, and realised that henceforth the comfort of his bed, the flavour of his cawl, and the lightness of his bread would be very uncertain, and he hastened at once to make amends by offering to fetch the delayed parcel from the ten-miles-distant station.

As for Gildas Rees, it was very evident that whereas a month earlier no man in the whole parish had been held in more high esteem, now, even between one sunset and the next, he had fallen from his pinnacle of honour, and it might take many a long year to reinstate him in the good opinion of his neighbours; for high and low the news had spread of his disaffection and open withdrawal from the church of his fathers, and when he caught up Captain Jack on the moor a glance sufficed to show the latter that the 'mishteer' of Scethryg was fully aware of the disrepute into which he had fallen. He saw the dark rings round the eyes, the hard set lips, and knew that the man whom he held in such high esteem was suffering, though he held his head as high and walked with as firm a step as ever.

'Well,' he said, answering the sailor's first remark, 'b't shwr, I didn't expect to see you up here.'

'On my way home from Tregarreg I am,' said Captain Jack. 'I started this morning before sunrise, thinking to be back before the sun got very hot; but he caught me up before I got there even, and all the way back he has been roasting me.'

'Where did you meet Gwenifer?'

'Well, when I reached the little Erva I thought it would be cooler to walk in the stream, and so I did till I met her doing the same thing as me, I expect, hiding from the sun.' Thinking that Gildas still looked dissatisfied, he continued, 'She was taking her new gown to Jinni the seamstress, so I came back a little way and carried her bundle for her. In my deed! I am glad to meet you here by yourself, because I can speak to you about something that has been in my mind to tell you, these days. 'Tis about Gwenifer.'

Startled, Gildas turned to look at him. 'What about her?' he asked.

'Well,' said Captain Jack, and in his eagerness he forgot the broad accent which he generally affected, and dropped into the refined manner of speaking that was really more natural to him. 'Well, then, in plain words, with your consent, I want to marry her – if she will have me,' he added humbly.

To say that Gildas was surprised would be but faintly to describe his feelings. He was astounded, and came to a standstill to turn round and look at the sailor.

'Marry her!' he gasped. 'Gwenifer? My consent? Man! what are you talking about? D'ye remember she is dumb?'

'And if she were blind also it would make no difference to me,' said Captain Jack.

'Gwenifer!' exclaimed Gildas again. 'Marry Gwenifer?' and through his mind and in his heart a host of bitter thoughts ran riot.

Who was this man of whom an hour ago he had felt a rankling jealousy, though he had been too proud to confess it even to himself? What were these terrible words that he had heard? Words that threatened to rob him of a light which he had unconsciously turned to in every event of his life. Live without Gwenifer! See that brown cot on the mountain-side in the grey of the twilight, and the blue of the dawn, and know that it was empty, that on a stranger's hearth that familiar form was sitting, and on a stranger those serene brown eyes were shining!

'*Never!*' And in the strength of his repugnance to the idea, the word escaped his lips unconsciously, though with great vehemence.

The suspicion that the man before him was he who had captured Nance's capricious heart had not taken deep root in his mind, so it was easily put to flight by the sailor's last words, but in its place a flame of bitter anger leapt up, as he realised the import of those words.

His love for Nance had received a shock that stifled and crushed his tenderest feelings, and was bringing out the hard antagonism which undoubtedly lay hidden somewhere in his proud nature.

Nance had wounded him, had insulted him; if she had ever cared for him, her love had vanished. Then let her go! He would live his life without her!

Indignation and distrust were laying a heavy hand upon his heart, with a weight that in a nature like his was not likely ever to be removed, though time might change it to a smouldering anger.

Captain Jack, startled by his sudden exclamation, stood still to stare at him in his turn.

'Never?' he repeated, colouring hotly. 'I know I am not good enough for Gwenifer – who is? But, Gildas Rees, I am not what you think me, I am not what I was; since I have been here, and in Gwenifer's company, and since I have been to Brynzion . . .'

'You have been converted, I suppose,' said Gildas, with a laugh that was full of bitterness and contempt.

'Well, no,' said the sailor, 'I am not much to boast of as a convert; but I am not ashamed to say that my eyes are opened to see that a man can do better with his life than I have done with mine. Converted! Diwss anwl, no! I don't want any one to think that of me, but if I can persuade Gwenifer to . . .'

'Does she know that you are thinking like this about her?' interrupted Gildas.

'No; I thought I had better ask you first, as in a way she belongs to you.'

'Belongs to me! What sense is there in that? No, she is as free as the birds in the air. Go and ask her, and, if she likes, she is free to marry you. But, listen you, Captain Jack, if she *did* belong to me I would never give her to you; never, *never!*'

'Why not?'

'Because you are not good enough for her – you have led a wild life, and the little good that is in you now you got at the Diwygiad, and it will pass away like *that*, before another corn harvest; and – you are a gentleman. You have cast in your lot with the sailoring and farming folk, but d'ye think we can't see the gentleman through all your rough ways? 'Tis in your voice, 'tis in your talk, 'tis in your walk.'

'And how can I help that? God knows I've done enough

to cast off the gentleman; and I must have more grace in me than I thought I had if any of it clings to me. Not that I want it – I have done with that part of my life; but that's *my* business: I don't want to talk about that, but just about Gwenifer.'

'Gwenifer!' said Gildas hotly; 'leave her out! She belongs to the moor and the sheep and the sea-wind. Queen of the Rushes! What do you want with her? She's not for you, man!'

'I'll not take your word for it, whatever,' said Captain Jack. 'Before another sun goes down I will ask her herself. I am sorry now I asked you at all; but I thought it would be – more honourable like.'

'Honourable!' said Gildas, and, looking his companion straight in the face, he added, 'Honourable! *Are* you an honourable man, Captain Jack, or not? I am not quite sure about you.'

This direct appeal had a strange effect upon the sailor. Every fault of his nature, every sin he had committed, every wild prank and every spree, rose in black array before him, amongst them his flirtation with Nance, which six months earlier he would have recalled without a qualm of compunction; now, recalled by Gildas's own words, it rose before him deep-dyed as any crime, rousing a sense of resentment against Gildas, who had thus disturbed his usually good-natured equanimity. To do him justice, he had not realised at first that his banter, his smiles, and the glances of his attractive eyes would make a deep impression upon the young wife; and being ignorant of her feelings towards him when she married another man, he was startled and somewhat taken aback when he found his compliments and glances so acceptable to her.

Latterly he had tried his best to correct the mischief he had done; nevertheless her too-evident predilection for his company flattered his vanity – and in a woman's presence it was impossible for Captain Jack to be otherwise than complimentary and pleasing. His first feeling of attraction towards Nance had soon changed into one of indifference and even disapproval, which, however, he had not sufficient strength of purpose to show plainly to Nance, who, her whole mind and character thrown off its balance by her complete surrender to the excitement of the revival, seemed less and less able to control her feelings, and she sought his company with an infatuation which she took little trouble to conceal. Thus he had drifted into the familiar intercourse with her which to him meant nothing more than a pleasant acquaintanceship, but to her was fraught with deadly peril.

Latterly the interest of the revival meetings, the pathos of the singing, the mystery of the dark meetings, had drawn them together a little more seriously; and Captain Jack put off the evil day when he should break off his friendship with the Mestress of Scethryg, and show her plainly that it was Gwenifer, and not her, whom he sought for on moor and cliff and shore.

Suddenly confronted by Gildas's keen black eyes, he stood self-convicted, and in a flash of temper answered hastily: 'I would have too much honour whatever to turn upon a man as you have done, when he came to you with a civil question. What is the matter with you? What can I help if you have chosen an apple that is rotten at the core?'

He would have given worlds to recall his words, but it was too late; they had been spoken in a moment of uncontrollable irritation, and he felt he had irretrievably alienated Gildas Rees, who, wounded to the quick, suddenly drew over his face the mask of coldness and hardness that hid so much and deceived so many.

They had unconsciously reached the middle of the moor, and, here coming to a standstill, Gildas pointed to a narrow sheep-path that wound its way between the clumps of heather.

'Here is your way to the village, captain,' he said. 'Seems to me we have wasted a lot of words. Bore da chi.'

Captain Jack muttered a 'dy' da chi' in return, and Gildas, taking a path to the right, was soon out of sight behind the furze bushes.

The bees hummed over the heather bloom, and in their murmur he seemed to hear the strange words, 'rotten at the core'; a lark rose almost under his feet, singing as she soared into the sunshine, and through her song the same words ran; the sound of his footsteps on the dry heather seemed to beat into his brain the same hateful words, 'rotten at the core.' It was not the heat of the sun that brought those beads of sweat upon his forehead, neither was it weariness of body that made his steps so slow and heavy as he drew near the home to which he had never before returned without a warm glow of pleasure at his heart.

His crops had generally been good, his harvests plentiful, and his modest account at the Caermadoc bank had shown a steady increase. He was a striving, healthy farmer, than whom no king need be happier.

But to-day, how different seemed everything!

Catching the first sight of the Scethryg chimneys, he turned his eyes hastily from them to the hazy blue bay, and wished he had gone to sea when a lad, and had never taken on the farm at his father's death; but crossing the 'clôs,' he was obliged to look round as a trim little figure emerged from the farmhouse door. It was Nance, dressed in her Sunday gown and hat; and as she approached over the shining straw, she picked up her skirts, displaying her neatly shod feet and slim ankles, and Gildas drew his tongue over his dry lips as he essayed a casual remark in passing.

'You are going out in the hottest part of the day,' he said, and still the words that Captain Jack had spoken seemed to burn in his brain.

'Yes, to the village,' she answered. 'Evan Roberts is arrived by now, and Nelli Amos has sent to fetch me. Gwenifer will give you your 'cawl'.'

With a wave of her hand she tripped lightly on her way, soon breaking forth into one of the favourite hymns at Brynzion, which, with all its solemn words, bore the inappropriate title of 'The Bottle Song.'

Her cheeks were flushed, her eyes had an unnatural sparkle, and there was a flighty buoyancy in her step that made Gildas look after her with surprise as well as annoyance. Behind the thorn hedge the sound of the old tune died away, and a look of contemptuous anger passed over his face.

'Revival, indeed!' was all he said; but he passed into the cool shade of the kitchen with a strong feeling, confessed to himself for the first time, that his marriage had been a mistake, that he was nothing to Nance – nay, more, that she was nothing to him, that she was 'rotten at the core.'

The misery that this awakening brought him was expressed in the attitude in which he sat down to his dinner. With his elbows on the table, his hands over his ears, he stared down at the seamed and time-worn board as if he hoped to read in it some explanation of his troubles.

His old proud spirit was not yet crushed, however; for as Het laid before him the simple fare, he drew himself up, and said in his ordinary tones:

''Tis a hot day, and no mistake.'

'Yes indeed,' said Het, 'but why are you going so far afield before the sun goes down? Ach-y-fi! I am not liking to see the dinner about in the afternoon.'

''Tis the turnip-field wants hoeing, and I went up to John Ty-rhyd's about it,' said Gildas.

'So it does, so it does. Well?'

'Well, he can't come. A funeral at Trefos.'

'But there's Jenkin Owen not half a mile further on.'

'He's cutting peat for Davies Lletyroen.'

'H'm!' said Het, setting her arms akimbo, and looking critically at Gildas. 'H'm, yes, that's it, you see. And listen you to me, mishteer: if this house were afire, one man would be busy cutting the peat, the other would be mending his 'clocs,' and the other would be trashing the hedges; but not one would throw down his tools and run to help Scethryg!'

'What dost mean, woman?' said Gildas angrily. 'Scethryg is not on fire, nor likely to be;' but deep in his heart there lurked a feeling that her words might be true.

'Here's what I mean,' she said, 'that no one will help the man who scorns the revival. I am telling the truth; no one would bring a bucketful of water! Except perhaps Gwenifer,' she added as she turned away.

Gildas finished his meal in silence, and at last rose and went out, turning towards the moor, where at least there would be peace and solitude; and as he trod the soft, crisp turf, a host of strange fancies assailed him.

Was the world turning against him? Was he going to be shunned by his neighbours and his own tenants, hated by his own wife? His black eyebrows knitted till they met in a dark line across his face; his square jaw seemed more pronounced than ever, and, as he walked under the hot sun with folded arms and lowering brow, another fear rose up and cast its shadow upon him. 'Except Gwenifer,' Het had said; but would she be left to him? The sound of the sea softened by distance fell soothingly on his ear, a breeze swept over its surface and reached his heated brow, the bees hummed musically over the heath – every sound, every sight, pressed home upon his simple rustic nature the presence of the immanent God; and coming to a standstill on the solitary moor, the strong man recognised that presence, and opened his heart to the comforting thought.

'God help me! God help me!' was all he said; but his brow cleared, his step grew firmer, and, raising his head, he unclasped his arms and squared his chest, and there was almost a triumphant smile on his lips as his steps took him more briskly on until, like a little brown mushroom, Gwenifer's cot stood before him on the heather, and, looking at it, Het's words return to his mind: 'Except perhaps Gwenifer!'

Yes, except perhaps Gwenifer! And the brave smile was still on his lips as he pressed the thumb latch, calling her name loudly. 'Gwenifer!' But there was no answer; the little cottage was empty. 'Why, of course,' he thought, 'she has not come back; there's moidered I am to-day! In my deed, Gildas I am ashamed of thee!' And entering further into the cottage, he saw the peat fire burnt out, the bowl of curds and whey half eaten; lying near it, a red ribbon which he had often seen on Gwenifer's neck.

He took it up and looked at it pensively, smoothing the creases out with his hard brown fingers.

And was it the fear of losing her bucketful of water that made him sigh as he laid it down almost tenderly before going out once more to the sunshine?

CHAPTER XI

The Evangelist

Captain Jack was little less disturbed in mind than Gildas when they parted on the moor, the one to return to his farm, the other to follow the path to the village, still shouldering his bundle, which did not grow lighter as the journey lengthened and the noontide heat increased.

His first feeling was regret for what he had said. 'I have a devil of a temper, and no mistake!' he thought, 'or else I would never have spoken as I did to Gildas Rees. Will he think I meant Nance, I wonder? Well! I didn't exactly; I was thinking of Gwenifer, and how much beyond his reach she was, while he had to put up with something much less worth having – that was my thought!' And Gildas was not the only one under that midday sun whose peace of mind was disturbed by the words 'rotten at the core.' Why had he spoken them? 'Why didn't I bite off my tongue sooner than say it to Gildas Rees? But he was nasty too,' and his thoughts ran into another groove.

'What made him turn upon me like that? In my deed, I think he's fond of Gwenifer himself, and perhaps poor Nance has more cause than we think for her discontent. Anyway, what they say about him is quite true: he's hard and cold as a stone.'

When he reached the village he was surprised to see several knots of people gathered here and there at the door-steps. 'Well, everybody's in the road,' he said to himself, 'except Fani, and Jinni Jones's new baby. What's the matter?' he asked as he passed one group. 'Evan Roberts has come,' said the man, taking a few steps towards him, and speaking in a solemn tone, 'Evan Roberts has come, and he's in John Parry's house.'

Captain Jack made no answer, but hurried into his lodgings, on reaching which he at once slipped his heavy bundle on to the table, which was ominously bare of any preparations for his midday meal. The large cawl-crock full of water hung over the fire, a piece of bacon, and a fowl making occasional visits to the surface, as the water boiled round and round. But where were the leeks, the white-hearted cabbages, the carrots, the potatoes? Captain Jack took the wooden ladle and turned it disconsolately in the crock. Nothing was there but the fowl and the bacon, and this would not satisfy a Welshman, so he went to the little sandy garden at the back of the house, and returned with a basketful of vegetables well washed in the spout at the back door. Flinging them into the crock and adding the oatmeal which he found ready mixed with water on the table, he waited impatiently for his hostess's return. With a sailor's deftness he soon laid the table in the usual simple fashion, and when a few minutes later Marged Jones entered the house she was full of compunction and excuses.

'Well, in my deed,' she said, 'this never happened to me before; and you so kind bringing this 'pack' home for me! But 'tis Evan Roberts you see arriving so sudden at twelve o'clock, and nothing ready at John Parry's; for Mari, poor old beetle, is always behind-hand, and that at the last, running about everywhere but the right way.'

While she spoke her fingers were busy with the bundle, which upon being untied disclosed a large ham.

'Well,' said Marged Jones, as though she were bringing a long argument to a close, 'it is no use to talk – the Almighty *does* watch over us; there's me now, vexing myself to death because there was nothing at John Parry's for the evangelist but tea and bread-and-butter, and now, you see, here's this ham, just in time to fry for him. I thought it was a gown my sister was sending me, but this is much better – I couldn't cut that in slices,' and she laughed gleefully as she cut a plateful of ham, and carried it hurriedly into John Parry's house. When she returned she sat down to her dinner perfectly oblivious of the fact that she had neither made the cawl nor laid the table.

It was not only Marged Jones who seemed excited by the event of the day, but every man, woman, and child in the village; and as it was now three hours since the evangelist had arrived, the news had been spread abroad into the surrounding districts as well.

Captain Jack did not wait for sunset before he went to meet Gwenifer, but sat for full two hours in the cool shade of the hazels and alders on the banks of the Erva. Here was the fair pool on which strand Gwenifer had stood when he came upon her through the branches, her brown looking expectantly for the approaching disturber of that sylvan retreat.

How beautiful she looked! What a fool he had been to let the precious moments slip by without telling her how he loved her, and how it was his dearest wish to make her his wife!

'That's me exactly,' he thought, 'with a foolish girl or a silly woman that I don't care a cockleshell for, I can talk or laugh by the reel; but here where my whole heart hangs on her answer, I haven't a word to say, I am dumb as a dog.'

He listened eagerly as a light step brushed the grass on the river bank, and, emerging into the sunshine, he intercepted Gwenifer herself as she came down the moor; astonished, she raised her hands and her eye-brows.

'Yes, 'tis I,' he said. 'Here's your old seat under the branches; won't you come and rest awhile?'

But she shook her head, and waving her hand towards the side of the moor where Scethryg lay, she imitated the action of milking.

''Tis not milking-time yet,' said Captain Jack, 'and I have something to say to you, Gwenifer – in my deed I have, something that is here, like a fire in my breast, lass, something that is ready to burst up into a beautiful flame, or else to turn into a ravaging fire that will burn my life out.'

She turned to look at him as Gildas had done, with utter surprise.

'Are you surprised, Gwenifer?' he said. 'Are you asking what I am saying? Well, let me tell you, lass; let me tell you how much I love you. Na, na, Gwenifer! don't shake your head, but listen to me. I love you, lass; my heart went out to you that first night I saw you by the kiln, and whenever I have seen you since, I have loved you more and more – until now morning, noon, or night, I am thinking of you; walking, resting, or talking, you are in my thoughts. What are you saying, pointing to your lips like that? You are silent, you are dumb – what does that matter to me? If you were blind it would be all the same; you are everything to me, and if you will not have me, Gwenifer, there will be a miserable man on board the *Liliwen*.'

Now, without invitation, the girl sat down upon the heather, and Captain Jack sat down beside her. She seemed strangely troubled. Disturbed as he had never seen her before, she looked round at the sea and sky, pointed to her lips, and clasped her hands, as if in deep distress.

'What is it?' he said, 'are you wishing you could speak to me?'

'Yes,' she nodded, and her eyes filled with tears.

'If you could speak, Gwenifer, would you tell me that you loved me?'

'No, no, no,' she said.

'Do you hate me, then?'

'Oh no,' still more emphatically.

'You like me, Gwenifer?'

'Yes,' she nodded, and smiled through her tears.

'Then marry me, lodes; I will make you love me in time; you shall have everything, Gwenifer, that my heart can devise for you. See that pretty new house that John Lloyd has begun, and can't afford to finish. I will buy it, and furnish it for you. Gwenifer, I will return from my voyages to our happy home, faithful and true to you.'

But still the girl shook her head more and more emphatically, though apparently with sorrowful regret. Once she raised her closed hand against him, and turned her head away as though bidding him cease his pleading; but he only seized the little brown hand, and carried it to his lips. She withdrew it ruthlessly, and again pointing to her lips, shook her head pitifully.

'No?' said Captain Jack. 'Won't you ever say 'yes'?'

'No,' said Gwenifer.

'Why not? What have I done so very bad that you can't forgive me? I ask you to marry me, lass, and I come to you for my answer. Come!' he said, 'tell me, is there some one else between us? Then I have no chance. Gwenifer, tell me the truth.' He fixed his light blue eyes upon her, and she felt constrained under their magnetic gaze to lift her own to his. He had often been conscious of a compelling power in his eyes; but had never exercised it with any intention or interest; his life had been too headlong and too adventurous for such useless problems. But now, with the eager desire to know her real feelings towards him, he looked fixedly at Gwenifer, and read the secrets of her heart.

For a moment a crimson glow dyed her face, but it faded out under that earnest and anxious gaze, and left her white to the lips, with a feeling that those compelling blue eyes were extracting from her the secret which she had hitherto kept so safely locked in her own bosom; and with a cry as if of physical pain, she hid her face in her hands. 'Oh, shame! shame!' was her thought. 'He knows what I thought no one but God would ever know.'

Captain Jack understood it all; he read the meaning of the crimson blush, the pain of the blanched lips, and filled with pity, he thrust from him his own bitter disappointment, and set himself at once to soothe the unrest which he had brought into the girl's life. Her secret was no longer one to him, but she should never know that he had discovered it.

'Gwenifer,' he said, taking her hand again, and somehow this time she let it rest in his. 'Don't cry, lass, because you cannot speak. I tell you it makes no difference to those who love you, unless, indeed, it makes them love you more. Forgive me that I have troubled you; you say you cannot love me, but at least you do not hate me. I will never trouble you more; when the *Liliwen* comes into the bay, I will sail away from Tregildas. Come, cheer up, 'merch-i; let it be as if I had never said a word to you. But if you change your mind, Gwenifer, remember that I will always be hoping for that; and when I cross the bay I will be looking towards Scethryg moor to see if a little blue handkerchief is fluttering from that mountain ash in the corner of your garden. I will know then that you have changed your mind, and that you are calling me back, and I will come to you, lass, as quick as the wind will carry me over the waves; but,' he added with a sigh, 'I don't expect such happiness as that will ever be my share. So good-bye, lass, our paths are parting here; and, Gwenifer, when you are saying your prayers, remember the captain of the *Liliwen*.'

The tears had been slowly chasing each other down her face, appearing to well up under the long black lashes that were cast down on her cheeks. She longed to be able to say

'Good-by, kind friend, it pains me that I cannot love you,'
but she could only sit on silently, looking after Captain Jack's
retreating figure, as he seemed to walk right into the golden
haze of the sunset. Then rising, she turned her face towards
Scethryg and walked rapidly over the moor, for milking-time
was past, and there was no room or time in Gwenifer's life
for useless regrets.

When Captain Jack reached the beaten track to the village
he was surprised to find himself continually overtaken by
groups of country people, who, having heard of the
evangelist's arrival, were trooping into Tregildas in the hope
of a 'meeting' at Brynzion. Square-faced farmers in their best
frieze coats, tanned sailors, buxom wives in good homespun,
farm lads in their Sunday suits, country girls dressed in town
fashions, aged men and women, the halt, and the blind!
Captain Jack found himself walking in a procession of them
all, and soon began to converse with his fellow travellers.
'Yes, he has come for certain,' he said, 'he was there when I
left the village at noon.'

'Well indeed,' said his companion, his curiosity roused at
once, ''twas something important no doubt that made you
go away just then?'

To this Captain Jack made no answer.

'Are you a stranger here?'

'Not quite that.'

'Well indeed; your ship is in port no doubt, because I see
you are a sailor.'

'Yes, yes,' said Captain Jack curtly.

'What chapel do you go to?'

'Brynzion.'

'Are you a member?'

'No.'

'Ts, ts, you haven't been converted, then?'

'Diwss anwl! no, man, leave me alone,' said Captain Jack

irritably, for he was in no mood to be questioned, and his answer had the desired effect.

'No indeed, so I see!' said his companion, hastily tacking himself on to another member of the group, and leaving the sailor to his thoughts, which were none of the happiest. He scanned the horizon anxiously, hoping for a sight of the *Liliwen* riding at anchor, for the mate had been gone some days with the intention of bringing her to Tregildas to pick up her captain before sailing up the Mediterranean to Algiers. 'What keeps him, I wonder?' mused the captain, 'she must be here to-day or to-morrow unless the wind changes. I want to be gone. I have made a 'cawdel' of everything on land – I wish I have never come, and yet . . .' And his eyes travelled over the broad moor, now growing grey in the twilight, to where a thatched cottage stood, scarcely distinguishable from the burnt heather around it; and though he said nothing more, it was with a sigh that he turned again to the village track. Reaching Tregildas, he found it alive with an eager throng, who swarmed around Brynzion chapel like bees round the hive. 'I want my tea, whatever,' he said, turning in at Marged Jones's door, which was wide open, and the kitchen empty. But this time his hostess had evidently thought of him, and prepared for his wants; the tea-things were laid, and the kettle was singing on the hearth, so it was not long before the handy sailor had prepared and partaken of his simple meal. Truth to tell, he was not very hungry; for beyond the tea-tray, and the little deep-set window, and through the subdued murmur of the crown in the roadway, he seemed to see Gwenifer's brown eyes raised to his almost beseechingly, as his earnest gaze drew from her the secret of her life, and he seemed to hear Gildas Rees's reproachful tones as he flung back, with scorn, the one word 'honourable!'

Leaving the house after his solitary meal, he found the

crowd had moved away from the chapel to swarm round John Parry's house. A murmur of disappointment rose from them as the twilight darkened and the moon rose clear above the moor, and still the chapel doors were closed.

'He can't come; the Spirit forbids,' passed from mouth to mouth, and as Captain Jack edged his way between them he heard sighs, and saw almost tears of disappointment.

In humble tones they asked each other what could be the reason that the Spirit still withheld its presence from them.

'There's something wrong,' said Jerri the boatman. 'Are we all at peace with each other?'

'Yes, so far as I know,' said Ebben Jones. 'John the cooper and Reuben the miller made up their quarrel of three years last night, and you know I forgave you the three-and-six you owe me since last fair.'

'Yes, yes,' said Jerri hurriedly, 'and I told you I would pay you at harvest-time, so it isn't we are at fault whatever. And,' he added thoughtfully, 'Gildas Rees is not coming near us now, so it isn't *he* is the cause of it.'

'What are you talking nonsense about?' said Nelli Amos, thrusting her shrivelled face between them. 'What is the distance of a mile, a rough moor, or a few fields, to hide things from the Spirit? D'you think he can't see Gildas Rees up there at Scethryg, setting his face as hard as iron against us? And the poor mestress doing her best to turn him from his ways. Ach-y-fi! I wish he was gone from the country, then we might hope for some answer to our prayers.'

'Well indeed, perhaps she's right,' said Ebben, but a sudden silence fell upon the crowd as the upper half of John Parry's window was lowered, and a figure appeared at it leaning his arms upon the window-sash and speaking in a clear, pleasant voice.

The evangelist himself, his face but indistinctly visible in the dim twilight, though the rays of the rising moon shone full upon it.

'Dear friends,' he said, and in the silence that followed the surging crowd held their breath to listen. The corncrake's cry came up from the meadows, the sound of the sea filled the air, until at last the evangelist spoke again. 'Thank you, kind friends, for the warm welcome, but it is not for me, I hope, but for Him whose messenger I am. You have been expecting Him long, but He still forbids me to enter Brynzion; to-morrow at this time I will come; go you to your homes to-night, and pray for the Spirit; but before you go let us sing together,' and with a musical voice he began the first notes of an old hymn, which was known to be a favourite of his.

In a moment the whole crowd had taken it up, and were singing with heart and soul in the words and melody, so that the corncrake's cry was drowned, the rush of the sea was hushed, and the whole air was filled with harmony – the voice of a multitude who had but one desire, namely, a blessing on the young evangelist, and the presence of the Holy Spirit.

Captain Jack, who had edged his way through the crowd, stood near the window, and, looking up at the face of the evangelist, felt strangely drawn towards him. A young face, a simple manner, a buoyant spirit, had ever a power to influence the impressionable sailor; and with the stirring refrain of the hymn in his ears, a new and strange enthusiasm awoke within him, as he joined in the singing through which every human heart in that surging throng seemed pouring forth its eager longing. It was his voice even that led the oft-repeated refrain, until at last the evangelist's eyes, roaming over the crowd, caught his earnest gaze. With a smile and a pleasant 'Thank you,' he waved his hand in recognition of the sailor's fervour, and, joining himself in the singing, such a volume of harmony went out upon the moonlit air, that the lonely fishermen on the sea heard it, and the cows on Scethryg moor raised their heads in wonderment. To Gildas

Rees, too, as he crossed the stubble yard, the night breeze bore the swelling tones, awaking within him a restless longing for the happiness and peace of mind which seemed to have gone out of his life.

The evangelist's glance of greeting and his brief word of acknowledgement sank deeply into Captain Jack's heart; it was just the touch of human sympathy that was needed to lead him captive. The preacher's earnest face, the swaying throb of the music, the picturesque setting of the whole scene, made an indelible though unconscious impression upon him; it soothed the feelings that had been sorely wounded by Gwenifer's refusal, and when at last the evangelist withdrew from the window, Captain Jack experienced a strange sense as of personal loss, and was filled with an eager longing to see and hear him again.

The enthusiastic crowd still sang on, their voices carried over moor and mountain; the moonlight flooded the valley with its silver beauty, the whispering sea, and the purling brook filled up the pauses in the music. The moon rose higher and higher, the wind grew cooler, and still the swaying harmony continued, while inside that open window the evangelist knelt in prayer, and wrestled with the mysterious power called by him and his followers 'the Spirit,' and which, whatever we may call it, bore without doubt a message from the spiritual world, a message to man of love, of warning, and of reproof.

Kneeling there, he continued wrapt in trance-like musings, while outside the singing still rose and fell, and the yellow moonlight streamed in.

An hour passed, and still he did not move, until at last with a sigh he rose, and waving his hand towards the window said:

'Bid them go now. To-morrow night I will speak to them; to-night I want rest – and sleep,' he added doubtfully, for it was well known that many a wakeful night fell to the share of the evangelist.

When John Parry appeared at the window, there was a pause in the singing, and such a silence that again the sound of the sea and the trickle of the Erva were plainly audible.

'He cannot come,' said the old man simply. 'Go you home, all of you, and pray for him, that he may have rest and sleep; to-morrow night at Brynzion he will speak to you.'

There was a murmur of disappointment as the crowd dispersed, and breaking up into separate groups they took their way over moor, field, and mountain, singing as they went, and the refrain of the evangelist's favourite hymn came back upon the air, filling the moonlit valley with music.

As the crowd dwindled away, a slim dark figure passed by in the moonlight, and Captain Jack recognised Gwenifer, who had lingered a moment, looking over the silver sea and listening to the singing as it died away in the distance.

Suddenly she saw Captain Jack, and almost unconsciously swerved a little from her path, and hurried on towards Scethryg; he saw her avoidance of him, and with a throb of pain turned towards his lodgings. 'She might have given me a 'Nos da',' he thought, but he was startled by a touch on his sleeve.

'Dear anwl!' said Nance, coming up with him, 'you're walking the other way so quick, I was afraid to ask you to come home with me over the moor. Ach-y-fi! I am never liking to cross it by myself.'

'Mestress!' exclaimed Captain Jack, and there was pleasure in his voice, for his heart was sore, and it was soothing to feel that here was somebody who cared for him. 'Why, of course! I didn't know you were here; but in my deed I am glad to see you; these people are all strangers to me. Come, then,' he added, 'this is the shortest path; though it is over the bog, 'twill be dry now.'

'Yes,' said Nance, wondering why he chose the shortest path.

'Where's Hezek?' he said, as they began their homeward way.

'Dakee? Didn't you know? He's gone away this fortnight,' said Nance, 'to the Wildrom mountains to look for some strange herb; he's always going this time of year. If he was at home there would be no need for me to trouble you to 'send' me.'

'Trouble, Nance!' he said. 'What are you talking about? Isn't it a pleasure for me, a sailor on shore, where there's nothing to do. Yes, and an 'onnore' too to take care of the Mestress of Scethryg, caton pawb! I am proud and glad to do it. Where is the mishteer to-night?' he added in an intentionally careless tone.

'At home,' said Nance, and there was a tremble in her voice that touched the tender-hearted sailor's feelings, for was he not feeling lonely and sore himself? 'Bending over his 'counts most like,' continued Nance. 'There's pity he didn't hear that beautiful singing! perhaps it would soften his hardness.'

'Perhaps it would indeed,' said Captain Jack. 'No doubt he is a hard man, but upright, Nance, and honest and true – that is what I have always thought him, whatever; but I can easily believe that his words are wounding you sore sometimes. 'Tis pity he didn't hear the singing. It nearly made a fool of me, whatever; seemed to carry me away from all care and trouble, you know.'

'You are wanting to be away?' asked Nance anxiously, but Captain Jack did not detect the eager tremble in her voice.

'Well indeed!' he answered, 'I am looking out for the *Liliwen* every day, 'tis time for me to be off.'

'Oh, no, no, no!' said Nance, 'oh, don't say that indeed. What will I do here by myself? Dakee away, and Gildas so cross to me,' and bursting into tears she forgot everything but her love for the man who was about to leave her. 'Don't go,' she sobbed, 'I shall never see you again, and I am so lonely, so lonely.'

Captain Jack was taken aback by this sudden outburst, and looking at the girlish figure, her golden hair catching the moonbeams, her smart hat hanging neglected over her arm, a wave of pity filled his heart.

'Nance, Nance!' he said, 'don't cry, 'merch-i,' and he drew her arm through his, as her footsteps swerved a little with her sobs. 'Don't cry; you will see me again right enough, for I tell you, when I am far away on the sea, my thoughts will be constantly turning to Tregildas, and when I come next 'twill be all right between you and the mishteer.'

'All right! Ach no!' she said, growing more excited, 'I can't bear to think of it, I hate him,' and she stamped her foot on the heather. 'I never cared for him when I married him, and I have got to hate him now. Oh, what will I do, what will I do?' and she dropped and swayed so much that Captain Jack was obliged to support her with his arm.

'Hush, Nance, hush!' he said, 'we are not far from Scethryg now, and somebody may hear you,' and he drew his hand pitifully over the golden head which was now leaning on his shoulder.

'I don't care,' said Nance, throwing all prudence to the wind, 'I will sail away with you on the *Liliwen*; I will never stay in Scethryg when you are gone. Take me with you, Jack anwl, take me with you.'

'Nance,' cried the sailor, now fully alive to his embarrassing position, 'Nance, hush, hush! for your own sake, 'merch-i; I hear a footstep coming down the lane. Goodnight, good-night; you are safe now, cheer up, and you shall come on board the *Liliwen* for a sail.'

'Shall I, shall I?' whispered Nance eagerly, and slowly

relinquishing his supporting arm, 'shall I then – indeed, indeed?'

'Yes, indeed then,' said the sailor, trying to get away.

'Where will we go then?' she asked excitedly.

'Oh, wherever you like,' he said, retreating hastily into the darkness. Before he had taken many steps in the direction of the village, he heard behind him Nance singing in loud shrill tones the refrain of the evangelist's hymn; and as he hurried on his way, and her voice died away in the distance, he shook his head, as he said to himself, 'There's something wrong there, and no mistake.'

CHAPTER XII

Upliftings

The next day was one of cloudless sunshine – a day on which the busy farmers worked hard amongst their green crops, so as to have their hands free for the harvest which was fast approaching, a day on which the sailors set their sails to welcome the breeze, a day on which the crisp waves danced and the seagulls called to each other on the bay; but a day at Tregildas when a spell of silence seemed to have fallen upon everything, a sort of sabbath stillness which no footsteps on the dusty road disturbed, no trundling cart, no straying horses, but only the sparrows cheeped and the swallows twittered under the eaves. Sometimes an adventurous pig would escape from his unwonted durance, and trot down the village road, wondering most likely, what had become of the friends whom he was accustomed to rub ears with. But he was quickly followed and shooed back to his sty. Truth to tell, the day had been an irksome one to the animals and the children, as also to Captain Jack, who was tired of looking out through his window at the deserted road and listening to Marged Jones's continual singing. One after another, and all in a minor key, she went through her whole repertory of hymns, until at last, irritated beyond endurance, her lodger took refuge in the sandy garden, and from thence, stepping over the low hedge of southernwood, roamed down to the breezy cliffs, from which he searched the horizon in vain for a sight of the *Liliwen*.

He was afraid to turn his steps towards the moor lest he should meet Nance, for her strange conduct of the night before had disturbed and startled him. 'Poor Nance,' he thought, 'what has come over her? 'Tis folly to think she could prefer me to such a man as Gildas Rees, and he her husband too. What has come over her? I have been joking too much, and talking too much nonsense with her! I think she'd give up everything, to sail away with me in the *Liliwen*. Poor thing. Her heart is sore, and so is mine: what if we *did* sail away together? No one would have a right to grumble. Gildas has turned against her, Gwenifer will have none of me. If it was Gwenifer now!' and he sighed as he strolled up and down the cliff, with his hands in the pockets of his wide trousers. 'Poor Nance,' he thought again, 'I can't be harsh to her.' His eyes strayed over the moor to the little brown cot, whose whitewashed walls the evening sunlight was beginning to gild. Gwenifer! If she would only listen to his suit! What a different man he would be! and he sat down on the heather, to think out *what* he would be. Well – happy, content, and – oh strong, like Gildas Rees, and then he laughed at his own childishness. 'In my deed,' he said, 'though I am such a hulking fellow, I believe I am only a child after all, else why would I be so restless, so easily led to any nonsense, as my mother used to say. Ach-y-fi, I am tired of myself! Yes, if any one wants the Diwygiad, 'tis Jack Davies, captain of the *Liliwen*.'

Down below the cliffs the sea splashed over the hard rocks, flinging its spray up into the sunset light; the breeze swept gently by him, he heard the seabirds calling over the water, and, throwing himself back on the soft grass, in a few minutes fell into a deep sleep. No wonder that he slept, for kind Mother Nature lulled him to rest with her soothing song of wind and wave. In all the crystal clearness of that evening air, no sign was there of any watcher over him; yet, riding hard upon the wings of destiny, powerful and fateful influences were reaching out towards Captain Jack. The lark rose singing from her nest beside him, and yet he slept; the grasses bent and brushed his face, still he slept on – until at last with a start he awoke and sat up, to see the sun just sinking behind the sea, leaving a shining path of gold upon the waters, at which he stared in bewilderment. The bark of a dog reached his ears, 'Cardi,' Jerri's dog. He knew it well! And surely there was the sound of a horse and cart. Hurriedly he looked at his watch, and seeing it was eight o'clock, realised that he had slept long, that Evan Roberts was to preach at Brynzion, and that he must hasten there if he was to gain an entrance.

On reaching the village he found the roadway thronged, as it had been the night before, with hundreds of eager men and women who had thought it no trouble to walk many miles from their homes on the chance of being able to hear Evan Roberts, or at least to catch a glimpse of him.

The chapel was full to overflowing, the courtyard too, and the surrounding slope. It was impossible any one could hear the evangelist, except those who were inside the chapel; but they could join in the singing, and perhaps the Spirit would visit them in the open air! So they adjourned to the flat on which the kiln stood, and there in the twilight they held their prayer meeting, with only the pale blue sky of evening over them.

When the singing from the chapel swept out on the breeze they joined their voices to the swelling strains, and the evangelist, standing in the pulpit, caught the sound through the open doorway, and was cheered and uplifted into a fervour of spiritual warmth which spread to the crowd around him. His clear earnest eyes scanned the throng of eager faces, he saw the rough hands clasped in nervous tension, and with the spiritual intuition of a 'Sensitive,' he seemed to feel the unrest of their souls, to hear the cry of their most secret longings; and moved to the heart by their expectant faces, he set himself to answer their call.

Outside, Captain Jack, having arrived at the doorway, found himself firmly wedged in the crowd, and almost despaired of gaining an entrance into the chapel; but when he desired anything, be it good or bad, he was not easily turned from his purpose, so by dint of sheer determination he thrust himself sideways through the human mass, and made his way into the centre of the building, where he was content to stand in the crowd, rejoicing to find himself near enough to see and hear with ease. Amongst the sea of human faces turned towards the pulpit, his would not have been noticeable had it not been for the determined manner in which he had worked his way through the crowd; but this seemed to have attracted the notice of the preacher, who, as soon as the sailor had come to a standstill, caught sight of the eager face, the bronzed skin, the light blue eyes so deeply shaded by their long lashes, and remembered the man who had led the refrain in the moonlight.

There was a flicker of recognition in his eyes; it was only momentary, but Captain Jack caught it as he stood there, his eyes fixed earnestly upon the evangelist. The look of recognition was followed by a smile, and the same wave on the hand with which he had shown his appreciation of the singing the night before. A fleeting smile, a transient look, perhaps, but one that laid hold of the sailor's warm impressionable heart. 'He knows me! He remembers me!' he thought, and during the ensuing three hours' service those blue eyes never wavered in their fixed and serious gaze; that restless heart never lost its deep interest in the simple words with which the evangelist riveted the attention of his hearers.

Often had they heard more fervid eloquence, more ardent appeals, from that pulpit. What was it, then, in the plain unadorned language of this simple son of the soil that spoke to their inner consciousness, and seemed to call to his hearers with a voice of awakening power? What but the Spirit of God, that poured itself into this earnest prayerful soul, and sent through him its message of love to the sad, the struggling, the sinning denizens of this lower world. What if the words in which that message was clothed by the imperfect human medium sometimes grated on ears sophisticated and tastes refined! What if they spoke of a narrow creed, a crude theology! How should this affect the heavenly message which burnt in the evangelist's heart?

Leaning over the pulpit, he preached not, but spoke to his listeners – one human soul conversing with his fellow travellers on the road of life, clothing his thoughts in simple words and graphic similes. His sympathetic voice reached every corner of the chapel, and spoke to it alone; his clear magnetic gaze compelled the attention, and seemed to read the very thoughts of those who hung so hungrily upon his words.

'Friends,' he said, 'have any of you seen, as I have, a balloon, just ready to commence its aerial flight? It has been made for that flight; every cord, every yard of silk, has been joined, and fitted together, for that purpose. It was the design of its maker that it should soar above the earth, should rise to higher altitudes than ours, to purer air, to clearer skies. And see! Though it is still bound to the ground, it begins to answer to its maker's designs, for a cord or two have been loosened! It rocks! it sways! it rises! but falls again to earth; and why? Because one cord still keeps it bound, one rope remains unsevered; and so that wonderful machine, with its graceful curves of use and beauty, remains attached to the earth, a useless object, a thing that does not fulfil the intentions of its maker! Alas, how sad! But see! The last cord is cut! the last restraining bond is broken! and lo! now it strains, it trembles, it rises, it soars above the clouds of earth, away, away towards the light. Do you see the simile, dear friends? Do you understand why the sight of that balloon bore in upon my heart the thought of you, of me, of all poor sin-bound creatures! Intended by our Maker to rise above the sordid cares, the gloom, the sorrows of earth, but fast bound to it by cords that keep us swaying between earth and heaven. Sometimes we rise a little, we feel the heavenly breezes, we reach towards the clear blue sky; but still we linger on attached to earth. Perhaps we have cut away and cast from us some of the cords that bound us, some of the sins that kept us grovelling on earth; and still we do not rise above the world, and why? Because one cord remains unsevered – one secret sin, the hardest of all, to overcome! Sever it! cut that cord! fling it from you, and behold! how you spurn the sordid things of earth! You rise above them, and away, away you soar, to clearer air, to bluer skies. God speed you on your way!' And kneeling down, the evangelist broke into passionate pleadings, which seemed to reach the very hearts of his hearers. The upturned faces flushed and worked with some strong yearning; and as if with one impulse the whole congregation burst into a volume of song, drowning the prayers of the evangelist, who rose from his knees and joined his voice to the impassioned harmony, in one of the old soul-stirring hymns which have so strong a hold upon the emotions of the Welsh; and as he sang with deep feeling, he looked round upon the crowd, and once again his eyes and Captain Jack's met in a long and searching gaze – a look that on the one hand seemed to ask, 'Friend, what is wrong with you?' and on the other to answer, 'I don't know, but *all* is wrong with me; give me peace, and give me happiness!' while the singing still went on, each verse repeated twice and thrice with increasing fervour.

At last it ceased, and a breathless silence fell upon the

meeting – the very air seemed full of a throbbing expectation; until from some mysterious depths there floated in upon their consciousness a *power, an influence*, indescribable, but strongly felt as if an invisible presence were amongst them. The Spirit! for whose advent they had prayed so long. The Spirit! who had raised so many of their friends from sin to righteousness, from darkness to light, had come; and Brynzion was no longer despised and rejected!

Suddenly the spell of silence was broken cries of penitence, songs of rejoicing, shouts of joy filled the air; and in their midst Captain Jack stood transfixed, bewildered, moved to his very soul. What was this mysterious influence that flowed in upon the roving sailor's heart? compelling him with irresistible power to turn away from the darkness of the past, and set his face towards the light, the peace, the purity which the words of the evangelist revealed. With a cry, as if of physical pain, Captain Jack succumbed to the strange power that fell upon his spirit; and although those who stood round him saw nothing of it, nor heard his cry of pain in that tumultuous sea of excitement, yet to him that single moment was the turning point, the climax, in his life of recklessness. They saw only his pale and haggard face, the look of startled anxiety, the beads of sweat upon his forehead; and recognising the signs of a spiritual upheaval, they endeavoured to make way for him, and to help him to reach the large square pew below the pulpit reserved for the newly converted. As yet it was empty, save for the presence of the evangelist, who had descended into it, and now stood looking at the moving mass of people. In a quiet voice that sometimes changed to one of almost anguished persuasion, he spoke of Him who stood waiting for them, even now; whose tender voice was calling to them; whose feet had trod the rough roads of Judea; who had lain sleepless under the starry sky of night, and had poured forth his soul in

prayers and vigils for the sinful and sorrowful. Almost
Captain Jack could *see* the face of heavenly beauty, could hear
the pleading tones, 'Come unto me . . . and I will give you
rest.'

But it was not to reach the evangelist that he was making
such strenuous efforts. In the sailor's heart a strong reaction
had set in, a tide of opposing feelings which made him
shrink from the publicity of the 'sêt fawr.' Yes, he thought,
he *would* turn from his evil ways, he *would* change his life,
but would not be forced into a public confession of his sins;
and with a wrench he broke away from this strange 'power'
that was painting his past in such lurid colours, and drawing
him, with bands that were irresistible, away from his old
familiar moorings. He struggled, almost fought his way
through the close-packed congregation, and, at last reaching
the doorway, staggered out into the cool night air. A few
moments he stood panting and inhaling long breaths of the
pure sea-breeze, then, turning his face towards the moor, he
hurried away, away, alone under the stars, where he could
face this mysterious power that was holding his heart in its
grip. But it was only to find that, walk he never so far, nor so
fast, neither moor nor mountain, nor time, nor distance,
could bear him away from the cry of an awakened conscience; and so absorbed was he in his self-communings
that he had not observed that his steps had taken him close
to Gwenifer's cottage, and he started when he saw the
glimmer of light in her tiny window.

Gwenifer! Oh for a touch of her little brown hand upon
his forehead! Oh for a look into her calm brown eyes! Never
had he longed so much for her presence, never had he felt
so unworthy of it. No! he would not even approach the
window, nor seek one glance at her face *until* – when, he
knew not, for, as he turned towards the bay, he caught sight
of a light that rose and fell with the heaving tide, and,

peering through the starlight at the black hulk, he recognised the *Liliwen* and her mast light. 'Thank God!' he exclaimed aloud. 'Out there on the sea I shall be safe. No more loitering on land for me, for it is full of pitfalls and temptations for a fool of a sailor'; and running down to Maldraeth, he scrambled round the base of the crags to avoid passing through the village, and, reaching Tregildas beach, unmoored Jerri's boat, and springing into it sculled towards the wavering light, with a feverish longing to leave the land behind him. When he reached the silent ship, he shouted 'Hoi, Hoi' and hearing the mate's answering 'Halloa,' felt more like himself than he had for some time. There was no further greeting than a smiling, 'Well, cap'n,' from the mate, and an answering, 'Well' from the captain, as he climbed on board; but later on, they descended to the cabin together, and by the light of the tallow candle discussed their business affairs – the cost of repairs, the nature of the cargo, etc., etc.. Suddenly John Davies looked critically at his friend.

'Well indeed, cap'n, you are not looking first-class. That's what I say; it's no good being too long on land. It's all right for a bit, but dei anwl! when I have been a fortnight ashore, I can't sleep, and I can't eat, and I'm quite ready for the ropes and the sails again.'

'That's it,' said the captain, 'I haven't slept well this week past; what with the dogs barking at night and the cocks crowing in the morning, 'twas impossible.'

'And how's the Diwygiad getting on at Tregildas? 'Spose you haven't been converted yet, cap'n?' said the mate, with a twinkle in his eye.

'Converted, no!' said Captain Jack, 'I am the same bad lot as ever, I'm afraid! Hark ye, mate, *there's something in it*. As sure as I am sitting here, there's something comes into those meetings besides the people.'

'Well, so I suppose,' said the mate, who was an observant

and by no means callous man, in spite of his boisterous manner. 'They've been praying so long for the Spirit that they've got an answer perhaps – if not, where's the sense of praying? Stands to reason.' But the captain seemed disinclined for further conversation.

'Will I scull in and take Jerri's boat in tow?' said the mate at last, seeing that his friend had what he called one of his 'moods' upon him.

'Yes, go you, and I'll go to bed, and see if I can sleep on sea, whatever,' said the captain. 'If I fail 'twill be the first time in my life,' and with scant ceremony he 'turned in.' But in spite of the familiar lapping of the waves on the ship's side, and the soothing sound of the breeze in the rigging, he lay awake in his bunk, and the pale dawn was beginning to grow rosy beyond the brown Scethryg moor before he fell asleep.

Allen Raine's house in Tresaith, Ceredigion.

Evan Roberts: The Welsh Revivalist.

CHAPTER XIII

Maldraeth

In Scethryg farmyard the milking-hour was always a sociable one, or had been until Nance had become so wrapt up in the chapel functions. The mishteer would saunter in to look over his herd, n'wncwl Sam would stand leaning over the gate with his pipe in his mouth, and often Hezek came home that way from his rambles over the hills, knowing that tea-time was near. Sometimes Nance herself would come out, with a bit of needlework in her fingers; even 'Juno,' the sheep-dog, and 'Betsen,' the old tabby cat, managed to be on the spot when the milk came frothing into the pails, and there was a chance of their pannikins being filled. But to-night neither the mishteer nor mestress were present. The former had gone to a hillside fair, and had not yet returned, and Nance . . .

'Oh, well!' said Het, 'of course we can't expect her, because, you see, she's stopping with Nelli Amos to say good-bye to the preachers when they go back to Tregarreg!'

For answer, Gwenifer raised her finger with a listening air, as over the moor came the sound of a woman's voice, singing.

'Yes, 'tis the mestress,' said Het. 'There's plenty of hymns she shows. Anwl! *She's* a good woman as sure as *I* am a sinner,' and she rambled on as she milked, not ill-pleased that Gwenifer was silent.

'I wish the meeting had lasted to twelve last night instead

of ending at ten. In my deed, I was just beginning to feel something fluttering here,' and she pointed to the region of her heart, 'and I thought I was going to be *seized* like Mari Jones by my side; but no! not a tear would come to my eyes, no more than if I was sitting here milking. Ach-y-fi, there's hard I am! and I'm no singer, so, in my deed, I'm afraid the Diwygiad will pass me by! Oh, she's got a book!' she continued in a disparaging tone, 'there's nothing in that! I could do it myself if I had a voice! There's pretty she is!' and she looked admiringly at her mistress as she stepped lightly over the stubble, her yellow hair shining like gold in the sunset light, her cheeks and eyes aflame with the fire of religious excitement which was consuming her.

Captain Jack's conduct of the night before had much disturbed her. Had he been converted? she wondered; then, indeed, her prayers had been answered, and he was hers – now nothing could come between them, neither distance, nor doubt, nor death itself could part them. But where was he, why had he fled from the chapel like one bereft of his senses? as those who were nearest to him had told her. Had he heard of the arrival of the *Liliwen*, and hurried on board to return soon to the woman whose prayers had saved him? and she entered the house with her heart full of restless questionings.

But when the evening hours passed on and still he came not, her anxiety increased, and she could scarcely control herself sufficiently to answer n'wncwl Sam when he returned from the village, where he had lingered longer than usual to see the last of the evangelist.

'The *Liliwen* is still in the bay,' he said, and Nance nodded, for her parched tongue refused to speak.

'The mate been in to pay Marged Jones; he's sleeping there to-night, and going back to the ship with the dawn, for they are sailing tomorrow to foreign parts.'

Nance started to her feet, and looked around as if she sought some means of escape.

She heard Gildas arrive in the farmyard, and as she caught the sound of the mellow voice, and the firm footstep, a strange look came over her face, so marked as even to disfigure it.

She threw back her head a little, and her eyelids drooped into a narrowing gleam of hatred, which, however, she managed to hide from the man who entered from the farmyard, carrying a parcel which he deposited on the table.

''Tis something Mrs. Jones Bryndu is sending you, Nance,' he said in a pleasant voice, and with something like his former manner. 'They are growing in her garden, and she says if you boil them and cut them in slices . . .'

'Ach-y-fi!' interrupted Nance. 'Old beetroots! I am not liking them,' and pushing them aside, she proceeded with her tea-making.

A hard and dour shadow fell again over Gildas's face, as he drew his chair to the table; and during the meal he spoke little, but showed no further sign of annoyance at his cold reception.

Nance seemed quite content with his silence, for she was too absorbed in her own thoughts to take much account of anything that was passing around her.

She went aimlessly in and out of the dairy, and stood long at the doorway, her eyes fixed on the sea, where a ship with a red pennon dipped gracefully in the rising tide.

More than once Gildas had asked her a question concerning his plans for the coming harvest; but she had not heard him, her gaze still fixed upon the glowing bay, her fingers working nervously in the folds of her gown.

'D'ye hear, Nance?' he said, his anger roused at last. 'Can't you turn your thoughts or your eyes to your own business? What is it so wonderful on the sea?'

For answer Nance turned round slowly with a look of defiant anger in her eyes; she spoke not a word, but turned to the clumsy staircase which opened up from the kitchen, and Gildas, as if regretting that he had shown his discomposure, calmly lighted his pipe and went out to the farmyard to pat Corwen's sleek sides, to rub Pinken's curly forehead, and to stand a moment by Gwenifer's fast-filling pail.

'Best cow of the lot,' he said, looking proudly round his herd, and Gwenifer nodded as she rose and rested the pail on her hip.

Gildas looked into the calm eyes raised to his, and felt inclined to open his heart to her – to ask what was the meaning of the cruel unrest that had come into his life, to complain of Nance's trying ways; more, even to confess to her that he had made a mistake, and that he rued the day when he had made Nance Ellis his wife! But it was only for a moment that this temptation assailed him; and he turned away with the now familiar pain gnawing at his heart, and the firm resolve to suffer in silence. What! complain like a child that his life was a miserable failure, tell another woman of his wife's faults and failings, even though that woman was Gwenifer, the silent, the tender, the true! And he was ashamed of having harboured the thought.

As he passed down the lane to the meadows his thoughts were still of Nance and her absorbing devotion to the revival. Was it that which had changed her so completely? No, he knew now, as well as though she had told him in plain words, that her heart was aboard the *Liliwen*; and the knowledge no longer wounded but only angered him, for his love had died out, the love that had never been founded on respect. He despised her for her falseness, and cursed his own folly in marrying her. What further harm could befall him? She had already held his name up to public contempt at the revival meetings, and a red flush of anger dyed his face as he seemed to hear again the words, 'Save Gildas Rees,' as they surged around him in that bitter hour at

Brynzion. What if she should bring further shame upon him, disgrace on the name he had always been proud of? 'In my deed I must guard her and myself,' he said, turning round and retracing his steps, urged on by suspicions and fears that were quite foreign to his nature.

Meanwhile, Gwenifer had finished her milking and carried her pail into the dairy. The clumsy door stood half open, and through the chinks by the hinges the old kitchen was visible, lighted up by the blazing fire which was always generously replenished with logs as the evening drew on.

Raising her eyes, she was surprised to see Nance take off her shoes, and, carrying them with her, approach the stairs on tip-toe. Had it been Het she would not have wondered, as it was a frequent custom to leave the shoes at the bottom of the stairs if soiled by walking in the garden or yard; but for the mestress to do so, and walk on tip-toe, was unusual, and Gwenifer was further puzzled by the noiselessness of her movements upstairs, where the bare, uncarpeted boards generally made every footstep audible.

The suspicions and fears which had only just gained an entrance into Gildas's heart had for some time haunted Gwenifer, for latterly she had seen more of Nance than her husband had, and had frequently been puzzled by her 'moods.' The curious mixture of religion and levity which Nance's actions evinced were new and alarming to her simple, straight-forward nature, and she kept a close watch over her mistress, fearing she knew not what, but at all events determined if possible to shield Gildas from further trouble.

The incident of the prayer meeting had wounded her quite as deeply as it had him, and she was earnestly desirous of preventing Nance's too frequent intercourse with Nelli Amos. It was for this reason that she stood perfectly still in the dairy when Nance had disappeared up the dark stairs.

She heard the slow opening of a drawer, the careful raising
of a creaking lid followed by a slight sound of soft footsteps,
and she watched intently when by-and-by Nance descended
carrying with her a small bundle. What could it mean? Her
heart beat loudly, he face flushed as she saw the mestress,
after putting on her shoes, pass silently out into the farmyard.

Where was she going? Should she follow and watch? She
hated to do it, but to save Gildas a pang and Nance from
foolish action she would have dared much, so she crossed to
the kitchen window, where in the deep recess Nance's
knitting still lay, the bright needles crossing each other as if
just dropped from the fingers.

'Oh, Nance!' thought the girl, 'we have been friends so
long! Where have you gone? What are you doing? Indeed,
indeed I must follow you, I must find you, for much I fear
there is something wrong.' She could not have told what her
fears pointed to – she had no time to think to-night, while
the evening shadows were falling so rapidly, while Nance's
blue figure was already disappearing through the gap into
the moor; so gliding noiselessly after her, she crouched
behind the hedge. Where was Nance going? To the village
again to have her mind poisoned against her husband? No!
rather would Gwenifer have followed her, have thrown her
arms around her, and implored her for the sake of their old
friendship to turn back to Scethryg. She watched eagerly
while in the darkening twilight Nance approached the spot
where the paths divided; one turning away over the moor,
the other to the village, and the third leading straight down
to Maldraeth. She stopped a moment and then took the path
to Maldraeth.

To Maldraeth! What did that mean? And catching sight
of the *Liliwen*'s tall mast against the sky, Gwenifer felt her
heart stand still, as she saw Nance stoop down and thrust

something under a furze bush, and then turning, come swiftly back towards Scethryg. Gwenifer had scarcely time to withdraw further within the thorn hedge; she held her breath as the flying figure ran through the gap, almost brushing her in passing, but she need not have feared discovery, for Nance was too excited to have noticed her.

Over the stubble yard she once more picked her way, and Gwenifer following entered the house to find the mestress sitting at the hearth with her knitting in her hand.

'Thee art stopping late to-night, Gwenifer,' she said, with a little angry gleam in her eye, 'thee canst go home now,' and Gwenifer went out into the soft twilight with her hands crossed on her bosom, and her head bent with shame and sorrow; over the moor, and along the path to Maldraeth, where under a furze bush she found the bundle which Nance had secreted there. Her hat, her jacket! oh! what could it mean? and she hurried on through the darkness, determined to hide herself in one of the caves on Maldraeth, and to watch till dawn, if need be, if so she might save Gildas from trouble and Nance from folly.

She had scarcely left the house when Gildas entered, and with a casual remark concerning the business of the farm, sat down to the supper of milk broth and brown bread which lay in readiness for him.

'Not coming to supper?' he asked, as Nance remained sitting on the hearth with her hand to her cheek.

'No, my tooth is aching shocking,' she said, and he saw she had wrapt her face in a band of red flannel.

'Hast caught cold?' he asked, a little tender pity for her pain inducing him to return to the more intimate 'thee' and 'thou.'

'Most like,' she said, and continued to sit by the hearth, rocking herself to and fro, until Gildas retired to bed.

'I would think bed would be the best place for thee, Nance,' he said, looking back with his foot on the first stair.

'Yes, yes, but go you; I will sleep with Het to-night then I won't be afraid of disturbing you with my toothache.'

'Well, good-night,' said Gildas as he turned away. He heard her close and bolt the door more noisily than usual, he heard Juno's last barking run round the premises, he heard Nance's step going up the stair to Het's room, and then he disposed himself to rest, but in vain.

He was careworn and heartsick; and to those who stand most in need of her, sleep often refuses her soothing presence, and Gildas Rees, who used to lose consciousness as soon as his head lay on its pillow, tossed from side to side, restless and sleepless. The hours passed on; ten o'clock struck, eleven, and still he lay wide awake. It was close upon the stroke of twelve; and he sat up listening, for surely he had heard a creaking stair; then all was silence, and he threw himself back on the pillow. But again he listened intently, for surely there was a soft footfall. Again a long silence, and then a cautious and almost noiseless drawing of a wooden bolt – the door is opened, it is closed again carefully and softly; but Gildas's keen ear is no longer deceived, and rising to the window he peers through the gloom and sees a silent figure that passes out through the doorway and crosses the stubble yard towards the moor.

In a moment he is dressing hurriedly, a terrible fear, an instinctive certainty, clutching at his heart and coursing through his veins. It is Nance! and he hastens after her across the stubble yard, possessed by the overpowering desire to save her and himself from the shame and disgrace which he sees threatening them.

When he reached the turning of the paths, she had already begun her way down the rugged cliff track to Maldraeth, and as Gildas followed swiftly, a host of bitter thoughts and memories rushed through his mind. How often had he met her here, when love was young and fresh and sinless! 'Oh,

God! what does it mean that Nance should be thus fleeing from me, that I should be seeking her through the darkness?'

Across the moor, down the rocky paths, and on to the pebbly strand he went, shoeless, and treading carefully, anxious to reach the truant without alarming her.

Arrived on the shore, Nance stood awhile uncertain. Was Jerri's boat there as usual? Yes, in the starlight she caught its outline; moored safely, with its keel already swaying on the edge of the full tide. With one hurried glance around, she prepared to draw it nearer through the surf, when a footstep crunched the gravel, a hand grasped her arm, and in the darkness Gildas stood before her.

The hushed silence was only broken by the plash of the waves, and his hard breathing. Frightened and speechless, Nance loosed her hold on the rope; but at once regaining her courage, she was the first to speak.

'What is it? Why do you follow me into the night? Can I never shake you off?'

'Nance,' said Gildas, his voice trembling. 'Where are you going, woman? What is the meaning of all your follies? Come back with me, come home to Scethryg, and this black night shall be as though it had never been. Come, Nance, be wise, 'merch-i,' and for a moment she faltered in her purpose, and whimpered a little as Gildas continued: 'Come home and let us begin our lives again; perhaps I have been hard to you. Come, Nance, and I will forgive and no one will ever know of this your folly. Have you forgotten everything? . . . the sunny day when the little bell at Penmwnten church rang out so merrily when we turned home to Scethryg together, so innocent, and so happy.'

In his eagerness he had clutched her arm once more, but she tore herself away.

'So innocent, and so happy!' she cried. 'Not me, not me! I tell you, man, I was miserable! I have been miserable ever since, and I cannot bear it any longer. Let me go!'

'Miserable!' said Gildas, and all the tenderness died out of him, and a hot tide of bitter anger filled his heart and barbed his tongue.

'False vilanes! Have you no shame? D'ye think I have not seen your wickedness, your smiles, your blushes? and all because a roving villain has crossed your path; and you a wife! Och-i! The wife of Gildas Rees! oh, shame upon you!' and clutching her arms firmly he turned her round, and made her face him in the starlight.

'D'ye think, woman, I could love you now, or care one cockleshell what in your mad folly you would do? Although I would still harbour you in my house, and hide your faith-lessness if possible, for my own name's sake. Come, choose! this is the last time you shall ever have the chance. Yes, by God! you shall choose between me and that devil Cap'n Jack.'

His angry tones, his firm grip, had roused in Nance a fierce daring which rose in arms against her accuser.

'Choose, woman,' he cried, but with a sudden wrench Nance loosed herself from his grasp.

'Cap'n Jack, then,' she cried, nay, almost screamed, so loud and excited were her tones. 'Cap'n Jack I choose, I choose,' and she broke into a shrill, mirthless laugh, that Gildas shuddered to hear.

It woke up the echoes in the silent cove, and from the craggy heights around, it still returned and seemed to fill his ears and smite upon his brain. He turned away without a word, and reaching the rocky path walked steadily upwards without casting a look behind; Nance, as if spellbound, watching him, until he disappeared over the edge of the moor and she was left standing alone by the surf, only the soft gurgling of the tide in the clefts of the rocks breaking the silence. The hours were passing, the tide was full: she must hurry and leave these taunts and troubles behind her

– away, away, on earth, sea, or sky, she cared not where as long as she might escape. And, lost to all sense of faith or honour, she turned eagerly to unmoor the boat; but once again a restraining hand was laid upon her arm, and she turned round fiercely to find Gwenifer facing her. She had hidden behind the rocks until she saw that Gildas's persuasions were vain, and until he was out of sight beyond the edge of the cliff; then she had slipped out from her hiding-place, longing as she had never longed before for words in which to clothe her entreaties. She could only seize hold of Nance, however, and try to draw her away from the boat; but not succeeding in this, she flung her arms around her neck, she kissed her and grasped her hands, wetting them with her tears, and pressing them on her heart to show how wildly it was beating. But all in vain, for Nance was no longer open to the call of reason or affection; her hot temper was up in arms, and, swayed only by the fierceness of her unbridled passions, she turned upon Gwenifer in a fury of resentment.

'Away, thou dumb fool!' she cried. 'Go back to thy cows and thy sheep! I go to the man whom my prayers have saved,' and she sprang into the boat and tried to loosen its prow from the strand. Its stern was already afloat, and in another moment would have cleared the surf. In that moment Gwenifer, light and agile, had sprung in after her, and with a lurch the boat floated on the tide, though it still remained close to the rocks; and the two girls stood up confronting each other with only the lapping sea around them, and the silent night sky above them. They could only see each other's outlines in the starlight, but that was enough to show that one was approaching the other with appealing hands.

In Nance's tortured heart a spirit of fierce anger had awoke, and with a cry of fury she sprang upon Gwenifer, overbalancing her, so that with a cry of 'Oh, dear God,' she fell over the side of the boat, striking her head on the rocks with such violence that she lost all consciousness, and remained still and white while Nance took the oars and rowed herself out into the darkness.

In a few moments Gwenifer had so far recovered as to sit up and stare at the dark, heaving sea, and wonder what had become of Nance, for all around her was silent as though Nance and her boat had never been.

Her experienced eye, however, soon detected a black speck upon the waters, in which she knew too well Nance was hastening to her fate. 'And what a fate, oh, what a fate!' thought Gwenifer, as the boat was lost to view in the darkness; and kneeling there upon the rocks she raised her clasped hands to the starry sky, the tears streaming down her cheeks, her eyes fixed upon the spot where she knew the *Liliwen* was riding at anchor. Suddenly, while she prayed, her memory awoke more clearly, the blood rushed to her heart, and flooded her face as a new and eager thought arose in her mind. Had she heard her own voice as she fell from the boat? Had she cried aloud, 'Oh, dear God'? And so intensely eager was her longing that it might be true, that she dreaded to put the question to the test, lest she might find it was a dream, and that she was still the dumb and silent Gwenifer! Should she dare to try? With her hands clasped and her eyes still fixed upon the glittering stars, she breathed softly the words that came most naturally to her lips, 'Oh, dear God.' Yes! she heard her own voice! Again, more loudly, and again she repeated the same words, and realised that mysteriously, as it had left her so many years ago, her speech had returned, and she was able to articulate freely and easily. When at last the blessed truth shone in upon her, in a full tide of overpowering joy and gratitude, she burst into a fit of wild sobbing; not only sobs of joy in the present, but also of self-

pity for the long silence to which she had been condemned
in the past. The long-restrained feelings, the serene patience,
gave way under the excess of happiness; and she sobbed
on, until quite exhausted she stretched herself on the rocks,
her head on a pillow of seaweed, to rest, to recover her self-
control, and at last to rise, her heart throbbing with happiness
in spite of the clouds that overshadowed her. Her first act
of calm consciousness was to kneel, and stretch her hands
towards the night sky, to breathe a prayer of gratitude, in
words that no longer died upon her tongue, but reached
her ears in the music of the human voice.

Turning to leave the shore where she had failed so
miserably in her attempt to save Nance, she strained her eyes
for a last look towards the ship, whose sails were beginning
to catch the light of the rising moon, continuing to use her
new-found powers of speech, fearing lest she might have lost
them again. 'Gildas, Gildas! Oh! Nance, come back to him,'
she murmured.

A solemn stillness reigned over the sea – a silence that
was suddenly broken by a distant scream, followed by
another, and another, and Gwenifer shuddered with horror
at she knew not what, stretching out helpless hands towards
the waste of waters. Helpless hands, and useless sobs! for
Nance was gone beyond the power of love to recall.

A faint hope still remained to her that the misguided
woman had returned to Scethryg while she herself had lain
unconscious, and climbing up the cliff path she determined
to go to the farm and find out. Not to tell Gildas of her
recovered speech – oh no, not now! Joy for her and sorrow
for him? No, she would keep her joy to herself as she had
kept her sorrow for so long, and wait at least until the first
pang of his grief had passed; and she ran up the cliff still
murmuring, 'Gildas, Gildas! Sorrow for you and joy for me.
Oh, how that spoils my happiness! No, I will not tell you
to-night.'

She made up her mind, too, not to tell Het, or Ben, until the next evening, hugging her happy secret to her heart.

When after her hurried walk up the cliff she reached Scethryg, she saw by the light that streamed out through the open doorway that Gildas was still up; and through the window, as she passed, she saw him pacing up and down with restless steps. Hearing her footsteps on the stubble, he hastened to the door, and with both hands outstretched called 'Nance!' There was relief, forgiveness, and pity in his voice; but he started back when Gwenifer entered.

'Gwenifer!' he exclaimed, 'what dost here so late?'

She pointed to the candle and to the light that streamed out through the doorway.

'Oh,' he said, 'thou saw'st the light and wondered what we were doing so late; well, 'tis Nance, thou seest; she has gone away somewhere, and I don't know in the world where. I'm thinking perhaps she's gone home to her father's house; she threatened it many times lately.'

Gwenifer nodded, and looked sadly into the darkness.

'Dids't hear a scream, Gwenifer, three times over? What was it?'

Pointing upwards, she flapped her hands like the wings of a bird.

'The seagulls, and at night? No, no! I cannot think it; go thou home and sleep, lass.'

She shook her head emphatically, but Gildas was firm.

'Thee'll do what I ask thee, I know,' he said. ''Tis my wish that thou should'st go and close thy door, and sleep.'

For he thought the wanderer might return, and to see Gwenifer there would but add to her humiliation. She bent her head, as usual acquiescing in Gildas's wishes, and passed out into the farmyard, leaving the restless man still pacing up and down the stone floor.

CHAPTER XIV

'On your Peril!'

Meanwhile, what had become of Nance? When Gwenifer had fallen on the rocks, and had lain so still and white where she fell, Nance, in a frenzy of excitement, had seized her opportunity and, leaving her without pity, had sprung into the boat and rowed swiftly into the darkness away from Maldraeth and towards the *Liliwen*, which was beginning to show like a ghost in the moonlight.

Over the dark waters her strong arms rowed the little boat, with only one idea in her mind – that taunts and misery were behind her, and happiness and rest before. In a short time she had reached the black hulk of the ship, where Captain Jack, leaning over the rail, had heard the sound of the oars in the rowlocks, and stood watching with great surprise the black speck approaching.

'Hoi, mate!' he called out, 'what's the matter?' but there was no answer from the fast-nearing boat.

'I thought you were stopping in the village to-night,' cried the captain; but again there was no reply, for Nance's courage had failed her, and she found no voice to answer. The moon was rising over the moor, and by her faint light Captain Jack saw it was a woman who had rowed so straight and swift over the dark sea, and a wild hope arose within him. Gwenifer! could she have relented? Was she coming to him for help of any kind? With eager hands he threw down the ship's ladder, and saw a woman grasp it and quickly climb up towards him; he stretched out his hands to help her, and in a moment she had stepped on board. Captain Jack recognised his midnight visitor and his heart sank like a stone.

'Nance,' he cried, 'you here? What is the meaning of this?'

'Yes, yes, Jack anwyl,' Nance answered, her heart beating almost to suffocation, ''tis me, Jack; I have come; I told you I would. I am coming to sail with you, to be your servant, your slave, only to be with you, Jack – oh! say you are glad to see me. Why do you stand aside like that? Hasn't the Lord given us to each other? I prayed for you by night and day, and He has heard my prayers, and given you to me, and me to you, to be together for ever and ever, in this world and the next.'

'Nance!' said Captain Jack, 'what do you mean? Where is your husband, Gildas, that noble man, that neither you nor I are worthy of? He flung the word 'honourable' in my teeth; and in my deed, if I did this wicked thing, he would be right; but bad as he thinks me, I will not. Nance, go back to him, to him to whom you owe your love and honour. Why have you done this foolish thing? Oh, Nance! Why have you come?'

'Why have I come?' said Nance, her arms dropping at her side, her face white, her eyes flashing. 'Why have I come? Because I love you, Jack, because I cannot live away from you, and because' – and she grasped his hands between her own, and bent her face upon them – 'because, Jack, you love me – yes, yes, I have heard it in the watches of the night, I have heard it in your voice, and seen it in your eyes when you came up so often to Scethryg; all the time I knew it was because you loved me, Jack! and because I loved you, and prayed for you.'

'Good God!' said Captain Jack, 'I have done wrong! Nance, Nance, come, be brave, 'merch-i! Remember you are a wife, and Gildas Rees's wife, too.'

A scornful smile was all Nance's answer, and the sailor

saw that to be kind he must first be cruel, and to awaken
Nance to a sense of duty he must show her the futility of her
mad passion.

''Twas never you,' he said, ''twas Gwenifer I sought;
'twas Gwenifer I loved, and though she refuses me 'tis
Gwenifer I will love for ever!'

For one moment Nance seemed dazed and stunned by this
sudden revelation. Gwenifer the dumb, the silent one, to dare
to come between her and the man who had been given in
answer to her prayers! 'No, no!' and she burst into a loud,
shrill laugh that startled the sailor; so fierce it was, so
mirthless.

'Come,' he said, 'you must get back, Nance. 'Tis a dream, a
fancy, that you have taken into your head. I, the roving sailor,
to be preferred to Gildas Rees; and he your wedded husband
in the sight of God and man! Oh, Nance, cast from you such
dishonour. I know to-morrow when you awake you will be
sorry for this wild freak; but no one knows it, save you and
me, and no one ever shall; I swear it, Nance. No one shall
ever know what has happened to-night if you will go back to
Scethryg; the boat is ready, I will help you down the side.'

'I will not go,' she cried, 'I will not go; never, never!' and her
voice rose into a frenzy of passion. ''Tis false, 'tis false that
you love Gwenifer!' Then her mood changed, and in tender,
sorrowful accents she pleaded, 'Oh, Jack, my heart is breaking; it is burning in my breast like a heavy burning stone!
And in my head a burning, too. Oh, Jack, say one kind word
to me to heal me of my pain.'

'Poor Nance,' said Captain Jack, touched by the sorrowful
appeal, 'you heart is sore! *I* know that heavy stone, that
burning heart. Come, I will help you into the boat; the path
of duty is hard sometimes, no doubt, but I believe 'twill bring
us peace at last. Then say so, Nance, whatever.'

'Peace?' said Nance, with a scornful laugh, 'in my deed,

no! Have you no word of kindness for me, when I have borne so much, and dared so much for you?'

'Not one word, Nance! Go back you must! At once! The moon is rising fast, we shall be seen, and you will lose your character for ever!' and laying hold of her hand he endeavoured to draw her towards the gangway, but her mood had changed again, and she struggled violently.

'Never, never, never!' she cried, and scream after scream rent the night air. Flinging her arms round his neck, she clung to him with mad tenacity; he tried to loosen her frantic grasp, but she burst into a loud peal of laughter again, laughter that made the sailor's blood run cold. Suddenly her grasp relaxed, and she fell into a fit of hysterical sobbing mingled with screams and laughter; she sank at last exhausted upon the deck, and Captain Jack seizing his opportunity lifted her tenderly, and with a sailor's deftness climbed down the ladder, and laying her down gently took the oars and rowed rapidly back towards Maldraeth.

When he reached the shore he raised her in his arms once more, and wading through the surf carried her safely beyond the reach of the tide, and set her gently on the sand.

'Now, mestress!' he said in a firm though not harsh tone. 'Awake! be brave! There's the path. Go home, and think no more of this dark night!'

She stood a moment as if dazed before she turned towards the dangerous cliff path; and Captain Jack shuddered as he saw her walk increase into a run, and dreaded lest a false step might hurl her to her death. But on and on she ran without a look behind, up where the steepness made the heart beat hard and the breath come quickly, up where the crooked track edged the scarped rocks, up to the very summit, and out of sight beyond the highest ridge. Here, when she reached the moor, she cast but one glance towards Scethryg, then turned, and fled as if for very life.

Away, away towards the cold grey hills that stretched eastward beyond the moor. The moon rose higher, the hours went by, but long after Captain Jack had reached the *Liliwen*, and thrown himself distressed and anxious into his bunk, Nance's face was still towards those bare grey hills; and on the wings of the night wind she was still speeding on. Away, away, she cared not where, for in her brain some cord seemed to have snapped, and all she thought of, all she desired, was to reach the Wildrom mountains where Dakee would pity her and comfort her.

The sun had scarcely arisen next morning when Gwenifer rose and went out in search of the cows. She had obeyed Gildas so far as to stretch herself on her bed, but not to sleep; the events of the preceding night had touched her so nearly that it was no wonder if her heart and mind and soul shared in the upheaval that had come into her placid life. Several times during the night she had risen, and peered through her tiny window at a tall familiar figure who paced up and down on the edge of the cliff. Full well she recognised Gildas's restless steps, and longed to join him even as she shared in his anxiety; but she waited in obedience to his wish until the sun rose, before she went out to call the Scethryg cows, where the heath tufts and the golden broom were just catching the glint of the sunrise. She knew it was not yet milking-time, so she turned from her path to join Gildas as he stood in deep thought, looking out over the bay where the *Liliwen* no longer flaunted her red pennon in the breeze. Her light footsteps made no sound on the dewy grass, so that when she laid her hand upon his arm as usual, he started violently.

'Caton pawb! Gwenifer, thou cam'st like a spirit over the moor. Didst do my bidding and go to bed and rest last night?'

'Yes.' And he started back two or three steps.

'What?' he said as if bewildered.

'Gildas, I can speak,' she said, with a light and happiness in her eyes that not even her sympathy with him could quench.

'Speak!' he exclaimed, 'speak!' and drawing near her, he clasped both her hands within his own. 'Lodes, what does it mean?' and a light and colour overspread his dark face that had been absent for many a long day. 'Gwenifer, I did not think that God would ever send such a gleam of light to brighten my darkness; but this, Gwenifer! 'tis more than I could ever hope for! I am glad indeed! indeed! I don't know what to say! Tell me, lass, how did it happen?'

''Twas last night,' said Gwenifer, 'only I wouldn't tell you when you were so troubled, mishteer. I was very unhappy, and suddenly I found I could speak. I cannot tell you more than that, mishteer.'

'No need, no need! Gwenifer can speak, so Scethryg is not quite accursed!'

'No, no, no indeed!' said Gwenifer. She would like to have told him that this was a dark and sinful suggestion, but her words still came with a little hesitancy, and moreover she knew that though speech is silver, yet sometimes silence is golden.

''Tis cruel to throw a shadow over thy happiness, lass, but I cannot help it. Nance has never come back, and now it is too late. I will go back to Scethryg and to my work, and forget her, Gwenifer, as though she had never been. Keep this all to thyself; but I needn't tell thee now any more than when thy lips were sealed. I will go home, and to my work; but Gwenifer, thou knowest me of old, the things I cannot speak about are here all the time,' and he pointed to his broad chest. 'Joy for thee, lodes, and thankfulness indeed! Art coming to the milking?'

She nodded, and they turned towards Scethryg together.

When after breakfast Het and Gwenifer entered the

turnip field, the mishteer and Ben were already bending over their work.

Gildas had eaten a hurried breakfast, and Het had attributed his silence to annoyance at having failed to procure labourers to help in the hoeing – an impression that Gwenifer did not attempt to correct, being thankful that as yet she had not discovered the true cause of his depression.

She had succeeded also in diverting Het's attention at breakfast-time from the mestress's empty chair, by launching her on the favourite top of her own sinfulness and hardness of heart.

'Yes, in my deed!' she said. 'Evan Roberts will have to knock pretty hard at the door of my heart before 'twill open! although, mind you, I'm doing my very best to be converted! 'Tis an odd thing, whatever. But come on, the weeds are growing while we are talking. There's late the mestress is to-day!' she added, as she went out, Gwenifer following with a heavy heart, for she had not failed to see Gildas's troubled looks.

A sleepless night and a wounded spirit had left their marks upon his face; there were dark rings round his eyes, and his lips were set and bloodless.

'Dear anwl, there's ill he looks!' said Het, as he passed them in the field. 'Yes, yes, the conscience is a troublesome customer to deal with! Oh, you may look black, 'merch-i! but depend upon it, 'tis his behaviour in Brynzion is weighing on him.'

Both she and Ben were under the impression that they had left the house to the care of the clever mestress, who would soon set all in order, and bring out their ten-o'clock lunch to the fields, as usual; ignorant of what Gwenifer and Gildas knew only too well – that the bustling housewife's place on the hearth and at the board was vacant, and would never more be filled by her. To Gildas, as he bent over his work,

that sunny morning was so fraught with gall and wormwood
that not only his mind and heart were aching, but his very
flesh seemed weighed down with a mortal sickness, which
darkened the fair scene around him and made him often
pause in his work and lean upon his hoe for rest. It was not
wounded love that was torturing him, so much as burning
shame and wounded pride; for his love had died out in bitter
anger and contempt, every scene in the tragedy of the night
before having increased that contempt and crushed his love
more completely. But the disgrace, the dishonour, the stain
upon his honest name, remained as a thorn in his flesh from
which he tried in vain to free himself.

What should he say when the terrible question was asked,
'Where is the mestress?' What but the truth could be the
answer to that? 'She is gone, gone for ever, from a happy
home to shame and disgrace and misery.'

His first impulse was to answer thus, to face the worst, to
stand up alone, and defy Fate that had already been so cruel
to him, to do its worst, for there was nothing more, he
thought, of misfortune or disaster that could be heaped upon
him! Poverty! How well he could have endured it, had he
only been able to keep his name untarnished! But shame! Did
not the old proverb say, 'Gwell angau na chywilydd'?
'Better death than disgrace.' Yes, indeed, a hundred times;
and under the brilliant morning sunlight there was
darkness, black as night, in his heart. Gwenifer, working
near, watched him from under her white sun-bonnet, with
cheeks as white and eyes as dark-ringed as his own.

It was nearing ten o'clock; she knew it by the look of the
sky, by the special flowers that waited for that hour to open,
by the length of her shadow on the leaves; oh no! no need of
watch or clock to tell her how the day was speeding. So,
being near the gap into the lane, she passed out unnoticed,
and hurrying back to Scethryg prepared the lunch of tea

and bread-and-butter and packing it into the usual basket carried it into the turnip field.

Gildas had just looked at his watch; yes, it was ten o'clock, and he must face the question, 'Where is the mestress?' But raising his eyes from his hoe, they lighted upon Gwenifer coming through the gap in the hedge, straight and slim, and strong of limb. She carried the round basket poised on her head, and he blessed the welcome sight, thankful for an hour or two's reprieve. She lowered her basket, and Het and Ben drew near, flinging away their hoes as they came; but Gildas went on working until Gwenifer went up to him and laid her hand on his arm as of old. He turned his dark face towards her, its expression so altered that her lips trembled nervously as she said, 'Will I go and prepare the cawl?' and she pointed to Het and Bryn.

'Yes, they will be wanting their dinner; and, Gwenifer, lass, I am not forgetting thy new happiness, though I am so silent, thou know'st me – 'the hard log' as people call me.'

'I know much better than that, mishteer,' said Gwenifer.

Gildas looked at her a moment with a wondering gaze.

'I think the fairies have been teaching thee in thy long silence: thy words are slipping from thy tongue like music!' he said.

As a matter of fact, Gwenifer's speech had returned to her without the rough country burr; there was a little hesitancy, sometimes followed by a rapid flow of retarded words, and the soft tones seemed to have caught somewhat of a foreign accent. But of this Gwenifer was unconscious; she revelled in her new-found power, and while she worked at her hoe she continued to murmur softly the words of some quaint old hymn, or a rhyme which had impressed her in the past.

'Go thou, and leave the turnips,' said Gildas.

She turned away at once, but he called after her, and she waited while he took a few steps towards her. 'Remember!'

Nance is gone away, but I don't know where, no more dost thou.'

She bowed her head slowly as she turned away. It would be long before she could avail herself freely of her restored gift of speech; indeed, she never entirely lost the habit of using her expressive eyes and eyebrows, her hands also, in conversation.

'Well, in the dear's name what's become of Gwenifer?' said Het, shaking the crumbs off her apron as she sought her hoe again. 'Perhaps the mestress wants her,' she muttered to herself, 'for it's Gwenifer, Gwenifer, from morning till night! Well, we'd better set to work, Ben and me, for it seems to me this farm is going to be left pretty well to us two!'

When noontide arrived, the cawl hung over the fire bubbling cheerfully; the bare table was laid with its blue plates and basins, and Gwenifer, hearing footsteps approaching over the stubble, hastily filled the basins from the big crock, and set the bacon at the end of the table. Through the open window came the scent of the gorse, borne in on the sea-wind, which had risen into a playful gale, tossing the spray into the sunshine, and racing the wavelets after each other, as though it said, 'See what a happy day we are having!' The smell of the seaweed, the odour of the brine, came in too, mingled with the sunshine through that open window, striking Gildas Rees, entering at the doorway, with an almost bitter sense of its purity and freshness, so different from his present state of mind and feeling that he almost turned away from the quiet calm of the old kitchen with loathing.

He cast one look round the table where Het and Ben were already seated, Gwenifer hovering around them. A glance at the vacant chair, one deep breath, and Gildas had conquered his weakness and taken his seat naturally before the dish of steaming bacon.

'Where is mestress?' asked Het between the sups of her cawl. 'Caton pawb! I have not seen her since tea-time yesterday!'

'She is gone,' answered Gildas slowly, as though he counted the words.

'Gone? Where?' asked Het, while Ben stared open-mouthed.

'I don't know,' was all Gildas's answer, and Het turned to question Gwenifer.

'Well, bendigedig!' she said, 'was ever such a thing? What has become of her? In my deed, mishteer, what will we do? Is she lost? She must be somewhere!'

Again Gildas's bare 'I don't know where she is,' and nothing more. He felt he had a right to say this, as when he saw her last Nance had been standing on the shingle at Maldraeth, as if undecided what to do, and he had yet a gleam of hope that she might have changed her mind and turned to Nelli Amos's for a night's lodging, that she might still return and so save her name and his from disgrace. It was only a faint hope and one that had in it but little comfort, nevertheless he felt it justified him in asserting that he was ignorant of her whereabouts, and that for her own sake he had better keep his fears to himself for a least another day. He had shaken from him the cowardice (as he considered it) which had overpowered him at first, and was quite prepared to face the talk and gossip of the neighbourhood; so that when Het followed up her fruitless questioning with a proposal that when work was over she should go down to the village and ask Nelli Amos if she had seen the mestress, he was able to answer calmly, 'Yes, perhaps thee'dst better do that,' and the meal proceeded in silence except for Het's continued speculations, some of them so ridiculous that Gwenifer, with all her anxiety, could not help smiling. Could the mestress have got shut up in one of the outhouses, and failed to make herself heard? Could she have met the Ladiwen that was said to haunt the moor, and swooned away in terror? In her deed, she would go round by the moor, and look for her, Ladiwen or not! And when she returned to her hoeing with the rest of the household, she continued her rambling suggestions until evening.

Gildas hoed on silently, only occasionally straightening himself to direct Ben, or remind him of a duty.

The lad seemed strangely absorbed and silent, keeping as near his master as his work permitted; once or twice helping him by picking up the hoe which had fallen out of his hand in a fit of abstraction.

'Mishteer!' he said at last, and Gildas looked up as though he scarcely knew him. He had liked Ben when he had been a careless, whistling farm-boy only, but lately, since the 'revival,' a change had come over him; and recalling that he had been present at Brynzion on the night when he had been insulted, as he considered, by the whole congregation, he had not felt so kindly towards the lad, although he had been too just to let any change be seen in his manner. For Ben was more punctual and steady in the performance of his duties than he used to be, and he had certainly been more truthful of late. Gildas started when he heard him a second time call, 'Mishteer, how far is it to Penwern?'

'To Penwern? Thirty miles. What of that?' said Gildas.

'Oh! then mestress will be a good while away. Because I suppose she's gone there. She told me last week that she would go one day and see her old home.'

'Did she? Told thee? How came that about, then?' said Gildas, catching at a straw.

'Yes,' continued Ben. 'She was telling me about the land over there, so flat and even, and the crops so rich, and I asked her, didn't she want to see the place sometimes? 'Yes,' says the mestress, 'and some day, soon, I'll take my pack on my back and walk, there, to meet Dakee, and see the old place again!' So no doubt she's gone, mishteer.'

'Very like!' was all Gildas's answer; and in his heart he knew that the lad had meant to throw a gleam of light upon his darkness.

'Perhaps,' he thought, 'Ben's suggestion was the real explanation of Nance's absence. Perhaps in a hasty moment she had set off alone to her old home'; but then came the memory of the words, 'I choose him, then; I choose, I choose Captain Jack!'

When the shadows lengthened, and supper-time arrived, Het hurried through her meal, looking often at the old clock in the corner, whose loud ticking seemed to resound through the house, so silent were they who sat at the table. 'Will I go, mishteer?' she said at last, 'and ask Nelli Amos if she has seen the mestress?'

Gwenifer shrank with repugnance from the thought; but Gildas answered, with quiet firmness, 'Yes, go, if thou pleasest, and tell them all.'

'I tell thee she's gone to Penwern!' said Ben hotly. 'No need to ask in the village. Didn't she tell me she was going!' But Het was not to be delayed, for had not mishteer said, 'tell them all if thou pleasest'? Here was licence indeed! And she was not going to be baulked of the pleasure of being the bearer of such news by Ben's foolish suggestions; so as soon as the supper was cleared away she set off, at first crossing the yard with leisurely steps, but no sooner had she gained the lane than her sedate walk changed into a run, which brought her quickly to the village, where in five minutes she was surrounded by a gaping crowd, who thoroughly appreciated her feast of gossip, in spite of the pity expressed on all sides for the mestress. 'Pwr thing, fach! To think it had come to this! To think Gildas Rees could be such a villain that she had to leave her home! Well indeed!'

'Didn't I tell you,' said Nelli Amos, 'that he was a cruel, hard man? You'll believe me now! Ach-y-fi! The sooner he clears out from here the better. But tell again, Het, where is she gone to?'

'He says he doesn't know,' said Het, 'and Gwenifer doesn't know, so there for you!'

'But I know,' said Ben, suddenly making his appearance among them. 'Didn't she tell me her own self about a week ago that she was going down to Penwern to see the old place, and to meet her Dakee? 'Tis there she's gone, of course! There's no need for Het to clabber, nor for the mishteer to vex, pwr fellow!'

'Pwr fellow?' said Nelli Amos, her eyes gleaming vindictively. 'Pwr fellow indeed! The man who drives his young wife away from home, and resists the Holy Spirit openly – 'Pwr fellow,' dost call him? Come away from Scethryg, my lad, before Gildas Rees turns thee to his wicked ways!'

'Wicked ways?' said Ben indignantly. ''Tis wicked ways to hound down a good man as thou art doing, Nelli Amos. I tell thee if every man was as upright as mishteer, there would be no need of being converted, and if thou hadst been truly converted thou wouldst know better what a good man is.'

At Ben's words, spoken with burning cheeks and flashing eyes, a moment's silence fell upon the group, a silence of shocked surprise. Could this be Ben Penpit – who had prayed so eloquently at Brynzion, who had been looked upon as the flower of the revival, a brand snatched from the burning? Was he now going to prove himself an apostate?

'Gildas Rees indeed!' cried Nelli Amos again, bringing her excited face close to Ben's. 'A good man, dost say? I am ashamed of thee! Wilt ask him a few questions for me? Ask him when he was last in a place of worship? Ask him what he had done with his wife? And ask him, how is he going to get his harvest in? There's three nice questions for thy good man.' And she laughed maliciously, but Ben only whistled as he turned away. Was he forgetting the Diwygiad, or was he putting its best principles into practice? However that might be, nothing availed to assuage the storm of indignation which Het's news had aroused. All Tregildas was moved, and in every one of its fifteen houses the mestress's disappearance formed the supreme topic of conversation for many days to come, the women without exception attributing her flight to her husband's hardness and cruelty. Some of the men, more lenient in their judgment, thought probably there were faults on both sides, and strongly advised non-interference, as the quarrels of a young married couple were soon made up, and no doubt the mestress would return when she had 'stopped a bit in her old home.'

Meanwhile, Gildas, when supper was over, had lighted his pipe at the wood fire, and leaving the house had turned away towards the moor, where a fresh wind was blowing from the sea, that tossed and foamed with the boisterous glee of a nor'-wester that has not its usual serious intentions. 'I mean no harm to-day!' it seemed to say, 'only a game of play with the waves and the seagulls!' and Gildas, well acquainted with every sound and sight of the broad bay, understood what the wind was saying, but only looked out to sea with never a smile on his stern set lips. With his hands thrust deep in his pockets he passed over the springy turf, unconscious whither his steps were leading him, until at last the deep channel of the little Erva stopped him where it fell over the cliffs to the sands below. He gazed a moment at its swift-flowing waters, before he turned and retraced his steps. Up and down, backwards and forwards, he continued to pace, until the sun had long set and the moor was growing grey in the twilight, unconscious of all but his anger and his bitter thoughts; until suddenly, catching sight of Gwenifer's brown cot, he stopped to look at it, for there was Gwenifer herself returning from the farm and lifting the latch of her door. He pictured her entering the empty cottage, kindling the fire of furze knots, turning gloom to brightness, and drawing the old oak stool to the cosy hearth. Oh for a few words of cheer and comfort from her! Should he follow her to the quaint low-browed chimney, and ask her help and guidance in his difficulties? No, he *must not*, he could not, he dared not seek the comfort of a word from her, for deep within his heart some secret instinct forbade his disclosing to Gwenifer the faults and sins of the woman whom he had chosen for his wife.

It would be an act of disloyalty, from which he shrank with distaste. 'Not until I am certain, whatever,' he thought; and even then, how could he sully this white-souled creature with the recital of such a story! No, he must bear his trouble alone. His face grew darker, his eyes flashed, his jaw showed out more square than ever, and, as if coming to a sudden determination, he turned round and walked hurriedly towards Scethryg.

Into the old kitchen, lit up now by its big log fire, where n'wncwl Sam sat by the hearth enjoying his evening pipe, Het returned from the village, clattering in and out of the dairy as of old. It was a bright and glowing scene, but Gildas saw nothing of it, as he went straight towards the old bookcase desk.

'Caton pawb!' said n'wncwl Sam, 'what is this I hear, that Nance has gone away? Where, then, in the dear's name?'

'I know nothing in the world,' said Gildas, 'but stop a bit till I finish here, and I will talk to you,' and sitting down to the desk, he drew pen and paper toward him, and began to write; n'wncwl Sam having perforce to be satisfied with his own ejaculations and guesses, aided by Het's rambling remarks.

Writing a letter was not a simple affair to Gildas Rees,

although he was by no means an ignorant or illiterate farmer.
He read his weekly newspaper with interest and pleasure,
forming his own opinions upon its political and religious
views; but he generally sat long with his pen in his hand,
gazing at nothing, before he was able to tackle a letter. This
evening, however, he seemed to find no difficulty, but dashed
straight into the subject.

'You villain! you villain!' he wrote.

'These few lines from Gildas Rees, Scethryg, to tell you
what he thinks of you, and to bid you beware of coming into
his presence, or on his lands again – on your peril. Do you
hear? on your peril.'

GILDAS REES

He folded and addressed it in his round plain handwriting
to –

> *Captain John Davies*
> *Of the 'Liliwen'*
> *Cardiff Docks,*

and hurried out to Ben's sleeping-room, a mere cupboard,
boarded off from the hay-loft, where he was startled to see
a light twinkling through the gaping boards. Ben was
supposed to retire with the sun, or if later, to undress in the
dark, for a light was not allowed so near the hay-loft; the
glimmering spark therefore must be extinguished at once,
and Gildas approached over the hay, his footsteps unheard
by Ben. He stopped a moment where the crack in the boards
gave a full view of the tiny room. What could the lad be
doing? He was sitting on the edge of his rough wooden
bedstead; in his left hand he held an old blacking-bottle, in
which a candle was stuck, by the light of which he was
reading a Bible, with a serious, earnest face. The mishteer,
astonished at the sight, stood still to watch, while the lad

who had had the reputation of being the 'wickedest in the parish' read on apparently with interest and pleasure. 'The revival!' was Gildas's first thought, and with it came the wave of resentment which the memory of the Brynzion prayer meeting always roused within him.

But surely that placid, calm face, that changed look of 'sweet reasonableness,' instead of the careless inanity which used to be the expression of Ben's face, spoke of some strange alteration in the lad. From Gildas's sore, embittered heart the contempt and hatred faded away, and he continued to watch the boy, his face showing both interest and surprise.

An instinctive feeling told him that, 'revival, or no revival,' here was the real thing! the changing of a wild reckless youth into an earnest, thoughtful man. Could this be Ben – the roystering, drunken blackguard of the fairs and markets? Closing his book at last, he blew out his candle; but the little room was not altogether dark, for the rising moon shone in upon the truckle bed and upon the lad's face as he knelt down for a few moments before getting into bed.

For the life of him, Gildas could not disturb him, but waited silently, while a few simple ejaculations rather than prayers expressed Ben's inmost feelings. The last of these reached the mishteer's ear through the rough bare boards, and fell with a soothing spell upon his troubled spirit, as though his mother's hand had touched his forehead.

'And oh, God, help the mishteer!' asked Ben, 'because he's in sore trouble, and I know it's not his fault!'

Then, after a moment's silence Gildas knocked softly in the darkness before entering.

'Ben! Wilt dress, and go down to the village for me?' he asked, and Ben started up in bed.

'B't shwr, mishteer. What for?' he asked.

'To carry this to the post. And I don't want any one to know the letter is from me, remember, or else I would go myself. Here it is, on the window board. I can trust thee, Ben.'

'Well, b't shwr!' said Ben, shuffling into his clothes; and Gildas went backwards down the hay-loft ladder, well knowing that in a few minutes his letter would be safe in the postbox in the village and beyond recall. He remembered the forbidden light which Ben had held so near the hay, but he said not a word of reproof, nor ever let Ben know that he had watched him through the partition.

CHAPTER XV

Sea Wrack

On a sunny morning in the following month, when the barley was ripe in the field beyond the creek, Gildas Rees, with a small band of reapers, crossed the shining water in Jerri's boat, as his father had done before him, so many years ago. Jerri himself was one of the reapers, having dared to defy the ill-will of his neighbours, in his desire to help the mishteer, for he had a heart somewhere under that sea-stained old blue jersey; and that organ had warmed up latterly in an unusual degree towards the man whom everybody else had turned against. Moreover, the strong, almost sacred, claims of the harvest had appealed to him as it had to the rest of the villagers, though with them the distrust and suspicion with which they looked upon Gildas had outweighed every other consideration. They risked the danger of being turned out of their homes rather than help the man who had wilfully opposed and rejected the more sacred claims of the revival; and he had come very near being left without hands to garner the crops, which Nature seemed to have lavished upon him with even more generosity than ever before.

'Look at the barley, woman!' Jerri had said one morning on the kiln, where Nelli Amos was basking in the sun. 'And the wheat-field next to it. Didst ever see such a crop? And if the Lord is willing to give him such a harvest, surely we can help to gather it in?'

233

'Why art so angry with the mishteer?' said Ben, stopping on his way to the blacksmith's. 'What has he done to thee? Dost not remember how kind he was to thee last winter when thou wert sick?'

'Oh, yes; I remember the bits of scraps and the shilling he sent me; and wouldn't I pay it back now in harvesting, if he had behaved himself? I have a good memory, thank God, and I remember, too, how his father turned my mother out of the house one day, because she spoke her mind to him about the path through the cornfield which he wanted to shut up. Oh, yes! I remember it all.'

'Why, Gildas was only two years old then,' said Jerri. 'What could he help that?'

'Two years old! I don't care if he was twenty.'

Ben turned away impatiently, but Jerri continued:

'Come on, Nelli fach, fetch thy sickle, and leave it between the mishteer and his conscience what he has done with his wife.'

What he has done with his wife! It had come to that in the village, for Gildas's continued silence had roused all sorts of suspicions, and he had come to be looked upon as a man of dark deeds, whom it was better to shun as much as possible; so that when he stooped his tall shoulders to enter the low-browed doorway in search of his usual complement of labourers, they had one and all refused, not openly and flatly, but with well-feigned excuses and looks of distrust.

Gildas saw it all, but was too proud to urge his request, or even to show that he suspected the truth.

'Well, b't shwr!' he said, 'if that is the case, you can't come,' and he had been prepared to attack the barley-field with only Ben and Het and Gwenifer to help him, until Jerri, shipping his oars, spat in his hands, and declared his intention of joining the reapers.

'Will you have me, mishteer?' he said. 'I'm better at the boats than in the fields, I know, but . . .'

'Yes, yes,' said Gildas; 'I'll be glad of thy help.' And they had begun their way from the rocks to the field, when a loud 'Hoi, hoi!' from the other side of the creek made them halt and turn round.

'Who can they be?' said Jerri, in astonishment, and Gildas felt a strong sense of relief when he saw two men evidently waiting to be rowed over.

''Tis Jones Bryndu and Seth his servant,' cried Ben joyfully.

'Jari! so 'tis,' said Jerri, pushing off from the rocks. 'Well, there's somebody don't think so bad of you, whatever mishteer!'

'Stop, I'll come across with you,' said Gildas stepping into the boat. 'And what do the others think of me?' he asked suddenly, and somewhat to Jerri's confusion. 'Now, *truth*, Jerri!' he added, 'thou know'st I hate a lie! What evil do they think of me? Make haste, or we'll be across.'

'Well then, mishteer, to tell the truth, they think you have been hard and cruel to your wife, because you didn't like the revival, and she did; and they are all saying that it's very strange what has become of her, and . . .'

'There's enough!' said Gildas. 'What matter what they say?'

'Well! If you can stop their mouths with a word, mishteer, why not say it? That's what I am thinking. 'Tis plain Jones Bryndu isn't thinking so bad of you, though!'

'Think so bad of me? What dost mean, man?'

'Well, that you have got rid of the mestress *somehow*, but in my deed I'm not believing them, whatever!'

'Good God! Do they think I have done her any harm? That I have murdered her?'

For the first time he realised the suspicions that hung over him, the dark thoughts that lurked in men's minds; and for a moment the shock unnerved him, and his strong arm trembled on the oar.

Before they reached the rocks on the other side of the creek, however, the sturdy independence of his nature reasserted itself, and the strong antagonism which the boycotting he had been subjected to had aroused in him awoke in full force in his heart.

He had done nothing wrong. Should he lay poor Nance's sins before these malicious gossips, and expose his own disgrace for their contempt? Never! And he stepped ashore firmly determined to keep his own counsel, and let Tregildas say what it would.

'Well, in my deed, this is kind!' he said, laying his hand upon Jones Bryndu's shoulder. 'What will I say? Only that Ben and I will be ready, sunlight or moonlight, to help with Bryndu harvest.'

'Twt, twt,' said Jones, stepping into the boat, followed by his man. "Twas hearing what heavy crops you had this year made me think of it, and the mestress saying, 'Go, of course, Will! for Gildas Rees is always ready with a helping hand.' Well, well!' he exclaimed as they landed under the barley-field, and looked up at its waving gold. 'Here's a crop! Indeed, I never saw a better!' and doffing their coats, he and his man were ready to set to, as soon as it was settled who should be leader, and strike the first blow at the ripe corn – this point being always considered important in the harvest proceedings.

'Wilt thou, Seth, be leader?' said Gildas, in deference to the man's greater age and experience.

Seth accepted the honour with due seriousness, and, under the gleaming sickles, the field was soon marked with lines of fallen grain.

They were too busily occupied during the first few hours for any conversation – moreover, Gildas and his friend worked somewhat apart; but when the morning waned a little, and Gwenifer appeared through the gap with her well-filled basket of provisions poised on her head, while from her right hand hung a bright tin can of steaming tea, the reapers were nothing loth to drop their sickles and draw towards the shade of the hedge where she was already spreading the food.

'Hello, Gwenifer!' said Jones Bryndu, 'how art, 'merch-i? There's glad we are, Betsy and me, to hear thou canst talk now like any other woman;' for the news of Gwenifer's restored powers had spread like wildfire through the neighbourhood. 'On my word, lass, thou'rt the prettiest flower amongst the barley! Eh, Gildas?'

Gwenifer smiled, and blushed a rosy red, wondering why so many people praised her beauty now, when her heart was full of pain and sorrow, whereas no one had noticed her in the days of old, when she had roamed the hills and fields of Scethryg content and happy, though silent. She knew not that every sorrow patiently borne adds a fresh grace to the human face; and so she wondered as she spread her simple store in the shade of the hedge.

She had been quick to notice that when Jones of Bryndu, in his rustic fashion, had drawn Gildas's attention to her by his 'Eh, Gildas?' the latter had fixed his eyes upon her absently, and as if his thoughts had been preoccupied; but she had not seen how the hard look on his lips had softened as she turned away.

'I don't see much change in her,' he said, as he and his friend stretched themselves in the shadow of the high hedge and watched the girl as she left the field. 'Gwenifer is like the sky above us, always the same.'

'Always the same!' laughed Jones. 'No indeed, then; the sky is very changeable with us in these parts, whatever.'

'Gwenifer has her shadows too, and her showers sometimes, I expect,' answered Gildas, smiling at his own bad simile; and they set to at the simple meal with appetites that are often absent from richer repasts.

The brown bread and butter, the hunches of cheese, the well-made tea, were all that they ought to be; but as the meal proceeded both men became silent and preoccupied, for in the minds of both the subject of Nance's disappearance was uppermost.

'Come!' said Jones at last, 'let us go to the shade of the thorn yonder, and let us have a talk about this strange thing that has happened.' And he began the way to the one tall bush in the hedge, Gildas following slowly.

'It is no use talking,' said the latter, flinging himself down beside his friend. 'I have nothing to say to you, only what I have said a score of times. Nance is gone, and I don't know where she is.'

'But, for sure, you have some guess, man!'

Gildas plucked at the dandelions and made no reply to this, and Jones continued, 'Most like you don't know how the whole parish is fermenting and talking about it, and a word from you would stop the talk; because, hark you, Gildas Rees, nothing that they can say will make me believe what they are hinting, that you have got rid of your wife in some bad way – drowned her or pushed her over the cliff or strangled her! What know they?'

'Do they think that of me?' said Gildas, 'and do you, William Jones?' And he sat up suddenly, leaning on his elbows.

'Caton pawb, no! Betsy and I we know you too well, man. Haven't we been friends since we were boys in school, you and me? Don't I tell you, I wouldn't believe if you told me *yourself* that you had been cruel to her. Ach-y-fi! Shame that any man should think such a thing! But, look you, Gildas, 'tis enough to make strangers and enemies think bad of a man when he won't say anything to clear himself but 'I don't know, I don't know!' If you can't tell them where your wife is, tell them where you think she is.'

'Let people think what they like of me,' said Gildas, his face falling into the set hard lines that had become habitual to it of late. 'I will never say more than Nance is gone away from Scethryg, and I don't know where she is. Look you, friend; I will say one thing to you that I won't to anyone else. I have done nothing wrong in this matter.'

'That I know right well, without your word for it,' said Jones. 'But haven't you left something *un*done? Have you tried to find her? Have you caused search to be made for her?'

'No,' answered Gildas.

'Diwss anwl, man! Why not, then? Don't you want her to come back to you?'

'No,' said Gildas again, still plucking at the flowers.

'Ts, ts! Well, in my deed, 'tis pity! Well, there's no use asking you, I see; so when Betsy asks me what did you say I can only answer, 'Nothing, and I believe you are right in your guess, Betsy, as you always are.' I believe sometimes Betsy is 'hysbys,' you know, she is so clear-sighted. 'Tell you what I think, Will,' says she . . .'

'Don't tell me what she said!' answered Gildas, standing up and taking his sickle, as if to end the conversation. '*I daresay she is right*, but I will never say a word against Nance. So there's an end of it, Jones, and if people like to talk, well indeed, let them; 'tis no concern of mine!'

'But, 'machgen-i,' said Jones, as they drew near the other reapers, 'they'll make it your concern if they go to Oliver, the lawyer, about it.'

Gildas only stooped to his barley, but after a few strokes of his sickle he straightened himself again, and said slowly:

'I am thankful to you, my dear friend, for your kindness. I will never forget it, but don't ask any more questions; 'twill be of no use.'

'Only this one,' said Jones. 'Are you *sure* she is not at her father's house, away in Glamorgan?'

'She may be,' said Gildas. 'That is what I am thinking sometimes, but I know nothing.'

'Know nothing! Know nothing!' said Jones, losing his patience a little. 'Are you mad, man? For God's sake say something to clear this up. You are doing yourself a lot of harm; perhaps you are twisting a rope that will hang you!'

Again that hard, mirthless laugh from Gildas as he answered: 'Well indeed! Perhaps Gildas Rees, Scethryg, will hang from the gallows in the end! I wouldn't wonder!'

'Well,' said his friend, 'I always used to think you had twice my sense, Gildas; but now, in my deed, I think I have double yours.'

An unusual silence had fallen on the barley-field, where laughter and jollity generally lightened the work, and only the stroke of the 'crymans' broke the stillness, as swathe after swathe of the ripe corn fell before the reapers, for everyone's heart was filled with doubt, if not suspicion. Jones Bryndu tried in vain to dispel the gloom with a joke or a merry repartee, but in vain, and the blue cornflowers and the golden marigolds fell with the barley in solemn silence.

When at last the shadows lengthened and the long day was drawing to a close, Gildas straightened himself, and, looking towards the blue hills that lay away beyond the moor, said, 'Who is this coming down through Parc melin?' and every questioning face turned to the north, and watched while a brown stooping figure drew nearer and nearer. Now it had reached the moor, and was crossing it with bent shoulders and lagging gait.

''Tis Hezek!' cried Ben; and every eye was turned upon Gildas to see how he would take this new development in the mystery that was exercising their minds so much.

'Hezek? So it is, in my deed!' said Jones, looking also at Gildas, who stood watching the old brown figure with a white troubled face.

''Tis Hezek!' he said, as the old man turned into the harvest-field. Conscious that the reapers were all watching him, he yet forgot for a moment that he was not alone. 'Poor old man! How will I tell him?' he said half to himself, and thrusting back his hat he wiped his heated forehead with his red handkerchief. 'I'd rather than fifty pounds if I was through with the job of telling him.'

'Will I go and break the news to him?' said Jones, seeing how hard a task it was for his friend.

'No, no; I wouldn't like him to hear it first from a stranger,' answered Gildas. 'He is fond of me, poor fellow; I must tell him myself.' And throwing away his sickle he advanced towards the old man, who had now reached the middle of the field.

'Fond of him? Yes, be bound!' said Jones. 'The warmest heart that ever beat has Gildas Rees! Don't I know him since he was *this* height; however he has got into this muddle! But listen you now before he comes back, friends. Whatever has happened, he's not to blame!'

'Why doesn't he speak plain, then?' was the only answer as they bent to their sickles, and that came from Jerri.

'Here they come!' he added, as the two figures approached.

'His heart has failed him,' thought Jones. 'He could not tell the old man.' For though the latter came very slowly towards them, leaning heavily upon Gildas's arm, his face was wreathed in smiles and wore a jaunty look, as though he had just heard something pleasant, if not amusing.

'Well, well!' he said. 'Reaping begun! And how are you all? I'll bring my cryman to-morrow; but to-night I'm tired, and will go home to bed. And so Nance is away, and the harvest begun! Well, well, she'll be home to-morrow, no doubt! Oh yes, she'll be home! She'll be home to-morrow!' he said, with a laugh that ill suited his drawn face and the hectic flush of excitement that reddened his cheeks. 'And Gildas doesn't know where she is! Naughty little lass to frighten him so! But we'll go down to Maldraeth to-morrow, 'machgen-i, and we'll find her looking for shells on the beach. Yes, yes, we'll find her there.'

'Come, then,' said Gildas, 'we'll go home to the storws; n'wncwl Sam is lonely without you, and you shall go to bed after tea, for I'm sure you are tired.' And they turned away together, Hezek still leaning heavily on Gildas's arm and continuing to mutter to himself, 'Yes, yes, she'll come home to-morrow!'

When Gildas had done all he could for him, the old man fell asleep, still muttering to himself, 'She'll be home to-morrow!'

'Poor old fellow! He's badly hit!' said Jones Bryndu, when Gildas returned to the field.

'Yes,' answered Gildas, 'but I don't think he is quite understanding his trouble, though I tried to tell him carefully. It seems as if a cloud was over his mind.' ('And, indeed, 'tis the best thing that could happen to him,' he thought.)

'Come on, 'tis supper-time,' he said; and they all followed into the big Scethryg kitchen, where the red sun was making flickering patterns on the stone floor of the ivy leaves that trailed over the window. Gwenifer had laid the supper on the long bare table, and now waited to serve the tired reapers. She had been startled an hour earlier by Gildas's sudden appearance at the door.

'Gwenifer,' he said, 'the old man has come home, very tired and footsore. He won't have any supper, and I have helped him to his bed. Wilt take him a cup of tea? Perhaps thou canst persuade him to drink it. I have told him Nance has gone, but he is dazed like, and says, 'Never mind, she'll come home to-morrow.' Poor old man!'

'Hezek come back! Oh, poor old man! Yes, I'll go to him, mishteer,' she answered, while she poured out the tea already made for herself; and she hurried out to the storehouse, to find the old man stretched on his bed, the pink quilt spread over him by Gildas's careful hands. He was looking at n'wncwl Sam, who sat smoking by the hearth, repeating continually, 'Never mind, she'll be back to-morrow!' and he received Gwenifer as though he had never left the old storehouse. 'Tea, 'merch-i?' he said, as she lifted him into a sitting posture.

'Yes, and this nice bread-and-butter,' said Gwenifer; and he showed no surprise at her restored speech.

'Well indeed! I suppose it *is* tea-time, and I have had no dinner. The little lass will be home to-morrow to tea. Eh, 'merch-i?'

N'wncwl Sam, who had taken his cue from Gildas, answered for Gwenifer. 'B't shwr, b't shwr! She'll be home to-morrow!' and Gwenifer, to hide her tears, hurried out to refill the empty cup. When the men came in from the fields she scarcely dared to look at the mishteer, for well she realised how Hezek's return must have put an end to his hopes that Nance was at her father's house, and must have brought home the fact that she was lost to him for ever.

The reapers were loud in their expressions of pity for the old man, and Jones Bryndu said as he took his departure:

'Let him be to-night, Gildas; sleep will make him either clearer in his head to-morrow, or else more dazed and contented;' and so he was left to himself for the night, though once in the moonlight a slender figure crossed the moor and crept up the storehouse steps, and after a long look at the wrinkled, sleeping face, retreated noiselessly down the crooked steps and turned towards the cottage on the moor which she called home.

In the brilliant light of the full moon the sea showed blue beyond the moor, where every little blade of grass and sprig of heather held its silver drop of dew; only the roar of the

surf on Maldraeth broke the silence; and as she walked alone
over the broad stretch of moorland it was no wonder that
she fell into a deep reverie, one of the fits of musing which,
in her silent past, had taken the place of social communion
with her fellow-beings. What had become of Nance? was a
question that continually haunted her. Was it possible that
Captain Jack, who had asked her to be his wife, could have
intentionally lured her away from her home? No, she could
not believe it. Her pure mind refused to harbour such a
thought – and yet Nance had rowed away in the darkness!
And what – oh, what meant those terrible screams? And
she lay long awake that night looking at the round moon
that sailed through the dark blue sky attended by one bright
star, and they had passed across her tiny window before
sleep had at last fallen upon her. She awoke again before
many hours had gone by, and before the lark had risen from
her nest she was out with her milking-pail, for there was
Hezek to be cared for before she began her day's work. He
slept late, according to Scethryg calculation, for it was near
eight o'clock when he awoke, and sat up with a pleased smile
and a contented look on his gentle face.

'Nance is coming to-morrow!' he said as he rose and began
to dress himself; and when he had eaten his breakfast,
Gwenifer attending to his wants with extra tenderness, he
shouldered his wallet and set off as usual in search of herbs,
returning in the evening apparently quite content with his
empty bag, and the happy prospect of Nance's return 'to-
morrow.'

It was the second day of the harvest, and the labourers
were beginning to look at their watches and to dry their
foreheads, for the afternoon was waning and supper could
not be far off.

Jones Bryndu and his man had come again to help Gildas,
and had promised to come till the harvest was over, as

Bryndu crops were quite a fortnight later than Scethryg's. 'Well, well,' he said, his eyes fixed on the moor. 'Here's somebody else coming to help us; 'tisn't old Hezek again. Who can it be? There's more than one; they're running! One, two, three, four. What can they want?' And he saw, as the line of moving figures advanced, that they were headed by Nelli Amos, who seemed to have regained the agility of youth, as she outstripped the others and came down the harvest-field, her grey hair blown about by the sea wind, her eyes flashing, her finger pointing at Gildas.

'What are you doing here?' she said, while the villagers who followed her crowded round with excited faces. 'What! you gathering your harvest in, and your poor wife lying dead on Maldraeth? Come down, for shame, and tell us what are we to do with the body! Ach-y-fi! you villain! Ach-y-fi!'

'The body?' gasped Gildas. 'What do they mean, Jones? I – I – I am rather moidered, I think,' and he sat down on the hedge-side, drawing his handkerchief over his white face. 'What do they mean?'

'What do they mean?' screamed Nelli Amos. 'Come down to Maldraeth and see, man! Isn't your poor wife lying there? what the sea and the fish have left of her! Her blue gown torn to ribbons and her beautiful yellow hair spread out on the sand! Och-i, och-i! That my eye should see such a sight! Come down, man, and tell us how she got into the water, or we'll see if the crowner can make you speak.'

'Yes, I will come,' said Gildas, rising slowly and stiffly, 'I will come, b't shwr!' and he began to put on his coat with hands that trembled.

'I will come with you,' said Jones, throwing down his sickle. 'What is the meaning of this noise?' he added, turning to the excited villagers. 'Is this the way you bring such a terrible piece of news to a neighbour? Shame upon you! Is this the way you show your Diwygiad?'

For a moment they seemed abashed, but Nelli Amos soon recovered herself. 'We don't show it by consorting with men who get rid of their wives in the night, and then say they don't know where they are!' she said.

'Come,' said Gildas, recovering his firmness. 'Come on and let them talk. Poor Nance, poor Nance!' and drawing his hat over his eyes, he began his way towards the rocks, going down to the creek and rowing across the tide to the village, where, on the beach, they saw a group of people awaiting them. Jones Bryndu was a man much respected amongst them, so that when they saw he was Gildas's companion, they received them with a more sympathetic manner than they were prepared to accord to Gildas alone.

'This is a shocking thing,' he said as he stepped ashore, 'and I am sure you will all sympathise with an old friend and neighbour in his trouble!'

There was a slight murmur of condolence from some of the group, as Gildas leaped out of the boat, but the greater number drew back as if afraid of committing themselves.

''Tis a dreadful thing, indeed,' said one, 'and we want to know how it happened. A young and happy wife (or ought to be happy) to be lost all at once, and then to be found a month after on the sands, drowned and sodden! Dear anwl! Such a thing has never happened at Tregildas before. Well, *we* have done what we could; we have sent for the crowner, and Ebben the carpenter has offered the coffin which he had ready for Jane Lewis's daughter; and we'd better take his offer, I'm thinking, for the mestress is lying on Maldraeth, poor thing, and we want to know where to take her.' And they crowned round Gildas with curious eyes, in which there was no spark of sympathy.

'Yes, that will be best,' said Jones. 'Go you home to Scethryg, 'machgen-i. I will see to all for you.'

Gildas thankfully took his advice, and in less than an

hour all that remained of the storm-tossed body was borne to Scethryg and laid in the big barn, for, as there was only one living-room in the farmhouse, and the stairs were narrow and crooked Jones Bryndu had decided, for sanitary reasons also, that this was the best arrangement.

It would be useless to try to describe Gildas Rees's feelings as he sat on his darkened hearth. The dread of shame and disgrace he was getting accustomed to, as it had hovered over him, waking or sleeping, for weeks; it was now giving place to pity and sorrow for Nance's sad fate, and to indignation against the neighbours who could suspect him of having compassed the death of his wife.

He was quite alone, not even Gwenifer hovered about, for, fearing to intrude upon his hours of mourning, she withdrew as much as possible to the solitude of her own cottage, where alone and undisturbed she thought over the strange events that had come into her once placid life.

Meanwhile at Scethryg the next day had dawned, a day which Gildas never recalled without a shudder.

The inquest was to be held at ten o'clock, the funeral as soon after as practicable, presumably before sunset. Soon after breakfast he saw that the farmyard was filling with a sombre throng, gathered together from the remotest parts of the parish, for the tale of Nance's disappearance and the suspicions of foul play connected with it had spread far and wide.

That hour was one of extreme bitterness to the proud, reserved man, who sat on the hearth in his best clothes, looking gloomily into the burning logs.

In his loneliness he longed for Gwenifer's soothing presence, but remembered with a groan that her heart, too, had gone forth to the sailor, and a longing for vengeance burnt up red-hot within him. He was roused by a knock at the door, which Het, dressed in the blackest of black clothes and with a suitable expression of countenance, opened to admit Mr. Bowen, the coroner, who, with his clerk, had driven noiselessly over the stubble yard. Gildas started to his feet as he entered, and the coroner shook hands with him in his usual friendly manner.

'I suppose the jury have not come yet – I am rather early,' he said, sitting down on the settle opposite Gildas. 'This is a sad thing, Rees,' he said, sympathetic but guarded.

They were interrupted by the arrival of the jury, who, in fact, had been waiting an eager half-hour in the lane.

The coroner looked at his watch. 'Ten o'clock; we had better adjourn to the barn. You will have to identify the body,' he said – 'a trying ordeal, of course, but necessary.' And, leading the way, he was followed by Gildas and the jurymen.

In the old dim barn, resting on its trestles, stood the long yellow box, so strange, yet so familiar, to us all. On the closed lid lay a wreath of harebells; and, with a pang, Gildas remembered they had been Nance's favourite flowers, and how often in the days of his wooing he had told her that their colour was that of her own eyes. Gwenifer, surely, must have placed them where they were!

On the further side the big barn door was closed and bolted, but it seemed as if the sunshine wished to enter and gild that sombre scene, for through the finger-hole a blue shaft of light poured in, shedding a golden radiance over the coffin and sparkling on its metal ornaments.

There was a little shuffling of feet as the lid was removed, and the gruesome wreck of humanity within was disclosed. One by one the jurymen approached and cast one glance upon the body; and, when his turn came, Gildas too drew near with a firm step and a face over which he had drawn that cold, impenetrable mask which so often hid his deepest feelings.

And when at last the whole gathering returned to the big

kitchen, and the coffin lid was screwed down upon all that had been saved from the sea, Gildas returned with the others, thankful that hitherto at least he had been able to endure in silence.

CHAPTER XVI

The Inquest

When Gildas found his old familiar kitchen filled with strange faces – the coroner sitting at the long table, his clerk beside him – he made his way to the hearth like a man in a dream. Everything seemed unreal to him, and, strange to say, it affected him little more than a dream would have done. He saw the blue business papers on the table, and heard the coroner's opening remarks without realising their import, so busy was his mind with the problem of how to speak the truth, and yet conceal Nance's folly. A tender pity for her filled his heart, but not even this could rekindle the love which had turned to ashes. He saw that his own name had already been hopelessly blackened, but he was doggedly determined that no word of his should smirch Nance's reputation. 'Poor Nance!' He repeated the words over and over again to himself.

'You have seen the body lying in your barn. Do you identify it as that of your wife, Anne Rees?' asked the coroner.

Gildas looked at him as if dazed. 'Yes, sir; but the face . . .'

'The face, of course, is injured beyond recognition. Have you therefore any doubt?'

'Oh no, no doubt; it is poor Nance. I recognised her hair and her gown. Oh yes, 'tis her, poor thing.'

'Have you any idea how she got into the water?'

'No, indeed I have not,' said Gildas firmly, beginning to awake to his surroundings.

'Now on Monday, August 14th, the day she disappeared, where did you see her last?'

'On Maldraeth shore, about ten o'clock at night.'

'Rather a late hour to be on the shore. Did you go down together?'

'No; I followed her.'

'Had you had any misunderstanding with your wife that day?'

'Not more than usual.'

'Did you object to the interest she took in the revival?'

'No, sir, not that exactly; but I wasn't willing for her to go so often to the meetings.'

'And did that cause a little friction – a little disagreement between you?'

'Yes.'

'Did this seem to depress or grieve her?'

'No, she was very high-spirited.'

'Had you any idea that she might put an end to her life?'

'No indeed.'

'What made you follow her down to Maldraeth?'

'Because it was so late.'

'Was there anything that might take her down so late?'

'Well, we had a lobster pot down there. If it had been moonlight, she might be going to look at it.'

'But it was a dark night. The moon did not rise till late?'

'No.'

'And when you reached her, what passed between you?'

'I asked her to come home. I said it was too late for her to be on the shore.'

'And what was her answer?'

'She bade me go home myself. She said I had no business to follow her, and she would stay as long as she liked.'

'In fact, you had a quarrel about it?'

To this Gildas made no reply, so overpowered was he by memory of that night; and the coroner pressed the question.

'Did you and your wife quarrel on the shore?'

'We had a few words. She was very excited.'

'And you were quite calm.'

'No, I was not.'

'Was she standing on the sand, or on the rocks?'

'On the rocks, close to the water.'

'And did you touch her? Did you lay your hand upon her at all?'

'Not to hurt her. Good God, man! do you think I would hurt my wife?'

'Never mind what I think, but answer me. Did you struggle with your wife?'

'I tried to draw her away with me, but she would not come.'

'And then what happened?'

'I changed my mind and left her suddenly, and I went home alone.'

'Now, might she not have slipped into the water during that struggle, or when you suddenly loosed your hold of her?'

'She might perhaps, but she didn't,' said Gildas, beginning to lose patience. 'I saw her still standing there when I was going up the cliff path.'

'On such a dark night?'

'Yes, 'twas not too dark to see her figure.'

'And do you think she threw herself into the water?'

'I know nothing about that.'

'Have you ever seen your wife alive since that night?'

'No.'

Here there was a movement of surprise and disapproval.

'All this month you have missed her and made no attempts to find her?'

To this again Gildas made no answer, and one or two of the jurymen shook their heads solemnly.

The coroner pressed the question, but failing to get any further information from Gildas, he was asked to stand aside while Ben was examined. His evidence, though meant to exonerate the mishteer from all blame, did his cause much harm, for it went far to prove that Nance had of late been an exasperating member of the family, and to have got rid her would have been a distinct gain to Gildas.

He withdrew well satisfied, however, feeling, that he had proved to everybody that Gildas Rees had been the best husband in the parish.

Het was the next witness, and very communicative. She had seen the mestress crying sometimes, and she and the mishteer did not live happily together of late. 'Caton pawb, no! it was easy enough to see that.' She had seen the mishteer go down to Maldraeth on the night when mestress was last seen. She and Nelli Amos had wondered what he wanted there so late, and had waited to see him come back. She would take her Bible oath that he had come back alone.

When asked if her master had shown any distress at his wife's disappearance, she said he looked black and sulky enough; 'but I didn't see any signs of sorrow in him, not I.'

This and much more was easily extracted from Het.

After Het, Nelli Amos was called; her evidence being much the same as Het's, except that towards the end of her deposition she drew from her pocket a small gold brooch, which she said she had picked up under the seaweed near to where the body of the drowned woman had been found. Gildas, recalled, identified the brooch as one he had given to Nance some weeks earlier. The sight of it seemed to affect him strongly, for it recalled to him vividly the evening when he had brought it home from the fair, when Nance had received it so coldly. He realised with bitterness of spirit that she had worn it on the night of her disappearance, not to adorn herself for his eyes, but for the sailor's.

'Then that settles the identity,' said the coroner.

'Yes, yes,' said Gildas, sitting down wearily on the settle.

Hitherto, all the evidence pointed to the fact that Gildas Rees and his wife had latterly lived at variance with each other, that she had disappeared suddenly, and that her husband had neither made any attempt to find her nor had he shown any grief at her absence; and there was little doubt that the jury had been impressed unfavourably towards Gildas.

One corner of the spacious Scethryg kitchen, well hidden by the settle, was given up to the storage of firing; not only logs for the hearth stood there, but also piles of brushwood and dried bracken, golden and brown from the side of the hill. On the day of the inquest, Gwenifer had hidden behind this pile of bracken listening with bated breath to the evidence, which seemed to point to Gildas with incriminating finger.

Oh! when would they call her? and how dared she appear before so many people? and how could she clear Gildas without exposing Nance? For she felt she would die rather than do this, as long as it was evidently Gildas's desire to shield her memory from blame.

Suddenly she heard her name called, and she emerged from behind the screen of bracken and took her place at the table.

Every eye was turned upon her; for the dumb girl, whose speech had been so miraculously restored, was an object of interest to the whole countryside.

The coroner settled his gold glasses on his nose, the clerk looked up from his papers, and the policeman from Caermadoc edged a little nearer; while Gwenifer, gathering courage, answered the preliminary questions quietly and calmly, the coroner's inquiries being put in a more gentle tone than those addressed to Gildas. There was a slight hesitancy in her speech, due to her long disuse of her vocal organs; but it was in no wise unpleasant – on the contrary, it had a quaint and piquant effect.

'You are, I believe – a – you helped Mrs. Rees in her work?'asked the coroner.

'Yes, sir. I am the Scethryg dairymaid.'

'Do you remember the 14th of August, the day on which Mrs. Rees disappeared?'

'Yes, quite well; because it was my birthday.'

'You have lived always at Scethryg, I think. Did you ever see or hear anything wrong in Gildas Rees's conduct towards his wife?'

'No, never.'

'Nor in hers towards him?'

'She was rather excitable of late.'

'Did they quarrel sometimes?'

'No, not quarrel exactly; they disagreed a little sometimes.'

'Did you ever see any reason to think she might put an end to her life?'

For a moment Gwenifer hesitated, then, looking up, answered firmly: 'No; but since the revival she was rather strange.'

'In what way?'

'Singing very loud and neglecting her work.'

'Neglecting her home and her husband?'

Here Gwenifer's head bent low; she was silent, and the tears gathered in her eyes.

'She was my friend,' she said at last.

'Now, on the 14th you saw her frequently during the day. Did she appear depressed or different from her usual manner?'

'Yes; rather excited.'

'Now tell us how you saw her last.'

'I saw her in the house after tea; then, when my work was finished, I went down to Maldraeth.'

'But it was dark. What did you want there so late?'

'I often go there at night – the sea is beautiful at night.'

'Well?'

'Then I heard a step crossing the shingle, and I saw it was Nance.'

At the words Gildas turned a startled look upon Gwenifer, and listened in silent surprise while she continued: 'I knew her by her walk.'

'Did she see you?'

'No; I was hidden by the rocks. I was just going to speak to her, when I heard another footstep on the shingle, and I saw it was the mishteer.'

A little movement of sensation followed this remark.

'And what then?'

'Then he went up to her and begged her to come home; but she would not listen.'

'Did he speak harshly or kindly?'

'Very kindly.'

'Did he lay hands upon her, or was there a struggle between them?'

'He took hold of her hands, and then her shoulders, and tried to turn her towards him; but she was angry, and would not listen – she shook herself free, and suddenly he let her go, and he turned away.'

'Now, did she fall into the water?'

'No: she stood still and looked after him as he went.'

'And what then?'

'Then I went and tried to persuade her to go home; but she was very angry, and pushed me aside violently. I fell and knocked my head on the rocks, and for a moment I didn't know anything.'

'For how long, do you think?'

'I don't know – not for long.'

'And when you came to yourself, where was Mrs. Rees?'

'She was nowhere to be seen.'

'Might she have thrown herself into the sea?'

'No, I don't think so,' said Gwenifer – 'but oh! whatever she did she didn't know what she was doing.' And quite overcome by her memories of that fateful night, she stopped and covered her eyes with her hands.

'Now listen, Gwenifer Owen,' said the coroner. 'Do you really mean you consider that 'the mestress,' as you call her, was not accountable for her actions? I mean, was her mind a little unhinged – was she 'not wise', as they say?'

For a moment Gwenifer fixed her eyes upon Gildas as she answered slowly:

'That is what I am thinking, whatever. I am thinking that her head had been a little wrong for some time.'

Here a movement of surprise and interest swept over the meeting, Gildas himself rising from his seat and fixing a glance of keen inquiry upon the girl. Gwenifer threw her head back and said firmly:

'That's what I'm thinking, and that's what I'm *sure*, whatever, that Nance did not know what she was doing, and that God will not call her to account for anything she did that night or for a long time before.'

The coroner looked up with fresh interest.

'And what do you think had caused her derangement – what had touched her brain?' he said, putting it more simply.

Again Gwenifer seemed to take counsel with her own heart before she answered.

'I think the Diwygiad touched her heart so deep her mind was not strong enough to bear it.'

This threw a different aspect upon the case. To Gildas it brought a sense of relief and gratitude, for the words which were beginning to throw a gleam of light upon Nance's strange ways. Her faults, her weaknesses – yes, her sins! – in this new light he could bear to think upon with tender pity; but by the jury the evidence was heard with different feelings.

There were few present who had not come into touch in some degree with the strong wave of spiritual awakening which was passing over the country, and there were few therefore who could not understand its possible effect upon a weak and excitable mind. To them the evidence seemed plain and reasonable; but to those who had touched only the froth and foam of the wave, joining in the frenzied prayers and cries of shallow excitement, the suggestion that 'the mestress' had been injured by her interest in the revival seemed like irreverence and blasphemy; but even they were impressed by the air of truthfulness with which Gwenifer gave her evidence.

Further questioning elicited the fact that she had made her way up to Scethryg when sufficiently recovered from her momentary unconsciousness, that upon approaching the doorway Gildas had appeared at it stretching out both hands and calling out 'Nance!' and that he had seemed much disappointed at seeing Gwenifer.

'Did you ask him what had become of his wife?'

'No, sir.'

'Why not?'

'I did not like to make him ashamed.'

'And what then?'

'He told me to go home and go to bed, and I went.'

'And neither you nor your master made any endeavours to find your mistress?'

'No, I didn't, whatever, because the mishteer had told me to go to bed; but I couldn't sleep, so I rose and looked out through the window several times before dawn.'

'And what did you see?'

'I saw Gildas walking up and down on the cliffs, and looking behind every bush and over the sea; he went down to Maldraeth twice, and he was calling 'Nance, Nance!' many times.'

'And did you go out to him?'

'Yes, but not until the sun was rising.'

'Did he tell you what he was looking for?'

'Oh yes, and I was thinking 'twas very sore his heart was. Many times since then I have sought for Nance on the cliffs and called to her on the shore, hoping she would come back, but she never came. And now I see why.'

With Gwenifer's depositions the inquest ended, and no one was surprised when the jury exonerated Gildas from all blame.

Nelli Amos alone was disappointed, for she had fully hoped that Gildas would not have passed through the ordeal of the inquest without danger to his liberty, if not his life.

It was late in the afternoon when the funeral at last started on its way to the little churchyard high up on the bleak hillside, where the countless grassy mounds and weather-stained headstones showed that, however strong had been the prejudice of the parishioners against the church during their lives, yet they loved to bring their dead to rest under the shadow of the ancient walls.

The mystery surrounding Nance's death had attracted one of the largest gatherings that had ever been seen in the parish, and among the women there was scarcely a dry eye when the Brynzion choir commenced the solemn hymn commonly sung at Welsh funerals.

As the coffin was raised high on the shoulders of the bearers it was visible to all the crowd. Every voice joined in the wailing melody, and as the procession wound its way up the rugged mountain road the mournful strains fell on the ear, and reached the heart, with unspeakable sadness.

Gildas, walking behind the coffin with old Hezek beside him, felt every rise and fall of the music; but his face showed no sign of emotion, and many a furtive glance of disapproval was cast upon him as he passed on his way.

'So high-headed, so hard!' they whispered to each other. 'What will bring his head down if this won't?'

Quite unconscious of their comments, Gildas found it all he could do to withstand the heart-searching strains of the music, and to bear unflinchingly the memory of the day when he had led Nance home from the little church, along the mountain road which they two were traversing now, with such a world of separation between them. But though the tones of that swaying hymn awoke sad memories and regrets, they brought with them no remorse.

'No, thank God!' was Gildas's secret thought. 'This dark day is none of my bringing.'

Hezek's was the only happy face in the procession.

Gwenifer had great difficulty in persuading him to leave his wallet at home. 'This is Nance's funeral day,' she had said, endeavouring to make him understand in some degree the solemnity of the occasion; but he had only smiled and said, 'Twt, twt, no! Nance will be home to-morrow;' so she had led him to Gildas's side with due injunctions that he was not to stray from him until they had returned safely to Scethryg. Nevertheless, he had scandalised the assembly as they drew near the churchyard by making a sudden swerve and gathering a flower which struck him as something uncommon. However, finding he was mistaken, he returned to his place with a penitent look.

There had been a change in the weather the night before, and, as they entered the churchyard, a sparkling shower fell upon them, though the sun was still shining; and as the solemn service proceeded, and the coffin was lowered into the grave, the raindrops fell upon it like a glittering shower of golden beads, while a robin perched on a neighbouring headstone sang so blithely that many a tearful eye turned towards it. Gwenifer even smiled through her tears upon the little feathered songster, who seemed to have come there to remind that sorrowful company that there was still love and light beyond the gloom of the present. Even into Gildas's sadness that sweet song had penetrated, and he turned away from Nance's grave with its echo in his ears and its gentle solace in his heart.

There were not wanting some in that mournful company whom pity had softened a little, and who would have wished to express their sympathy with the man whom they had suspected and condemned; perhaps even they had heard that tender bird-song and been unconsciously moved by it, for nothing is too small or insignificant to bear the messages of the Most High. Gildas, however, gave no one the opportunity of speaking to him, for, on returning to Scethryg, he passed straight into the house, and through the dairy door made his way to the moor, where the evening sun was gilding the raindrops on furze and heather, where the passing shower had freshened up the dry grass, and where the pearly grey sky opened out in the west to the shine of the sunset, and the broad illimitable sea seemed to speak of the peace and rest which his sore-stricken spirit longed for. Bitterly wounded by the events of the day, he was indignantly hurt by his neighbours' attitude towards him, and his proud spirit rebelled against the idea of receiving their condolence or sympathy.

CHAPTER XVII

Inside the Red Gate

The harvest all over the coast hills that year had been one of unusual fulness and beauty – of almost unbroken sunshine all day, and brilliant moonlight at night, the latter being no small factor in the ripening of crops, according to the farmers; at all events, it had added much to the beauty of the season. It was past now – the heavy crops of golden grain, the song and shout of the harvesters, the swish of the scythes, and the clash of the 'crymans' – and the soft grey days of St Michael's summer had come.

Gildas Rees had good reason to be grateful to Jones Bryndu, for he had given him daily and unceasing help until the Scethryg crops were safely garnered; while Betsy Jones had made him feel, without a word spoken, but by her kindly grip of his hand, that he had her confidence as completely as he had her husband's. One thing had grievously upset her – why had she not been called at the inquest?

'In my deed, Will,' she said, 'I could have made everything plain to the coroner in two minutes. I could have told him what I know, and then he would have seen that Gildas Rees, instead of being a wicked man, is the most long-suffering, and the kindest, and the bravest.'

'Stop, stop! Where do I come in?' laughed her husband.

'Of course, in the right place, at the top! But why wasn't I called?'

'Nonsense, 'merch-i! What facts hadst thou to mention?'

'Facts!' said Betsy Jones, with supreme contempt. 'Facts! What does a woman want with facts when she knows? Tell me that, Will! Don't I *know* that Nance Rees was fond of Captain Jack? Well, there, then! 'Tis plain enough why Gildas Rees got to look so dark and sad. And don't I know, as well as if she had told me so, that she sailed away in the *Liliwen* with him that night on Maldraeth, when Gildas tried to persuade her to go home with him? Yes, yes, I know it all! And then Captain Jack got tired of her and cross to her, and at the first port she ran away again, and roamed back to Tregildas cliffs, and then she fell from there in the dark, or perhaps, indeed, she threw herself over. Why, you men must be blind as moles not to see it yourselves! And if you had only let me speak at the 'quest I would have settled it all in a moment, and there would have been no need of a 'quest at all.'

'Well, too late now, 'merch-i! Come to supper,' and Jones Bryndu sat down to the table thoughtfully, pondering over Betsy's suggestions, for, in spite of her disregard for facts, he had often found that his wife's mind reached a correct conclusion with a sort of kangaroo leap, while he waded slowly to the same point, to find her standing triumphantly on the rock of verified intuition, with a patronising 'didn't I tell you?' to greet him with.

At the same time Gildas was at work in one of his fields. Spade in hand, he dug and delved, and mended the gap that the brindled cow had made in the hedge, in one of her mischievous raids upon the clover in the next field. The passing weeks seemed to have brought some measure of peace and rest into his life; his face had regained much of the colour and spirit that before the trouble of his unhappy marriage had made it so pleasant to look upon, in spite of its rugged features; the sparkle in his eye returned sometimes, when Juno forgot her dignity in a sudden excitement over a rabbit or a rat, or when Hezek told some marvellous tale of mysterious adventures in his mountain rambles.

He could not shake himself free from the conviction that not only Nance had been contaminated by Captain Jack's company, but that Gwenifer too had given her heart to the roving sailor. Was it possible, he asked himself sometimes as he watched her cross the moor or stoop to her pail, that that sweet face could blush and that pure heart could beat faster for one so unworthy? and his own heart answered yes, for he knew from his own experience that Love could hide the blackest sins, until one day Time and Truth joined hands and tore away the clinging folds, and the idol was seen in its true colours.

For the time he forgot his bitter memories of Nance, his wounded pride, his indignant resentment at his friends and neighbours' treatment of him; for the murmur of the sea was in his ears, the smell of the fresh earth was in his nostrils, the sense of all-conquering work nerved his arm, and almost Gildas Rees was the strong, the energetic, the hardy farmer of old.

The peaceful calm of the autumn days flowed in upon his spirits, and stooping, he picked up a tiny blue flower of which he had seen a bunch at Gwenifer's neck the day before. He added another and another; perhaps she would like a posy! and he looked with a smile at the tiny nosegay. But a sudden change came over his face – his lips took a hard curve, his black eyes flashed, and with a scornful gesture he flung the flowers over the hedge, and went on with his work, digging hard and fiercely into the forget-me-nots, and turning them ruthlessly face downwards on the broken gap.

While he turned up the soil, he fell to thinking of a project which had been no stranger to his mind of late. He would

let Scethryg, he would leave the land of his forefathers where
he had been so badly treated. It would be better for him to
spend his energies in some other country, where he could
forget the past, his old home, and his unhappy marriage.
Gwenifer would look after his interests for him; in time she
would regain her peace of mind, would forget the unworthy
sailor, for surely she would not marry the man who had
brought so much misery to Scethryg.

Raising his eyes over the edge of the bank between the
wind-worn grasses, he saw the silvery grey of the sea, and
as he stood a moment to rest, and gaze upon it, round the
horn of the bay there came into sight a fair ship, ploughing
the waters bravely and flinging the white spray from her
prow like showers of snow. Gildas needed not to ask what
name was written on her stern – for well he recognised that
streaming pennon of red which fluttered at her masthead.
An indescribable change came over the face of the man who
watched those graceful lines, those swelling sails. His eyes
positively flashed with anger, his hands closed on his spade
handle with a fierce clutch, and, turning his back upon the
bay, he began to dig again with an energy which gradually
seemed to relieve his feelings, and enable him to subdue and
control his passion; so that when at noon he returned to
Scethryg, and found the dinner laid, Ben and n'wncwl Sam
and Hezek already sitting on the bench drawn up to the
table, while Gwenifer moved about between them and the
hearth, he was able to sit down calmly to his meal, although
in his lowered eyes and in his heart burnt a fire of fierce
resentment.

'What'st think!' said n'wncwl Sam, with the first sups of
his cawl. 'What'st think! the *Liliwen* is in the bay. In my deed
I'm glad. We'll be hearing some of the cap'n's stories of
foreign parts again.'

Gildas made no answer, but, looking towards Gwenifer,

saw a crimson tide of colour rise suddenly into her face, and as quickly recede, leaving her features blanched and pinched. What was this storm of feeling? What should disturb her placid countenance? What meant those drooping eyes and white lips, if not love? His food seemed to choke him, a hot unreasoning anger rose within him, and he scarcely heard n'wncwl Sam's platitudes and Hezek's conjectures, but finished his meal in silence, brooding over a crowd of suspicions and an eager desire for revenge; while Gwenifer, instinctively conscious that he had seen her sudden blush, fumbled awkwardly with the bowls and platters. But Gildas saw no more, for he had quickly finished his meal and was already striding across the field to the damaged gap, where he attacked the clods once more with renewed energy.

'We'll have to hang a plock round Seren's neck,' cried Ben, who passed on his way to his own work. 'There's no hedge will stand against her, and Corwen and Folant are beginning to learn her bad tricks,' and he whistled as he went, leaving his master to his work and his angry thoughts.

The day wore on, the afternoon light was fading, for a bank of heavy cloud was rising seawards; the crows and seagulls returned from their inland expeditions to the shelter of the cliffs, the young geese in the stubble fields clacked and cried as they flew over the hedges, feeling the strength of their growing wings; but Gildas dug on unconscious of them all, until wearied with his exertions he stood up and stretched himself. Flower, the brown mare, was grazing in the foreground. Beyond, the field sloped up to the moor. The whole landscape had grown grey and sombre, the red gate in the opposite hedge being the only bit of colour in the scene, and on this Gildas's eyes rested vacantly.

Suddenly the pupils dilated, his face, his figure, became rigid with interest, as the red gate slowly opened and a familiar figure entered the field – a man above the middle

height, supple and strong-looking, though of slimmer proportions than Gildas; he walked with a free swinging step,
the step of the sailor ashore, and Gildas recognised his enemy
Captain Jack. There was no indecision in his gait, but he
walked like a man who had something to say to the other,
who awaited him with a fierce look of anger in his eyes, the
muscles of his hand upon his spade quivering. 'That devil,'
were his thoughts, 'on my land, in my field! How dare he?'
But Captain Jack evidently dared with intention, and
advanced steadily; he had already reached Flower, who
raised her head to look at him, when Gildas called 'Halt! No
nearer!' but still the sailor walked on unheeding.

'Back, man,' shouted Gildas, advancing a step or two in a
threatening attitude, 'or I swear I will dash your brains out.'
All the savage instincts of the primitive man awoke within
him; his reason and conscience seemed to swoon under the
strength of his wrath, and Gildas Rees for a moment was a
dangerous foe, conscious only of an eager desire for revenge.

'Strike, if you like,' said Captain Jack. 'I am ready; but I will
not strike in return.'

'Coward! Hound!' cried Gildas, whose blood seemed
boiling in his veins; his voice was hoarse with passion, his
white lips parched, and as the sailor moved still a step
towards him, blinded with fury he brought his ponderous
spade down with a crash. Unconsciously he had allowed for
a shrinking aside on the sailor's part, and, answering to his
instinctive impulse, the spade had fallen a little to the left,
striking the man's arm only, and leaving him still standing
erect and firm.

A moment's silence fell on the two men, who looked at
each other with a stern, unflinching gaze, while through the
soft evening air there came the sound of peaceful rustic life;
Flower's grazing, crisp and regular, the whirr of a covey of
partridges, the tinkle of a sheep-bell, the neighing of a horse

– they heard them all, and mingled with them, and distinct from all, the sound of a girlish voice came down from the moor, a voice that called the cows to the quiet milking, 'Corwen and Cochen and Seren, Trwdy, fach! come home, come home;' and the clear tones seemed to fall like a spell on the two men.

All this passed in a moment, but in that moment Gildas had realised what he had done and what he had failed to do. A hot flood of shame suffused his face. 'A murderer!' and the soft, clear voice that came down the mountain-side seemed to call to him 'Shame, Gildas; for shame!'. With a strong swing of his arm he flung the spade away from him, and drew his hand over his dark face. 'Now,' he said, advancing close the sailor, 'we are equal; defend yourself;' but Captain Jack stood immovable.

'You may strike if you like, Gildas Rees,' he said again, 'but I tell you I will never strike you in return.'

'Not strike! Coward, you must!' said Gildas, exasperated beyond measure at the other's calmness, and with furious passion he struck at his foe; but the sailor, supple and strong and lithe of action, grasped his arms in the act of striking, and, holding them as in a vice, looked steadily into the fiery gleam of his antagonist's eyes.

Baulked of his immediate revenge, Gildas stood astounded and overpowered by the sailor's unshaken demeanour, so different from his own mad passion; his arm fell nerveless at his side, and in the moment's silence that ensued he seemed to awake from a fit of frenzy, and though he still trembled with anger he became calmer and more reasonable.

'And what of Nance?' he asked hoarsely, and he pointed to the side of the hill, where the whitewashed walls of the little church showed clear against the grey sky. 'Carried up from the sea to that lonely churchyard, her heart broken, her name blackened, and all through you – villain! How dare you stand before me? Take your cursed blue eyes off me; keep their uncanny looks to draw some poor weak woman from her home again, but don't try them on me.'

'Gildas Rees, my eyes are as the Almighty made them; but in my deed I am glad if they have power to make you listen to me, for I tell you, man, you may strike me, you may kill me, but you will be killing an innocent man. Listen, then, for I think what I have to say may be of some comfort to you.'

'Comfort! *You* to speak to me of comfort? Didn't you get my letter that I sent after you to Cardiff?'

'Letter? No,' said the sailor, 'I have had no letter from you; no doubt 'tis waiting for me.' He raised his left hand, and for the first time Gildas saw that blood was dropping slowly from the sleeve of the other. 'As God is my witness,' he said, 'I knew nothing of your wife's sad death until I rowed in from the *Liliwen* to-day. I sailed into the bay this morning, and my eyes turned at once to Scethryg and the moor. I hoped to find you all at peace and happy as you were when I first met you.'

An exclamation from Gildas interrupted him, but he held up his hand and went on. 'I sculled into Maldraeth and climbed that sheep-path up the hill, and over the hill to Gwenifer's cottage. You know, for I have told you, why I went there; I found her in her garden, but she charged me with having lured your wife away from you, with having turned her adrift, with having compassed her death by some foul means, and for the first time, Gildas, I heard of her sad end. It was long before I could persuade Gwenifer to listen to me, but she did at last. She believes me, and so must you, when I tell you what happened on that black night. She agreed with me, too – and that is what I think will comfort you – that your wife was not right in her head, Gildas; for a long time I am sure her mind had been unhinged, Gildas, she was 'not wise,' as we say, and so was not accountable for her actions.'

He stopped a moment as if considering.

'Go on,' said Gildas sternly. 'You are forgetting your sailor tongue; but I think I understand you' – for in his excitement the sailor had dropped his sea brogue, and was speaking in the refined tones that were more familiar to him.

Near them stood one of the many grey boulders that strewed the upland fields, and sitting down upon it, Captain Jack continued.

'When first I went to Scethryg I saw Nance Ellis in the old storws before you were married. She was a bonny lass and full of fun and life; we had some jokes and laughter together, a little flirting, a little nonsense, but nothing more, I swear to you, Gildas Rees. I cared no more for Nance Ellis than I did for Het or Jenni the seamstress, and when I heard she was going to marry you I was glad, because that would leave me free of her. At Scethryg, after you were married, I got to like her better, as a friend; and though I am willing to confess now that I was too free and foolish in my talk and jokes with her, 'twas only to hide my liking for Gwenifer, and an excuse for going often to Scethryg; and I was surprised and shocked one day when I saw that Nance was fond of me, and not ashamed to show it. Then, Gildas, I tried to draw back, to show her how wrong, how foolish, she was; but very gently, because, though I am but a rough sailor, my heart is very tender with women, and I could not be harsh with her, when I felt I had been so much to blame myself. I am afraid my love for Gwenifer made me selfish, and I scarcely noticed nor cared that Nance was getting more wild and excited, less anxious to hide her fancy for me.'

He stopped again, for he wished to hide Nance's folly as much as possible from her husband. ''Twas the night after the revival meeting when I sailed away from Tregildas. Gwenifer would have nothing to do with me; and that night I saw plainly the best thing, and the right thing for me to do, was to keep away from Scethryg. And out on the bay, in the dark and silence, many things became clear to me, many things that had pressed on my heart in the Diwygiad meeting, and seemed too sharp and strong for me to bear. Well! the next night we were sailing. I had seen Gwenifer and begged of her if she ever changed her mind to send word to me or let me know; and I was leaning over the rails, and thinking of this. The mate had gone into Tregildas to settle up for me with his old aunt, and the cabin boy was spending his last hours with his mother, so I was alone. Well, my thoughts were full of Gwenifer, when I heard the sound of a boat coming out from Maldraeth. I wondered why the mate didn't row out from Tregildas, and then a strange thought came into my mind – could it be Gwenifer? Had she changed her mind? (Have patience!) The boat came nearer, and I saw a woman in it, and I was fool enough to believe it was Gwenifer. I called out, but there was no answer; I threw down the ship's ladder, and she climbed up. I helped her on deck, and than I saw it was Nance, and my heart sank like a stone – it was very dark, but I had lighted a lantern, and then . . .'

'And then?' echoed Gildas, with intense eagerness, for as he had listened to the captain's story an instinctive belief in its truth had taken possession of him.

'And then – how can I tell you, Gildas Rees? Isn't it enough to tell you that your poor wife did not know what she was saying – I saw I had better tell her the truth, that I loved Gwenifer, that it was her I had always sought for at Scethryg, and that I had no other love in my heart. Gildas, she was quite mad, she screamed terribly, and fell to the ground in a kind of fit, and before she came to herself I had lifted her into the boat and rowed her back to Maldraeth; she was quite calm then, only rather bewildered. I pointed to the path, and bade her make haste home to her husband, and I watched while she went up and up; and at last, when I lost sight of her over the edge of the cliffs, I had no doubt she would go back to Scethryg and no one would know of her folly. I rowed back to the *Liliwen*, and with the first streak of dawn we sailed away, and to-day for the first time I heard of your dreadful trouble. Poor thing! Poor thing! Forgive her, Gildas, for no doubt the tremendous truths that the Revival pressed in upon her conscience were too strong for her, and unhinged her mind. Forgive *me*, Gildas, for my folly and my nonsense.'

'Has Gwenifer forgiven you?' said Gildas, with parched lips, though his passion was dying out.

'Yes, she has forgiven me; but she will not have me. How can I expect her? And when next I sail away you will never see the *Liliwen* in the bay again.'

'And will you forgive yourself?' said Gildas sternly. 'Out there on the bay, man, will it be as nothing to you that your foolish jokes and nonsense have led a woman to such a fate?'

'No,' answered Captain Jack, 'the wind may blow, the waves may race, the ship may sail, but I can never leave behind me the memories of Scethryg. Rest satisfied, Gildas, if it will be any comfort to you to know, that I am a miserable man.'

''Twill be no comfort to me,' said Gildas, 'but it is as it ought to be, I think. I am not wishing you ill, Cap'n Jack, and I believe now that if poor Nance's mind had been all right her heart would have been truer to me, so good-bye to you.'

'Will you shake hands with me before we part?' said Captain Jack.

'Shake hands with you? No,' said Gildas. 'Do you think, man, such wounds as mine can be healed and mended by a little talk like this? Will it bring cheer and brightness back to my hearth? Will it restore to old Hezek his little lass that he loved so much? No, you may be telling the truth – I think you are, and you are less to blame in this matter than I thought you were; but I cannot shake hands with you, and I wish only never to see you again.'

'I am going,' said Captain Jack, and as he moved Gildas saw a little pool of blood had dropped from his sleeve.

'I have wounded you sore, I'm afraid; 'tis of God's mercy that my spade swerved, and I am not a murderer.'

'Twt, twt, that is nothing,' said Captain Jack. 'The mate has a wonderful salve for a cut. I will go back to the *Liliwen*, if I may take Ben from that field to scull for me?'

Gildas nodded.

'And when I sail away in a few days, you will never see me more in Tregildas bay, and that is why I wanted to shake hands with you. But if you won't – well, good-bye! I would have done much to be friends with you, Gildas Rees, but it is not to be, it seems, so good-bye.'

'Good-bye,' said Gildas, and Captain Jack walked away towards the field where Ben was at work, while Gildas turned back to his spade, and dug at the brown clods more vigorously than ever.

The shadowy night drew on apace; the sun set in a bar of golden haze, underlying the leaden bank of clouds that had lifted from the horizon.

Strange as it may seem, his interview with Captain Jack, a meeting which he had dreaded, and yet desired with a vengeful anger, had in a great measure lightened his trouble; and even as that heavy bank of grey was lifting from the west, so, as he turned homewards through the hawthorn lane, a renewal of life and hope flowed in upon him, and led him onwards, with a feeling that for him too, in the future, there might be a golden haze beyond the heavy clouds that had of late darkened his life.

CHAPTER XVIII

The Fire

A few days later in the same week, a bright log fire was burning on the Scethryg hearth, for it was supper-time, and the mishteer was just home from his work.

The leaping flames lighted up every corner of the quaint old room, and showed up the glittering pans and platters of an earlier generation which were ranged above the wide-browed chimney. Inside, in the full blaze of the fire, hung the cranks, the cranes, the ladles, and the bellows in a friendly company, the two broad settles flanking the walls beneath them.

Here sat n'wncwl Sam and Hezek, each in his corner, waiting for his supper which was evidently cooking in the large crock hanging down from the chimney.

Cawl, is it? No, for the table is laid with plates and knives and iron forks.

On the middle of the board stands a giant jug of butter-milk, while the end of the table bears a large platter of roof beef, salted and dried under the rafters and boiled in the day-before's cawl. Hard it is, no doubt, but not too hard for Gildas's strong white teeth, nor yet for the girl's, who takes her portion and arranges the plates on the table.

Now she lifts the lid from the streaming crock, and pours into a huge wooden bowl the mealy potatoes, bursting through their grey jackets; the brown bread and cheese is added, and they draw round the board with healthy appetites. Gwenifer sits at the side; she is losing the quaint, pretty break in her speech, but Gildas still thinks there is something unusually musical in her voice. ''Tis as though the thrushes are talking soft in the evening sometimes,' he had said one day, and he thought so to-night, as she recounted her simple tale of the day's work and events – the red cow's persistent attempts to get into the garden, Juno's frivolous games with the gander, the little brown lamb that had grown into a sheep all too soon, the simple things that make up the life of a farm; and Gildas listened with a pleased smile as he ate his salt beef.

Yes, poor Nance was sharing the fate of many a better woman; her hearth and her board knew her no more; her husband's heart was closing over her loss, and was opening out to a new happiness that seemed to glide into it with the simple joys of his home life – the glowing light on the hearth, the pleasant, cosy meal, which Gwenifer was clearing away, his seat in the firelight, the puffs of blue smoke that curled up from his pipe, it was all very pleasant, and he stretched out his feet to the blaze and laughed at the old men's gossip as they talked across the fire.

'Yes, in my deed, then, if you are not believing me,' said n'wncwl Sam, ''tis as true as I am sitting here; so John 'Crydd' told me, whatever. 'Twas the shepherd of Voel was looking for a sheep that had strayed down here to the moor, and coming he was towards Gwenifer's cottage, and he saw it plainly crossing his path in the moonlight; it went out of sight between the bushes, and he says he will swear he heard a sigh t'other side of the broom bush.'

'Tush,' said Gildas, ''twas the wind,' and he blew a fresh puff from his pipe.

'Most like,' said Hezek, looking into the burning logs, 'though Phil is a truthful man.'

'Was it the wind, then,' said n'wncwl Sam doggedly,

'that Michael Brynderw saw in the churchyard one night about a fortnight ago walking in between the graves? He's a bold man, is Michael, and he followed it across the churchyard, but it disappeared under the yew-tree, and when he went there, it was gone; ach-y-fi!' and he shuddered as he knocked the ashes out of his pipe.

'Nonsense!' said Gildas. 'There's no such thing as a ghost; those are all superstitions and old wives' fables, come down from the past – we are wiser now. What d'ye say 'bout it, Hezek? You've got more learning than we.'

'A ghost?' said Hezek, holding his thin fingers to the blaze and turning his dreamy eyes upon Gildas. 'Well, I don't know about ghosts; but 'spirits," he said, 'I don't know why spirits would not be seen sometimes.'

'Twt, twt!' laughed Gildas again; and as Gwenifer passed he laid hold of her sleeve. 'Here's one now ought to tell us all about it if any one can; so many long years alone on the moor with only her thoughts for company! Come, Gwenifer! tell us, lass, what dost think about it?'

'Yes, Gwenifer knows very likely,' said Hezek, the far-away look in his eyes brightening for a moment.

'Say, Gwenifer, come! Has't ever seen a spirit?'

'No, indeed,' said Gwenifer, 'I have never seen one. But I think there is more in the silence and solitude than we know of; it is full of spirits to me.'

'Caton pawb!' said Gildas, laughing, ''tis all nonsense, lass, and superstition.'

'Look you now,' said Hezek, 'you are too hard on super-stition, as you call it. Hark you, boys! there is much to be said for superstition.' His eyes brightened, his figure straight-ened, as in fancy he addressed his 'boys' at St. Austin's school, and Gildas listened with a smile as he harangued his imaginary class. 'Mind you, boys, I wouldn't have you believe every marvel, every ghost story, every old legend;

sift them out, find the truth, let the light in upon them, and cast away all that is foolish and baseless; but, after all, keep a place in your hearts for the spiritual side of life, for there is much that your dictionaries and your mathematics cannot explain. And as for poor old Superstition, I don't want her back, boys! She had her follies and weaknesses; but she's dead and gone, and we have buried her with scant ceremony.'

N'wncwl Sam and Gildas could only listen in silence, the latter with an indulgent smile on his lips and a twinkle in his eyes, while Gwenifer sat down and waited, for well they knew how impossible it was to stop the old man's flow of speech when he addressed his boys.

'Yes, yes!' he continued. 'We have buried her safe; the parson, the lawyer, the doctor, have all had their say about her, and the schoolboard master has clapped a tombstone upon her, and there's an end of her, they think; but mind you, boys, now that she's gone, don't you think we've hustled her away too hastily?' and he pointed his finger at n'wncwl Sam, who sat about the middle of an imaginary class.

'Mind you,' repeated Hezek impressively; and n'wncwl Sam moved a little nervously, and unconsciously dropped his pipe into Het's clothes-basket, which stood beside him on the settle.

'Superstition was not all bad,' continued Hezek, 'and when we got rid of her so hastily and so unceremoniously I am not at all sure that she did not carry away with her in the folds of her grey robes, much of the romance and poetry that made life full of beauty and interest in the past; and remember you too, boys, she was first cousin to Faith, and I, for one, have still a tender place in my heart for what they *call* superstition.'

N'wncwl Sam broke the thread of his argument by exclaiming, 'Dei caton pawb! You can preach like a parson, man, but I don't know what's it about.'

The light died out of Hezek's eyes, his hand fell to his side, and, looking round as if dazed he sat down, and, filling his pipe, bent over the hearth with his usual placid far-away look.

'Well, in my deed!' said Gildas indulgently. 'You are a clever speaker, Hezek, and you make us have more respect for our old grandmother's stories.'

Hezek made no answer, looking silently into the fire; but n'wncwl Sam, thinking the argument had turned in his favour, said triumphantly, 'Well there, then, that's all I said; that the shepherd of Voel saw the 'ladiwen,' or the 'ladilwyd,' running across his path like a mountain cloud.'

'Well indeed!' said Gwenifer, 'I saw something strange on the moor one night when I was going late from here; 'twas something crossing my path like what Phil y Voel saw; but it might be the grey heifer from Wern, she's always straying.'

''Twas that most like,' said n'wncwl Sam. 'I wonder will the *Liliwen* sail before dawn?'

A crimson blush dyed Gwenifer's cheeks, which she was careful to hide by stooping over the fire, while a little constraint came into Gildas's voice.

'What is he stopping for?' he asked.

'Oh, waiting he is for the *Speedwell*; she is bringing him something from Milford, some iron goods they are taking to Spain. What for didn't he come to see us this time, I wonder? First-class man is Captain Jack.'

'Yes,' said Gildas; 'I have nothing to say against him.'

'Caton pawb, no!' said n'wncwl Sam. 'What dost think of him, Gwenifer?'

Confused and startled, she could only answer, 'I don't know – yes, indeed, I think.'

''Yes, indeed,' 'I don't know,' and 'nothing against him!' In my deed, if that's the way my friends speak of me behind my back I'd rather be without them,' blurted out the old man.

Both Gwenifer and Gildas tried to laugh away his indignation, but the spell was broken, the cheerful sociability of the evening had departed.

''Tis getting late,' said Hezek, rising from his corner.

'Art going home, Gwenifer?' asked Gildas. 'Will I come with thee over the moor? Art afraid, perhaps?'

'No, no,' said Gwenifer. 'I am sleeping here to-night, for 'tis churning to-morrow morning. I am waiting for Het – she is not home yet from the meeting; here she is on the word!' and Het arriving, n'wncwl Sam, with a 'Nos da' to all, followed Hezek out to the old storehouse.

Soon after, the lights were put out, and darkness and sleep fell over all at Scethryg.

Out on the bay, the *Liliwen* rising and falling slowly with the lapping tide lulled John Davies and the cabin boy, each in his bunk below, more soundly into the land of dreams. The captain should have been sleeping too, for, safe anchored in the bay, there was no need of watch or compass; but a throbbing pain in his shoulder, added to the restlessness of his mind, had banished sleep, and he had risen to pace up and down in the darkness where the only sound was the lip-lap of the sea under the ship's keel.

When he entered the bay he had hoped to find the usual domestic happiness restored to the inmates of Scethryg; now he was full of troubled thoughts as he recalled his meeting with Gwenifer, and later with Gildas.

As his ship had ploughed her way through the green waters his longing desires had far outstripped her speed, and he had ventured to hope that time might have softened Gwenifer's disinclination for him, but now – he had had his answer; and there was nothing for him but to sail away, and bid good-bye for ever to the sight of the humble thatched cottage where his strange, erratic heart had at last cast anchor.

In a rift between the clouds he caught a glimpse of the moon, and in her light he saw the little white cot with its thatch of brown on the edge of the moor, and the grey walls of Scethryg with their dark clumps of ivy at the shoulder of the hill; but only for a moment, for the thick bank of clouds had obscured the moon again and the familiar landscape was lost to his sight.

Suddenly he stared eagerly through the gloom, for what was that pale cloud that rose over Scethryg?

A grey cloud curling into billows of yellow and brown, and tinged now with red! He called hastily to the mate and the cabin boy, and in an incredibly short time they were rowing towards Maldraeth, their eyes on the billowy smoke that rose without doubt from the walls of Scethryg. The mate and the boy rowed hard, the captain, with his disabled arm, steering straight into the little cove where Gildas and Nance had quarrelled and parted.

'Make haste to Tregildas!' said Captain Jack to the lad, 'call them all up, bid them bring pails and follow us to Scethryg,' and the boy ran with his heart in his throat, calling as he went, 'Tân! Tân!' till the villagers roused from their sleep, came out to their doorways, and, seeing the glow in the sky, hurried up to the old farmhouse.

Het's prophecy, 'No one will come to help Scethryg,' was not verified, for, as the grey smoke burst out into flames, and showers of sparks rose up into the night sky, there were scores of busy helpers. Every man bore his pailful from the rushing spout or horse-pond in the yard, and, amidst cries and shouts of encouragement, the fire fiend was attacked and fought by willing hands, urged on by eager hearts; for through the whole neighbourhood the tide of public feeling had turned, and there was scarcely one in the parish who did not regret the bitterness with which he had resented Gildas Rees's objection to the excitement of the Diwygiad, for already that feverish excitement was passing, and calmer and more reasonable sentiments were taking its place.

After all, they argued, every man had a right to his own opinions, and no doubt Gildas Rees had seen cause to fear the effect of the Diwygiad upon his poor wife's mind. And they rushed at the fire with an energy born of regret and remorse, which before long began to tell upon those leaping flames.

Foremost amongst the workers were Captain Jack and the mate. There was no time for conjecture or questions. They could only rush from the house to the spout and back again; while the flames towered high through the gaping roof, and the roar and the crackle of the sparks filled the air.

Suddenly a hand clutched the captain's sleeve, and Gwenifer's face, lighted up by the glow, was full of anxiety. 'Gildas,' she cried, 'where is he?'

'Oh somewhere at work,' said Captain Jack.

'No, no,' said Gwenifer excitedly, 'he is not here. I thought he was getting the horses out of the stable, but he is not there. Oh, Captain Jack, where is he?'

'Not here?' said Captain Jack. 'Has nobody seen him?'

'No, no; nobody.'

'Then God help him! he must be still in his bed. A ladder, Gwenifer! – a ladder up to his window!' And in a moment Gwenifer had brought the ladder, and together they stood under the smoke-blackened walls. Captain Jack catching at her shawl wrapped it round his head, and climbed up the rungs as a sailor only can climb. It would have been impossible to reach the room in the ordinary way, for the fire seemed to have started in the centre of the house, and the rickety old staircase had burnt completely away, while the outside walls were as yet intact. An opening in the roof made a furious draught, towards which the force of the flames seemed to converge.

In the red light the surging crowd watched Captain Jack's brave attempts to enter the house – attempts which they feared were doomed to be fruitless, for no sooner had he opened the window than a cloud of smoke rushed out. Blinded and almost suffocated, but undaunted, he thrust himself through the small aperture, for Scethryg windows were only made to open half-way.

The crowd below stood watching breathless while he disappeared, and a cry of dismay escaped them as a long, lithe flame leaped out through the kitchen window and licked the rungs of the ladder.

Within the smoke-clouded room Captain Jack, holding his breath, reached the bed, only to find it empty.

Thank God! Gildas has escaped. And he returned to the window, where shouts and groans reached him from below, and where he saw the ladder was already charred by the flames. Realising his danger, he turned in despair to the doorway. Here the small crooked landing was full of choking smoke; the old stairway had already fallen to the ground – a heap of charred wood.

That way, escape was impossible, but crossing the landing he stumbled blindly into a little doorway which led into the cheese room, from which he remembered a few steps led down to the dairy. He hurried across the room almost suffocated, but stumbled again over something that lay in his way; he stooped, and found it was Gildas himself. Roused by the smoke and the cries of the villagers, he had awoke, half stupefied by the fumes of the fire, and, dazed and alarmed, had started up and realised at once what had happened.

The house was on fire! Some enemy had done this, and the pang caused by this thought was more sharp and cruel than the scorch of the long flame that reached him as he rushed out, to find the stairs ablaze. He turned towards Het's room, for had not Gwenifer said, 'I'm sleeping here to-night'? What if she had slept to her death! But no! the room was empty of all but smoke. He staggered out again, blinded and choking and overcome by the fumes, and fell heavily on the floor at the top of the little flight of steps leading down to the dairy.

Here Captain Jack found him, unconscious but living; for he groaned as the sailor lifted him and with almost super-human strength carried him down through the dairy to the stable-yard, where the crowd, soon learning the good news of his safety, gathered round him.

It was Gwenifer who had first remembered the little-used dairy door. ''Twas there I thought I heard the mishteer calling us,' she said, 'and I thought he was safe down here; but Het and I climbed down the elder tree which grows so near our window, and in the hurry we forgot the dairy door;' and she ran round the house to find her hopes realised, and Gildas lying safe on the stubble with Captain Jack bending over him, bathing his face and holding a flask to his lips.

'He will cough,' he said, looking up at Gwenifer.

True, Gildas did cough, and opened his eyes; and Gwenifer, assured of his safety, quietly drew back, leaving the two men together.

'They will make friends better alone,' she thought, 'and Gildas will know who saved him.'

Mingling with the crowd, she was soon aiding their endeavours to extinguish the fire, which was now giving way to their vigorous exertions. The flames were dead, the smoke was lessening, the air was clearing, the fire fiend was conquered.

In the stubble yard Gildas was rising to his feet and steadying himself by a hand on his rescuer's shoulder. It was his wounded shoulder, but he did not wince; he would have borne much more for the sake of that friendly pressure.

''Tis the arm I hurt, too,' said Gildas.

'Caton pawb! I had forgotten it!' said Captain Jack, laughing outright. ''Tis you will have to wear the sling now, for I saw your sleeve flaming on your arm.'

'Yes, and if it wasn't for you I'd have been flaming all over by now, I expect. You have saved my life, captain;' and he held out his hand, with a smile of meaning which the sailor understood. He grasped the hand, and a warm pressure spoke for Gildas more than any words could have done.

'Come, then,' he said, 'help me to the other side; there's surely something we can do;' and with the sailor's help he walked, though unsteadily, towards the group of workers, who were still busily engaged in extinguishing the small flames that continued to burst out here and there from the smouldering débris.

'Thank you, kind people,' he said, appearing amongst them. 'Caton pawb! I didn't know I had a friend in Tregildas!'

'There's your mistake,' said Owen Hughes, one of the deacons at Brynzion. 'You must forgive our zeal for religion; it had made us over hasty, lad. We forgot that 'the wind bloweth where it listeth'; and though it blow like a gale over Brynzion, it may whisper like a still small voice in the heart. Yes, yes, you have friends; to-night has shown you that.'

'It has shown me I have enemies, too,' said Gildas bitterly. 'Who lighted this fire, think you?'

'That question,' said Owen Hughes, 'came into my mind when I first heard the cry of 'Tân!' I am troubled sore,' said the old man, looking down at the ground. 'I had hoped that the pure flame of the revival spirit had burnt out every stain of malice from our midst; but I'm afraid – I'm afraid,' he added, shaking his head again sorrowfully, as he turned away and left Gildas standing alone watching the ruin of his house. A group of women stood near, looking on, like himself, at the scene of devastation. 'Dear, dear!' said one, 'there's a pity! In my deed, I am sorry for Gildas Rees. How did it happen, I wonder!'

''Tis the arm of the Lord,' said Nelli Amos. ''Tis plain to see nothing but trouble has followed him since he turned against the Diwygiad.'

'Twt, twt,' said the first speaker, 'his harvest was the fullest in the parish, his barns are bursting over with grain; the Lord has blest him there, whatever, and I am thinking 'tis some man, or woman perhaps, who has done this wicked deed, and not the Lord. With Het and Gwenifer so careful, it couldn't be an accident.'

'It might be an accident,' said Nelli Amos, 'and yet be the hand of the Lord. Well, it's put out now, whatever, and I am going home to bed.' And she turned away in the darkness towards the village. Soon afterwards Gwenifer came up to Gildas, and, laying her hand on his arm with her old habit, said: ''Tis put out now, mishteer, and Het and I have made up a bed for you in the storws. Go you and lie down; we will watch here till the morning, for fear a fresh flame may burst out. You can trust us.'

He could see her face in the faint moonlight, and, looking into the dark brown eyes, he said: 'Yes, I can trust thee, Gwenifer. But listen, lass; come here and let me tell thee my thoughts and my troubles, as I used to do when I was a lad. It has long been in my mind, Gwenifer, and to-night's work has settled me in my plans. I will leave the old country – I will let Scethryg. Will Jones would be glad to take it and farm it with Bryndu; I can trust him, too. I will go away and work in some foreign land, Gwenifer, where I can forget my troubles and the hatred of my enemies. Dost hear? Dost understand?' he added, finding she made no answer.

'Yes,' she said at last, and the darkness hid the signs of sorrow in her face.

'Thou wilt keep watch over Scethryg for me; and out there perhaps, with hard work calling for all my strength, some day these bitter things will pass out of my life. I don't want to be a hard, gloomy man; in my deed I believe the world is full of brightness still. The earth smells sweet, the grass grows green, the birds sing blithely, and the good God is over all; but somehow, lass, I have missed it all. If you take a wrong step 'tis hard to find the right path again; *but if there is a right path, I will find it in spite of my enemies.* Who, dost think, did this cruel thing?'

'Oh, Gildas!' said Gwenifer, steadying her voice and gulping down her sobs. 'One person only in the whole parish would do this evil deed.'

'Nelli Amos?' he asked.

'Yes. I am sure the fire was safe; I put out the last log and I swept up the hearth. Go, Gildas, to bed; we will watch by the burning.'

He turned away towards the storehouse, feeling for the first time in his life overwhelmed by his troubles. Hitherto he had held his grip on the rudder, and had felt the power to steer between the rocks of danger to a safe anchorage; but now he was shaken and storm-tossed, and sought the shelter of the old storehouse in a frame of mind which was quite new to him. Rest, sleep, oblivion, had become desirable things to the man who had always sprung to meet difficulties and toils, and had enjoyed the struggle. He sighed as he reached the steps, and looked up at the red door, which he called to mind had been the portal through which he had passed to meet misfortune.

He heard the talk and the calls of the neighbours, who still worked at the smouldering embers, but felt too weary and sick at heart to join in their exertions.

'Caton pawb, Gildas Rees!' he said to himself. 'Art going to be beaten at last?' and in sheer exhaustion sat down on the bottom step; the burn on his arm, though not a serious one, beginning to make itself felt more acutely.

'I wish I had asked Gwenifer to see to it,' he thought,

'but, dear anwl, I must learn to do without her, too. She will change her mind and marry the captain after all; he will persuade her, I am sure, for I think she likes him now. Well, he's a straight man and a kindly, after all; yes, I believe that,' were his thoughts, as he sought and found n'wncwl Sam's greasy candlestick. 'If he was foolish and wild – well, I believe he is changed. Yes, yes; I know very well as Owen Hughes said, that 'the wind bloweth where it listeth,' and although I don't like the smoke and the glare of the Diwygiad, I know what the flame of the Spirit can do.' And, lighting his candle, he sat down in Hezek's chair to await Gwenifer's return.

'I must learn to do without her; but can I? It will be like tearing the life out of me!' And he fell into a fit of sombre musing, from which he awoke with a start, as he heard footsteps coming up the steps. 'I have been a fool,' he said, 'and now I must bear my punishment.'

Gwenifer came, ere long followed by Hezek, whose sympathy was almost outweighed by his satisfaction at having Gildas, the sceptical, as a patient, and eagerly requesting a soothing salve.

When the arm was bandaged and the old man's remedy had begun to lessen his pain, he turned to Gwenifer. 'Go thou now, lass,' he said, 'and can diolch. I will try to sleep, for in my deed I don't know myself in this weak plight.' The pale dawn was beginning to brighten the sky in the east, and throwing a cold, weird light upon the groups of busy helpers who still stood round the smouldering débris, conversing together in subdued tones. The consensus of opinion was that 'an enemy had done this thing,' and though no name was mentioned, yet suspicious looks were cast towards Nelli Amos's cottage, whose chimneys came just in sight above the sloping path to the village.

'We must see to this,' said Ebben the carpenter. 'A

righteous indignation is one thing, but a bitter malice is another. You understand, friends, we must see to this in Brynzion.' And they lingered round the still smoking house until every vestige of danger had disappeared.

When Gwenifer returned from the storehouse she was met in the yard by Captain Jack and his mate. In the pale grey dawn the former looked haggard and white, his arm once more adjusted in its sling.

'Dear, dear, is it burnt?' said Gwenifer. 'There's a pity! Come you then at once, and Hezek's herb oil will cure you.'

'Twt, twt!' said Captain Jack, while he called to mind vividly the blustering night when he and his mate first entered that ill-omened red door. 'Caton pawb, no! We must sail in half an hour.'

'Well,' said the mate, 'I will leave you to say 'good-bye,' captain, while I run down to Maldraeth to see is the boat there, because we were in too great a hurry to fasten it safe. Fforwel to thee, Gwenifer; we will bring thee a ribbon from foreign parts when next we come into Tregildas bay.'

'They don't want me,' he thought, as he hastened down the moor. 'I have long seen how the wind lies in that quarter. 'Tisn't the slopes of Tregildas nor the friendship of Scethryg that is drawing the captain so often to this bay. 'Tis Gwenifer; and in my deed, if there's a maid in the world is good enough for my captain, 'tis the sweet 'Queen of the Rushes,' as they used to call her.'

When he had disappeared the two persons in question were left alone in the dim, dawning light. The sun was approaching, for behind the highest edge of the moor a rosy flush was spreading, which lighted up Gwenifer's face with a faint colour.

'Gwenifer,' said the sailor, holding out his left hand, 'if it must be 'good-bye,' let it be soon over, lass. Must if be?'

The girl's eyes filled with tears.

'Yes, indeed it must be,' she said, 'and 'tis sorry I am in my heart that you have set your love upon me. 'Tisn't that I don't value it, Captain Jack. From the first day I saw you I liked you, and I wish – oh, I wish – you were my brother. But I can never marry you, never; so put me out of your mind, if you can't feel to me as a brother.'

'Tush!' said Captain Jack, with an impatient gesture. 'If I can't love me, Gwenifer, I want nothing else.'

She shook her head, while the tears that had gathered in her eyes stood on her cheek, and she placed her hand in his.

'Fforwel, lass,' he said, 'I have lost something here at Tregildas; but I have gained something too. Good-bye; may God bless thee! One thing I will always remember with gratitude. Gildas Rees has shaken hands with me; tell him, Gwenifer, how glad I am. Where is he?'

'He's sleeping in the storws,' said Gwenifer – 'quite tired and worn out.'

''Tis no wonder he is worn out. Well! bid him 'fforwel' for me. Fforwel to you, lass.' And with a warm pressure of her hand he dropped it suddenly, and turned away down the path to Maldraeth.

It was a pathetic, lonely figure that Gwenifer strained her eyes to watch through the morning mist.

Perhaps she was unstrung by the events of the night and the previous day; perhaps she was wearied in body; perhaps in her tender heart the sailor had held a warmer place than she was aware of. At all events, she sought the dim grey garden, and, finding a secluded corner, buried her face in her hands and cried silently.

She heard the bustle and the talk in the yard, where the neighbours and helpers were gradually dispersing; she heard the songs of the birds, and, drying her eyes, returned to the stubble yard, where she found Het preparing for the milking, and washing her pails under the spout.

'For seems to me,' she said, 'everything will smell of smoke after this night. Ach-y-fi!'

Gwenifer called the cows as usual; but it could not be 'Corwen' or 'Seren' that she was thinking of as she said with a sigh, 'Poor fellow! poor fellow!'.

The milk frothed into the pail, the sun rose higher above the moor, and, looking over the bay, she saw that the rosy beams were catching the white sails of a ship.

Through the clear air she heard the clink of the anchor-chain, she saw the red pennon flutter as the vessel answered to the swelling breeze and sailed away into the golden haze which hid the horizon.

A fresh breeze rose, the clouds parted, the sun shone out bright and strong, and into the golden haze the *Liliwen* sank, Gwenifer watching the last glimpse of her sails with tearful eyes.

CHAPTER XIX

A Face at the Window

The month which followed the fire was one of dull inaction at Scethryg. For a time Gildas Rees seemed stunned by the catastrophe, a fresh proof, as he considered it, of the unrelenting anger of his neighbours.

Ere long, however, he began to revive, to recall his old powers of resistance, his dogged determination to fight and to conquer the mishaps that seemed to crowd round his path.

'He would rebuild Scethryg,' he said, as Jones Bryndu and he stood looking at the débris of the fire. 'After all, 'tis only the old stairs that are gone and the roof at the top where the laths caught fire. The stairs were shocking rotten, and now we can have a handrail to go up, like Bryndu.'

'Yes, you are right,' said Jones. 'You can let the house, and I will take the land off you if you are determined to go; but, indeed, Gildas, 'twill be strange here without you for Betsy and me, and I think we will have to come after you.'

'Well, come!' said Gildas, 'we'll work hard out there together, and make our fortunes, and come back here to end our days in our old homes; that is my plan, whatever, though 'tis hard to leave the old country.'

Will Jones looked soberly down at his earth-clogged shoes. 'Well indeed,' he said, 'I'm thinking such jobs as this fire are punished in this world, without waiting for the next. There's Nelli Amos – shrivelled up, a bag of bones! She took to her bed the night she was turned out of the seiet, and Peggy

Hughes had her place as chapel-keeper, and Nelli has never got up since.'

'What did they turn her out for?' said Gildas, 'because no one saw her do this; only Ben saw her peeping over the garden hedge late that night; but she was on her way home from Voel, she said, and Jerry the boatman saw her arriving home with a heavy bag of potatoes on her shoulders.'

'Well,' said Jones, 'they had other things against her: she didn't keep the chapel so clean as she used to, and her tongue is too rough and bitter for Brynzion. But in truth, 'twas the burning of Scethryg was the real cause of her being turned out, and she knows it well, the old hag.'

'I suppose she did it,' said Gildas, looking at the charred and blackened heap. 'I can't believe any one else would do it, bitter as they are against me.'

'No one, no one; if it wasn't an accident.'

'Couldn't be; Gwen and Het are so careful of fire.'

Here they were joined by n'wncwl Sam and Hezek, who spent much of their time in strolling round the ruins, speculating upon the origin of the fire, and suggesting alterations when the rebuilding began.

'Tom Williams and Dafydd Jones Penrhiw will be here to begin on Monday, no doubt,' they said, 'for we must make haste to get the work done before the frost comes,' and so the event had at least brought a fresh interest into the lives of the two old men.

'Come here!' shouted Jones Bryndu, who had crossed to the centre of the pile and was raking away at the ashes. ''Twas here it began, I'm thinking – 'twas just here the stairs went up.'

'Yes,' said Gildas, drawing near. 'What have you found? The cupboard under the stairs was where you are standing.'

'Well, somebody had been smoking his pipe in the cupboard, I suppose, for look you here!' and he held up a short clay pipe.

'In my deed, 'tis n'wncwl Sam's!' said Gildas. 'Did you hide in the cupboard to smoke that night, n'wncwl? or did you throw your pipe in there? See, 'tis your pipe that you bought in the fair, with a woman's face on the bowl; 'tis burnt whiter than ever, but not a crack in it.'

N'wncwl Sam approached, and taking the pipe in his fingers, examined it narrowly; and while he looked at it at arm's length, close to his eyes, through his spectacles, and over them, he went through an exhaustive list of ejaculations.

'Jari! so 'tis; there's the face quite plain! In my very deed, 'tis mine! Well, well! Caton pawb! there's an odd thing! In my deed, I never saw such a thing! 'Tis my pipe and no mistake!'

''Tis your pipe, I'm thinking, set the house on fire,' said Gildas, 'but how did it get under the stairs?'

'Stop you a bit now,' said n'wncwl Sam. 'There's nothing like using your senses.'

'When you have got any,' interpolated Hezek.

'Look you here now,' continued n'wncwl Sam, 'call you Het and Gwenifer here, and I will make a confession. Dear anwl! how one's sins find one out!'

'What's the man talking about?' said Jones Bryndu impatiently. 'Did you set the house afire?' Nevertheless he shouted for Het and Gwen, and they both came out of the barn together.

'Come you here,' said n'wncwl Sam, 'and listen to me. Mind you, I haven't passed through the Diwygiad without learning my duty; and now that I see my pipe, my conscience won't let me rest till I've told you everything,' and again he held the pipe close to his eyes, and ejaculated, 'Howyr bach!'

. 'D'ye remember the night of the fire we were sitting together round the hearth?'

'Not *me*!' said Het, 'don't bring me into your fire or pipe, if you please.'

'Taw, fool! and listen. I was sitting on the settle, and smoking my pipe as innocent as a child unborn, and Hezek

there was preaching about the 'ladiwen'; and all of a sudden
he pointed his finger at me, and sort of frightened me, and
I dropped my pipe into a basket of clothes that was standing
on the settle by my side; and look you, Gildas! I was meaning
to look for it before I went, but Hezek's preaching put it out
of my mind; and as sure as my name is Samuel Watkins, I
never thought of my pipe from that moment till now. I had
an older one in my pocket that I liked better, and so I forgot
the new one; and on my word, Gildas, there's the whole
truth for you. Forgive me, 'machgen-i, thou know'st 'tis the
fault of an old man's memory.'

'Yes, yes, I see that,' said Gildas, 'but how did the pipe get
under the stairs?'

'Caton pawb!' said Het, 'I don't know anything about it;
but of course, when I came in from chapel and saw the
clothes-basket on the settle, I knew the folded things would
get too dry for ironing, so I whisked it away at once to the
cupboard under the stairs; and I suppose they'll be turning
me out of chapel now, and whispering everywhere that I set
fire to Scethryg.'

'Nonsense, Het,' said Gwenifer. 'Art not glad that the truth
is plain and that poor Nelli Amos will be cleared?'

'Poor Nelli Amos? – umph, umph,' said Het. 'I don't
know but she deserves what she's got, turning my sweet-
heart against me, and talking to him about Laissabeth
Penlan!' and she tossed her head as she turned away.

'This clears up everything,' said Gildas. 'Well indeed, I'm
glad; though it won't pay for the repairs,' and they moved
on with Jones of Bryndu, to take a last look at the filly in
the field, which was soon to be transferred to the Bryndu
pastures.

N'wncwl Sam climbed up to the storehouse, still
ejaculating, and treasuring his pipe as if it had been some
trophy of a well-won victory.

That night the long windows of Brynzion chapel were once more ablaze with light, for within a service was being held. There had been earnest prayers and fervid singing, but none of the extravagant expressions of penitence, the cries and groans which had marked the first advent of the revival; for the flame and smoke had died out, and given place to the calm, steady glow of true religious feelings, which, as time went on, made Brynzion and its congregation a shining light in the religious world.

Outside, the waves fell with the same monotonous plash that had beaten time on the shore for centuries; a host of brilliant stars crowded the sky. Up from the village, and from the grey hills, the congregation were dropping in one by one, amongst them a man from the moor, stalwart and tall, broad-shouldered, and firm of step. Without hesitation or pause he entered and walked straight across to the Scethryg pew, where n'wncwl Sam was already sitting in solemn solitude. He stared in astonishment as Gildas entered, and although no outward sensation marked the event, a flutter of interest passed through the congregation.

'Had he seen the error of his ways and returned to the church of his forefathers? Well indeed, God's ways were wonderful!'

And while they marvelled and rejoiced, Gildas bent his face over his hat in the orthodox fashion, and hung it up on the rail at the back of the seat, as though nothing unusual had happened in the weeks that had passed since he and Nance had sat there together.

One of the deacons rose in the 'sêt fawr' and spoke the customary words: 'There will be a 'seiet' after the service.' The preacher mounted the pulpit stairs, and a hymn was sung with evident feeling and appreciation of the words.

Everybody listened with rapt attention, an earnest reverence pervaded the whole congregation, every face was alive with fervour and interest; but there was an entire absence of the tumultuous excitement which had characterised the earlier gatherings.

With true Christian humility the preacher, who had willingly effaced himself, and gladly consented to take a subordinate place during the religious crisis, now with praiseworthy readiness took up his work once more, never resenting the greater popularity and success which had attended the efforts of the younger and more gifted teachers. Once more he looked down upon the upturned faces of the flock to whom he had ministered for thirty long years without any visible signs of success, thankful to see the awakening fire for which he had hoped and prayed so long, although kindled by others' hands.

Gildas, sitting in the corner pew under the gallery, noted the temperate tone of the meeting.

'Dear anwl,' he thought, 'if it had always been like this I would have been saved much trouble. But there, that is passed. 'Tis no use thinking about that.'

The words were easily said, but not so easy was it to banish the memory of the painful events which had caused him to absent himself so long from the place of worship with which his earliest recollections were entwined.

He remembered his father and his mother as they led him by the hand to the old seat in the corner. In later years how proud he had been to see Nance in all her buxom beauty sitting beside him in the same old pew! And while the familiar service went on, a host of bitter thoughts and memories passed through his mind, and so embittered had be been by all that had passed, that he longed for the closing hymn which should set him free to turn his steps from the chapel and once more reach the open moor.

'No,' he thought to himself, 'not yet can I come back to Brynzion; but when things that are passed are not so fresh in my mind then I will join the old chapel again. After all, a man's life doesn't seem complete without some place of worship to go to.'

When the service was over and the congregation dispersed some remained for the seiet, amongst them the Mishteer of Scethryg; he listened patiently while a knotty point of church discipline was discussed and settled, after which the deacon asked the usual questions.

'Does any one feel inclined to make any remark?'

'Yes,' said Gildas Rees, rising to his feet, 'I do,' and there was a furtive glancing towards him.

'Very good,' said the deacon, 'we will listen with pleasure to anything you have to say; and I will take this opportunity of telling you that I am sure there is no one in this meeting to-night who is not gratified and thankful to welcome our brother amongst us once more. What have you to say?'

'Well,' said Gildas, 'I have ventured to come amongst you to-night, because as far as I have heard you have not formally cut me off from membership of this congregation.'

'No, no, no,' said the preacher, rising hastily. 'Certainly not; welcome back, 'machgen-i.'

'I have come to ask you a favour,' said Gildas. 'I hear you have turned out Nelli Amos from her old place in your midst, and I am thinking that perhaps the story I have to tell you may make you inclined to change your minds about her. I know nothing about your reasons for expelling her, but when you have heard what I have to say perhaps you will reconsider the matter,' and he recounted the finding of the burnt pipe in the centre of the charred and calcined wreck of the Scethryg stairs, and n'wncwl Sam's explanation of the matter.

'It is quite plain, you see,' said Gildas, 'there can't be any doubt about it. N'wncwl Sam dropped his pipe into the basket, and forgot to take it out again; well, Het came home from chapel, and says she carried the basket to the cupboard under the stairs; the pipe was smouldering in it all the time, no doubt. I am not very fond of Nelli Amos; but she's an old woman and lonely, and I do not like her to be wrongly suspected on my account.'

'Dear, dear!' exclaimed the deacon. 'Thank the Lord it has been made so plain, so that no innocent persons may be wrongly suspected! You, Gildas Rees, I must say have acted towards the old woman in a more Christian spirit than she has shown to you.'

'Now comes my favour,' said Gildas. 'Will you take Nelli Amos back to your midst?'

There was a short consultation between the grey-headed deacons and their minister, during which Gildas Rees stood up in his pew.

'Yes, 'machgen-i,' said the leading deacon, 'gladly we agree to your request; and thank God you have shown us reason for reconsidering the matter. Nelli Amos shall be restored to her place. Let us pray, and thank God for clearing our path,' and the old man knelt in the sêt fawr, and spoke out his thanks to his Maker with the simple earnestness of a child. There were many ejaculations of 'Amen' as he brought his prayer to a close; and Gildas Rees, without hurry or disrespect, was yet the first to emerge from the heated atmosphere of the chapel to the cool night air, where the stars were still glittering in the sky, and the waves still breaking on the silence of the night. With the satisfied air of a man who had gained his point, he turned his face towards the moor, and strode on over the springy turf where the rising moon was beginning to throw long shadows from the furze bushes.

There was always a glow and cheer in the old storehouse which made it a pleasant place to return to from a night's walk, and Gildas hurried homewards with a brisk, light step. He had forgotten Nelli Amos, forgotten the fire, too, for his mind at every spare moment turned to the plans and projects which had latterly dawned upon him, of life and work, and perhaps success, far away in the woods of Canada.

He had reached the middle of the moor. Gaunt thorn bushes here and there stood up in the heather as if to defy the sea-wind which whistled through their branches and bent their round shoulders towards the east; but so wrapt was Gildas in his own thoughts that he saw nothing of his surroundings, until suddenly in the dimness of the cloudy moonlight a grey figure stood before him straight in his pathway.

Was it Gwenifer going so late to the village? and he called aloud with a pleasant ring in his voice, and a feeling of welcome in his heart.

'Gwenifer, lass, is it thou?' The grey figure made no answer; like a shadow it passed behind the thorn bush, and Gildas stood still, uncertain what to do. 'Why, follow of course,' he said, 'if I want to find out,' so he swerved to the left and walked round the bush; but in vain. Nothing was there save the wind from the north bearing tales of far-away frost and snow; nothing but the grasses waving on the ground, and in the sky the grey clouds chasing each other across the moon.

Gildas stood in surprise. 'No one here? In my deed there was somebody!' and turning to look round, he saw the same mysterious form – or was it another? – disappear swiftly into the shadow of the furze. 'What! Is the place full of witches?' thought Gildas, a little annoyed; but before he had taken many strides further, his mind returned to its former groove, and he was steering his boat over some lonely lake or felling down trees in the tangled forest of a strange country. Life and energy were in his brain and in his strong arm; but deep down in his heart a tender regret refused to be stifled.

Suddenly he stopped again, for surely behind him there was a sigh on the air, a footstep that brushed the grasses; or was it the wind coming up from the sea? and turning round he thought he saw the same grey figure disappear in the winding path through the furze.

Now for the first time he remembered the tales he had heard of the ghost that so many of the villagers declared they had seen of late on the moor, and he laughed at his own fancies, as he turned once more and looked over the many sheep-paths that wound through the heather. 'Perhaps it was a rabbit!' and he kicked at a clump of scrub and fern; but no! no white-tailed rabbit scuttled away, and he advanced a few steps, but stopped to listen as a long low wail caught his ear like that of some creature in pain or distress. 'In my deed,' he said taking off his hat and rubbing up his hair, 'there's something here besides the wind and the heather! We must find it out or else nobody will cross the moor in the darkness; but it's too late to-night,' and at last he went on his way, though frequently stopping to look back in puzzled curiosity and to listen, soon, however, forgetting the whole subject in his desire to reach the old storehouse and smoke his pipe in the blaze of the hearth.

When he reached the red door it was opened by Het, for Gwenifer, she said, had gone home, 'gone home to that old bwthin, if you please, instead of sleeping with me in the hay-loft. Ach-y-fi! and she not fit to be by herself.'

'Why that?' said Gildas, sitting down to his supper 'she is used to being by herself.'

'Yes,' said Het, 'but I don't know what was the matter with her to-night. She went out after tea with a bunch of flowers from the garden – and there are not many left there now – and went up to the churchyard like she used to do; and when she came back, she was as white as a sheet, and wouldn't stop to taste the uwd or the cawl, or anything. Ask you Hezek, then,' and she pointed her thumb at the old man, who was bending over his herbs.

'Yes, indeed!' he said, ''tis quite true. Gwenifer is always pale, but she's not white, as she was to-night. Look you here now, there are many shades of white in nature; now, the snowdrop and the hawthorn are both white; but . . .'

'Oh, never mind them,' said Gildas impatiently. 'Was Gwenifer sick, dye think?'

'Yes, I am thinking, indeed,' said n'wncwl Sam, 'there was something odd about her; perhaps she'd seen the ghost.' And Gildas remembered the grey figure that had flitted round him on the moor; he could imagine its frightening a girl, and he finished his supper hurriedly.

'I'll go and see what is the matter with Gwenifer,' he said, turning to the red door, 'perhaps she has been frightened.'

'Well, in my deed,' said Het, 'I wouldn't wonder! Up there in the churchyard by herself and the ghost so often appearing on the moor.'

'Foolishness all!' said Gildas scornfully as he went out; but as he heard the wind that came sighing up from the sea he recalled what he had seen on his way home from the meeting, and wondered whether Gwenifer had seen the same mysterious figure.

When the twilight was falling, she had made her way, as was her frequent custom, to the little churchyard on the side of the hill, to place a few flowers on Nance's grave.

Up there on the bleak shoulder of the hill the wind blew with a steady force, rushing through the little belfry, sweeping by the old porch, and whispering in the yew-trees – like some living creature, Gwenifer thought, as she entered the churchyard, and sought a shelter from the blast in the quiet corner where Nance's grave lay.

She drew the flowers out separately from her hastily gathered bunch, and with a very pensive face laid them gently on the grave; only the common flowers of the country garden – southernwood, wallflowers, primulas, roses, and lilies – but Gwenifer laid them down reverently and with a sigh whispered 'Poor Nance' as she turned to retrace her steps to the churchyard gate. Raising her eyes to the narrow window which overlooked closely the spot where Nance was buried, she saw a sight that seemed to freeze the blood in her veins, that chained her footsteps to the ground, and riveted her eyes on the long church window, for within it she saw dimly but distinctly a white face, with hollow eyes, that looked down upon her where she knelt.

For a moment she saw it, plainly in the gloom; but even while she looked the phantom seemed to fade, or to recede into the background. Slowly she moved away, and her courage returned, as, passing the porch she saw the church door was open. 'Perhaps, then, someone had entered, had climbed to the high window-sill, and looked down on her. Yes, it must be so, and yet, and yet . . .' and she hurried on in the twilight.

'Could it be? Oh, surely no,' and with some mysterious fear clutching at her heart, she ran the rest of the way back to Scethryg, to bid Het not to expect her to supper, and then home over the moor, the wind in her ears whispering its weird and mournful secrets; but Gwenifer ran with her heart beating fast to the shelter of home, where she bolted her weatherworn door, and sat on the fire bench to recover her breath and her courage.

She pressed her hand on her throbbing side, for a terrible fear had darted through her mind at the sight of the pale face at the window – a suspicion that refused to be banished, even by the shelter of home and the glow of the bracken which she soon kindled in the little grate.

She bustled about with her tea-things, she lighted her candle and tried to forget her fears; but ah! when she looked towards her tiny window, which had never known a blind, *there was the face*! more terrible far in the quiet of home; for here it pressed close against the pane, and, as if grown more bold, stared in at Gwenifer with lack-lustre, meaningless eyes. Again that terrible thought! and Gwenifer hid her face in her hands and trembled like a leaf.

She who had lived alone with Nature so long was now overwhelmed by nervous dread; but it was not the foolish fear of the ghost, the blind terror of the ignorant, that had overcome her, but the power of that strange thought that had darted through her mind in the churchyard, and that now with double force took possession of her. What should she do? She must open her door and let the phantom enter if such was its desire; she must open her heart and welcome it there too! 'O God, give me strength,' she cried, and looking again at the window, she saw the white face still there, the hungry eyes still fixed upon her; and burying her face once more in her hands, she sat down to try to grasp the terrible idea. Yes, gaunt and hollow-eyed though it was, she recognised the face of Nance, and felt instinctively that it was neither ghost nor spirit that haunted the moor of Scethryg, but Nance herself returned in the flesh; and into her mind came rushing the thought of all it would mean for Gildas and for her, and in her heart too she felt that between her and him once more there stood a strong barrier that nothing could bridge over.

Turning her eyes again to the window, she saw that the ghastly face had disappeared, and then a fresh tide of feeling swept in upon her . . . Nance, her friend! the playmate of her childhood, the unhappy one who had strayed through tangles and briars and found her way back again to the old home. From such a one she had turned away! Had allowed her to drift once more to the wild moor and the bleak grey hills! Oh, shame!

She went to the door, and throwing it wide open waited silently within, in the hope that the wanderer might enter. She listened intently, and on the night air came the sound of a step that approached on the soft grass. Surely she was coming! and every thought of self died out in Gwenifer's heart, while she waited there to welcome and comfort the woman who could bring nothing but disappointment and cruel tension into her own life.

The step drew nearer, firm and steady; no ghost or phantom this, and Gwenifer, agitated and perplexed, saw Gildas enter.

'Mishteer!' she exclaimed in astonishment, 'so late!'

'Yes, so late, and thy door so wide open! Who wast waiting for, lass! Didst think I would come when I heard thou wast sick?'

'Oh no, indeed,' said Gwenifer in dire confusion. 'I didn't think such a thing, mishteer; but thinking I was that I heard a step on the heather, and waiting to see who it was.'

'Art disappointed then, lass?' he said laughingly, and taking the seat placed for him in the ingle nook. 'There's glad I am to see thou art well and hearty; Het and the two old men made me think there was something the matter with thee, so I came to see what it was; but on my word thou art better than ever, I think. What was it, then, Gwenifer?' and he puffed at his pipe and stretched his feet to the blazing hearth. 'In my deed,' he said, 'there's no one knows how to make a comfortable hearth like Gwenifer,' and he looked round the tiny room with pleased enjoyment. 'But come, lass, sit thee down, and tell me what was the matter.'

'Oh, nothing!' said Gwenifer. 'Only frightened I was, at something passing quick through the twilight – nothing at all only that, mishteer;' and while she spoke, glancing towards the bare window, she saw again, though a little withdrawn into the darkness, the face that had startled her before. Every vestige of colour, which excitement had brought to her cheeks, faded out, and left her deadly pale – so white, so stricken, that Gildas observed the change.

'What is it, lodes?' he said, rising to his feet. 'Thou art not a girl to have foolish fancies. Where is it, then, this creature that is frightening thee? Was it the grey thing they call the ghost, Gwenifer?'

She made no answer, for she still saw the white face faintly marked against the gloom.

Following the direction of her eyes, Gildas looked too and thought he saw a faint shadow flit away. In a moment he was at the door.

'Ghost or not,' he said, ''twill have to gave an account of itself to me. Caton pawb! Are you to be haunted on your own hearth? Let me go, Gwenifer!' for she had placed herself between him and the doorway. 'Art thou become a coward? or am I a child once more? Art afraid the bwcci will have me?' and he laughed, with the ringing heartiness of earlier days; and still determined, he gently thrust her aside, and made straight for the door; but Gwenifer was as determined as he was. What! let him go out into the darkness, to meet face to face the woman who he thought was dead and buried! No! she must detain him at any cost, and she grasped his arm, and clung to him desperately, at last flinging her arms round him and looking up into his face with such beseeching eyes, that for very shame he desisted in his struggle, and grasping her hands in his, held them pressed to his breast, while he returned her imploring look with one full of something that she had never seen there before.

'Gwenifer, lass,' he pleaded, and there was a passionate tremble in his voice, 'put thine arms round me again, and tell me thy heart is mine;' but with a sudden wrench she drew her hands from his grasp, and turned away her face, no longer pale, but blushing like the dawn.

'No, no,' she said, 'I cannot, I must not, Gildas; you must

not say that to me,' for even while his words made her heart burn with happiness, she remembered the face at the window that might even now be looking in upon them, and she drew herself away and left Gildas standing as if stunned.

For a moment, while he had felt the warm clasp of her arms, and held the little brown hands in his own, his face had lighted up with the fire and energy that had marked it of old, his eyes had flashed, the old merry smile had curved his lips; but when Gwenifer had turned away from him so resolutely, had wrenched her hands from his grasp so ruthlessly, an angry flood of colour had risen to his face, but had receded and left him white and still, his lips set in the old hard curve.

'Thou must forgive me, Gwenifer,' he said. 'I forgot myself, lass, and I did not know it was so with thee, but I remember now. I will never offend thee again; thou know'st me, that I always keep my word, so thou need'st not fear me.'

Gwenifer had seated herself on the old oak stool by the fire. She was faint and torn with conflicting feelings; the hope of her life had been fulfilled, and at the same moment she was called to resign it. She tried to speak, but her lips refused to utter a word; and Gildas, looking down at her, seemed equally unable to express his feelings.

At last turning to the door he stopped with his hand on the latch, and trying to throw off the silent embarrassment that had fallen upon both, he asked in his ordinary voice, 'Would'st not like to come home to Scethryg to-night if thou art frightened?'

She bent her head to hide the tears that had gathered in her eyes.

'No, mishteer,' she said, 'I will stop here to-night.'

'As thou pleasest,' he answered. 'Good-night, then,' and without another word he walked out into the darkness.

CHAPTER XX

Betsy's Plans

There was no sleep for Gwenifer that night. It was not only
the strange discovery that Nance was still alive in the flesh
that disturbed her, but underlying it was secret sorrow which
she tried hard to stifle. She opened the door wide, and,
leaving a friendly light in the window, went out over the
moor and cliffs, calling softly, 'Nance! Nance fach! is it thou
indeed?' but in vain she called, and strained her ears to listen.
There was no answer on the night wind, no sign of the grey
figure flitting between the furze bushes. Many times in the
long hours between night and dawn she went out and
roamed about, herself like a wandering ghost, ever calling
in persuasive tones, 'Nance, Nance! Come home, 'merch-i,
come home!' But when the night was spent and the sky
began to lighten in the east, and still there had been no
response to her call, she returned to her cottage, and
throwing herself on her bed, intending to rest a few minutes,
fell asleep, and did not awake until the sun was risen high
in the sky; until the sea was sparkling and dancing under his
beams; until the little sea-crows and the gulls were already
winging their way to an inland reedy river-bank.

She started up, and, dressing hurriedly, ran out into the
bright morning air. 'Oh anwl!' she cried, racing over the
grass. 'Dear, dear! What is the matter? Everything seems
upside down to-day: sleeping so long, and Het milking the
cows for me.'

Breathless she entered the kitchen, where Gildas sat at his morning meal.

'Oh, mishteer!' she cried, trying to speak naturally. 'Dear anwl! I have overslept myself.'

'Never mind,' he answered. 'Het has milked for thee.' He finished his breakfast, and made his arrangements for the day's work as usual, and at last went out to the barn, apparently unmoved by any disturbing memories.

"'Twas a dream!' said Gwenifer to herself, as she turned to her work in the dairy; but, as she skimmed the wrinkling cream, and cleansed every speck and spot from the stone slabs, her heart contradicted the words, crying with every beat, 'Not a dream, not a dream; but, Gwenifer, thou must forget it!'

In the afternoon a round red sun shone through the autumn haze upon Gildas, working in the field beyond the creek; and his hand was not less steady, the long furrows none the less straight, because in his mind there remained the memory of a glowing hearth, of his own momentary loss of self-control, of a girl who turned away from him and wrenched her hand from his grasp with cruel firmness. 'Well, doubtless she had given her promise to the sailor, and there was nothing more to be said about it.'

'Yes,' he soliloquised, being quite alone in the broad ploughed field, with no one to hear him but the crows and seagulls who followed closely at his heels. 'Yes, in my deed, I have loved her all my life – when I was a boy, and played with her on the shore; when I was a man I loved her too; now it is all over. Gee up, Flower! Come up, Darby!'

The plough did not swerve from its line, and the green sward grew smaller and smaller as the afternoon waned. Turning the corner, he heard a loud call from the hillside, where two figures were rapidly approaching the Scethryg fields. His face lighted up with pleasure, as he raised his hand in welcome; and a few minutes later Jones Bryndu, accompanied by his wife, came in at the gap, and skirted the field towards Gildas.

'Here she is!' he cried, jerking his head backwards towards his wife, who was plodding after him through the upturned clods. 'She would come with me. I don't know is she welcome or not.'

'Twt, twt,' said Betsy, waving her rough brown hand. 'I'll take my chance of that, and we'll come home to tea with you, Gildas.'

'Well, b't shwr,' said the toiler. 'Wo, Flower! We'll be glad indeed to see you, if you don't mind tea in the old storws, for you know we are not back in Scethryg yet.'

'No, no,' said Jones, 'we know that. Go you on with your ploughing, and we'll go on to the storws to tell them we're coming.'

'Yes,' laughed Betsy, 'and that you will be in soon to your tea; for I see you'll have done the field in half an hour.'

'Yes, yes, go you on,' said Gildas. 'I'll soon be at home;' and Flower and Darby were again set going, and the keen bright plough with its red handles went on cleaving the sods.

When Het, from the vantage ground of the storehouse steps saw the two figures enter the field where her master was ploughing she was plunged into a whirl of excitement. 'Diwss anwl! here's Jones Bryndu and his wife coming – coming to tea, be bound; and we in the old storws without a cup or a plate in the place it ought to be; and everything so nice in Bryndu. Ach-y-fi! Gwenifer gone out to the milking, too! What *will* I do?' and she rushed about at railway speed, until she had hunted out the best tea-things and laid them on the table – had hidden away the old brown teapot, and brought out the brilliant china one which she had bought at the fair.

The kettle was boiling and the tea-cakes were toasting

when Betsy Jones reached the top of the steps. 'Well, tan-i-marw!' said Het, as the visitors came in at the red door. 'Well, who'd think to see you here, Mr. Jones and Mrs. Jones? There's a good thing now that I've got the tea ready for mishteer. Not expecting company I was, so everything's very plain on the table, Mr. Jones and Mrs. Jones. I wonder now Juno did not bark, or something to show me you were coming; but you must take us as we are.'

'Oh, everything is first-rate, Het,' said Betsy Jones, 'and the mishteer will be home in half an hour.' Her face was set in a sedate company look, for she had on her best gown and hat; but she smiled, and very broadly within herself, at Het's pretences. As plainly as if she had been present, she saw in her mind's eye the scuffling and hurrying that had preceded this triumph of festal array.

'Well indeed!' said Jones. 'Who would think you could be so comfortable in the old storws? But there, Het, you and Gwenifer are good managers; and how's the dun cow getting on?' and the conversation fell into a pastoral strain; the pigs, the sheep, the fodder, filled up the time of waiting for the mishteer and the tea. He came at last, followed by n'wncwl Sam, always punctual at meal-times, and always in a hurry to get out again, as if the whole work of the farm depended upon him. Gwenifer, too, came in from the dairy, but Hezek was absent, 'roaming after those old smelling weeds,' Het said; and they sat down to as good a meal as could have been served in palace or farmhouse: the thick golden cream, the brown bread and butter, the new-laid eggs, the ham, and the tea-cakes; and, crowning all in Het's opinion, the brilliant china teapot. Gwenifer stared a little at the unaccustomed display.

Mrs. Jones made the tea, and Het waited.

Betsy's mind, like nature, abhorred a vacuum, and while she had followed her husband to Scethryg that day she had evolved a 'plan' in her mind which should restore peace and happiness to Gildas Rees's household. It was entirely without foundation, born of her own busy thoughts and kindly instincts – but what did that matter to Betsy Jones?

As she sat at the tea-table, she felt she had 'managed' more unlikely affairs, and brought them to a successful issue. She looked at Gwenifer's downcast eyes, she saw the blush that dyed her cheek when Gildas spoke to her, and her keen insight was aware at once of some constraint in his manner. Something had passed between these two, and what more fitting? She must 'manage' it; and she chattered cheerfully, and filled up the teacups with thorough enjoyment, not only of the pleasant meal, but the prospect of 'business' before her.

Under the genial influence of the fragrant cup, with its accompaniment of chat and laughter, Gildas grew more cheerful, more like his old self, and discussed with his friend his preparations for leaving the old country.

'I met Oliver the lawyer on the road yesterday,' he said, 'and he will have the papers ready before long; I told him I wasn't going till the spring.'

'What's the hurry about the papers?' said Betsy, 'perhaps you will change your mind, man! Indeed, there's foolish you are; take my advice now, and stop where you are. There's no man in the whole neighbourhood more honoured and respected than you are, whatever you may think,' but Gildas shook his head.

'No,' he said, 'I would be better away from here, for a few years at least; I want to forget the past, and begin again. I have plenty of work in me, and dear anwl, don't think I am going to break my heart. No, no, if the clouds are ever so dark, the sun is shining behind them, and perhaps it will shine upon me in another land; certainly I have not seen much of its light lately. That's what I think, Jones, a man makes his own fate, and I have begun wrong. I'll try again in another country.'

'And why not here?' said Betsy. 'Look round you, man, and see for yourself; some people miss the flowers at their feet by looking over the distance.'

But Gildas only shook his head soberly.

'Well,' said Betsy, 'you'll go your own way, of course, like every man; but remember you, Gildas, I am dead against it, and somehow or other I often get my own way.'

'True enough,' said her husband parenthetically. 'Well yes; and we'll talk about this again when it's nearer the spring,' continued Betsy, without heeding the interruption. 'Well indeed, these tea-cakes are nice, there's eating I am! And here's Gwenifer now! Time for her to be looking out for a husband, for she's got a tongue now, to give him a trimming sometimes. What d'y think, Gildas?'

'Well,' said the latter, 'I'm thinking she knows her own mind on that point;' and Gwenifer rose hastily to help Het in the waiting, and to hide her confusion.

'Oh, no doubt,' said Betsy. 'When I know his name, 'merch-i, I'll wish him joy from the bottom of my heart; for I think he'll be a lucky man.'

'Yes, in my deed,' said Jones jocosely. 'If it wasn't for Betsy here, now, I'd try my luck myself; but she stops the way, you see. Would I have a chance – eh, Gwenifer?'

'Well yes; I'm thinking, indeed, a very good chance,' laughed the girl, taking the joke in good part, and glad to have an excuse for her blushes. The laugh went round the table, Gildas alone being silent; a fact that was not lost upon the shrewd Betsy.

They were, to all appearances, a merry and light-hearted company, when suddenly they heard Hezek's voice somewhere from the stubble yard, conversing as he walked, or, rather, soliloquising, for there was no answer to his remarks. 'Come on! come on, then dear heart! We are nearly there now. Up these steps, and we are at home.' And they heard him ascending, and, with his, another footstep, slow and lagging. In another moment he appeared at the doorway, leading by the hand – a girl, a woman, a wraith? What was she? Clad in rags, bent with fatigue; yet, altered as she was, they recognised in the tattered figure, Nance – the lost, the drowned.

Had a thunder-bolt fallen in their midst, they could not have been more startled and alarmed. Betsy Jones dropped her tea-cake and stared open-mouthed at the stranger; Gwenifer started up and covered her eyes with her hands; Het screamed and ran into hiding somewhere; Jones Bryndu rose to his feet, bewildered; Gildas alone sat on immovable – as if turned to stone, he stared at the unkempt waif before him. Amazement, horror, were in his gaze; but no joy, no greeting.

'Didn't I tell you?' said Hezek, breaking in upon the silence. 'Didn't I tell you the little lass would come home? She was lost between the bushes on the hill-side, but *I* found her; and here she is now, all ready for her tea.'

Only for a moment was Gwenifer overcome by the unexpected sight. Before Hezek had finished speaking, she had hastened to the forlorn-looking creature, who stood there like a stranger, her eyes fixed on the table. With a cry as if of pain she stretched her hands towards the food, tottered, and would have fallen had not Gwenifer caught her, and, with the help of Betsy Jones, who had now recovered her senses, placed her in a chair.

'Starving, poor thing!' she cried. 'A cup of tea, Gwenifer, and some bread-and-butter.' They held the cup to her lips, and she drained it eagerly, but turned her head away from the more solid food. The refreshing meal that had so often been longed for had come too late.

Meanwhile, Gildas had sat on at the table as if stunned, his eyes fixed on the busy group and the unhappy object of their care.

Starting to his feet he cried: 'Stand aside!' They obeyed, and drawing nearer he stood straight and tall and unbending before the wreck of humanity which he had once called wife.

'Nance!' he cried – and there was a tremor of suppressed feeling in his voice – 'Nance! Do you hear? Do you know me?' But there was no answer from the blue lips, no sign of recognition in the vacant eyes.

Gwenifer, who stood behind her, held one of the wasted hands towards him, thinking such was his desire; but he made no answering movement to take it, and she laid it down again on the ragged gown.

'Nance!' cried Gildas again, 'listen, 'merch-i. I am Gildas Rees of Scethryg – your husband. Look at me, if you can, and say do you know me?' But the eyes still roamed vaguely; from her lips came only a little moan, a little gibbering; and with a shudder Gildas turned away.

'Thank God!' he said, as Jones Bryndu tried in his clumsy fashion to show his sympathy. 'Yes, thank God, Jones! since this is His will, that I find her like this. If she were in her right senses, knowing me and able to talk to me, I am afraid I could never forgive her; but now like this, I can say, 'Poor thing! poor thing!' and – I can try to forgive her.'

Hezek sat enjoying his tea in perfect content; he had found a rare and long-sought-for herb that day, and in seeking for it had lighted upon his little lass, the wretched condition in which he found her making no impression upon his unbalanced mind; for had he not brought her safely home? And he was the only member of that little company who was undisturbed by the wanderer's return.

Gildas had not even glanced at Gwenifer; nor had it struck him that Nance's return would in any way affect their relations to each other, for the girl's firm repulse of the night before had thrown him back upon his proud and defiant nature. He would forget that he had been a fool, he would live his life alone, and no one should know of his weakness. Nevertheless, his very soul was disturbed and upheaved as he sat by the hearth, and looked at the woman who had brought such misery into his life. He could not lay all the blame of her strange deviation from the path of wifely duty to the excitement of the Revival, for he remembered that she had married him without love, had deceived and humiliated him; and as he looked at the lack-lustre eyes, the meaningless smile, he could only be thankful that he was able to say, 'Poor thing, poor thing.'

Meanwhile Betsy Jones had been thrown into a turmoil of mixed feelings: thankfulness that she had been present on such an eventful occasion; that she could say to her friends, 'I was there, I saw it myself'; sorrow for the trouble that she saw was weighing upon Gildas; and pity for the unhappy creature who had been cast upon their hands.

What will we do with her? was already a pressing question. 'Go you out,' she said to the men, with a wave of her hand, getting rid of them as the first step in the rearrangement of her flustered ideas. 'Caton pawb! we can do nothing while the men are maundering about! Now they're gone, better settle what we're to do with her. Put her to bed, of course, poor thing! But where? There's no room here.'

'No,' said Gwenifer, 'but we have made up the beds in Scethryg, thinking to go back there to-morrow; now, 'tis a good thing we can put her in her own bed, and I can sleep with her and tend her;' and with Ben's help they bore the helpless, almost inanimate form; and thus did Nance, the bold and blooming, recross the threshold of her husband's home.

Where she had spent the weary weeks, since on that dark night at Maldraeth she had climbed the rugged path to the top of the cliff, and then with clouded brain and aching heart had turned towards the bare, grey northern hills, they never discovered with any certainty; they could only conjecture that she had suffered much, from her rambling and incoherent words when, returned to her old home, she lay exhausted on her bed, and when neither care nor tenderness availed to recall her from that bourne on whose banks she had arrived.

Sometimes the watchers, bending over her, tried to catch her indistinct mutterings. "'Tis cold o' nights on the Wildrom mountains!' they heard her say. 'The paths are long and rough.' Once she cried with a shudder, 'The shepherds have fierce dogs on the Wildrom mountains!' And Gwenifer's eyes were full of tears as she tried to soothe and reassure the way-worn wanderer.

By night and day she was unremitting in her attention to the invalid, and, helped by Betsy Jones, she soothed the last hours of the ruined life. To Gildas these last days of lingering sickness were a severe ordeal. He roamed for hours about the cliffs and moor, often returning to ask for news of the sufferer, but never entering the room; for he shrank with an uncontrollable aversion from the sight of his unhappy wife. He impressed upon Het and Gwenifer, however, his wish that everything possible should be done for her comfort; 'and if she comes to herself,' he said, 'call me at once; but, like this, to see her would do no good to her or me.'

But there was no reawakening to consciousness for poor Nance, no return of reason; and when at last the flickering spark of life went out, nothing but pity filled the hearts of those who watched beside her.

Hezek alone was still untouched by care. 'The little lass had come home; she was tired, she was resting in bed with Gwenifer to nurse her,' so he set out on a long ramble with a happy smile on his placid face; and when he reappeared at Scethryg, Nance had been a fortnight in her grave. Her return had already slipped out of the old man's memory, and he continued to solace himself with the words, 'she'll come home to-morrow.'

The news of the unexpected event which had so much disturbed the Scethryg household had spread like wild-fire through the neighbourhood.

Betsy Jones had taken care to return home by the village, although it was quite out of her way, for such an opportunity for reproving the Brynzion deacons was not to be lost. She was fortunate enough to meet the whole congregation just emerging from a prayer meeting. 'You see!' she said, haranguing a group who were standing outside the chapel, 'how you have all wronged Gildas Rees – almost calling him a murderer; for in spite of the 'quest and the crowner, you still suspected he had got rid of his wife by some foul means; and here she is come back to Scethryg and her senses gone.'

'The mestress come back!' they gasped. 'Caton pawb! is that true?'

'True as the sun is shining!' said Betsy. 'I was there myself. Will and me!'

'Yes indeed,' said her husband more calmly, ''tis quite true poor Nance has returned.'

'Come back?' they exclaimed again. 'Where has she been all this time, then?'

'Oh, the Lord knows! Roaming the world over, I should think by her shoes; and her clothes in gibbets and her senses gone, poor thing! Don't you see, John Parry?' she said, turning to the chief deacon. 'Don't you see? Gildas Rees knew what he was about when he tried to keep her from the Diwygiad meetings. Didn't he see the excitement was too much for her? And there she is in bed, with Gwenifer to nurse her, and poor Gildas telling them to give her every-thing she wants, and walking about the cliffs he is, like a man demented. He must have suffered a lot! Between the loss of his wife, and your black thoughts, for of course he knew them all.'

'Yes indeed,' said the preacher, who had joined them in the roadway. 'This is a strange happening, and it behoves us to confess our fault, Mrs. Jones; we were too hasty, and we must ask his pardon.'

'Well yes,' said Betsy, 'but some other time. Now he is too upset with a wife that he thought was drowned and buried, coming back to him suddenly when we were all at tea.'

There was a chorus of 'Dear anwls!' and 'Caton pawbs!' during which Betsy Jones and her husband left, the former delighted with the sensation she had created.

Her departure was followed by the question 'Who, then, did we bury and hold the 'quest upon?' But such an event as this was not wholly unknown where the wild sea was ever rushing up against the rugged coast, and where Maldraeth's curved bay was ever the trap which caught so much of the wrack and refuse of the angry waves; and they agreed 'twas some poor creature drowned at sea, who by a happy chance had had a Christian burial in a quiet grave.

Gwenifer called to mind the little storm-tossed ship which she had seen one evening in the twilight, and felt secretly convinced that the presentiment of danger to Gildas which it seemed to threaten and which had haunted her so persistently had been fulfilled in the mistaken identity of the body found on Maldraeth, and she never forgot when she laid her simple flowers on Nance's grave to scatter a few also upon that of the unknown woman. Hitherward Gildas's footsteps never turned. He accompanied the funeral up the stony mountain road, his face set in that impenetrable mask which hid his feelings so completely, that though no one said he had shown any signs of sorrow, yet no one remarked upon his callousness, and that was all that he desired.

As the weeks sped on, and winter set in with frost and snow and storm winds from the bleak north, the outdoor work on the farm had perforce to be discontinued, but that did not mean an idle time for the inmates of Scethryg. Het clattered in and out in her wooden shoes as vigorously as ever, the two old men worked at the beehives and 'whintell' baskets, clumping in through the snow in the evening, to finish their day with a smoke before the blazing logs.

Gildas was busy with his preparations for departure in the spring, though it must be confessed that as the time drew nearer, the stronger seemed the cords that bound him to the old home and the old country; and any dreams of success and riches which he might sometimes indulge in drew their chief charm from the prospect of their happy climax in a speedy return to the land of his birth, and a peaceful rest at the end of his days in Scethryg.

There were visits to the tailor and the shoemaker to fill up his time, new garments to be stowed away in the big box, strong shoes to be dried under the rafters, and, above all, tools of every kind and fashion to be collected and packed in an iron-clumped chest, which, to judge from its appearance, might already have crossed the Atlantic many times.

Gwenifer was often absent from the household circle. She attended to her duties as regularly as ever, but when the day's work was over she generally took her way over the moor to her cottage, whose brown thatch only showed above the soft white mantle of snow. There sitting alone by her tiny hearth, where, however, the peat and furze crackled and blazed cheerfully, she sat and wove her dreams and fancies, as she had been accustomed to do when her lips were sealed and silent.

She hummed to herself as she knitted, or worked at her bright patchwork, and surely there must have been some pleasant thought behind that calm and even frame of mind, that happy smile, and the tender lustre of her dark eyes. Yes, she was very happy; for in her heart a new and eager project was forming, in her mind a forceful purpose was daily gathering strength. It required much planning, much consideration, and all must be done in secret, and by her alone; so it was no wonder that her thoughts were busy while her needles clicked, no wonder that she hummed and crooned her simple old hymns and mountain lays, for plans, anxieties, and dreams were all pointing to a bright and successful issue. The wind might blow keen from the north, the snow might fall in whirling flakes, her pathway to the farm might be hidden under the drifts; but still in Gwenifer's heart, in spite of wind and storm, a bird of summer and its song of hope and cheer.

As the days grew shorter and darker and the year grew nearer to its close, the old farm kitchen seemed to Gildas to have lost something, he could not tell what, but something that had brightened the fire-glow, that had sweetened the laughter, and lightened the gloom.

He scarcely realised that it was Gwenifer's absence which made this blank in his home-life; but when at evening she crossed the farmyard on her way to her cot for the night, his eyes followed her with regret, and when morning brought her again his face lightened, and he went to his work with content.

'And yet,' he thought one day as he went out to see how the sheep had fared in the night, 'and yet he was going to leave it all. Gwenifer! he would miss her sorely! But, dear anwl! was he a woman to grieve and fret over a slip of a girl who had shown him plainly that he was nothing to her – nothing but the mishteer? Once to be a fool was enough, then; for surely, ere long, a bright red pennon would again flutter against the grey sea, the sailor would return, the timid half promise would be changed into a plighted troth, and Gwenifer would marry him!'

There was gall and wormwood in the thought.

'Well,' he said, leaning over the hurdles and forgetting

the sheep, 'let me be gone first. Let the sea roll between me and that wedding-day! Perhaps 'twill be nothing to me when I come back here some day in the future.'

Jones Bryndu and Betsy came often to the farm in the afternoons, when Het, no longer taken unawares had the china teapot always ready, the tea-cakes in the oven, and sometimes the lightcakes on the griddle to greet them; and drawing round the fire when the meal was over, the wind roaring in the chimney, they chatted and laughed and sometimes sang together – for Jones and his wife were good singers, and Gildas's voice had a mellow ring in it that added to the fulness of the harmony. What pleasant times they were! Hours to be remembered, the latter thought, when he was working hard on some lonely farm in Canada. Yes! the clouds were lifting from his life, in spite of one secret regret.

'Where is Gwenifer?' said Betsy Jones, who had once more begun to evolve her little plans. 'Indeed, 'tis not like Scethryg without her. Where is she, then?'

'Gone home, I think,' said Gildas, looking after the blue cloud which he was puffing up the chimney. 'She goes home early now the days are so short.'

'Yes,' said Het from the background. 'And what do you think she is doing there? I followed her one night and peeped through the window – why, sorting out new clothes, she was! In my deed, I think she must be going to be married. Captain Jack will be in the bay soon, I suppose, for I think he is the man!'

'Captain Jack!' exclaimed Betsy – and through her mind darted a host of arguments, pro and con – 'why, of course! Hadn't he been always ready to talk about her? But then, wouldn't he look higher than Gwenifer? And wasn't he rather 'wild'? And yet, hadn't he once said he had never seen a woman to compare with her? And now that it was proved that he had nothing to do with Nance's disappearance – why, of course, it must have been Gwenifer whom he was always looking for at Scethryg!'

All this passed through her mind as she turned inquiringly to Gildas.

'Captain Jack! Is there anything in that?'

'Yes, I suppose,' said Gildas, 'but indeed I don't know – they have never told me.'

'Well, well, dear anwl! I suppose it would be a good thing for her, for they say he's saving money, and he has turned very steady lately.'

And not even Betsy's keen eyes detected the shrinking pain which Gildas hid under his quiet answer.

'No doubt, then, thou are right, Het,' continued Betsy, 'and she's beginning to prepare her stafell. Well indeed, he's a lucky man, too. I couldn't think what he was asking John Lloyd about his half-finished house for; no doubt 'twas for Gwenifer to live in, and she'll have to leave her little bwthin now.'

'Stop, stop, 'merch-i!' said her husband, with a laugh. 'Thou art building too much upon Het's fancies; the house that's built without a strong foundation is apt to fall into ruins.'

'Oh yes; thou should'st have been a preacher, Will; seems to me quite plain. Dost think she wouldn't have him?'

'She would never marry him,' said her husband. 'I am certain she doesn't care for him.'

'Where are thy reasons, thy facts, then? as thou art always saying to me.'

'Oh, I haven't got any,' said Jones, laughing, 'but, like thee sometimes, 'merch-i, *I know*!'

'Not marry him!' said Het indignantly. 'The girl who was as dumb as a post for all those years, and who nobody looked at until her tongue was loosened; and now everybody is flattering her up and calling her pretty! Pretty, indeed, with her pale face! Yes, she'd take Captain Jack, and be thankful.'

'Would you be willing, Gildas? because in a way she belongs to you,' asked Betsy.

'Dear anwl, no!' he answered. 'She doesn't belong to me. Captain Jack's a brave man, and saved my life in the fire; I have nothing to say against him.'

'I have, then,' said Jones. 'Nobody would ask me, I daresay; but if they did I would never be willing.'

'Caton pawb, thou indeed!' was all Betsy could ejaculate. She was flustered and annoyed at having been so blind as to what had been happening around her; moreover, she had always asserted that her husband could not see further than his nose. As that was a very short one, his range of vision must have been very limited, but in this case Jones could see further.

'Well,' he said, rising and stretching his gaitered legs, 'We must go. Seems to me there's more snow coming. Come, 'merch-i, the moon is calling us. The new year is close upon us, so perhaps we won't meet again this year.'

'Well,' said Gildas, 'if we don't, a happy new year to you both!'

'The same to thee, 'machgen i,' said Jones, with a warm grip of the hand, for they had been friends from childhood; 'and the wish of thy heart in the new year – Nos da!'

CHAPTER XXI

The Joy of the Moor

The winter was over and gone, and the spring had come with its chorus of blackbirds and thrushes, and the song of the lark was thrilling over the moor.

Awakening life was everywhere, and beauty overflowing, in field and garden and hedgerow; even the sea seemed to share in the joy of the springtime, sparkling and dimpling, and reflecting the blue rifts in the clouds. The lambs frisked about on the hillside, the ploughboy whistled at his work. Yes, no doubt spring had come! but Gildas Rees still lingered at home and acknowledged to himself that it would have been better to have left the old country in the autumn when the days were shortening, the leaves fading, and when the moor was bleak and bare. Now it was decked with beauty, the furze was already blooming, the blackthorn spread its white mantle over the crags, the primroses peeped out between the heather, and in the hollow the bluebells were braving the wind.

As for the Scethryg garden, it was entrancing in its early budding charms; on the sunny side of the hedge the bees were humming round their straw hives, the brown earth was cracking and bursting with the tender seedlings that thrust up their little green hands to greet the sunshine; the daffodils were growing up everywhere, and standing, as their old Welsh name suggests, like gold-crowned kings, surrounded by their spearmen.

Het and Ben worked busily between the bushes, and Gildas sauntered through in the evenings, when the setting sun sent his slanting beams to gild the scene. The apple-trees were rosy with buds, the gooseberry bushes, like green lace-work, were crowded with tiny fringed berries; the wall-flowers, golden and brown, mingled their fragrance with the southernwood and ribes. All was tenderly alluring to the man who had grown up in their midst, and was now about to break the cords that had bound him so long to his old home. He heard the big clock in the kitchen strike seven, with its loud metallic ring; he heard Ben's voice in the stubble yard, and Het's wooden shoes in the dairy. In the clear evening air every sound fell distinctly on his ears, and, as he sauntered there in the gloaming, seemed strangely appealing – awakening in his mind a question that had long lain there hidden. He had not hitherto looked at it closely, because he was ashamed of it, but now he let it find expression.

Was he obliged to go? that was the question that had awoke within him; and as he stood in that old garden, listening to 'the sounds so familiar to his ear,' his feelings seemed to change, the former bitterness and anger against Brynzion died out, and his determination to leave his home and seek forgetfulness across the seas presented itself to his mind in a new aspect.

The sun went down, the moon like a silver boat sailed through the sky, the soft grey shades of evening gathered round him, the stars came out one by one, and yet he paced up and down the time-worn paths, filled with restless thoughts and longings. 'Hiraeth,' that sad-eyed visitant, so ready to take up its abode in the heart of a Welshman, stalked by his side, and he knew would follow him across the sea.

What had happened to alter his feelings so completely – to make the project of emigration, which had been a consoling thought to him a few weeks earlier, now appear in the light of a duty only? What had filled him with restlessness and indecision? To-night he faced the question, and in his honest rustic mind he saw the answer clearly written. Gwenifer! it was she alone who held him back; from here, therefore, he must fly. And when at last he heard the old clock striking eight, he turned towards the upland field, where he continued to walk and meditate for full another hour.

When at last he drew under the shadow of the big chimney, and let his musings follow the smoke from the kindling logs, he was still unsettled, still in the clutches of unrest and discontent, and he rose the next morning after a sleepless night, unrefreshed.

'Caton pawb!' he said as he hurried to his work, 'what has come to me I can't think!' and he dug fiercely at the sods with but little consciousness of what he was doing.

Late in the afternoon when he returned to his tea he found Jones Bryndu and his wife already seated on the settle.

'Up from the village we have come,' said Betsy, 'and there we have been hearing wonderful news, and I thought I would come and tell Gwenifer about it.'

'But why tell her?' said Jones, 'what is it to her more than to all of us? We are all proud when a Welshman does a grand thing. 'Tis Captain Jack . . . ' But he wasn't allowed to proceed further, for Betsy had come with the express intention of seeing how Gwenifer would take the news. The latter entered the house at the moment, carrying in one hand a bunch of daffodils, in the other a bowl of eggs from the hay-loft.

'Hast heard the news, Gwenifer?' she asked. 'There's a piece as long as my arm in the paper about Captain Jack.'

'Thy finger, 'merch-i,' interpolated Jones.

'Twt, twt – finger, then,' said Betsy, and she gazed at the girl with a smile of satisfaction, for over her face a conscious blush had spread – a tell-tale blush, Gildas thought. As a matter of fact, it had no tale to tell, except of the interest which a tender woman seldom loses in the man who has offered her his love.

'Listen,' said Betsy, 'I have brought it with me,' and she drew from her pocket a Welsh newspaper from which she read the following:-

'During the late severe gale which swept so disastrously over the Irish coast, a crowd of people was gathered on the pier at Ballenport, watching, with distressed faces, a derelict bark which the storm was driving in upon the rocks outside the harbour. The lifeboat was launched, but owing to the jagged rocks it was round impossible to reach the ill-fated ship. There was no living creature to be seen on board, except one small black figure, that of a child, who was seen to run distractedly from one side of the half-submerged hulk to the other. The sea was running mountains high, and there seemed no hope for the solitary child, until a sailor standing among the crowd seemed suddenly to make up his mind. Taking off his outer garments, and supplied with a life-belt, he dashed into the foaming breakers and literally fought his way to the rescue of the terrified child and brought him safe to land.

'There is a romantic sequel to this tale of heroism, for, finding that the boy was a friendless orphan, the sailor resolved to adopt him, and take him with him on board his own ship, which happened to be in port. The boy, Robert Owen by name, is a bright and intelligent lad of twelve. The unfortunate vessel, whose captain and mate were lost, was the *Andronica*, of South Shields.

'It will further interest our readers to learn that the brave sailor who thus imperilled his life to save a lonely boy was none other than our well-known and popular friend Captain John Davies of the *Liliwen*, or, as he is generally called, Captain Jack. Hir oes iddo!' (Long life to him!)

'There for you!' said Betsy Jones.

'Well indeed!' said Gwenifer, who had conquered her blush, 'I am very glad; I knew he was a brave man;' and placing her daffodils in a glass on the table, she carried her bowl of eggs into the dairy.

'So the shipwreck was a lucky thing for the boy after all,' said Het. 'I suppose he'll be bringing him here with him next time he comes.'

'No doubt,' said Gildas. 'Well, he's a brave man, and no mistake.'

'No denying that,' replied Jones, 'but 'twasn't to talk about Captain Jack I came here to-day, but to tell you Reuben my brother is coming here next week to look at the house if it is convenient.'

'Well, b't shwr; 'tis full time.'

''Tis only for a year he wants it, while his house is building; but that will give us time to look around for another tenant. And here's the paper from that shipping place that I sent for; plenty of ships, and all the cost marked plain; but ach-y-fi! I am hoping still you'll change your mind.'

Gildas took it with a word of thanks, thrusting it into his pocket. 'I'll look it over to-night,' he said, 'and I'll come up to Bryndu to tell you what I've settled one of these days.'

Het was already hunting for the china teapot, but Betsy Jones was firm in her resolve to go 'straight home at once; because I am not easy in my mind about the new cow; she was not chewing her cud when I left. No, Will! we must go straight home. And come you back, 'merch-i,' she called to Gwenifer with a mischievous smile, 'I am going, and there won't be anyone to tease you any more about Cap'n Jack.'

There was a general laugh, which, however, Gwenifer evaded by keeping still in the dairy.

'Too shy to come out, you see,' said Betsy, with a knowing wink, pointing towards the dairy door, at which, however, Gwenifer suddenly appeared.

'Indeed, there's nonsense you are talking, Mrs. Jones!' she said. 'My blushes are coming and going when they like without asking me; I wish I could stop them. But they don't mean anything, you can believe me.'

'Yes, yes, we know all about that,' said Betsy. 'Good-bye 'merch-i, thou art a lucky girl, I think. Though I had other plans for the Queen of the Rushes, Will,' she added, as they crossed the clôs together, "tis at Scethryg I'd like to see her.'

'Well, stick to thy plans, 'merch-i,' said her husband, 'they generally turn out right.'

That evening it was rather a silent, preoccupied group who sat down to tea together at the farm. Het bustling about had most of the conversation to herself.

'There's a funny woman Betsy Jones Bryndu is,' she said, 'with always a joke, and a merry word; but she's talking a lot of nonsense sometimes.'

'Well, when people talk a great deal, some of it is bound to be nonsense,' said n'wncwl Sam pointedly, for between him and Het there were wordy encounters sometimes.

'Betsy's a fine woman,' said the mishteer, 'she knows more about the farm than Jones does himself, and she's a good wife, whatever.'

Gwenifer said nothing, and finished her meal in silence.

The sun was in the west, but an hour from his setting, as they could see by the slanting rays on the table.

'There's a fine bed of leeks sown,' said n'wncwl Sam. 'Ben and me we've been trashing the hedge a bit, to let the sun shine more upon it.'

Gildas made no answer, but rising went out into the stubble yard, and from there to the moor, to which from childhood he had resorted whenever his will seemed unduly thwarted. If a stolen holiday was discovered and punishment was imminent, if a lesson too long neglected required special study, if his father forbade a visit to the fair – there was solace for everything on the moor; so now, when the experiences of life seemed intricate or disquieting, it was natural to him to turn to that broad expanse.

To-day his mind was disturbed; he was dissatisfied with himself – indeed, he was dissatisfied with everything; and as he walked to the edge of the cliffs, he felt he must put an end to this state of indecision so foreign to his nature. Stretching himself face downwards on the grass he drew from his pocket the paper which Jones Bryndu had given him, and leaning on his elbows set himself to study its contents. 'The *Livonia*, the *Campania*, the *Prudentia*; why not the *Livonia* – yes, that would do.' He drew his brown finger over the lines, and for the next ten minutes his face looked like hard thinking.

At last rising he set out for the creek, and the fields beyond; this led him by Gwenifer's cottage. But the door was closed, no smoke curled from the chimney, so he knew she was still at Scethryg dairy; perhaps when he returned she would have come home, and he could tell her of his final decision. But why tell her, what was it to her? what was it to anyone that he was tearing himself away from the land he loved. And why? Simply because in a moment of anger he had determined to do so – and was Gildas Rees going back on his word? And besides this, he confessed to himself, there was the underlying dread of seeing Gwenifer married and borne away to a stranger's hearth. No, that thought was intolerable, and he walked restlessly on. He would have a look at the dear old farm, its bare craggy knolls and its grassy uplands. The sea stretched out before him smooth and opal-tinted to where the sky was already hanging its curtains of purple and gold for the red sun that was hastening to his rest.

In the golden light of the day's last hour, the field and moor were glowing with an unearthly splendour, like the beauty of a dream, and Gildas's face lighted up with pleasure

as he gazed at the scene. Turning his face homewards, he
soon came in sight of Gwenifer's cottage, and saw that she
had returned, for there was the blue smoke rising up from
the chimney; and there was the girl herself sitting on the
garden hedge-bank, and looking out over the sea to the
gorgeous colouring which was spreading over the west.
Was she thinking of a white sail which might come into the
sunset? Banishing this thought, Gildas drew nearer, and
climbing up the bank sat down beside her amongst the
daffodils. She started a little with surprise, for, lost in
thought, she had not heard his footsteps on the grass.

'Dear anwl!' she exclaimed as he suddenly appeared.
'Mishteer, I wasn't thinking to see you.'

'No,' he said, 'thy thoughts were far away, I could see that.
Where were they, Gwenifer!'

Ah, where were they? In dire confusion she bent her head
and Gildas's heart sank, but he continued quietly.

'But there, I have no right to ask that; and whatever they
were, they were just right. I have finished packing my tools,
in that box in the barn, and my clothes thou has packed for
me. I thank thee, lass; thou has been very kind and ready to
help in everything.'

'Well indeed,' she said, 'you haven't asked me to come
with you, mishteer.' Her eyes were fixed upon the setting
sun, not in abstraction, but in the eager desire of impressing
him with the earnestness of her purpose; so she did not see
the start with which he had heard her words, nor the colour
that reddened his dark face. There was a moment's silence
while both looked out over the sea, and when Gildas at last
spoke there was a tremor in his voice, and he unconsciously
crushed the daffodil which he held in his hand. 'Come with
me? What dost mean?'

'Yes, come with you,' said Gwenifer, turning her face
towards him, and clasping her hands. '*Yes indeed*, I am

coming,' and once the ice was broken, she poured out the flood of reasons and arguments which she had prepared in many a day's musing, and many a night's vigil.

'Oh, let me come, Gildas! You will want a servant. You cannot do things for yourself like many men; you couldn't sew a button or mend a hole; you can only do a man's work. You will hire a servant as soon as you go out there; let me come, then – hire me now, and let me come with you. I will do all the work and live upon whatever food is cheapest there. Do you think, Gildas, that after being with you all my life I could let you go over that far sea and stop here after you were gone? No, no indeed, that I could never bear. I have got all my clothes ready; I am your servant, and belonging to you ever since my mother died. Don't turn me off now, when you want me more than ever.'

He had turned to stare at the beautiful face looking up at him, the imploring gestures, the pleading eyes, and his whole being was flooded with a sense of some strange awakening. What did this mean? Gwenifer! whom he had thought beyond his reach! from whom he was tearing himself away with the hard-won victory over his tenderest feelings!

Was he dreaming, or was she fooling him? and there was a hard, almost harsh, tone in his next question. 'What dost mean, lodes? Art asking to come to a foreign land as my servant?'

'Yes.'

'Art willing to leave thy home and thy friends?'

'Yes. Haven't I always been your servant?'

'*No, never*,' said Gildas emphatically. 'Thou hast been my sister, my friend, but never my servant, lass; and that thou canst never be.'

'Why, then?'

'Why?' said Gildas, starting to his feet. 'Because I love thee, lass; because I cannot bear to be near thee unless thou wilt promise to be my wife.'

'Gildas!'

'Gwenifer!' and there was a pause of conscious silence between them, during which he sprang down the hedge-bank on to the moor, and turning held both his hands towards her. She took one timid step down the bank, but Gildas, raising his hand as if to forbid her coming nearer, said 'Art coming as my wife, then? If so, trust thyself to me. Art coming, Gwenifer?' and he looked up at the slender form that wavered a little in the sea-wind.

'As my wife, Gwenifer?'

'Yes, then, Gildas,' she said, and stooping took the upstretched hands. She sprang, and was caught in his strong arms.

'Mine for ever, Gwenifer?' he questioned, as she slipped to his side, her head upon his breast.

'Yes, Gildas, for ever and ever,' she whispered.

He passed his arm round her waist, as he had done in the cottage when she had repulsed him so firmly.

'Thou wilt not turn away from me as thou didst that dark night, Gwenifer? That night that has cost me so many uneasy hours. It has kept me awake at night, lass, and followed me to my work by day.'

They were walking now towards the cliffs, bathed in the sunset light, their long shadows following them on the green-gold grass.

'Come, tell me, lass, what made thee turn away from me as if thou hatedst me?'

'Oh, Gildas!' she said, 'the ghost! The face at the window! I knew thy wife was living, was looking in at us.'

'What art saying, Gwenifer?' he exclaimed. 'That grey ghost! Was it Nance, then, that haunted the moor, that stood before me in the twilight, so near!' and he shuddered visibly. 'But not my wife, Gwenifer! that she was never as thou will be – the wife of my soul, as well as the wife of my heart. Is it true that all that dark time has passed and gone for ever? And Cap'n Jack, what of him? Dost know, lass, how I have dreaded to see his ship in the bay?'

'Well, what about him, Gildas? Why are people always bringing his name before me? Poor Cap'n Jack! You have no need to fear the sight of his red pennon.'

'Is it true, then, what I am hoping now – that he is nothing to thee?' and holding her face between his hands he raised it to his, and looked into the clear brown eyes.

'Nothing, Gildas.'

'And is it true that I am everything to thee?'

'Everything.'

'Come then, lass, and let me tell thee what thou art to me.'

And together they walked into the sunset light, all rosy and golden like their hopes.

How many questions had he to ask! How much had she to tell of the long silent years, when, in spite of her sealed lips, his name was familiar and beloved!

Yes, they had much to say to each other, as lovers always have; but when the sun had set, and the twilight gathered round them, they turned towards home together, and it was plain to see that every cloud had vanished, every doubt had been set at rest; and Gwenifer, as if forgetting that Gildas had been the mishteer, had already fallen naturally into the familiar 'thee' and 'thou'.

One subject they had both avoided – the long voyage before them, the banishment from their native land. Once, when she had alluded to it, he had by a very simple but effectual method sealed her lips. 'Hush, lass!' he said, 'let us leave that till to-morrow; to-night the world looks too beautiful, the sky is too clear, and the moon is too bright to talk of anything but joy.'

'Yes, but, Gildas, I mean to make it happy for thee out there too,' she answered.

'Happy? Yes indeed, if thou art there, Gwenifer,' and the glow on his dark face and the light in his eyes reminded her of the Gildas of old.

It would never have done for them to return to the farm together – all the rustic proprieties would have been outraged; so in the lane where the hawthorns were growing thick and green they parted, he to return to Scethryg, and she to run back to the little brown cot which had never sheltered so happy a being before.

And what a different world was that upon which the sun rose next day! To Gildas, as he went out to his plough, it seemed as if the lightness and zest of his boyhood had returned. He looked at the broad blue sea that scintillated under the morning sunbeams, and no longer dreaded to see a red pennon on the horizon; he looked at the brown furrows which the tender blades were already tingeing with green; he saw the wide purple moor where he had found his happiness, the tiny cot to which his eyes had always turned with interest – and surely over all there was some light more golden than the sunlight, more crystal than the sky, a 'light that never was on sea or land'; and through it all he heard a woman singing in a soft low voice, and knew it was Gwenifer, who was bringing the early lunch down the hawthorn lane.

He saw her enter the gap and spread the contents of her basket in a sheltered nook; he saw Ben and Het draw near; but he did not see the conscious look of love which Gwenifer directed towards him as he ploughed in the further corner of the field. Perhaps he felt it, for he whistled at his work, and his eyes followed her with a benison as she withdrew through the lane without approaching him. It behoved them to be careful now, and keep their happy secret to themselves, for Gildas had not lost his horror of being talked about; and so they spent their days apparently apart, but ever conscious of each other's presence.

When the moon rose, however, and flooded the upland fields with her silver radiance, two figures might be seen who walked together in the moonlight, their shadows blended into one, their voices sometimes low and tender, sometimes raised in merry laughter, for surely never were man and maiden more happily betrothed than these two whom fate, and the blindness of one, had so nearly separated for ever.

Hark to Gildas's hearty laugh. 'Well, in my deed,' he says. 'I can give a different answer now when people say 'Gwenifer belongs to you'. There's angry I used to be; now I can say, 'Yes, she does belong to me!' But listen, lass, I have something else to ask thee to-night. Thou hast shown thy love to me by being so willing to give up thy home and everything for me, and proud I am of that; but harken thee, I have another boon to ask.'

''Tis granted indeed,' she answered, 'but what is it, then?'

'Wilt stay at home with me, Gwenifer?'

'*What*?' she said, turning to look at him in amazement.

The moon shone full upon her, and Gildas might be excused for thinking it could not shine upon a fairer face.

'What, Gildas? Stay at home with thee? Not go across the sea? Not leave old Scethryg and the moor? Is that what thou art saying?' And the look of rapture that illumined her face needed no words to express its delighted consent.

'Yes indeed, that is my thought; why would I go when every dark cloud has rolled away, when I have gained the prize for which I was always hankering? Yes, since I was a boy! Why would we go when the reason for going is cleared away? In my deed, Gwenifer, I think a man may show his firmness sometimes as much in changing his mind as in keeping a useless resolve; the world has changed for me since last night. Will I be a fool, then, and give up this happy home and leave 'hen Gymru wen' just because I said I would? No; let them laugh and say, 'Gildas Rees is a reed shaken by the wind' – very well, what the worse will Gildas and Gwenifer be of that? 'Tis only Jones Bryndu and Betsy who know how full I was of going, and they will rejoice with us. Art glad as I am, Gwenifer? for thou art very silent;' but when she turned to him in the moonlight, he saw her eyes were full of tears.

'Oh, Gildas,' she said, ''tis only now I know how hard it was to go, and how thankful I am to stay; and Gildas, when I am happiest, then I am silent.'

* * * * * *

The crops are gathered, the air is crisp and fresh, and laden with the scent of autumn; the grain, the apples in the orchard, the blackberries on the hedges, the odour of the sea-breeze, all add their sweetness to the subtle fragrance.

Once more we enter the old grey farm with its uneven gables, and its ivied chimneys, but little altered by the fire and the subsequent restoration.

'Tis Sunday morning, a few days after Gwenifer and Gildas's marriage. A bright fire blazes on the hearth, the simple breakfast is laid, and Gwenifer moves about from hearth to table, from table to dresser, with little careful touches adding to the comfort of the old room and evidently waiting for somebody, who comes at last down those new stairs, berailed and polished, which have risen from the ashes of the old staircase – Gildas, his dark face full of life and energy, his black eyes bright and sparkling as of old! no shadow of care or trouble there, but full content and happiness. Dressed in his best, he looks, as he descends into the old living-room, with his firm step and open countenance, a husband to be proud of, and so Gwenifer thinks as she greets him with a little raillery.

'Dear anwl, Gildas,' and she raises her hands as if in amazement, 'dear anwl, there's smart thou art! Art going to be married, then?'

'Yes, if thou pleasest! I wouldn't mind a dozen times if thou wert the bride, lass! Thou art very smart, too, Gwenifer! That black with the yellow spots is suiting thee well indeed; but everything suits thee, even thy red petticoat and thy little white hood. In everything thou art like a queen!'

'Oh yes, Queen of the Rushes!' laughed Gwenifer. 'But where art going, indeed, Gildas?'

'Oh, to Brynzion, of course,' he said, attacking his breakfast. 'Isn't it Sunday morning? And don't husband and wife always go to chapel together? Art not going, Gwenifer?'

'Well, of course, if thou art.' And when half an hour later she appeared in her new white hat, with gloves and scarf to match, Gildas thought no lovelier woman ever walked by her husband's side.

We have followed them through the shadows and rough places on the road of life, and now we must leave them as they walk together into the sunshine; for darkness has flown away, and from henceforth it seems as if the wheel of fortune had turned – flowers lie in their path, hope and joy dwell in their hearts.

Glossary

Ach-y-fi!	Exclamation of distaste.
Anwyl, anwl	Dear.
Bachgen or *'machgen i*	Lad, or my lad.
Bendigedig!	Blessed!
Bore da chi	Good morning.
B't shwr	Certainly.
Bwthin	Hut.
Caton pawb!	Save us all!
Cawdel	Muddle.
Croten	Homely name for lass.
Clocs	Wooden shoes.
Clôs	Farmyard.
Crydd	Cobbler.
Cwrw	Ale.
Diwygiad	Reformation, the Revival.
Hen Gymru Wen!	Dear old Wales!
Hiraeth	Longing, home sickness.
Lodes, los	Girl, lass.
'Merch-i	My daughter, my dear.
Mishteer	Master.
Nos da chi	Good-night.
N'wncwl	(my) Uncle.
Penstif	Obstinate.
Sêt vawr or *fawr*	Big seat, deacon's pew.
'Stafell	Bride's possessions.
Tân	Fire.
Vach, fach	Little or dear.
Whintell	Willow basket.